D1173393

Stephen Booth is the internationally bestselling, CWA Dagger-winning author of the acclaimed thrillers featuring Cooper and Fry. The series is in development as a TV programme. Booth lives in Nottingham.

Find out more at www.stephen-booth.com or follow Stephen on Twitter @stephenbooth.

Also by Stephen Booth

Black Dog
Dancing with the Virgins
Blood on the Tongue
Blind to the Bones
One Last Breath
The Dead Place
Scared to Live
Dying to Sin
The Kill Call
Lost River
The Devil's Edge
Dead and Buried
Already Dead
The Corpse Bridge
The Murder Road
Secrets of Death

STEPHEN BOOTH

DEAD IN THE DARK

sphere

SPHERE

First published in Great Britain in 2017 by Sphere

1 3 5 7 9 10 8 6 4 2

Copyright © Stephen Booth 2017

The moral right of the author has been asserted.

All characters and events in this publication, other than those clearly in the public domain, are fictitious and any resemblance to real persons, living or dead, is purely coincidental.

All rights reserved. No part of this publication may be reproduced, stored in a retrieval system, or transmitted, in any form or by any means, without the prior permission in writing of the publisher, nor be otherwise circulated in any form of binding or cover other than that in which it is published and without a similar condition including this condition being imposed on the subsequent purchaser.

A CIP catalogue record for this book is available from the British Library.

Hardback ISBN 978-0-7515-6758-8
Trade Paperback ISBN 978-0-7515-6759-5

Typeset in Meridien by Palimpsest Book Production Limited,
Falkirk, Stirlingshire
Printed and bound in Great Britain by Clays Ltd, St Ives plc

Papers used by Sphere are from well-managed forests
and other responsible sources.

Sphere
An imprint of
Little, Brown Book Group
Carmelite House
50 Victoria Embankment
London
EC4Y 0DZ

An Hachette UK Company
www.hachette.co.uk

www.littlebrown.co.uk

To Lesley, as always

No one wants to die in the dark. To lie alone in the blackness, feeling the chill of death creep slowly over you. Shut away from the light as the fear numbs your limbs and chokes the breath in your throat. The long, long sinking into the cold depths. And then to sense that slipping away. The final slipping away into nothing.

Do you feel that stab of pain as it shoots through your chest? Try to make your breathing more shallow. You have several broken ribs, a fractured arm, perhaps a punctured lung. You can hardly know, in the dark. But you can feel the internal bleeding, the seeping blood as it squeezes your internal organs, bloats your stomach and intestines. You know your injuries are fatal.

That fear of the dark is overwhelming. Because this is true darkness, an eternal night in which your eyes have become useless. Your heart thumps uselessly as you strain to see where you're lying. You can sense space around you, a slight movement of icy air, a shifting of heavy masses, a solid weight way above your head. A sharp, stabbing pain is in your back from something hard you're lying on. This isn't a grave. But it is your tomb.

Does your fear of the dark make any sense? When you're dead, you go into endless blackness. Yet you've always hoped you would get one last glimpse of the light, always prayed that you wouldn't die alone.

Well, that's not going to happen. There's nothing for you to see here. Not a glimmer of light, not a flicker of hope. Only the darkness.

A creak and a rattling makes you freeze. Is someone here? Or some thing? But no . . . you breathe out and release the pain. The noise has quite a different meaning. It's something huge shifting overhead. It signals the end, the approach of your death. You're about to be crushed completely.

2

Day 1

Flies buzzed around the armchair. A mass of them covered a tiny window, like a moving black curtain. Detective Sergeant Diane Fry watched from the doorway as figures in scene suits moved around the overheated sitting room. Apart from the chair, there was little other furniture. A small table in one corner, a TV set on a stand, a stack of shelves containing two candles, a statue of the Virgin Mary, and a half a dozen books in Polish.

In a tiny kitchen area, there was barely enough room to turn round between an ancient gas cooker, a fridge and a sink. The off-white paintwork was scuffed, and the wallpaper looked damp, with a sheen of black mould under the window. Dust had gathered along the skirting boards and a trail of mouse droppings lay scattered near the bin.

Fry sniffed. The smell in the flat wasn't the stink of death, though it soon would be. The aroma was a mixture of rancid pork and fried onions. A thin, half-eaten sausage lay on a plate. The door of a wall-mounted cupboard hung open, revealing a row of cans and a few cups and plates. A plastic bag stood near the door. Fry glimpsed a loaf of bread, a carton of milk, some pots of yoghurt. Somebody's shopping.

The body itself lay curled in an awkward position, its head tilted back, one arm hanging towards the floor. Where the tips of the fingers touched the carpet, the skin was a livid purplish red. Blood had pooled to the lower parts of the body, red cells sinking slowly through the serum in the arteries when the victim's heart stopped pumping. The carpet was so thin that the blood from the victim's head wound would soon have soaked through to the floorboards and dripped on to the ceiling of the shop below.

'There's a trail of blood all the way from the alley, Sergeant. As far as we can tell, that must be where he was attacked.'

Detective Constable Jamie Callaghan was standing outside in the yard, looking up at her from the bottom of a narrow metal stairway. Yellow evidence markers had been placed on the steps, marking the blood spatter left by the victim as he climbed unsteadily up to the flat. A smear of blood left on the handrail halfway up showed the clear impression of a palm print.

From her position above him, Callaghan looked tall and lean, the darkness of his eyes emphasised by the yellow glare of a security light overhead. It had been daylight for a couple of hours, but it still hadn't gone off. Perhaps something had triggered the motion sensor.

'So instead of seeking help, he came back here and sat in his chair to die,' said Fry. 'Why would anyone do that?'

Callaghan shrugged. 'He probably didn't realise how serious his injuries were.'

Fry looked at the splatter on the stairway. 'Perhaps. But he must have seen how much blood he was losing.'

'Shock?' said Callaghan. 'You can't expect people to use sensible judgment in those circumstances.'

'Are there any witnesses, Jamie?'

'We're still looking. Nothing so far.'

'Well, keep trying. It seems very unlikely that no one would have seen either the attack itself or an injured man bleeding his way back to this flat. The distance between the two scenes is . . . what? A hundred yards or so? And right in the middle of town.'

'We've got some local officers on it,' said Callaghan. 'No one is being very helpful at the moment.'

'Isn't that always the way?'

'In this part of the world, yes.'

Fry turned back to the room. The victim was a man in his late thirties, heavily built around the shoulders and thickening at the waist. His fair hair was cut short, and he had at least a day's growth of beard. He was dressed in jeans and a bloodstained blue T-shirt, and he was still wearing trainers, which had left damp prints on the carpet. A padded jacket lay where it had been dropped on the floor by the armchair.

Fry's boss, DCI Alistair Mackenzie, was deep in conversation with the crime scene manager, who she didn't recognise. The forensic medical examiner straightened up from her examination of the body and turned to the doorway, narrowing her eyes as she peered at Fry's face. She looked as though she was about to diagnose an unusually serious medical condition from her appearance.

'Do you want my initial assessment, Detective Sergeant Fry?' she asked.

The FME was an Asian woman wearing a hijab below the hood of her white scene suit. Fry vaguely recalled meeting her in the Accident and Emergency department at Edendale General Hospital once, when a recently arrested suspect had required urgent medical attention. As a doctor, she must have become tired of the day-to-day stress of A & E, so had moved to something more stable, like sudden death and the examination of detainees in police custody. Fry couldn't remember the doctor's name, though. She could have asked, but it probably wasn't important.

'That would be helpful,' she said. 'I imagine that's why you're here, doctor.'

The FME began to strip off her latex gloves, carefully peeling them from one finger at a time.

'Well, the cause of death appears to be a substantial loss of blood from the stab wound in the left side of the thorax. The weapon entered through the ribs here, as you can see from the extent of the bloodstains on the clothing. But there's also an extensive head injury, which is serious enough in itself to have caused concussion.'

'So he may have been in a confused state after the assault?'

'Almost certainly.'

Fry pointed. 'And the blood on his hands?'

'His own, probably. Most of the blood is on his left

6

hand. I imagine he would have clutched it to the wound. It wouldn't have done much to reduce the flow. On the other hand, if he'd received immediate medical attention, it would have been a different matter.'

'So he could have been saved?'

The FME nodded. 'A paramedic would have been able to reduce the loss of blood. An ambulance could have got him to A & E in ten or fifteen minutes. King's Mill Hospital is only seven miles away.'

Fry looked at the dead man's blank eyes. Seven miles was a long way when you were dying on your own, weakened by loss of blood as it pooled on the floor around you. And there was no sign of a phone for the victim to have dialled 999. No landline, which wasn't so unusual. But no mobile either. That was odd for a man of this age.

'I see there's post-mortem lividity,' she said.

'Yes, particularly noticeable in the right hand where it's close to the floor. If the pathologist finds similar lividity in other areas of the body, it will confirm that the victim died in situ and hasn't been moved since.'

'What does it tell us about time of death, doctor?'

'Well, livor mortis starts from about twenty to thirty minutes after death, but it isn't usually observable to the human eye for two hours or so. The pathologist may be able to give you a more accurate estimate after she's assessed the point of maximum lividity.'

'So he's been dead for two hours at least?' persisted Fry.

'Yes, at least.'

7

'But how long did he take to die?'

'Now, that's an impossible question to answer,' said the FME. 'He looks a strong, healthy individual. It could have been several hours.'

On the victim's dangling arm, the purplish-red colour of the hand was very noticeable. But Fry was looking at the fingers where they touched the floor. The tips were oddly pale in comparison to the rest of the hand. Strange, when the fingertips were the lowest point of the body.

The doctor followed her gaze.

'Of course, the discolouration of livor mortis doesn't occur in parts of the body that are in direct contact with the ground. The contact compresses the capillaries.'

'Thank you, doctor,' said Fry.

The FME flapped a hand in front of her face, as if waving away Fry's thanks. But that wasn't what she was doing.

'I must say, these flies seem to have found the body very quickly,' she said.

Fry looked around the flat. 'No, doctor,' she said. 'I think they were here already.'

For a few days the weather had been unseasonably warm for September. But on the previous night a storm had hit after darkness fell. Heavy rain and gusty winds had battered the Peak District for six hours until daylight came.

This morning, the roads were littered with broken branches as Detective Inspector Ben Cooper drove from his home in Foolow. In low-lying lanes, soil and leaves had been swept into the middle and piled up on the bends as road surfaces turned temporarily into rivers.

Cooper was feeling optimistic this morning. He couldn't explain why. It was a sensation he wasn't used to experiencing as he headed to work. Not recently, anyway. Since he'd become a DI and taken on management responsibilities, the burden on him had increased rapidly. Sometimes he felt as though the ground was constantly shifting under his feet and he didn't know what to expect next.

On the descent into Edendale, a farmer was cutting a fallen chestnut bough to clear a field entrance, the whine of his chainsaw sounding angry and spiteful in the bright, clear air. Cooper slowed the Toyota as he edged past the obstruction. He gave the farmer a friendly nod, but got only a blank stare in return.

He had a new CD in the player that someone had asked him to listen to. He liked discovering new music and new bands. And this one was certainly different. They were called Stary Olsa, a Belarusian folk band who covered classic rock tracks on medieval instruments. It shouldn't have worked, but Cooper found himself singing along to a version of Pink Floyd's 'Another Brick in the Wall' played on flute and Belarusian bagpipes. That was definitely new.

In Edendale, the police station in West Street looked much the same as it had when it was built back in the 1950s. But nothing stayed the same in policing. There were only two divisions of Derbyshire Constabulary now, where once there had been five.

The old alphabetical system had been abandoned completely. In the latest reorganisation, E Division had been become just one part of North Division, which covered all but the city of Derby and the southern fringes of the county. It was properly known as the Eden Valley Local Policing Unit, neighbouring the LPUs of North East Derbyshire, High Peak, and Derbyshire Dales.

Stary Olsa were getting into Black Sabbath's 'Iron Man' as Cooper drew into the secure car park at West Street and keyed the code number to enter to building. After so many years based here, he found it strange and disorienting to realise there was no longer a divisional organisation in Edendale. He didn't even have direct access to his boss. Detective Superintendent Hazel Branagh was now based twenty miles away in Chesterfield. In some ways it gave him more autonomy and freedom, but he'd come to rely on the guidance of Superintendent Branagh. A more distant physical relationship changed things for everyone.

The corridors of the station had been feeling empty for months. Cooper supposed it was only a matter of time before someone at headquarters in Ripley decided it would be a good idea to sell off some of the buildings. *Disposal of surplus assets to meet a revenue shortfall.* He could see the words quite clearly at the head of a report. Yes, an email would drop into his inbox one day. And it wouldn't be long before it happened.

But that seemed to be his job now. Every day of his working life was spent adapting to change.

When he reached his department, Cooper went

straight into the CID room. As usual, Detective Constable Carol Villiers and Detective Sergeant Devdan Sharma had arrived before him. It was as if they were engaged in an unspoken competition to see who get could into work first.

'DS Sharma. What's happening this morning?'

'Not much, sir,' said Sharma gloomily. 'It's pretty dead around here as usual.'

'Not dead. Just under control,' responded Cooper.

'If you say so, sir.'

Cooper laughed. But Sharma just gazed at him, his dark brown eyes unblinking. Sharma was about as impenetrable as anybody he'd met. This was hard work.

When asked, Cooper had said several times that DS Sharma would fit in. But he wasn't sure it was true, rather than just something you said when you were asked. He knew a little about Sharma, but it was only superficial information. Though he'd been born in the Peartree area of Derby, Sharma's family were from the Punjab, where Hindus were in a minority to Sikhs. Cooper had learned that his wife's name was Asha, that they had no children yet, that they attended the Geeta Bhawan Temple on Pear Tree Road in Derby. But he still didn't feel that he knew the man, even though he'd been based in Edendale for several months. Perhaps it would take longer.

But would his DS stay that long? For months now, Cooper had been trying hard to be positive about him, but he couldn't resist a niggling doubt, a suspicion that he and the Eden Valley LPU were being used, treated as a stepping stone to something else, something better.

DS Sharma was destined for higher things.

He recalled Sharma telling him that he'd applied for a transfer to EMSOU's Major Crime Unit from D Division, but didn't get it. Cooper had wondered whether he knew Diane Fry. He'd denied it at the time, but they had worked together since. Cooper mentally corrected himself. By 'worked together', he meant Fry had used Sharma for her own reasons. She had a habit of doing that. It meant nothing to her that an officer was a member of someone else's team.

Carol Villiers had said Sharma was 'full of himself, thinks he's God's gift'. Was there a reason she resented him so much? On the other hand, Sharma had made a good impression on Gavin Murfin. A retired DC working as civilian support might be easily impressed, though – even if Sharma had been winding Gavin up. It was hard to tell whether he had that kind of sense of humour, or whether he had a sense of humour at all.

Before that, Murfin had made a reference to Devdan Sharma 'doing his diversity training' by transferring to the rural territory of North Division. Was it really just part of the relentless drive to create a service that reflected the diverse population it served? Up here in the High Peak and Derbyshire Dales, ethnic minorities represented only two per cent of the population. Police officers recruited from the Asian community were in such short supply that they were most often deployed in areas where their presence might help community relations, as well improving the public perception of the police.

Carol Villiers couldn't wait to chip in.

'Another farmer lost a barn full of hay last night,' she said.

'Arson?' asked Cooper.

'Of course.'

'No animals killed this time? No vehicles burnt out?'

'No,' said Villiers. 'But it's still someone's livelihood.'

'Yes, yes. I know.'

Cooper felt momentarily irritated that Villiers should feel it necessary to point that out to him. Was she suggesting that he'd forgotten his own history, abandoned his own background? He'd grown up on a farm, for heaven's sake. His brother was still in farming. He could hardly escape it, or leave it behind. Yet it seemed as if Villiers thought he was becoming a townie, like Dev Sharma. But surely he wasn't?

Sharma was definitely a city boy, though. He had no idea what a barn full of hay was worth to the owner, and no idea how easily it could be destroyed in a fire. In a way, it was just like with Diane Fry all over again.

Cooper sighed. The optimism he'd set off with from Foolow this morning seemed to have dissipated pretty quickly.

Cooper fetched himself a cup of anonymous brown liquid from the vending machine, then went into his own office and began to check his emails.

He was becoming far too familiar with the jargon used in the internal memos. He'd even fallen into the trap of using some of the phrases himself when he was writing a report. *Re-prioritising resources. Due diligence.*

Overarching strategy to ensure best practice. They seemed to leap naturally from the keyboard to the screen. He imagined a superintendent or chief inspector at headquarters in Ripley nodding in approval when he read them. The words might not mean much, but they ticked all the boxes, rang all the right bells. So why did he feel so guilty about doing it?

Within a few minutes there was a knock on his office door and Carol Villiers appeared.

'Carol, come in.'

'Have you got a few minutes, Ben?'

'Of course,' he said. 'Sit down.'

There was just enough room for a couple of chairs on the other side of the desk. Cooper had thought about asking for a move to more spacious accommodation, which now lay vacant on another floor. But he was nervous about the answer he might get. Someone was likely to tell him that his next office would be in the storage shed at the back of the yard.

'Is everything okay?'

'Yes, fine,' she said.

Cooper studied her expression, hoping it wasn't too obvious that he didn't believe her.

The woman sitting across the desk from him was a different Carol Villiers from the one he remembered when he was growing up. When she returned to Edendale, she was older, leaner and more tanned. And there had been something else different, an air of self-assurance, a firm angle of the jaw. He still sometimes saw her as she was in her military photograph, the uniform with black-and-red flashes, her corporal's stripes on her sleeve, an MP's badge. And there was that extra dimension – a shadow in her eyes, a darkness behind the professional façade.

Since he'd moved to Foolow, Cooper now lived only a few fields away from Carol Villiers. Her parents ran a bed and breakfast on Tideswell high street. But had it really brought him any closer to her?

'You must be wondering when you'll stand a chance of getting promotion,' he said, forced to guess at the reason for her visit in the face of her silence.

Villiers shook her head. 'Not really. It's not something worth worrying about. It's probably never going to happen anyway.'

'Oh, it will. There just isn't a vacancy right now.'

'I'm not waiting anxiously to push Dev Sharma out of the way.'

'Do you like working with him?'

'Of course,' said Villiers. 'He's fine. He's a good DS.'

Cooper nodded. 'You're loyal. That's one of your best qualities. I wouldn't want to change it.'

Villiers looked at him quizzically, but didn't ask any more.

'I bet you're sorry you ever left the RAF Police to come here,' said Cooper. 'Derbyshire Constabulary has probably been a disappointment to you.'

Villiers smiled. 'Not at all. It was the right time for me to get out of the Snowdrops when Glenn was killed. And where else was I going to go?'

Cooper wondered if it had been insensitive to remind Villiers of her husband's death. They had both been serving with the RAF Police, whose white-topped caps gave them the nickname 'Snowdrops', when Glenn Villiers had died in an incident in Helmand Province. But as he watched Carol now, she seemed calm and unperturbed. Her eyes narrowed in the familiar way as she brushed back a strand of hair from her forehead. She still looked the tough, competent ex-servicewoman he'd seen that day at West Street when she joined E Division CID. Derbyshire hadn't softened her in the meantime. Not too much, anyway.

'I wanted to tell you about a report DS Sharma didn't mention,' said Villiers. 'He doesn't think it's important, but . . .'

Cooper was intrigued. 'What is it, Carol?'

'A misper.'

He frowned. 'A priority case? A child?'

'No, an adult male in his early forties.'

'So why are you bothering me with it? You know we won't take any action on a missing adult unless they're vulnerable or there's a reason to suspect a crime.'

'Well, true. But you might remember this one.'

'Someone I know?'

'Sort of.'

'Who is it?'

'A gentleman named Reece Bower. He has an address in Bakewell.'

'Reece Bower . . .'

The name was certainly familiar. Cooper felt sure it must be an old case he'd been involved with, but years ago. So many names passed in front of his eyes, written in reports that came across his desk or listed on his computer screen that he couldn't possibly remember more than a fraction of them. Yet his team seemed to expect him to have an encyclopedic memory stacked with the details of every major case from the past twenty years.

'Reece Bower,' said Cooper again, reaching for his keyboard to search the database.

'There's no need for that,' said Villiers. 'I can tell you the basics. I looked up the case.'

'Go ahead, then.'

'Ten years ago Mr Reece Bower was the primary suspect for the death of his wife Annette, and was subsequently charged with her murder.'

Ah, now that rang a bell.

'I remember,' said Cooper.

'I thought you would.'

'It was a very unusual case.'

Villiers nodded. 'It certainly was.'

'But that case is more than a decade old,' said Cooper. 'Why are you telling me about it now?'

'Because this time,' said Villiers, 'it's Mr Bower himself who has disappeared.'

3

Ten years ago

It started with a single drop of blood. There was almost nothing to see – a splash, a spatter, a fading stain on the laminate flooring. When she first saw it, Frances Swann's initial reaction was to reach for a handful of paper towels from the cupboard. A drop of washing-up liquid in water should do the trick. Or at least, it did on the carpets in her own house. Did it work on laminate?

The thought made her pause, worrying that she might make the stain worse. She was in her sister's home, after all. It was only then that she began to wonder where the blood had come from.

Frances looked up. The dogs were out with Adrian and the children were at their granny's. Reece was in the garage tinkering with the car, polishing up the chrome or something like that.

Puzzled, she stared at her own hands, turning over the palms to examine them. Had she scratched herself on a nail, cut herself on a knife? But there was no visible mark. No trace of an injury on her skin. So the blood wasn't hers.

She crouched to look at the stain, as if it might tell her something. She felt like a forensic examiner who'd forgotten to bring her equipment today. If she looked closely enough, the blood might tell her whose it was. Was it even human, though? How could she possibly tell?

From that moment, she had a strong impression that whatever she did next might be very important for someone's life.

Reece Bower pushed the curtain aside and gazed out of the window of his house at the empty road. He seemed to be watching for someone, but no one came. Frances Swann paced impatiently across the room. She was finding his reluctance infuriating.

'We must do something, Reece,' she said. 'She's been missing for hours now.'

He turned back towards her, but she couldn't read his expression. It was as if he expected something else to happen, and she was disappointing him.

'Yes, all right,' he said in the end. 'But Annette won't thank us for it when she gets back. You know how she hates a fuss.'

'I'm sure something's happened to her,' said Frances.

'And I'm sure it hasn't. Everything will be fine. You'll see.'

'Well, I hope you're right. Are you going to phone, or shall I?'

Bower shook his head. 'No, I'll do it.'

'You'd better tell them the truth,' she said.

He paused with his hand on the phone.

'What do you mean? What truth?'

'You two had a fight, didn't you?'

Bower withdrew his hand and held it up in a defensive gesture.

'No,' he said. 'No, of course not. What on earth makes you think that, Frances?'

'I saw the blood,' she said. 'Reece, there was blood on the floor.'

'On what floor?'

'In the kitchen.'

He smiled. To Frances, it looked like relief. 'Annette cut herself chopping vegetables. That's all it was, an accident. She must have missed cleaning a few spots up.'

She said nothing. She didn't believe him, but wasn't in a position to argue – not until they found out where Annette was, and what happened to her.

'Is that all it was?' said Bower. 'Frances, really. I'm surprised at you.'

He took a pace towards her. Frances tensed, but stood her ground. 'This is why we need the truth, Reece.'

'Okay. It's fine. We'll do it. Though I trust you're prepared for the consequences.'

Frances watched him dial and lift the phone to his ear.

'Yes, I'm prepared,' she said quietly. 'I hope you are, Reece.'

Within a few hours, a search team had been through the house. It was normal procedure, Frances had been told. It was common in these cases for the missing person to be discovered close to home, often right inside their own house.

There had been a lot of questions for Reece to answer. A lot. There was an absolute bombardment from the detective in charge of the case. And Frances could see he was very unhappy about it. *When had he last spoken to his wife? Had she said that she was going anywhere? Might she just have forgotten to tell him? What possessions did Annette have with her? A phone, a purse? How much money would she have on her? Cash? Credit cards? How was she dressed when she left the house? Had he checked the wardrobe to see if she'd taken any clothes with her, or personal items? Was there any reason she might have decided to leave? Had he noticed anything suspicious? Had he seen anyone hanging around the house?*

Reece had become exasperated very quickly. He couldn't take questioning like that. It wasn't in his character. He was used to being in control and he became offended within minutes at the detective's questions. Frances couldn't see, but she could imagine them glaring at each other with a growing hostility. Reece wasn't doing himself any favours. But she wasn't sorry to see that.

And then came Frances's turn to answer questions.

'So Mrs Bower's disappearance was reported by her husband,' said the detective when he came to interview her.

'Yes,' she said. And then she added: 'Eventually.'

He'd looked interested then.

'Did you think he should have reported it earlier, Mrs Swann?'

21

'I do,' she admitted.

'And you had a disagreement about it?'

She looked at the officer more closely. She hadn't said that, but he'd read it in her manner. Frances realised that she had been underestimating him.

'Detective . . .?' she said. 'I'm sorry, I didn't take in your name. Everything has been so mad.'

'Detective Inspector Hitchens,' he said. 'Paul Hitchens.'

She smiled at him. Somehow knowing his name made him more human.

'Yes, we did disagree,' she said. 'I urged him to phone earlier, but he kept saying he was sure Annette would come home soon. And she didn't, of course.'

'We do ask people to be certain a person is missing for no good reason before they make a report,' said DI Hitchens gently. 'We can waste a lot of time otherwise, if someone is just late, because they've got stuck in traffic or their car has broken down. Sometimes they don't have a phone, or the battery has run down, or it isn't possible to get a signal. There are all kinds of innocent reasons.'

Frances shook her head. 'It isn't anything like that.'

'Well, the other possibility is that Mrs Bower went away for a reason and is deliberately not making contact.'

Frances felt a flood of relief. He'd seen exactly what she was thinking without her having to say it. She would have felt guilty volunteering her suspicion. Disloyal. Of course, her true loyalty was to her sister, not to Reece. Yet she felt as though she was interfering in their relationship, coming between them in a way her sister would object to. She was afraid of what

Annette would say about it when she came back. But that was *if* she came back.

'It's all right to tell me what you're thinking,' said Hitchens. 'I assure you it won't go any further, Mrs Swann.'

'Very well.' She took a deep breath. 'Reece and Annette have been going through a difficult patch in their marriage. My sister confides in me, you see. She told me they've been having arguments recently.'

'What about?'

Frances hesitated. It was getting personal now. 'Oh, the usual things.'

'I don't really know what the usual things are,' said Hitchens. 'I'm not married.'

'Well . . . I mean money, for a start. Annette likes to spend it. Reece is more cautious. He thinks she's too extravagant.'

'And that's been causing arguments. Serious ones?'

'Not violent, if that's what you mean. Just an ongoing niggle and resentment.'

Hitchens didn't look impressed. 'Anything else?'

'Well, a few years ago Reece had an affair. Annette was very upset about it, as you can imagine.'

'That I can understand.'

'It was with a colleague of his at work. Her name was Madeleine Betts.'

Hitchens consulted a notebook. 'Mr Bower works at Chesterfield Royal Hospital, I believe.'

'That's right. In the finance department. I'm not sure about the Betts woman, but he must have met her through the job.'

'How long did the affair last?'

'I can't tell you. I don't think Annette ever got the full truth out of Reece. But he told her it was over and the woman was being moved to another department.'

'So that was it?'

'It took them a long time to get over it and go back to normal. In fact, I'm not certain they ever did get back to normal. It's not something you forget very easily, that kind of betrayal.'

'But this was some time ago,' said Hitchens.

'Yes, it must be a couple of years now.'

Hitchens narrowed his eyes, and she knew nothing was going to escape him. 'But more recently, perhaps . . .?' he said.

Frances sighed again. 'I think Reece has been doing the same thing again.'

'He was having another affair?'

'It seems like it. I gained the impression from a few things Annette said, small incidents she mentioned. She didn't say straight out. I think she was ashamed.'

'Ashamed? I don't understand.'

'It's a bit hard to explain, but Annette made that decision two years ago to forgive him, and stick by her marriage. If she had to admit the same thing was happening again, it would mean she'd made a mistake. That she'd failed. I think she saw it as her fault. That was why she didn't come straight out with it, I'm sure. She would normally have confided in me, but in recent weeks I could tell there was something she was holding back.'

'It's hardly evidence, I'm afraid,' said Hitchens. 'But if you could give me more details of what your sister said to you, we can follow it up and see if there's any substance to your suspicions.'

'I understand.'

'I'll get Detective Constable Murfin to come and take a full statement from you.'

'Very well.'

While she waited, Frances went into the kitchen. Her instinct was to make a cup of tea. Some of these police officers would probably like one. It wasn't her house, but she felt it was her role. Something she could do, at least. Something other than answering questions.

To her surprise, she found Reece collapsed on a chair at the kitchen table. He looked exhausted. His face was pale and his hair was untidy, as if he'd been running his hands through it. She had never seen him look so dishevelled. Surely just answering questions wouldn't have drained him like that? He was probably too tense. He must be hiding something. She was sure of that now. Trying to conceal a secret under questioning was very hard work.

Reece didn't look up as she came into the room. He was staring at his hands where they lay on the table. Frances imagined he was picturing what his hands might have done. She could feel the guilt oozing from his pores. What should she do? What could she say to him?

Frances cleared her throat.

'Do you want a cup of tea?' she said.

She couldn't even bring herself to say his name. A conviction was growing inside her and she couldn't fight it. She didn't want to fight it. She had no doubt in her own mind now that he had done something to Annette.

'What?' He looked up, as if dazed. 'Oh, yes. All right.'

Frances boiled the kettle and took some mugs out of the cupboard.

'I thought I'd make one for the detectives. There's one coming to take my statement. Or do you think they'd prefer coffee?'

Reece seemed to jerk back to alertness. 'Your statement? *Your* statement?'

'Yes. I don't know how much I can tell them that will be of any help.'

'No, nor me,' said Reece.

He was staring at her now. Frances began to feel a little afraid. She could see two police officers in the garden. They were standing near the flower bed where Reece had dug out some hydrangeas. He'd said they were getting too big, killing off everything else around them. Annette had liked them, but she'd been unable to convince him to keep them. He'd dug them up by the roots, cut them up and burned the branches by the shed at the bottom. You could still see the black embers of the fire where he'd poked at it with a stick to make it flare up, as if he was tending a barbecue.

Now the detective inspector was speaking to the two policemen. Hitchens, that was his name. Frances saw him nod seriously, then he turned to look back at the house. She made a show of turning on the tap and wiping a cloth round the sink. She knew it was futile.

He wasn't stupid. He would know perfectly well that she was watching.

'Are you making that tea, or what?' said Reece crossly from behind her.

'It's coming.'

Frances clanked the mugs, popped in teabags, poured boiling water. Through the steam, she glimpsed Detective Inspector Hitchens walking down the garden to the burned patch. She saw him pick up a stick – probably the very same stick that Reece had used – and he poked carefully at the ashes before dropping the stick and pulling a phone out of his pocket.

She walked quickly to the fridge and took out a carton of milk before coming back to the window. It was too interesting to miss, like watching a TV detective drama but in real life, right there in her sister's garden.

Now it was her turn to feel guilty. This wasn't entertainment. This was about her sister's life.

'Mrs Swann?'

Frances turned and saw a new visitor standing in the doorway of the kitchen. A middle-aged man shaped like an egg, wearing a scruffy suit and tie pulled loose at the neck. Surely this one couldn't be . . .?

'Detective Constable Murfin,' he said. 'I'm here to take your statement.'

'Yes, I'm ready for you.'

The newcomer glanced at the milk carton she was holding and the steaming mugs.

'You wouldn't happen to have a piece of cake to go with that?' he said.

*   *   *

Just over two weeks later Frances Swann stood and watched as her brother-in-law was handcuffed by police officers and led away to a car. She didn't know what she felt as she saw him being driven away. Her emotions were conflicted. It was hard to accept that she had played a part in bringing Reece to this disaster, yet it was the only thing she could have done for Annette. Her sister still hadn't been found, and everybody was certain now that she was dead. Reece Bower would have to explain that.

Frances hadn't been able to figure out how he'd done it. Oh, it was easy to kill someone. Far too easy, in fact. But disposing of a dead body was much more difficult. The policeman, Detective Inspector Paul Hitchens, had told her that. You had to work very hard, or be particularly clever, to make sure the body of your victim was never found.

Frances turned away as the police cars left. That was what puzzled her most. In her experience, Reece Bower wasn't a man who would work very hard at anything, not if it involved physical effort. And he certainly wasn't particularly clever.

So how had he done it? Was it possible that someone had helped him?

4

'Zalewski. Krystian Zalewski.'

Detective Sergeant Diane Fry looked at the passport in her hand. 'You said that well, Jamie.'

'I've been practising.'

DC Jamie Callaghan pulled out his notebook. 'Mr Zalewski is a Polish national, as we know. He's been living in this country for more than two years, the last eight months of that here in Shirebrook. He rents this flat from the owner of the shop downstairs.'

'Our Mr Pollitt.'

'Right.'

'Any family that we know of?'

'Zalewski is apparently unmarried and he lived here alone,' said Callaghan, with a glance around the tiny flat. 'Well, you wouldn't want to bring children up here, would you? There's hardly room for two people.'

'True.'

The body had been removed by the funeral directors' van to the mortuary, and the room looked almost undisturbed, except for the bloodstains on the carpet and on the side of the armchair.

The crime scene examiners had finished with the flat and moved on, leaving traces of their fingerprint powder, steeping plates around the chair, and a bare patch of floorboard where a rectangular section had been cut out of the carpet. A separate team was still working in the alley a hundred yards away, where the attack was thought to have taken place, judging from the evidence.

Fry's boss at EMSOU, DCI Mackenzie, was still in Shirebrook. He'd been at the scene when Fry and Callaghan arrived, but he'd left them to it and was now at a meeting with local councillors and representatives of other agencies. Apparently, a tense situation was developing in the town in the wake of the murder. But that was Mackenzie's job to deal with. Fry felt much happier here, at the scene of the death, looking at a bloodstained carpet.

'Mr Pollitt thinks there was a mention of a brother living in the Derby area,' said Callaghan. 'He can't remember the name, though.'

Fry picked up a diary and flicked through the pages. There was a list in the back that looked like addresses and phone numbers. She couldn't see a Zalewski, but then you probably wouldn't enter your brother in your address book under his surname.

'We'll have to start working our way through these numbers,' she said. 'We'll need a Polish speaker.'

'There are plenty of those in Shirebrook,' said Callaghan.

Fry ignored the comment. She pointed at a pile of papers on top of the bookshelves.

'And we'll have to get someone to go through this paperwork. There might be some letters from a family member.'

'Same Polish speaker, I imagine.'

'Was Mr Zalewski in employment?' asked Fry.

'Yes. When he first rented the flat he was working at the big distribution centre just outside town. But he left there after about four months. He got six strikes against him.'

'Strikes?'

'Time-wasting offences, that sort of thing. Since then, he's been employed in a hand car wash.'

'We need to talk to his employer then.'

'Already on it.'

'And still nothing from the immediate area, I suppose? No witnesses?'

Callaghan shook his head. 'You know what they always say. No one saw nothing.'

The statuette of the Virgin Mary seemed to be winking at her from the shelves, until Fry realised a fly had landed on the Virgin's head.

'In that case,' she said, 'we'll have to make a point of talking to some of the other Polish residents.'

'But for that—' began Callaghan.

'Yes, yes. We'll need a Polish speaker.'

At West Street, Ben Cooper had stood up from his desk, but found there was no room to pace the carpet. Instead, he leaned against the wall and stared out of the window. From his first-floor office, he was looking out over a corner of the football ground. Edendale FC

31

were doing well in their amateur league, according to the officers who followed football. All that Cooper noticed was the cars clogging up the roads on a match day.

'There were several things that made the Annette Bower case unusual,' he said.

'Oh yes,' said Carol Villiers. 'For a start, the victim's body was never found. And it still hasn't been found, ten years later.'

Cooper nodded. 'That was a major problem.'

He knew just how hard it was to get a conviction for a murder without a body. You had to satisfy a jury that someone was definitely dead and not going to walk into a police station next day, looking surprised at all the fuss.

A murder investigation with a missing body followed specific lines of inquiry. The first consideration was to establish when the victim was last known to be alive. From there, officers had to prove that all normal behaviour by the victim had stopped suddenly and completely. No mobile phone use, no bank transactions, no contact with friends or relatives.

Often the irresistible temptation for the killer was to get their hands on the victim's money. Fraudulent use of a bank account was a giveaway. So were letters claiming to be from the victim. Handwriting experts could examine documents to confirm they were forged. A claim on a pension or an insurance policy were an indication that the subject was considered dead. In many missing body murder cases, the killer attempted to imitate the victim in an effort to prove they were alive. In others, they moved house straightaway, putting distance between themselves and the location of the murder, the burial place of the body.

The body was very helpful if you wanted to learn exactly how someone was killed, or if you wanted to find evidence of the killer. But sometimes the body wasn't that important, particularly in a domestic crime. There was always a lot of cross-contamination if people were connected. In some cases, finding the actual body didn't prove anything that wasn't already known.

'It didn't used to be possible to convict anyone for murder without a body at all,' said Carol Villiers. 'It was that way for hundreds of years.'

'The Campden Wonder,' said Cooper.

'The what?'

'A notorious seventeenth-century case in Chipping Campden. When a man disappeared without trace, three people were hanged for his murder. The following year, the alleged victim reappeared, saying he'd been kidnapped and sold into slavery in Turkey.'

'It was a bit late by then.'

'Exactly. Convictions without a body became a potential minefield for miscarriages of justice. But the law was changed following a murder case in Wales in the 1950s. The last hanging was in 1964, and capital punishment was abolished a few years later. Now there are a couple of murder cases every year where no body has been found. Of course, the situation is different with modern technology. It's difficult just to disappear, unless you're dead.'

Cooper recalled reading about the case of a Polish

ex-serviceman who bought a farm in South Wales after the Second World War and went into a partnership. Police who came to the farm to carry out routine foreigner checks found the partner had gone. Despite the Pole's claim that his other man had returned to Poland, the inquiry discovered complaints of violent behaviour and money left in the victim's bank account. They became convinced the body had been chopped up and fed to the pigs on the farm.

At the trial, the jury heard evidence of more than two thousand tiny bloodstains found in the farmhouse kitchen. The defendant said they were animal blood from skinning rabbits. In the twenty-first century, there would be no doubt about the origin of the bloodstains. DNA would have identified the victim.

Cooper thought that murder inquiries like this might happen more often, if it wasn't for the difficulty in disposing of a dead body. It was the main obstacle to committing the perfect murder. In a crowded island it was just so difficult to get rid of a corpse. Most of the time it would turn up. If it didn't, that was a huge stroke of luck for the killer. In Cooper's mind, it had been a massive stroke of luck for Reece Bower.

In a town, the police could use CCTV footage to trace someone's movements and get an approximate time and place for their disappearance. The missing person's actions could reveal a lot. It could establish whether the disappearance was intentional or not. But cameras were few and far between in this area.

'Is Gavin in today?' asked Cooper.

'I think he's just arrived.'

'See if you can tear him away from his second breakfast.'

'I think it's his third breakfast by the time he gets to his desk,' said Villiers.

Cooper laughed. 'Just brush the crumbs off him, then, and steer him in here.'

While he waited, Cooper looked up the details of the inquiry. The Bower case had occurred only ten years previously. On 29 October that year, Annette Bower had allegedly disappeared while walking her dog on the Monsal Trail near Bakewell. That afternoon, after several hours, she was reported missing by her husband Reece.

A week later Derbyshire Constabulary launched a high-profile public appeal for information. They even issued a statement saying they believed Annette might have been the victim of a criminal act, though the basis for that claim so early in the investigation was unclear to Cooper.

Statements were issued by Annette Bower's family saying that her disappearance was completely out of character. Was that enough to suspect a crime? Within a few days, the police announced that they were treating the inquiry as a murder investigation.

Searches had already begun on the Monsal Trail and in the nearby industrial estate. Now the garden of the Bowers' house was dug up. Police said they were anxious to trace the movements of a red Nissan seen being driven by a man near the scene of Annette Bower's disappearance.

Despite the lack of direct forensic evidence, police

believed Reece Bower had killed his wife and hidden her body. In the middle of November, Bower was detained in connection with the disappearance and processed through the custody suite here at Edendale.

Cooper had seen people who hated being shut up in a cell or an interview room so much that they'd do anything to get out, including making a false confession. The fact that it might mean them ending up in prison didn't come into the equation. It was that need to escape from the immediate situation that blocked out long-term thinking, or any consideration of the consequences.

Reece Bower hadn't been one of those people. His time in the custody suite had been extended to ninety-six hours before he was charged. The hope had been that he would give away important information under questioning, or that some evidence would lead to the discovery of his wife's body. Neither of those things had happened.

At the end of the extended detention period, Bower was charged with murder. All the case files had been prepared, and a trial date had been set for the following year, when new evidence came to light.

'Oh, Reece Bower,' said Murfin when he appeared. 'Has that thing surfaced again after all this time?'

Cooper wasn't sure whether he was referring to the case as 'that thing' or to Reece Bower himself.

'It looks like it,' said Cooper. 'Bower himself is missing.'

'Well, that's nothing to cry about.'

'You were on the inquiry team, weren't you, Gavin?'

Murfin nodded. 'I was working with DI Hitchens' team under DS Osborne. Those were the days. Bill Osborne was quite a lad. I remember once—'

'Yes, Gavin, thanks. I think you've probably told us all the stories from the old days.'

'Oh. Well, they're all gone, except for me. Bill went on extended sick leave, then retired on health grounds. He's living in the Channel Islands now. DI Hitchens went off to Ripley, didn't he?'

'Yes, to work for RIPA.'

'Well, that's it, then. The whole team has gone. Except for me, and I'm only half here, so to speak.'

'You always were, Gavin.'

'True. But at least I was building up my pension fund.'

'Did you meet Reece Bower?'

'I certainly did.'

'And I take it you didn't like him.'

'I don't think anyone on the team did. He was a creep. No one was in any doubt that he was guilty. As far I'm concerned, it was written all over him. Right across his forehead.' Murfin made a scribbling gesture above his eyes. '*Guilty*, it said. Spelled properly with a "u" and everything, so it was official.'

Villiers had brought a file containing Reece Bower's details. She unclipped a photograph and slid it across Cooper's desk.

'That's the bugger,' said Murfin, twisting his head to peer at the photo. 'You can see what I mean from here.'

Cooper had to admit that the smile on Bower's face looked insincere. It was an expression he'd seen often on people who were guilty, a fake attempt at ingratiating sincerity. But everyone was guilty of something, weren't they? It didn't have to be a crime as serious as murder to make you look shifty and evasive.

Bower was in his early thirties in this photograph. It dated from the time of the earlier case and had been taken in the custody suite downstairs. Detention officers weren't known for their expertise as photographers. They could make any suspect look like one of the Kray Brothers. Even the women.

And it was also quite rare to see someone smiling for the camera as they were processed. Would he still have been smiling after fingerprints had been taken, and a mouth swab for DNA, and a blood sample, and finally the slamming of a cell door?

Cooper was reminded of a famous mugshot of the Hollywood actor Steve McQueen after he was arrested for drunk driving, smirking at the police photographer and giving a victory sign, as if knowing that he would never face the full penalty of the law.

'Is there a photograph of his wife too?' he asked.

'Sure.'

Villiers slipped another photograph on to his desk. Annette Bower looked two or three years younger than her husband. Cooper wouldn't have put her much above thirty. She had auburn hair, unfashionably long for the time. In the photo she was facing the camera, smiling, with an open, friendly expression that appealed to him straightaway. He could see how anyone might have fallen for this woman, as presumably Reece had.

Cooper felt a cold certainty grip his heart. This woman was almost definitely dead. And no one had found her, or brought her justice. That seemed so wrong that he knew he had to do something about it, if he could. The idea of her lying somewhere, undiscovered, her body turned to bones and eventually to dust . . . well, it didn't bear thinking about.

'Reece Bower is currently a logistics manager for a steel fabrications company in Chesterfield,' said Villiers. 'Ten years ago he was working in procurement at Chesterfield Royal Hospital, near Calow. His job was negotiating with suppliers. At that time, Mr Bower was accountable for more than five million pounds of expenditure on clinical supplies each year.'

'A responsible job. I suppose he lost it when he was arrested.'

'Well, a murder charge doesn't do much for your reputation,' said Murfin.

'And it was a thorough investigation.'

'Oh yes. The inquiry team combed through his entire life. They traced his movements, his relationships, his finances. They searched his house and dug up his garden. There was strong circumstantial evidence that made him look guilty. But the Crown Prosecution Service decided not to take it to court. They said the case against him wasn't strong enough to achieve a conviction.'

'Why not?' asked Villiers.

'Well, they never found Annette Bower's body, for a start.'

'It's possible to get a murder conviction without a body,' said Villiers, 'if the rest of the evidence is compelling enough. It has been done.'

'I know. And it almost went that way. Except . . .'

'What?'

'The inquiry suffered a serious setback,' said Cooper. 'Didn't it, Gavin?'

Murfin nodded.

'A witness turned up while the case was being prepared for court. He claimed to have seen the victim alive and well, days after she was supposed to have been killed. The statement this witness gave was pretty sound. It undermined the whole case. Reece Bower had maintained his innocence from the start and offered plausible alternative explanations for each item of forensic evidence. Without any proof that his wife was actually dead, there was just too much scope for reasonable doubt.'

Reasonable doubt. Cooper nodded. The great dread of prosecutors and police officers in a jury trial. It was always impressed on jury members that they had to bring a 'not guilty' verdict if they felt there was reasonable doubt.

From a police officer's point of view, some jurors seemed to experience doubt at the slightest prompting from the defence. Sometimes twelve ordinary members of the public turned into a roomful of Doubting Thomases, unconvinced by even the most powerful evidence, refusing to accept anything they were told, dismissing statements made by the police, disregarding the opinions of forensic experts. In this case, the CPS had probably made the right decision. A consistent and convincing witness was hard to ignore.

'This witness,' said Cooper. 'Remind me who it was.'

'Oh, a very reliable person in the eyes of the CPS. The person who claims to have seen Annette Bower alive was Mr Evan Slaney. Annette's father.'

5

It wasn't quite five p.m. on a Monday, yet the shutters were down on almost all the shops in the centre of Shirebrook. Diane Fry had parked her Audi in the deserted marketplace, where acres of free parking stood empty and unused. Apart from hers, just two cars occupied the whole area. This would never happen in Edendale, let alone in Nottingham, where parking spaces were at a premium, a privilege you had to pay through the nose for.

A group of children ran past her. Their chatter was in a language she couldn't understand. She could see the only shops doing business were Maxi Foods *polski sklep,* the Polo Market, and Zabka European super-market. She turned to look the other way. Oh, and Bargain Booze.

First-floor flats over every shop were occupied, and above them the attic rooms had been converted to living space, with curtains in tiny dormer windows. Men yelled to each other across the square from one betting shop to another, from William Hill to Betfred. In the alley by the Co-op the paving was littered with cigarette ends. A few people stood smoking outside the working men's club.

And a few yards away, Krystian Zalewski's blood was still soaking into the carpet and dripping through to the ceiling of the shop below.

Fry watched a group of press photographers clustering at the corner of the square with their camera bags slung over their shoulders. Reporters had been in town earlier, stopping people at random in the street to get their instant reactions to the murder. Shirebrook would be on the news tonight.

She found DCI Alistair Mackenzie at the crime scene in the alley, talking to a very tall uniformed constable from the Shirebrook Safer Neighbourhood Team who was acting as scene guard.

The entire alley had been taped off, with a guard posted at each end. A forensic tent had been erected at the spot where the attack appeared to have taken place. A pool of blood was drying on the brick paving, and the crime scene examiners had lifted shoe marks from prints left in the blood. A clear trail of blood spatters led away from the marketplace to the street entrance, highlighted by a zigzag series of yellow evidence markers. From there, it was only a short distance to the yard at the back of the shop.

Mackenzie nodded at Fry as she arrived.

'The crime scene guys say it's difficult to know how many people were here at the time of the attack,' he said. 'There seem to be at least three distinct shoe types, one of which is a match to the trainers Zalewski was wearing. But there could be other individuals who stayed clear of the blood. We have no way of telling.'

'I don't suppose there's any sign of Mr Zalewski's phone, sir?' asked Fry.

'Yes, in a way. Not a sign of its presence, but its absence.'

'I'm sorry, sir?'

Mackenzie pointed into the opening of the tent. 'In the middle of the patch of blood there. A clear spot the size and shape of a mobile phone. Perhaps a Samsung Galaxy, or something similar.'

'So he dropped his phone when he was attacked,' said Fry.

'And someone picked it up, yes. If we find the phone, it will have traces of Mr Zalewski's blood on it.'

'Any other traces that would help us, sir?'

'We've had officers doing a fingertip search the length of the alley.' Mackenzie screwed his face in disgust. 'I don't need to tell you everything they found. There was nothing useful, except this.'

He held up a sealed evidence bag. Fry had to look closely to see what was glinting inside.

'An earring?' she said.

'Exactly. And Krystian Zalewski doesn't look the sort of man who would wear them.'

'The earring is significant, then.'

'It may help an identification,' said Mackenzie. 'It's covered in latent prints and possibly DNA. But we'll have to send it to the lab at Hucknall.'

'It might mean one of his attackers was a woman. If there was a fight, she could have lost that earring in the struggle.'

'You'll see that there's no lighting in the alley,' said Mackenzie. 'Nothing along this whole stretch between the market square and the street that runs at the back there.'

'A perfect place for someone to lie in wait.'

'It seems Zalewski was on his way back from the shops when he was attacked.'

'The *polski sklep*?' said Fry.

'Of course.'

'He took his shopping with him after the attack. We found it in his flat. Bread and milk, nothing of interest. Zalewski seems to have been a perfectly ordinary, law-abiding citizen.'

'Do you know,' said Mackenzie, 'one of the residents here has kept a file of offences that migrant workers have been charged with. A sort of diary or scrapbook. His file goes back years, from when the first East Europeans started arriving in Shirebrook, just after Poland and a bunch of other countries joined the EU in 2004. The information has been gleaned from court records and various items published in local newspapers.'

'What sort of offences?'

Mackenzie shrugged. 'Run of the mill, most of them. One man was convicted of driving without a licence or insurance, taking a vehicle without consent and being over the breath alcohol limit. Another stole a beard trimmer from a pharmacy in Mansfield. A third admitted affray and actual bodily harm after a fight in the street here in Shirebrook. It's pretty much what you'd expect in the courts every week.'

'Anything serious?'

'No serious convictions. There was a sexual assault on a woman a few weeks ago. Everyone seems to believe the perpetrator must have been a migrant worker, but there's absolutely no evidence of it. A suspect has never been identified.'

'So it could have been anybody.'

'Absolutely. But that fact doesn't convince anybody.'

'I'm not surprised.'

Mackenzie looked at her closely and lowered his voice.

'You've read all the intelligence reports on the shop-keeper, Geoffrey Pollitt?' he said.

'Yes, I'm up to date.'

'It may not be relevant to the present inquiry, but keep it in mind. Mr Pollitt has been flagged up on multiple occasions for his right-wing extremist connections. But don't alert him yet to the fact we know about his activities.'

'I'll treat him like any other witness, sir.'

Mackenzie smiled. 'I suppose that will have to do.'

At the side of the market square, the bus shelters were plastered with posters printed in English and Polish. And another language in Cyrillic script. Russian? Bulgarian? Fry wasn't sure. But they all set out the conditions of a three-year Public Spaces Protection Order, the geographical version of an ASBO.

Some of the corners of the posters were torn off. They spelled out the warning of a one hundred pound fixed penalty or a fine of up to a thousand pounds on conviction. The order covered the whole of Shirebrook and neighbouring Langwith Junction, including the huge distribution centre on the former pit site.

No person shall consume alcohol. No person shall have an unsealed vessel containing alcohol in their possession. No person shall urinate other than in a public toilet. No person shall dispose of any litter other than in the bins provided. No persons shall congregate in groups of two or more within the alleyways which lead to Shirebrook Marketplace.

Someone had burned cigarette holes in the plastic cover of the bus timetable. Shan and Ryan had added their names in graffiti.

Other signs here warned that arson was a crime. Why would you need to explain that to anyone? Well, it must have been considered necessary in Shirebrook.

Incidents of arson had been increasing in the last couple of years, mostly in Nottinghamshire but spreading across the border into Derbyshire. A lot of them were in and around the old coal-mining towns too. Perhaps there was some deep-seated psychological reason for it.

Jamie Callaghan loomed up behind her and peered over her shoulder at the posters.

'Should we arrest Shan and Ryan? It would be a result of sorts.'

Fry turned. 'What have we got?'

'Well, we've got a couple of potential witnesses who are willing to talk,' said Callaghan, 'which is a bit of a minor miracle. They don't look very hopeful, but it's all we've got. They're scheduled for interview tomorrow morning.'

'English or Polish?' asked Fry.

'One of each.'

'Okay. Then we'd better talk to Mr Pollitt before he disappears.'

'He'll be waiting for us in the shop,' said Callaghan.

They made their way across the square to the shop. The sign on the fascia was broken in half, as if it had been torn away by a strong wind. The only word left was 'Shirebrook' followed by the start of another, a capital 'P'. What had the name of the shop been? Shirebrook Pets, Shirebrook Portraits? Shirebrook Pound Shop?

Like everywhere else, a shutter was down on the window, but the door was still open. Fry knew that the shop owner locked up at the end of the afternoon and drove out to his new-build semi on a Bellway estate in Warsop Vale, retreating across the border into Nottinghamshire when he wanted to escape Shirebrook for the night.

'How do you want to handle this?' asked Callaghan.

'We play it absolutely straight. Mr Pollitt will expect to be interviewed again. He'll know it's normal procedure in a murder case. If we left him alone, it would make him suspicious. So just treat him like any other witness.'

'Understood.'

'Lead the way, then.'

The shopkeeper was a stocky, middle-aged man with a barrel chest and incipient beer gut. The width of his torso forced him to carry his arms away from his chest.

Fry noticed that he held them awkwardly, like a gunslinger constantly about to go for his guns. He was wearing baggy jeans and a black T-shirt. A leather jacket slung over the counter suggested that he was ready to leave and go home to Warsop Vale, perhaps on a motorbike.

'I'm Geoffrey Pollitt,' he said. 'Everyone round here calls me Geoff.'

'I know you've already been spoken to, Mr Pollitt,' said Fry, 'but we'd like to know as much as we can about your tenant, Krystian Zalewski.'

'He weren't no trouble. Not like some of them. I'm open-minded, me. Poles are as good as anyone, as long as they have the money.'

Fry turned to look at the shop. There wasn't much to see. A bare counter ran most of its length, with an electronic till and a card reader at one end. A display case down the middle of the shop floor contained a few tools in blister packs. Hammers, screwdrivers, chisels, a lot of loose nails and tacks. A thin covering of dust lay over many of the items on display. The shelves on the back wall were empty, but for some posters advertising heavy metal concerts. Savage Messiah and Rob Zombie at Bloodstock in Catton Park. Slipknot and Marilyn Manson at the Download Festival. All the posters were a couple of years out of date.

'Is business not very good, Mr Pollitt?'

'What?' He looked startled. 'Oh, the shop? I haven't really got it up and running properly yet.'

'How long have you been here?' she asked, though she knew the answer perfectly well.

49

'Just a few months, like.'

Fry nodded. She knew it was more than a year, of course. It was in the intelligence reports. But it looked as though Mr Pollitt was making no attempt to establish a viable business.

'It's hard to compete these days,' said Pollitt, as if that explained everything.

Fry's foot hit something solid but yielding on the floor. She looked down. A bag of cat litter. A stack of similar bags stood against the counter, with some trays of pet food tins.

'Is this a hardware shop?' she said.

'You might call it that.'

Jamie Callaghan had drifted along the far wall towards the back of the shop as she was talking to Pollitt. She could see the shopkeeper's eyes never left him as they followed his progress. Right at the back was a door marked 'Private', which presumably led into the storeroom or an office of some kind.

'I'm trying to give customers what they want,' said Pollitt. 'If they come in here and ask for dog food, then that's what I get in for them. The thing is, I can order in anything they want, get it next day from the cash and carry. So I might look as though I don't have much stock in, but the turnover is better than you think.'

'Isn't Shirebrook a pretty quiet place?'

'It looks quiet now, but we have markets four days a week here. Tuesday, Wednesday, Friday, Saturday. It's cheap, too. A ten-foot pitch with a council stall only costs twelve pounds. But it's the hours that are a problem. You have to be there for a six-thirty start in the morning, and the market closes at two-thirty and gets dismantled. Shift change is at three.'

'Shift change?'

'When the workers come out from the distribution centre.'

'Oh, I see.'

'After that, there's no point staying open.'

'So you pull the shutters down for the night.'

Pollitt gave her a sideways glance. 'It's a lot safer that way.'

'You get trouble?'

'Not me. But some of the other shopkeepers, they've had problems.'

'Problems with the Polish people?'

Still Pollitt didn't rise to the opportunity.

'There's quite a lot of them in Shirebrook,' he said with a smirk, 'as you've probably noticed.'

Callaghan had completed his slow tour of the shop and arrived at the counter. He casually ran a finger along the surface.

'Tell us again about when Krystian Zalewski first came here. How did Mr Zalewski find out you had a flat vacant?'

'I advertised it in the Polish shops,' said Pollitt. 'I got a girl in one of the shops to write it out for me in their language. I knew it would get a response pretty quick. They all want somewhere to stay, don't they? And I don't charge much for the rental.'

'The flat isn't exactly luxurious, is it?' said Fry.

Pollitt shrugged. 'It has all you need.'

'And it's small.'

'One bedroom. It might suit a couple at a pinch, but I was happy to have a single tenant. Less chance of rows, you know.'

'Mr Zalewski seems to have had a violent row with someone,' said Fry. 'A fatal row.'

'Well, I can tell you straight, I don't know nothing about that. As far as I'm concerned, he were a good tenant.'

'And it was you who found the body this morning?'

'Yeah. I had to go up there to see what was wrong.'

'Had to?'

'Because of the blood. Look, you can still see the stain,' said Pollitt almost proudly, pointed at the ceiling.

A red patch had gathered near a light fitting, where blood had soaked into the plaster and spread sideways, forming uneven tidemarks and darkening in the centre as it dried.

'I'm afraid it will be there permanently, sir, unless you redecorate,' said Fry.

'Aye, I reckon it will.'

Looking round the shop, Fry thought that prospect was unlikely. It hadn't been decorated in here for some years.

'That's what told me something was wrong,' said Pollitt, still craning his neck to admire the stain.

Fry stared with distaste at the view she was getting of his double chin, covered in a patchy stubble.

'Well, you did the right thing, sir,' she said.

'How long had he been dead?' asked Pollitt. 'Do you know?'

He was asking too many questions now. Fry's instinct

told her that his interest was prurient. People she met were often like this, peripheral witnesses to a violent crime who felt they'd earned an entitlement to all the gory details.

'We're not sure,' she said.

'Oh.'

'What time did you notice the blood on your ceiling?'

'About seven-thirty, when I opened the shop.'

'You were here early, sir.'

'You have to open up early to get the customers,' said Pollitt. 'Passing trade, like.'

'Passing trade?'

'People call in for odds and ends.'

Fry knew she mustn't push it. There was a fine line between not asking enough questions and seeming to know too much. Best to stay focussed on the main issue for now.

'Mr Pollitt,' she said, 'did you ever see anyone visiting Krystian Zalewski?'

He shook his head. 'No. But then, I wouldn't. You've seen it – you get into the flat from the backyard. And the lad was out most of the day. If he had visitors, maybe they came in the evening after I locked up the shop. The only day I even knew he was here was on a Saturday now and then. He reckoned to work about every other weekend. If he was at home I could hear his radio sometimes. That was it, really.'

'You never had to go up to the flat to speak to him?'

'Only once or twice,' said Pollitt. 'He didn't know how to use the wheelie bins – what rubbish to put in which one, you know what I mean? I had to explain it to him. They won't take your bin if you've put the wrong stuff in.'

'What about collecting the rent?'

'I didn't have to bother. He put it through the door of the shop once a week without fail. Cash in an envelope. He always paid in full and never fell behind. Like I said, he were a good tenant.'

'So you'll be sorry to lose him,' said Fry.

Pollitt shrugged. 'There'll be another along in a day or two. There're plenty of migrants. It's one thing we're not short of around here. Not until Brexit, anyway.'

6

Ben Cooper was getting his new home straight, after a fashion. The cat, Hope, had settled in, which was the most important thing. She came and went through her cat flap as if she'd been doing it all her life. She'd developed a knack of catching the flap with the tip of her tail as she went through, and letting it bang with a noise that she seemed to find satisfying, and which alerted her owner to the fact that she'd gone out, or had just come in and was ready for food.

She'd also made friends with a ginger-and-white tom that belonged to the old lady next door. Hopes had been spayed and the tom was neutered, so there was no chance of any unexpected kittens.

The cat's satisfaction with her new home made Cooper himself feel more relaxed. A couple of the neighbours had called by to say hello. He'd popped into the local pub, the Bull's Head, and no one had stared at him too much.

In fact, Cooper had begun to meet a few people in Foolow. He'd learned from some of the older residents to call it 'Fooler', though if he used that name anywhere else no one would know where he was talking about. That was normal in the Peak District. Eyam was 'Eem', Edensor was 'Enser', Tideswell was 'Tidza'. It was a sign of ownership of the landscape, adopting a version in the local accent that outsiders wouldn't recognise.

The village nestled in a cluster of trees, barely a stone's throw from where he'd grown up. Its name meant 'Bird Hill', bestowed by some ancient Scandinavian settler. One of his English teachers at school had been an enthusiast for the study of local place names and their origins. He'd made an analysis of etymology and the mixing of elements from different languages an unofficial part of the syllabus. So Cooper knew it was a peculiarity of Peak District names that one of the words for a hill was 'low'. It looked odd when you came across a place called High Low. And it was all due to the pesky Scandinavians.

On the village green at Foolow stood an ornate cross and a former bullring. St Hugh's Church looked old but had been built in the nineteenth century, which was practically yesterday in the history of this area. Lead mining had been one of the major occupations here since the fifteenth century. Mounds and hillocks around the parish marked the sites of former lead mines, and sinkholes caused by the mine workings were a problem. The most recent had appeared about four years ago, he'd been told.

Tollhouse Cottage was nearly three hundred years old, built for farm labourers or estate workers at a time when houses were intended to last several lifetimes. The walls were solid, not those timber and plasterboard things you could put your fist through. Without the door or a window open, he could hear nothing from outside. Its limestone walls oozed with history and the steps to its front door were worn smooth by generations of previous occupants. It was squeezed into its village setting as if it had always been there, as if it had grown organically over the centuries, jostling with its neighbours for the available space and light, as much a natural part of its environment as the trees and the grass and the heather on the hills.

On summer evenings he was able to sit on the patio in the backyard, open a bottle of beer, and take in the view and the evening air. The view from here was the attraction that had swung his purchase of the house. When he looked out over the patchwork of fields, the sun broke through the clouds sporadically, highlighting one field and then another, changing the colours in the landscape as it went, catching a white-painted farmhouse here, casting shadows from a copse of trees over there.

The tracery of white limestone walls was like a map laid over the landscape, so painstakingly constructed that it seemed to hold the countryside together. He sometimes thought that if you followed the right lines on that map you could discover any story, find the clues to any mystery. All the answers might lie caught in this gleaming web.

Over a low wall, he occasionally saw his neighbours from up the row going to and from their houses. And Gavin Murfin had been right when he called at the cottage that first week. The 'old biddy' next door was no trouble once he'd made a fuss of her cat. She'd even made him an apple pie not long after he'd moved in. Two doors down, the teacher and her husband were a bit more distant, but they nodded and smiled whenever they saw him.

The wood-burning stove would be able to keep the cottage warm when the weather turned cold – it was a smaller version of the one at Bridge End Farm and he knew it would be cosy in here during the winter. Although the cottage was small, there was still a lot of empty space. He'd meant to get more stuff when he'd finished the decorating, but he seemed to have forgotten.

Tonight Cooper was on his way to a different pub a couple of villages away – the Barrel Inn at Bretton, up on the top of the ridge. Laying claim to being the highest pub in Derbyshire, it was also where he'd first talked to Dr Chloe Young, apart from a conversation over a post-mortem table in the mortuary.

Dr Young was the newly appointed Eden Valley pathologist, currently assisting Dr Juliana van Doon so that she could work part-time as she coasted towards retirement. Cooper's relationship with Chloe Young had been progressing slowly but steadily. But that was fine with him. There was no rush.

Young had come to the house in Foolow in her yellow VW Beetle. He was always surprised how different she looked outside the mortuary. The first time they'd met off duty he'd hardly recognised her. That was the way it could be with people you only saw in particular circumstances, in a specific role or location. They became one-dimensional figures, and it was disorienting to find they were real people with unexpected aspects to their lives. Chloe Young had her hair down, which instantly transformed her from the professional in a mortuary apron and scrubs, with a complicated hair knot tied up under a hat. He liked the way she dressed too, casual but stylish.

'So they do let you have some time off?' said Young when he let her into the cottage.

'Of course. Why wouldn't they?'

'Well, you hear stories about police officers. Dedicated to their work, always on call. They say they're married to their jobs. You know what I mean.'

'Not me,' said Cooper.

'Good.'

While he put on his jacket, Cooper sneaked a glance at his phone. No messages, so far at least. Perhaps he should turn it off for the evening? But he hesitated. Well, he'd set it to vibrate on silent anyway.

'Do you have a murder case, or is it just a missing person?'

'Well, we have no body,' said Cooper. 'Correction – *no bodies*.'

'And you're attempting to find them?'

'Of course.'

'So you're trying to make work for me after all. I see.'

Cooper's Toyota was parked on a bit of rough ground at the back of the cottage, while Young's Beetle was on the street.

'I'll drive,' she said cheerfully, jangling her keys.

He wanted to argue, but it obviously made sense. The VW felt a bit cramped when he got into the passenger seat, but it was okay. At least, it was okay until he discovered how fast Young liked to drive. He was jerked back against the seat as she took off through Foolow and swung into Bradshaw Lane.

'There's a speed limit, you know,' he said.

'But no speed cameras. And no patrolling policemen, because they're too short-staffed.' She glanced at him. 'Not ones who are on duty, anyway.'

'Just make sure we get there in one piece.'

'I'm an exceptionally good driver.'

'If you say so.'

Luckily, it wasn't far to the Barrel Inn. And like so many Peak District roads at a quiet time of the year, they met hardly any traffic coming the other way. A tractor or a milk tanker on a narrow bend would have been a different matter. They might never have made it to the pub at all.

Dr Young was no more than five feet six, possibly less, with hair that was dark, almost black. Cooper recalled the first time he'd met her, the sheen of it catching the light reflected from the stainless steel dissecting table, the French twist knotting it at the back of her head to keep it away from her face.

And then, when she'd removed a pair of protective glasses, he'd seen those cool green eyes, verging on hazel. She was so different from his idea of what pathologists looked like, such a contrast to the lean, hunched posture, sharp eye and disapproving expression of Dr Juliana van Doon that the image had stayed with him for some time, until he was able to meet her again.

Chloe Young was originally a Sheffielder, but after graduating from Cambridge she'd done postgraduate work and had a spell in a research position in London. Then she came back north to work in Sheffield. When he met her that first time, Young had been taking part in a neurobiological study of suicidal behaviour. She was present in Dr van Doon's mortuary to take samples of brain tissue from suicide victims before they degraded too much to be useful in her study. It hardly sounded like a promising start to a relationship. What Cooper remembered most was when she later described her career up to date and said: 'I don't know where I'll end up next.' Yet here she was, still working in Edendale. Something must be keeping her here.

She seemed quite unselfconscious and at ease with him, as if she'd known him all her life. For a moment, Cooper wondered whether she did know him. Perhaps they'd encountered each other at some time in the past and he'd forgotten – though she was the sort of person he was unlikely to forget.

She'd told him that the Peak District was one of the factors that had encouraged her to return to the north. He liked that. Cooper always imagined that if he ever had to leave the area for some reason, it would be these hills and valleys and moors that would draw him back as irresistibly as a magnet. Young had said that she used to feel it was her own personal national park. That was the way he felt too.

'What would you like?' he said when they got to the bar at the Barrel.

'Vodka,' she said.

'And?'

'Just vodka. It's like a little black dress. It goes with anything.'

'Are you sure?'

'Don't worry,' she said. 'I'll only have one. Got to be careful with a police officer in the car.'

They found a table by the window and Cooper wondered how to start the conversation. He didn't know her well enough to ask after her family, or to have any idea what else was likely to be going on in her life except a constant flow of dead bodies through the mortuary.

But Young had the advantage of him.

'How's Carol?' she said. 'I haven't seen her for a while.'

'Oh, she's fine. Busy, you know. Like we all are.'

It was an awkward reminder that Carol Villiers had known Chloe Young long before he'd met her. Villiers had even been out with her brother for a few months, many years ago. The Young family were from Sheffield, a city that sat right on the Yorkshire edge of the Peak District. It was Villiers who Chloe had got in touch with when she came to work in the Eden Valley. It had always bothered Cooper that they might talk about him to each other. But you had to have trust, didn't you? That was important, both to his connection with Chloe Young and in his working relationship with Villiers.

'Have you decided what you're going to do next?

Will you take the full-time vacancy when Dr van Doon retires?'

'It's one of the options,' she said.

It wasn't like her to be coy. Was she just teasing him? Now, that he didn't like much. He was aware that Chloe Young was extremely well educated. *'Qualifications coming out of her ears'* was the way Villiers had expressed it.

Cooper had managed a few A levels before he joined Derbyshire Constabulary. He'd watched the influx of younger graduates over the years with some uneasiness. He knew it didn't make any real sense, but he still felt a twinge of inferiority when he was talking to people with that level of education. Chloe Young's qualifications were part of who she was. She was a forensic pathologist with a specialty in neurobiology and the study of brain tissue samples. He was a copper who'd managed to work his way up to inspector rank.

'You've never gone far away from Edendale, have you?' said Young. 'Not for any period of time.'

'I've never wanted to,' said Cooper.

'So you must have seen a lot of changes in this area.'

Cooper laughed. 'Changes? I've seen things change so much. When I took my A levels at Eden Valley College and joined the police service, life looked very positive, and I don't think it was just my age. Now, it's very different.'

Young looked serious. 'How do you mean?'

'Well, there are so many things. I see people working really hard, but existing on wages so low that they couldn't afford the lifestyle they once expected, people who can't afford to pay a mortgage without doing at least two jobs. Young people can't get on the housing ladder, tenants are struggling with soaring rents. Disabled people lie awake at night worrying about their benefits being cut. The unemployed on jobseeker's allowance feel they're being pushed from pillar to post to avoid being sanctioned. I meet all these people in my job.'

'I'm sure you do.'

'Oh, on the surface it doesn't look too bad. Visitors to the area don't see it. But I know there's a waiting list for appointments at the Citizens' Advice Bureau to get debt counselling or advice about eviction. The number of food banks has been expanding – there are three in Edendale alone now. Some households can't afford to get a broken refrigerator or a cooker repaired.'

Cooper took a long drink of his beer.

'I met an outsourced care worker recently,' he said. 'She was driving from one fifteen-minute appointment to another, going from door to door trying to deal with people who need full-time care. Out here, in some of these villages, the social institutions are being eroded. Churches are becoming redundant and closing and clergy are thin on the ground and stretched across six or seven parishes. Where are people supposed to go for support?'

'I don't know the answer to that.'

'No, of course you don't, Chloe. No one does.'

'I do see the results of this,' she said. 'Right at the end of the process, I suppose. We're very rarely aware of what's gone on before. But you see it all at the blunt end, don't you?'

Cooper nodded. 'Do you know, there was a case recently where we went to the house of an old couple. The wife was disabled and her husband had cancer. She told us she lived in fear of her disability living allowance being stopped and losing the car she uses to ferry her husband to hospital for treatment. They both dread the postman delivering a brown envelope from the Department for Work and Pensions, containing bad news.'

'That's sad.'

'It makes them feel worthless, Chloe. That's something that shouldn't happen to anyone. And we're right in the middle, ill-equipped and untrained to help.'

'Is this the police service you came into as a teenager?' asked Young.

'No, it isn't,' said Cooper. 'It isn't even the same world.'

Cooper stopped, aware that he'd been talking more in the last few minutes than he'd talked to anyone for months and months. How did Chloe Young get all that out of him, things he'd been feeling but hadn't ever expressed before, even to himself?

He smiled. No, he didn't know how she did it. But it certainly made him feel better getting it out of his system. It felt almost as good as sitting across the table from her here in the Barrel Inn.

'Change of subject,' said Young.

She placed an envelope on the table in front of him and tipped something out.

'What are those?' said Cooper.

'Tickets.'

'I don't recognise them.' He picked one up. 'Oh, Buxton Opera House. I've never been there.'

'What, never?' said Young.

'Well no, that's not right. I think I went to some Gilbert and Sullivan thing once. It was years ago, though, when I was a teenager.'

'That long ago?' laughed Young. 'Good grief.'

'I went with my parents. They dragged me along against my will, because some relative was in the chorus. One of my cousins, I think. Not that we could have recognised them under the make-up.'

'What did you see?'

'I think it was *The Pirates of Penzance.*'

'Ah.'

'What do you mean "Ah"?'

'"*A Policeman's Lot is Not a Happy One*",' she sang.

'Of course. I remember it now.' He smiled at the recollection. 'My mother sang along, but my father wouldn't join in. It was beneath his dignity, I suppose.'

Young looked more serious. 'Yes, he was in the police too, wasn't he?'

'A sergeant,' said Cooper, then hesitated. 'Did you hear about it? What happened to him, I mean.'

He knew the answer, of course. Everyone knew about the way Sergeant Joe Cooper had died. If Chloe Young didn't know when she came back to Edendale, she would have been told by Dr van Doon when she began working at the hospital, or by Carol Villiers. It wasn't something he could keep private, even if he'd wanted to do so. Over the years he'd become accustomed to the idea that everyone knew. But he could never be sure whether the knowledge made people look at him differently. Was Chloe Young looking at him differently now?

'Yes, I did hear,' she said after a moment's pause. 'I'm so sorry.'

'It was a long time ago,' said Cooper.

'Not long enough for you to have forgotten it.'

'No.'

Cooper was forced to look away for a few seconds. There was another tragedy in his much more recent past, one he could never forget. And he was certain Chloe Young would have heard about that one too. He began to feel uncomfortable in her presence, as he questioned what might be going through her mind. She wasn't a suspect in an interview room, so he couldn't interrogate her. He had to accept that her thoughts were her own, unless she decided to share them with him.

'Anyway,' she said, more brightly, 'back to the tickets.'

Cooper looked down at the table. He'd forgotten the tickets. They'd slipped from his mind in that flood of memories, a chain reaction of recollections sparked by the mere mention of Buxton Opera House and *The Pirates of Penzance*.

'Oh, the tickets,' he said, knowing he must sound stupid.

'You'll notice I have two,' said Young.

'What are they for?'

'*Tosca*. The English Touring Opera production. Are you a fan of Puccini?'

'Of course.'

She looked at him more closely. 'It isn't Gilbert and Sullivan, you know.'

'Now you're being patronising.'

'I apologise.'

'Accepted.'

'So – are you free on that day? I hope you are. No urgent cases to investigate?'

'Hopefully,' said Cooper. 'And no dead bodies waiting for you to cut up?'

'None that won't keep in the freezer for a few hours.'

'Thank you. It's a date then.'

Young smiled. 'So it is,' she said.

7

Diane Fry felt exhausted as she drove back into Nottingham that night. Shirebrook had tired her out.

The act with Geoffrey Pollitt had been difficult to maintain. Fry knew far more about him than she could have admitted. Yet, in the Zalewski case, he was supposed to be a secondary witness who might have some information about the victim. She had to treat him as an innocent bystander. And Pollitt had to believe that's what he was.

On the way back towards Wilford, Fry drove over Clifton Bridge and pulled into the forecourt of the BP filling station on Clifton Lane. She withdrew some cash from the ATM, filled up the tank of her Audi, and bought a couple of bottles of water in the shop. She didn't need the cash – she hardly ever used it. But it had become a habit. Cash, petrol, water. A steady routine that kept her grounded and reminded her that she had a private life, such as it was, out of the office.

She crossed to the bank of InPost lockers in a corner of the forecourt next to the air pump. She had a medi-um-sized locker for items she'd bought online. She scanned the QR code from her phone to open the locker, conscious of the CCTV camera focused on the lockers. Today there was another yellow box waiting for her to collect. She slid it out and clicked the locker shut.

When she reached her apartment, she remembered she had no food in. She'd been used to that at the old flat in Edendale, of course, but somehow she'd imagined it would be different in Wilford, as if the apartment would resupply itself. It had every other modern convenience, so why was the fridge always empty? Something wrong there, surely.

Fry sighed. So it was a takeaway. Domino's Pizza or Oriental Express? They were both near the Tesco store at Compton Acres. It was a Monday, so the Oriental Express would be open. Tomorrow, the choice would be more limited. After a second's hesitation, she dialled and ordered a Yuk Sung Chicken with mini vegetarian spring rolls.

While she waited, she performed some exercises to wind down from the day. She became absorbed in what she was doing and stopped in surprise when the buzzer sounded.

'That was quick,' she said. 'They must be quiet tonight.'

She grabbed a couple of notes, left the apartment, and went downstairs to the outside door to collect the takeaway. She never knew what to say to the delivery people, so when she opened the door, she began: 'Thank you. That was—'

And then she stopped.

'Oh, were you expecting someone else, Sis?' said her visitor. 'Anyone nice?'

'Angie?'

Fry gritted her teeth. Why did her sister always do this, arrive for a visit when she was least expecting her? It was almost as if Angie was trying to catch her out.

'No one,' she said. 'I wasn't expecting anyone. Particularly not you.'

Angie smiled. 'Are you going to invite me in, then? If I'm not intruding?'

'I suppose so.'

Fry took a step out of the door and looked round the parking area in front of the apartment block. No sign of any unfamiliar vehicles. Angie had a mysterious boyfriend who Fry had never managed to meet. But if he'd dropped Angie off, he'd made a very quick exit.

Angie was already on her way upstairs. She knew her way to the apartment, because she'd been here before, staying for a few days after another unexpected visit. Fry realised her sister wasn't carrying anything but a small shoulder bag. No change of clothes, nothing for an overnight stay. So it would only be a quick visit. And there were no bottles, teats, wet wipes, or packs of nappies either.

'Where's – er . . .?'

'Where's what?' said Angie. 'Who?'

'The baby. Zack.'

'I know what my baby's name is. Sonny is looking after him.'

'Really?'

Fry had formed an image in her mind of Angie's

boyfriend. He drove a Renault hatchback and was involved in some kind of business that brought him to Nottingham occasionally. She was sure it was dodgy, probably illegal. She deliberately hadn't asked. And looking after a baby for the day didn't suit her mental image.

'Actually,' said Angie, 'it will be Manjusha who's looking after him.'

'Manjusha?'

'Sonny's mother.'

Angie had dropped into an armchair in the sitting room and kicked off her shoes.

'Wait a minute,' said Fry. 'Who's Sonny? I thought your boyfriend was called Craig something?'

'Oh, him,' said Angie with a dismissive wave of her hand. 'He's old news.'

'But isn't he the father, of er . . .?'

'Zack? Maybe. But he wasn't much of a dad. Never showed any interest. I couldn't have left Zack with *him* for the day, let alone his mother. She's a drunken old slag.'

Angie eyed the gin bottle on the table. It was half-full, or half-empty, depending on your point of view. There was a glass next to it, but only one. Fry took the opportunity to slide the yellow box out of sight under her jacket on a chair.

'Now, Sonny is a different matter,' said Angie. 'He's very good with Zack.'

'So how long will he last? Or are you planning to move on to someone else soon?'

Angie yawned. 'No, he can stay for a bit.'

'Is his name actually Sonny? It makes him sound like a boxer.'

That made her sister laugh. 'He's nothing like a boxer. Well, if you must know, his name is Sunil Kumar. Everyone calls him Sonny. Though I've always thought it ought to be Sunny, with a "u". He's quite a laugh.'

Angie had managed to control the weight she'd put on after the pregnancy and was starting to recover her old angular body shape. Her face had changed, though. That was probably permanent. Fry realised it must be the approach of middle age. Angie had started having children relatively late, as many women did now.

Then Fry checked herself. *Started having children*'? That raised the possibility there were going to be more little versions of Zack. She wondered what those would be called. Zane, Zappa, Ziggy, Zeus?

'I'm glad you're happy,' said Fry.

'Thanks, Sis. I suppose you want to know all about him.'

'Only if you want to tell me.'

'Is there any chance of a cup of tea?'

'Of course.'

The door buzzed again. Before Fry could move, Angie had jumped to her feet and run to the window to peer out.

'Oriental Express,' she said. 'That's great. It looks as though I'm just in time for supper.'

Shane Curtis scrambled awkwardly through the opening and clung for a second to a beam before dropping on to a bale of straw.

This barn had been disused for years. The old man who owned the farm had used it for overwintering his suckler herd. But there were no signs left of the cattle now, except a layer of trampled straw and a whiff of dung from the breeze-block stalls. A much bigger, steel-framed barn stood a few yards away, stacked to the roof with huge bales of straw.

Shane settled into a dark corner where he couldn't be seen from the doorway. He found a dry patch and squatted on a pile of empty feed sacks. The place must be crawling with insects, but they didn't bother him. They couldn't do him any real harm. Only humans did that.

A trickle of moonlight crept through the gaps in the corrugated roof, and a movement of air stirred a vast spider's web strung between the beams. There was no sound, except for that persistent coughing. Cough, cough, cough, like a coal miner with emphysema.

Shane tugged a can of lager from the pocket of his coat, popped the tab and took a long swig. He fumbled in another pocket and found his tin. A couple of feeble-looking joints lay inside. It wasn't the best stuff, but it was all he had. His usual dealer had got himself nicked a couple of weeks back, the idiot. Someone else would take over his customers, but for now Shane had to rely on some blokes who came out from Mansfield and went round the pubs. It was expensive too, but they charged what the market would take. Pure capitalism.

He lit one of the joints and lay back in his corner, smiling to himself. This was his idea of the way to live. Away from all those drunks and junkies and the stupid women who got themselves pregnant at the drop of a hat. There was only one thing missing.

Cough, cough, cough. Out there in the darkness, somewhere between the barn and the house.

Shane laughed at the sound. Things like that out in the darkness didn't scare him either. He'd been in juvenile detention for eighteen months after twocking a few cars and pinching a bit of stuff from the shops in the market square. Werrington Juvenile Centre. That was pretty bad. But it hadn't scared him. Not at all. He was as tough as any of those kids in there, and he could prove it if he had to.

He sat up suddenly, clutching the joint. The coughing had stopped. Instead, he heard a soft thud of hooves on the muddy ground. Something or someone was coming this way. Those sheep had heard it before he did and they were leaving in a hurry. It was time to be ready.

Then Shane sniffed. He could smell something more than mouldy straw or the whiff of cows. What was it? It took a few moments for him to identify the smell. Then he had a memory of the party at his uncle's back in July. Out in their big garden on a warm summer evening. Burgers and cold beer. Uncle Rick himself presiding over the barbecue with his apron and tongs.

Shane jumped to his feet, spilling the last bit of lager from his can. Yes, it was smoke. He could see it now, grey tendrils of it creeping under the barn door. It stank of burning wood, acrid and toxic.

'No! Not now!'

He scrambled to his feet and ran to big double doors.

But the bar across them was too heavy to lift, the hinges too rusted to shift. He banged on the wood.

'Hey! There's someone in here. Let me out.'

There was no response. Only the increasing noise of flames crackling, the *whoosh* of a bale of straw igniting in the hayloft, showering sparks on to the floor below. The fire had started right here in the barn. Someone had done this deliberately.

Shane coughed as a blast of smoke filled his lungs, the hot fumes scorching his airways until he could barely croak out a breath.

'Hey! Someone! Please!'

He shouted and banged on the door for as long as he could, until finally the smoke overwhelmed him and he sank to his knees, his throat raw and his eyes streaming.

And still there was no reply. Even the sheep had moved away from the barn to leave him to his fate.

8

Day 2

Ben Cooper stepped out of his Toyota. He didn't need to sniff the air to know what had been burning. The air was still thick with charred embers of straw drifting on the breeze. A shower of black specks were settling even now on the paintwork of his car and on to his face as he turned to look up at the burnt skeleton of the barn. The ground around the building was muddy and running with channels of water from the fire-fighters' hoses. The smell of hot steam mingled with traces of acrid smoke that stung his nostrils.

He looked around for the duty DC and found both Luke Irvine and Becky Hurst on the scene. The two youngest members of his team were very different. Irvine could turn a bit bolshie, if he wasn't reined in. Cooper had overheard political arguments between him and Hurst and Irvine was definitely somewhere out on the right wing. Hurst was like a little terrier, no job too much trouble. She had good instincts too. When Carol Villiers wasn't around, Cooper often looked for the coppery red of her hair behind a computer screen.

'Another arson?' he said.

Irvine nodded. 'No doubt about it.'

'Dry straw goes up so easily. It wouldn't take much to start it off.'

'And don't these kids know it.'

'Kids?' asked Cooper.

'Well, it must be, mustn't it? Some youths who get a kick out of setting fires and watching them burn. They like to see the fire appliances turn up. It's like they're watching the telly, but in real life.'

'There's no evidence of that, is there?'

'We just haven't identified the right suspects,' said Irvine. 'Because no one is talking. They never do – even if it's a murder case.'

Castle Farm stood in a small valley to the north of Edendale, at the end of Reaper Lane. It would once have been remote, lying at the foot of the moorland that separated the Eden Valley from the Hope Valley. But, as the town grew, the housing estates on its northern outskirts had crept nearer and nearer to Castle Farm, filling the bottom of the valley and coming within a few fields of the farm itself.

The mass of housing was visible to Cooper from the gate of the farmyard. The fields, barns and outbuildings were near enough for youngsters from the estates to reach in twenty minutes on their bikes. The old farmer was the last generation of the Marston family to run it as a going concern. Other Marstons had left to take jobs in Chesterfield or Sheffield. When Ron Marston retired or died, the farm would become vacant. The sheep would be sent off to market, there would be another farm machinery sale in the yard, and developers would be competing to get their planning applications in for a series of barn conversions.

'We're not classifying this as a murder case,' said Cooper. 'Not unless there's any clear evidence. On the face of it, it seems unlikely to have been a deliberate killing. It was arson, certainly. But it looks as though Shane Curtis was in the wrong place at the wrong time. So manslaughter at most, I'd say.'

'Of course, he might have been in the right place at the right time,' said Irvine.

'What do you mean?'

'It's quite possible he was one of the arsonists, isn't it? Why else was he in the barn?'

Cooper looked at Hurst, but she shrugged. 'It's true we haven't found any legitimate reason for him to be here.'

'So Shane and his mates came along to have a bit of fun and set fire to the barn,' said Irvine. 'And somehow it all went wrong and he was trapped inside when it went up.'

'So you think it was his own fault?' said Hurst.

Irvine was unmoved. 'Death by misadventure,' he said.

'Have you talked to Mr Marston?' asked Cooper.

'Yes,' said Irvine. 'He had the usual complaints about kids trespassing on his property and causing damage, or injuring his livestock. It's true, too. Some of the incidents are on record. But he didn't know any of the kids by name. Shane Curtis meant nothing to him. He didn't see them either, but he doesn't go outside much after dark.'

'He lives alone?'

'Apart from a couple of dogs. Long-haired German Shepherds, and they're a bad-tempered pair. They're chained up in a shed across the yard from the farm-house. Mr Marston heard them barking last night, but he says the dogs often bark at foxes and badgers when they get their scent, so he didn't go out to see if there was something wrong. Not until he noticed the fire, anyway.'

'Surely he doesn't work this farm on his own? He isn't a young man.'

'No, he uses a couple of part-time employees.' Irvine held out his notebook. 'He's written the names down for me.'

'Written them down for you? Have you lost your ability to write?'

'No, just these names. His workers are both East Europeans.'

'Where is Mr Marston now?'

Irvine inclined his head towards the farmhouse. 'He's watching us round the corner of the barn. You're welcome to see if you can get anything out of him, boss. I can't.'

Cooper found the old farmer leaning on a gate. Marston could have been any one of scores of farmers he'd seen leaning on the pen sides at the cattle market in Edendale, or grabbing a handful of fleece on a sheep at Bakewell Show. He wore the flat cap favoured by the older generation, rather than the baseball caps their sons and grandsons had opted for, and a pair of brown corduroy trousers tucked into his boots.

'Mr Marston? Detective Inspector Cooper.'

'Are you the bloke in charge here?'

'Yes, sir. I gather from one of my officers that you have two East European men working here at the farm.'

'You're not immigration enforcement, are you?'

'No, sir. Edendale CID.'

He scowled. 'Same thing.'

'I just wanted to ask a few questions about your workers.'

'Look, those two lads have been helping me out on the farm,' he said. 'Feeding the pigs, moving arks, scraping muck off the yard. They're hard workers and they've never been any trouble.'

'Do you talk to them much, Mr Marston?'

'Well, not beyond the basics. They don't speak much English. I show them what to do and they get on with it. We don't exactly socialise.'

'So you don't really know anything about them, do you?'

'I know all I need to,' said Marston obstinately. 'If you want to know more, you'll have to ask them yourself.'

Cooper saw this kind of obstinacy often. Perhaps it was a characteristic of people living and working in an environment where you needed a powerful streak of stubbornness to survive. No one wanted to admit they were wrong, or give in to what might look inevitable from the outside. He could admire that pig-headedness sometimes. But not always.

He went back to the barn, where Irvine and Hurst were waiting.

'Keep talking to people,' said Cooper. 'DS Sharma will

be here soon. He's dealing with the parents and getting a formal identification. You'll report to him, okay?'

Irvine and Hurst nodded and Cooper turned away to walk back to his car, stepping over the still smoking remains of a charred lump of straw.

In a field nearby he heard sheep coughing and stopped to listen. In a human, he would have thought they were affected by the smoke. But this was a different type of cough.

'Lungworm,' he said.

Irvine heard him, and stared across in amazement, as if he thought Cooper had just insulted him.

'The sheep,' called Cooper. 'They've got lungworm.'

Back at his office in West Street, Ben Cooper found a message waiting, asking him to call Detective Superintendent Hazel Branagh urgently. He picked up the phone straightaway.

'Ben, thanks for getting back to me so quickly,' said Branagh.

'No problem, ma'am. What can I do for you?'

'I've just seen a request from you to give priority to a missing person case in Bakewell.'

'That's correct, ma'am.'

'Why do you want pursue it?' she said. 'It's just a missing person report. An adult missing from home, no indication of a crime or any other cause for concern.'

'Because of the background,' said Cooper. 'The history, I mean – the Annette Bower case from ten years ago.'

'I remember it well, Ben. You don't have to tell me about it. I was the senior investigating officer.'

'Of course you were.'

'I've looked at the available information regarding the apparent disappearance of Reece Bower. I don't think it can be regarded as a priority at the moment. Not with your arson death and the spate of armed robberies and everything else that's going on in the division. You must see that, Ben.'

Cooper bit his lip. She was right, of course. Without further evidence, it was officially low priority. But still . . .

'Understood, ma'am,' he said.

He heard Branagh hesitate. 'I wish I was still there in Edendale, you know,' she said. 'But I'm sure you'll be fine.'

'Of course. But it's sometimes difficult to know when I can use my own initiative and when I need to refer things up the chain of command.'

There was a short silence. Cooper thought he might have gone too far. But it turned out that Superintendent Branagh was thinking something quite different. When she replied, she had lowered her voice to a more confidential tone. Cooper instinctively leaned forward to listen what she had to say. He felt like a conspirator, worrying about electronic bugs in the light fittings of his own office.

'Between you and me, Ben, I was always disappointed in the outcome of the Annette Bower case,' said Branagh. 'It felt like a personal failure for me as SIO.'

'It was a CPS decision not to go forward with a

prosecution,' said Cooper.

'Of course. But that just meant the evidence we'd gathered wasn't considered strong enough. One contradictory witness cancelled out everything we'd done. All those weeks we'd spent working on the inquiry counted for nothing.'

'They might have been right to make that decision,' said Cooper cautiously. 'A jury—'

'Yes, yes. Perhaps it was right by their criteria. Reasonable doubt and all that.'

Branagh made the phrase 'reasonable doubt' sound like a curse.

'I take it you didn't agree, ma'am?' said Cooper.

She was firm in her answer. 'No, I didn't. The Bower case was a miscarriage of justice. Oh, I know people usually take that phrase to mean someone who's wrongly been found guilty. But it applies in these circumstances too. As far I'm concerned, Reece Bower escaped justice.'

'A lot of people seem to share that view, ma'am.'

'It's also important to me personally, Ben. It's been concerning me for ten years, ever since I saw Reece Bower walk free.'

Even though he hadn't been on the inquiry team, Cooper could remember the atmosphere in the station when the news came through of a new witness and an apparent sighting of Annette Bower alive and well. At first, the response had been sceptical, even dismissive. It always happened in a missing person case, or in the hunt for a wanted suspect. Sightings came in from all kinds of unlikely people and places. They had to be

84

checked out, but it was rare they came to anything.

In this case, everyone had been so convinced that Annette was dead that the report of a sighting barely caused a ripple. Perhaps they'd all been steered towards that certainty by the confidence of their SIO, Detective Chief Inspector Hazel Branagh.

But, gradually, the faces of the officers assigned to interview the witness told their own story. His statement was consistent; his account couldn't be shaken; the witness would perform well on the stand under cross-questioning. In the end, DCI Branagh had returned from a conference with the lawyers of the Crown Prosecution Service with a face like thunder. On balance, there was insufficient prospect of a successful conviction against Reece Bower.

Cooper noticed the photograph of Annette Bower sticking out from a folder on his desk. He drew it out and looked at her as he spoke. Her eyes seemed to be trying to communicate with him across a decade. But what was she trying to tell him?

'Do you think Reece Bower has done a runner, ma'am?' asked Cooper frankly.

'Maybe,' said Branagh. 'But why would he do that ten years later? If he did kill his wife, he knew long ago that he'd got away with it. Mr Bower has settled down, changed jobs, started a new life with a new partner, and had another child. There's no reason for him to abandon all that. He hardly sounds the sort of person who'd suddenly be overcome with guilt.'

Cooper smiled as he recognised how thoroughly Detective Superintendent Branagh had kept up to date with what had happened in Reece Bower's life since the original inquiry. That was more like the senior detective he knew and admired.

'What if Mr Bower was aware that some new evidence was about to come to light?' he said.

'Mmm. Well, that's possible. But what sort of new evidence? The one piece of evidence we needed most was the body. But if that's about to turn up somewhere, how come Reece Bower knows about it – and we don't?'

'I can't answer that, ma'am,' said Cooper. 'Not without making further inquiries.'

Superintendent Branagh was so quiet that he could hear the voices of people walking down the corridor near her office. Then he thought he heard her laugh quietly.

'Detective Inspector Cooper,' she said, 'I'd appreciate it if you could find the time to come and see me this afternoon. Towards the end of the day, if possible. Shall we say about five p.m.?'

Cooper smiled. Five p.m. A time when most of the office-based staff would be going home.

'Yes, that will be fine.'

'And I dare say you might happen to pass through Bakewell on the way here?'

And that was even better.

'It would be a pleasure, ma'am,' he said.

After he'd finished the call, Cooper picked up the photograph of Annette Bower, gazed at it for a moment, then slipped it into the pocket of his jacket.

9

Tammy Beresford was first on Jamie Callaghan's list. A single mother in her late twenties, wearing clothes that smelled of charity shop. She looked from Fry to Callaghan as if they were aliens just arrived from another planet.

'I don't know what I can tell you,' she said.

'Anything would be helpful.'

'You'd better come in, I suppose.'

She showed them into the kitchen, where she began folding a stack of washing from a basket. T-shirts and socks hung over the radiator. A kettle and microwave were plugged in on the worktop, but there was no offer of a cup of tea.

'Is this your house, Miss Beresford?' asked Fry.

'It's rented. I live here on my own with my boy, Jayden. He's ten.'

'Is he at school at the moment?'

'Of course. Why wouldn't he be?'

'No reason.'

Fry looked around for a chair. She moved a pile of towels to make room on a dining chair at the table.

Callaghan remained standing by the door and Tammy Beresford ignored him.

'You know why we're here,' said Fry. 'We're making inquiries into the death of Mr Krystian Zalewski. He's a near neighbour of yours. Or he was.'

Tammy beat a sweater flat. 'Yes, I heard.'

'Did you know him well?'

'Hardly at all. We don't know any of them. I tell Jayden to stay away from them at school, but he can't avoid it.'

'Them?'

Tammy sneered at her. 'The Polish. Don't you know anything?'

'You have a problem with the migrant workers in Shirebrook.'

'A problem? Yes, I'll say there's a problem. Why should people have to put up with them camping in front of our homes, sleeping in garages and sheds? You have Poles and the rest sleeping rough, using hedges and alleys for toilets, and looking in recycling bins for clothes. You try to get an appointment at the health centre because your child is sick and it's booked solid, and when you go all the names being called out are Polish. They love our health service. And there's rubbish everywhere. You can see it yourself. We're a dumping ground. They've swamped us.'

'I can see you're angry—'

Tammy slammed the basket back down on the tiled floor.

'My dad was a miner,' she said. 'One of the last men working at Shirebrook pit. He says this place was brought to its knees in the 1980s by the closures at Shirebrook and Langwith. It put hundreds out of work. He feels so let down by the government – not just this one, or the one in the eighties, but all of them. And so do I. We've been ignored for too long now – like my dad says, British people are second-class citizens in their own country.'

'Are you going to say "I'm not racist, but . . ."?' asked Fry.

The woman flushed. 'It's all right for you to sneer. But I bet you don't live in a place like this.'

Fry opened her mouth to explain that she lived in the city of Nottingham, which was much more multicultural than anywhere in this part of Derbyshire. But Tammy didn't give her a chance.

'You can see perfectly well what the problem is,' she said. 'The Polish use their language as a barrier to keep separate from us. Yes, it makes me angry that a place where everyone used to help each other has become like this, with people divided into different groups, speaking in different languages. We're not a community any more. I'd like to get Jayden away from here, but I don't know whether I can afford it.'

Fry glanced at Callaghan, who gave her an ironic smile. She thought he had probably known what she was letting herself in for with this witness.

'We wanted to talk to you specifically about Krystian Zalewski,' she said.

'Well, go ahead then.'

'How often did you see Mr Zalewski?'

'We've seen him at the back from time to time, going up the stairs to his flat.'

'Did you ever see anyone with him?'

'No.'

'Never?'

'He seemed to be one of those loners that you hear about.'

'Yes, I think he was,' said Fry. 'Go on.'

'But then one day we went down to the Polish shop, Zabka.'

'You shop in the *polski sklep*?'

'What else is there? Besides, Jayden likes the sausage.'

'Kielbasa?'

'That's it. I have to get it for him, or he nags me about it.'

'I see. So you were in Zabka—'

'And he was in there too, this bloke.'

'Mr Zalewski. Did he speak to you?'

'Not exactly. Jayden spoke to him, because he saw he was buying the same type of sausage. He's a friendly kid, you know. A bit too friendly sometimes. I've told him not to talk to strange men, but he'd seen Zalewski a few times and knew he was a neighbour. I suppose he hasn't learned yet that a neighbour can be just as dangerous as a stranger.'

'Especially those loners,' said Fry.

Tammy scowled at her. 'Well . . . yes.'

'And did Mr Zalewski seem to present a danger to your son?'

'Obviously not, or I would have done something about it. He was surprised to be spoken to at first, but he smiled and was quite pleasant actually. Jayden liked him, though he told me the man spoke a bit funny.'

90

'Mr Zalewski's English wasn't very good?'

'A bit basic. But at least he had *some* English. Some of them don't bother.'

'When was this meeting in the shop?'

'Sunday teatime.'

'That was the day he was killed,' said Fry.

'I suppose so.'

'Did you see him speak to anyone else?'

'He was still in the shop when we left.'

'Was there anyone in the street outside?'

Tammy shook her head. 'No more than the usual. Nobody I would have looked at twice.'

Fry wondered if Tammy Beresford looked at anyone twice, or whether she took the trouble to look at anyone at all.

'Could you describe Mr Zalewski?' she said.

'I told you – I'd seen him going up the stairs to that flat above the shop. I knew it was him.'

'So you recognised him, but you can't describe him.'

'What's the difference?'

'Thank you, Miss Beresford,' said Fry. 'I think you've told us what you can. I assume you'll be around if we need to speak to you again?'

'I suppose so. But I'm not sure I'll stay in this town for long,' she said.

'But you'll be here for the foreseeable future?'

Tammy peered out of the window to see who was down there in the market square.

'It's all these takeaways I don't like. People eat at those places for breakfast, lunch and dinner. They probably nip in for a snack in between to see them through.

Then at night you get a group of Neanderthals fuelled up on Tennent's Super Strong, roaming around looking for someone to fight. A punch-up outside a fast-food place doesn't even raise an eyebrow. It's just the evening's entertainment.'

'Is that the East Europeans, Miss Beresford?'

Tammy looked at her with a sneer, but didn't reply to the question.

'Are you done now?' she said.

Next on Jamie Callaghan's list were a Polish couple, Michal and Anna Wolak. They had rented a two-bedroom terraced house only a street away from Tammy Beresford and Krystian Zalewski.

'I came here because of my sister,' said Michal. 'She came to Britain before me. She told me this was a place you can get work if you do not speak English.'

Michal Wolak was a fair-haired young man with neat sideboards and pale blue eyes. He wore a loose, short-sleeved shirt, which revealed powerful muscles in his forearms, covered in dense blond hairs.

'It must be hard to get a job anywhere else if you don't have the language,' said Fry.

'Yes. I couldn't speak English too well when I came here, but I took a course. I'm better now, do you think?'

'Yes, your English is fine.'

'And then I met Anna. She comes from the same town as me, Góra Kalwaria. Both of our fathers used to work in the sports equipment industry, but the factories closed. They are no longer in our town.'

Anna Wolakowa was darker, smaller, and very quiet. She sat close to Michal, squeezing his arm occasionally.

'We were married by our parish priest, Father Posluszny,' she said.

'Which church is that?'

'*Kościół pod wezwaniem Matki Bożej Ostrobramskiej i Święty Barbary*. The Church Of Our Lady of Ostra Brama and St Barbara. It's in Mansfield.'

'I don't know it.'

'We were part of the Polish baby boom,' said Anna with a smile at Michal.

'Baby boom?'

'During martial law in the 1980s,' explained Michal, 'under Jaruzelski's military government. There was a curfew, you see. People couldn't go out after dark, so the baby boom was the result. And when we all came of age at the same time, there weren't enough jobs for everyone. So we had to become migrant workers. We came here to the UK.'

'And you work at the distribution centre outside Shirebrook?' said Fry.

'We both do, yes,' said Michal.

Fry knew the distribution centre had opened the year after Poland joined the European Union. Michal Wolak was just one of thousands of workers who had subsequently come in from Poland, Latvia, and other countries of Eastern Europe. It was said that they didn't ask too many questions, and were willing to accept the terms of employment. In return, they earned more in a week than they would in a month back home.

'This place has changed, though,' said Michal, shaking

his head sadly. 'Now people feel frightened and threatened. Our children get problems at school. "When are
you going home?" they say. "We're sending you lot
back." It's been the same ever since the vote.'

'The EU Referendum?'

'Of course. People say they have never been frightened here before. But some of them are frightened
now.'

'How do you know Krystian Zalewski?'

'I met him at the distribution centre when he was
working there. He wasn't very good at the job. I don't
think the work suited him. He got into trouble a lot.'

'Trouble?'

'He broke the rules. He arrived a few minutes late,
he took too long going to the toilet, he was slow in
his work. If you get six strikes against you the agency
has to let you go. There are plenty of others waiting
for the work.'

'You talked to Mr Zalewski?'

'When I got the chance. He was from a different
part of Poland, down in the south, near Kraków. His
English was not so good, so he liked to be able to talk
to someone in Polish.'

'Was he friendly with any of the other employees?'

'No, I wouldn't say so. He was very quiet. Very . . .
solitary.'

'A loner,' said Fry.

Michal nodded. 'I was sorry when he left. He just
couldn't fit in. But I saw him one more time after
that.'

'Where was this?'

'At the car wash. We have a Ford Focus. It's quite old, but we like to keep it nice. I took it to the hand car wash one day, and I recognised one of the men there. It was Krystian.'

'This was recently?'

'Just last week. I didn't know he was working at the car wash until then.'

'Only a few days before he was killed . . .'

'It seems so.'

'Did he speak to you?' asked Fry.

'He said "hello". We chatted for a while in our own language. He asked how Anna was, and whether we had a baby yet. We've been trying for one, you see.'

He looked at Anna, who gave him a big smile. Fry wondered from the smile if she was actually pregnant, but it didn't feel appropriate for her to ask. The other question that came into her mind was whether they intended to have a baby here, in Shirebrook. Or in England at least. If so, what nationality would the child be brought up as? What language would it grow up speaking?

'Krystian told me they wanted him to work night shifts at the distribution centre, and he said "no". He thought he was being picked on after that, because they wanted to get rid of him. But I'm not sure. They're just very strict on rules of timekeeping. Krystian wasn't very good with time.'

'Why didn't he want to work night shifts? Would it mean working with someone he didn't like, doing a different kind of job?'

'No, it was nothing like that. It was a silly thing, I

thought. Krystian just didn't like the dark. He wanted to go to work and come home in the light. The car wash suited him, because they only get customers during daylight.'

'That's odd for an adult male.'

Michal shrugged. 'Perhaps there was some reason for it. If there was, he never talked about it to me.'

'So did Mr Zalewski ever mention having trouble with anyone?' asked Fry.

'Trouble with local people?'

'Well . . . anyone. Had he been involved in any arguments or disputes that you know of? Was there anyone who might intend to do him harm?'

'He didn't say anything like that. Not at all. He was a very nice man, Krystian. He didn't really have friends. But I don't know of any enemies either.'

Fry noticed Anna fidgeting in her seat as if she wanted to interrupt.

'What do you think, Anna?' said Fry.

'I'm sorry, but . . .' she began.

'Yes?'

'Well, for some people here, we're all the enemy, aren't we?'

'You mean there are people who resent all Polish workers.'

'More than resent. They hate us.'

Anna's English was better than her husband's. She had very little accent that Fry could detect.

'Can you identify any individuals who hate Polish workers so much that they might attack Krystian Zalewski in that alley and stab him to death?'

Anna exchanged glances with Michal.

'We don't know their names,' she said. 'We've seen them, though.'

'Here in Shirebrook?'

'We don't know if they live here. We just see them sometimes. They stand outside a pub, or one of the shops, and they stare at us as we go past. It's quite . . . intimidating.'

'One of the shops?' said Fry. 'Any particular shop?'

'It's difficult to say. They're usually there after dark, when the shutters are all down. A group of men. They dress in black, sometimes with leather jackets.'

'There is one shop,' put in Michal. 'I've never been inside, so I don't know what it sells. Even when it's open, it looks empty. There are posters in the window.'

'Posters? For heavy rock concerts?'

'Heavy rock . . .?' said Michal, with a look at Anna.

'Black Sabbath, Iron Maiden,' she said.

'Ah yes. And Rammstein.'

'That's what I'm thinking of,' said Fry.

'The posters are so big that you can hardly see through the window without getting very close,' said Michal. 'I wouldn't dare to do that.'

'If we see those men, we walk the other way round the market square to get home,' said Anna.

'Have you heard of any actual attacks on Polish people?'

'Not that anyone talks about. They may keep it to themselves.'

'That's the wrong thing to do,' said Fry. 'You must tell someone. Tell the police if it happens to you. Will you promise me that?'

'Of course.'

'There's a Public Space Protection Order in force, so they shouldn't be gathering in groups and intimidating people.'

'Oh, we know about that order,' said Anna. 'They say it was our fault.'

'There was a problem with Polish men drinking in the street.'

Anna became animated for the first time.

'You know, the English people used to drink in the street,' she said. 'And they urinated in doorways. The English people used to gather in groups in the alleys too. Now they blame us because they can't do it without getting moved on by the police or arrested. We stand out more because we're Polish. It's easy to point the finger at us.'

Fry nodded at Callaghan, and she got up to leave. Michal and Anna accompanied them politely to the door.

'My uncle Tomasz runs a shop here in Shirebrook,' said Anna, as she looked outside at the street. 'He works night shifts at the distribution centre, goes home to kiss his wife and son, then opens up his shop.'

'So he's a hard worker,' said Fry.

'Yes, he is. So are we.' Anna Wolakova gestured at the houses around her. 'The people of Shirebrook are getting older, or they're sick. None of them are working. So who would be paying tax if we Polish weren't here? A few bad people give us all a bad name. People drinking in the street? There were ten of them, maybe. And now suddenly "all Poles drink in the street".' It's not true. Most of us are normal people. We have jobs and families. We live our lives like everyone else does.'

At the scene in the alley where Krystian Zalewski had been attacked, Diane Fry noticed that the crime scene examiners were already starting to dismantle their forensics tent and pick up the evidence markers. Everything had been carefully photographed and videoed in situ. It would be unrealistic to try to keep the scene contained any longer than absolutely necessary.

DCI Mackenzie looked unhappy and dissatisfied.

'How is the community cohesion going, sir?' asked Fry.

Mackenzie snorted.

'I keep being asked over and over, "Is this a hate crime?" Do we have any evidence of that, Diane?'

'None at all so far,' said Fry.

He nodded. 'It would be better if it isn't.'

'Why?'

'Why? Just think of all the attention we'd get. All the national media – tabloid newspapers, TV crews. The Police and Crime Commissioner would be here. There'd be questions asked in Parliament. It doesn't bear thinking about.'

'We're getting some of that already. There's been a bunch of reporters around Shirebrook asking questions, getting knee-jerk responses from the public. I think they're probably looking for a pub now.'

'Yes, we had photographers taking pictures of the tent and the scene guard too.'

'But that tells them nothing.'

'No. And that's what we should carry on doing,' said Mackenzie. 'Telling them nothing.'

'Of course.'

'How did you manage with Mr Pollitt?' he asked.

'There's something going on in the shop – if you can call it a shop. From what I've just been told by a witness, there may be suspect individuals meeting there.'

'What do you mean?'

Fry repeated what Michal and Anna Wolak had told her about the men outside the shop with the heavy metal posters in the window.

'We ought to get a look in the storerooms at the back of the shop,' she said.

'We don't have any justification,' said Mackenzie. 'Not on that basis.'

Fry sighed. 'I suppose not.'

Mackenzie checked his phone for messages. 'I'm sorry, but I'm going to have to go,' he said.

'I'll make sure everything is being done here, sir.'

Mackenzie looked up from his phone.

'As you know, Diane, I've been asking for the appointment of a new DI.'

'It's long overdue,' she said.

'We were expecting to get a DI seconded from Nottinghamshire, but they say they can't spare anyone. Apparently they have a shortage of experienced officers at that rank.'

'Hasn't everyone? But there must be someone in Derbyshire, or perhaps a DI might want to transfer from Eastern Command. It's hardly a million miles from Lincoln to Nottingham.'

Mackenzie put his phone away and fastened his coat.

'We'll carry on hoping. I just wanted to keep you up to date.'

'I appreciate it, sir.'

When Mackenzie had gone, Fry stood for a while and looked at the alley. With the crime scene examiners' lights dismantled she realised now how gloomy this alley was. As DI Mackenzie had pointed out, there was no lighting for its entire length.

And Krystian Zalewski had hated the darkness. Perhaps that explained it. Explained why he'd staggered away from the scene of the attack, growing weaker and weaker as he gushed blood from a fatal knife wound.

He'd made his way back to his little one-bedroom flat, with the damp in the walls and the mouse droppings on the floor, just so that he wouldn't die in the dark.

10

A hospital mortuary was always located near the boiler house and laundry, well out of the way of living patients as they came and went to their appointments. When you arrived for the first time, you looked for the chimney.

'So you found me a body after all,' said Dr Chloe Young. 'You didn't have to do that.'

'I'm sorry. Was it a nasty one?'

'Young people,' she said. 'They're always difficult. They have all their lives ahead of them. Or they ought to. They shouldn't be lying on my examination table.'

Cooper nodded. 'I feel the same, you know.'

'Of course you do, Ben. I know.'

Against his own better instincts, Cooper had spent his time on the way here picturing Shane Curtis in a hospital shroud, with a tag on his wrist and a tag on his ankle, and the grey, drained face of the dead. He'd seen the funeral directors collect the body at the scene of the fire and transfer it feet first to their vehicle, the way funeral directors always did.

Of course, he could have left this one to Dev Sharma.

In fact, Sharma had assumed he would be coming. He knew his DI had good reasons to avoid post-mortems on this kind of victim. But something had encouraged Cooper to make time for the call at the mortuary today.

'His name was Shane Curtis,' he said. 'Eighteen years old.'

Dr Young didn't need to look at her notes for the details.

'He wasn't very well-nourished for a young man of that age,' she said. 'I imagine he had a substandard diet. So many people I see in here do. He also had substantial amounts of alcohol in his blood. Cannabis too. They're familiar lifestyle signs. But he died of smoke inhalation from the fire. He has thermal damage to the respiratory system, burns around the mouth and nostrils, pulmonary swelling caused by carbon monoxide and various toxic gases. *That* couldn't be called a lifestyle choice.'

To Cooper, the physical details sounded all too familiar. For a moment, he couldn't say anything. The words wouldn't come out of his mouth, because the images in his mind were too clear.

Young looked up, immediately sensing his discomfort.

'Oh, I'm sorry,' she said. 'A fire death victim. You should have sent someone else. Why didn't you?'

Cooper shook his head. 'I can't avoid these things. They're part of the job.'

'Yes, but the memories must still be very painful. You were there at the scene when she was killed, weren't you?'

'Actually,' said Cooper, 'that's not the problem. It's the good memories that are the most painful.'

Young put a hand on his arm. He found her touch reassuring. Cooper took a deep breath, filling his lungs with the antiseptic smell of the mortuary.

'There were no traces of accelerant on the swabs from the victim's hands,' he said. 'We're working on the assumption that someone else set the fire.'

Immediately Young became professional again.

'So your job is to find out whether it was an unfortunate accident, or if young Shane's death was deliberate,' she said.

'And who started the fire,' said Cooper. 'That will be the first step.'

Young looked at him closely. 'What would be the most likely scenario from your experience?'

'It would be someone Shane knew, possibly a friend. An escapade that went wrong. Our suspect will already have the death of a friend on his conscience, I'm afraid. He may be injured too. Those two factors will make it easier for us to identify him.'

Young tapped a pen on her desk. 'Sometimes,' she said, 'I think your job must be a lot worse than mine. Dealing with the living is so much more complicated than handling the dead, isn't it?'

'I'm afraid so,' said Cooper. 'No matter what our skills and experience are, the living still tend to behave in completely unpredictable ways.'

'That's so true.'

Cooper had his car keys in his hand, but turned back to look at Chloe Young.

'When will I see you again?' he said.

'Well, Thursday night. We've got the tickets for Buxton Opera House, remember? *Tosca.*'

'Oh, sure. But not before?'

Young smiled apologetically. 'Sorry, it's a bit busy at the moment. People keep bringing me bodies.'

Cooper felt irrationally disappointed.

'Just one more of life's unpredictabilities,' he said.

At West Street, Ben Cooper looked around his team as they came back from their assignments. Dev Sharma was on the phone and Luke Irvine had his head down over his computer. Gavin Murfin was looking for something in his desk drawer. And he couldn't ask Carol Villiers.

Cooper wandered over and hovered near Becky Hurst's position. She looked up expectantly.

'Sir?'

'Do you listen to opera, Becky?' asked Cooper.

'Yes, a bit.'

'So what is *Tosca* about?'

'Oh, the usual,' said Hurst. 'Murder, torture, suicide.'

'Great.'

'But in a good production it can be done really well. Who are you going to see?'

'English Touring Opera.'

'You'll be fine, then. I'm envious.'

He saw Villiers glance across and wondered what she'd caught of their conversation, and what she knew already.

'There's been another armed robbery reported,' said Dev Sharma when he saw Cooper had returned. 'This one was at a corner shop and off-licence.'

'Here in Edendale?'

'Yes, on Buxton Road. At Singh's Stores.'

'I know it,' said Cooper. 'Was anyone hurt?'

'No, but Mrs Singh was a bit shaken up. Two men entered the shop at about ten forty-five this morning and threatened her with a baseball bat and a knife. She gave them all the cash from the till.'

'Sensible. From what I've seen of her husband, Mr Singh might have acted differently. He would probably have tried to resist, or even fought them.'

'That could have ended badly,' said Sharma.

The Singhs' shop was close to where Cooper had lived until a few months ago, just across the other side of Buxton Road from his old flat in Welbeck Street. He'd visited the shop many times and remembered both the Singhs, as well as their daughter, Jatinder, who'd attended Eden Valley High School a couple of years below him. Mr Singh had once beckoned Cooper into the back of the shop and showed him his *kirpan*, the ceremonial knife that he wore under his clothes. It was only a few inches long, but Cooper had been unsure at the time of its possible illegality as an offensive weapon. Mr Singh had assured him that a *kirpan* was kept sheathed except when it was withdrawn for an occasion such as a religious ceremonies.

'It is not a weapon, Mr Cooper. Not even a symbolic weapon, any more than a Christian cross is a symbolic torture instrument. Do you understand?'

Mr Singh had shown him the *kirpan* because he knew Cooper was a police officer. It made Cooper smile even now when he thought of all those individuals whose arrests he'd been involved in, who'd gone to great trouble to conceal their blades from the police.

'Gavin has been down to the shop to take Mrs Singh's statement and make initial inquiries,' said Sharma. 'He brought back some CCTV footage.'

'Excellent. Have we got the suspects on camera?'

'Very much so. Take a look.'

The CCTV images from the shop were excellent. Good resolution and in colour – and pretty accurate colours by the look of the background. One of the robbers was wearing a blue top and a black baseball cap, with a blue scarf covering his face. The other was dressed in a grey top, blue tracksuit bottoms, and was wearing a motorcycle crash helmet. He had a scarf over his face too. Cooper looked a bit closer. The crash helmet was red and covered with a distinctive pattern of white stripes and black stars.

'That gives you a reasonable chance of making an identification,' said Cooper, 'if you can find some possible suspects.'

'I'm sending Gavin back out to canvass the neighbouring properties. Initial reports suggest the two men left on a motorbike, possibly a Kawasaki, heading away from town. I've asked for CCTV from the cameras at the junction of Buxton Road with High Street, in case they came from that direction.'

'More likely they came in and went out the same way,' said Cooper, 'rather than risking the area where there are most cameras.'

'I thought it was worth a try.'

'Of course, Dev.'

Cooper looked at the map of Edendale on the wall of the CID room. What was further up the Buxton Road?

'The convent,' he said.

'I'm sorry, sir?'

'The convent. Sisters of Our Lady. The nuns are very security conscious. They have a comprehensive CCTV system covering the gates. They might have caught a motorcycle passing with the two suspects.'

Sharma looked doubtful. 'Who should I send to a convent of nuns?' he said.

Hurst and Irvine both looked up as if their names had been mentioned.

Cooper smiled. 'You could go yourself, Dev. Consider it part of your acclimatisation to the local community.'

'There have been a spate of robberies over the past few weeks,' said Sharma. 'Not just in Edendale, but all across North Division. Some have been raids on businesses like the Singhs' shop, some have been street robberies. They're all opportunistic offences. They see a chance, and they go for it. They seem to be travelling around the area after dark looking for a target. The only common factor is the use of a motorbike.'

'A red crash helmet?' asked Irvine.

'Not always.'

'There may be more than two suspects, then. More than one motorbike.'

'It looks like it. The descriptions from witnesses differ in some details. The height and build of the suspects, the colour of their leathers and helmets. Oh, and there was some variation in the accents they spoke with. Some witnesses say they were local, others couldn't identify the accent. One victim said in her statement that they had Manchester accents. She's from the area herself, so she recognised it.'

'Manchester isn't the best known of accents, not like Liverpool or Birmingham.'

'I can't think what it sounds like at all,' said Hurst.

'Think of Oasis,' said Irvine.

'The Gallagher brothers?'

'That's it.'

'Oh, did they call people scrotes and muppets?'

'No,' said Villiers, 'but before they left one of them did tell the other it was "sound".'

'Which means "okay".'

'Right.'

'I don't like it,' said Cooper. 'If we have two or more pairs of suspects carrying out these attacks, it suggests some level of organisation.'

'We'll keep on it,' said Sharma.

'What about the boy who was killed in the arson attack at Castle Farm? Have we spoken to his family?'

'Yes, we've interviewed Shane Curtis's mother,' said Sharma. 'Martina Curtis. There doesn't seem to be a father. She's distraught obviously. But she's got friends and relatives there with her now. A support network.'

'Are there any other children?'

'A daughter about sixteen, three more boys of fourteen, twelve and nine.'

'And no father?' asked Cooper.

'It would probably more accurate to say "no fathers". I don't think there was just one.'

'Five children. She already has it pretty tough, then. And now this . . .'

'They're all on benefits, of course,' put in Irvine. 'Mrs Curtis spends a fair part of her allowances on fags and booze. And she told us she buys National Lottery tickets every week, scratch cards and all.'

'Waiting for the moment that will change her life, I suppose. A moment that will never come.'

'It doesn't do any harm to keep your hopes alive,' said Hurst.

'Oh, fine. But she's doing it on taxpayers' money.'

'What did she tell you about Shane?' asked Cooper.

'Well, she says Shane was no angel,' said Sharma.

'But then, they always do, don't they?' added Irvine.

'Does she have any idea what he was doing in the barn at Castle Farm?'

Sharma shook his head. 'No, not a clue. But I got the impression she never knew where he was anyway. *"He does his own thing"* was the way she put it. He was unemployed, though he seems to have had a bit of money to spend, over and above his jobseeker's allowance. I'm sure he didn't get it off his mother. She says he liked to go out on his own for hours on end. She doesn't seem to have any idea what he was doing all that time.'

'Well, from the forensic evidence,' said Irvine, 'he was clearly drinking lager and smoking pot. And considering his criminal record . . .'

'. . . he was probably getting up to other things too,' put in Hurst. 'The logic of prior conviction.'

'He does have a record,' said Irvine. 'So he was almost certainly involved in drugs or petty crime.'

'A record?'

'Well, it's true Shane was no angel. He spent eighteen months in juvenile detention at Werrington Youth Offenders Institution.'

'In Staffordshire, isn't it?'

'Yes, near Stoke on Trent.'

'You've got to wonder who he met in there,' said Irvine. 'It often leads kids into worse things when they get out.'

'What were his offences?'

'Taking a vehicle without consent, driving without a licence or insurance, theft, shoplifting, possession of drugs. The usual sort of list, really.'

'No mention of previous arson offences?'

'No. But that doesn't mean—'

'It doesn't mean anything, Luke. Keep an open mind.'

Irvine scowled. 'Yes, sir.'

Cooper was starting to get worried about Luke Irvine. He'd started off so promisingly when he first transferred from uniform into CID. He'd been a bit naïve, but keen. He'd reminded Cooper of himself when he was at the same stage of his career. But now he was beginning to get awkward and opinionated. His mind wasn't as open as it should be. Cooper didn't know what was having this effect on him – perhaps it was something going on in his private life. He would have to make a point of sitting down and talking to Irvine seriously about it when they both had time.

'What about his friends?' asked Cooper.

'A loose association of youths of a similar age around the Woodlands and Cavendish estates,' said Sharma.

'A gang?'

'Mrs Curtis would never have used that term.'

'And I suppose she doesn't know the names of any of them?'

'Shane didn't exactly bring them home for tea,' scowled Irvine.

'So we're no closer to knowing who he might have been planning to meet there at the barn. Or if he was planning to meet anyone at all. He might have been the victim of a rival gang who took the opportunity of trapping him inside.'

'You mean a rival loose association of youths,' said Irvine.

Cooper shook his head. 'Whatever the circumstances, I don't think Shane intended it to end up that way.'

Then he looked around the CID room.

'DC Villiers,' he said, 'are you free at the moment? I'd like you to come with me.'

'Where are we going?'

Cooper waited until they were out of the room before he answered.

'To Bakewell. We're going to talk to Naomi Heath.'

'Reece Bower's partner?' said Villiers. 'I thought you'd be interested.'

'You know me so well. I could use your opinion on this one.'

Cooper decided not to mention his call to Superintendent Branagh. He would wait until after his meeting this afternoon. Things might have changed by then. He didn't want to involve Carol Villiers too deeply if he could avoid it.

So he was very quiet as they left the building and walked to the car park. The words of Detective Superintendent Branagh were echoing in his mind. *The Bower case was a miscarriage of justice.*

Cooper knew there were many ways for a miscarriage of justice to happen. Derbyshire had experienced its fair share of cases. But as he got into his car he was thinking of a much older one – the story of the notorious Dr Hawley Crippen, who was hanged at Pentonville Prison in 1910 for the murder of his wife. It was a case that he'd studied as a police cadet when the history of criminal justice was one of his obsessions.

In that instance, Cora Crippen had disappeared from the family home after a party. Her husband told everyone that she'd returned to the United States and that she'd later died and been cremated. Crippen had immediately moved in his lover, Ethel Neave. Under questioning, he admitted that he'd made up the story to avoid having to explain that Cora had left him for a music hall actor. The Crippen house was searched, but nothing was found and the police had no option but to conclude he was innocent. Yet Crippen panicked and fled to Canada with Neave.

It was only their disappearance that led Scotland Yard to carry out three more searches of the house. On the final search they found a human torso buried under the basement. A mark on the skin of the abdomen was said to match a scar Cora had. Otherwise, the evidence against Dr Crippen was entirely circumstantial. And still he had been hanged.

'Ben, the barrier's open.'

Cooper realised he'd been distracted and his car was sitting motionless in the entrance to the car park. He was aware that Villiers was staring at him.

'Oh, yes.'

'Is something wrong?'

'No, not at all.'

He drove out on to West Street, back into the modern world of policing. He reminded himself that many years after Crippen had been hanged for the murder of his wife, DNA techniques were used to establish that the remains from the basement were not those of Cora – and weren't even female. Some said the police had planted the body parts to use as evidence, after becoming convinced of Crippen's guilt by his attempt to escape.

That wouldn't happen these days. But when a suspect attempted to escape, it usually pointed quite clearly at their guilt. Reece Bower had evaded justice once. Was he trying to do the same thing again?

11

The road twisted and turned constantly on the way from Baslow into Bakewell. They called this stretch Thirteen Bends. Cooper thought there might actually be fewer than thirteen, but he'd never managed to count them, being too busy steering his car round one sharp curve after another.

He drove down the hill past the Peak District National Park headquarters and arrived in the centre of the town near the visitor centre and the Old Original Bakewell Pudding Shop, with the Rutland Arms hotel looking out over a little square.

Bakewell was only a small town. Its permanent population was about four thousand, but in the summer it was full of visitors. It was also the market town for the surrounding area. On cattle market days the streets were thronged, the car parks packed. Busiest of all were the two days of the Bakewell Show early in August. The police station here no longer had a front counter and wasn't open to the public, though some officers were still based here.

A few miles down the A6 from here was the

wonderful Haddon Hall, one of his favourite places to visit, when he had time.

The Bowers' home was on Aldern Way, a curving cul-de-sac on the edge of Bakewell, with views across to Chatsworth estate in one direction, and down over the town in the other. The spire of All Saints Church stood out clearly on the skyline.

The house was a stone-built three-bedroom detached with two short driveways down from the road and an attached garage. The driveway Cooper and Villiers used was short, but steep. An iron rail had been placed to assist in icy conditions.

Naomi Heath was aged in her thirties, so must have been ten or twelve years younger than her partner. She had short blonde hair and wide cheekbones, and she'd used make-up to disguise dark shadows under her eyes. She was dressed in jeans and a T-shirt, and was clutching a mobile phone in her hand.

'The postman slipped on the ice once and bruised his arm,' she said when she saw Carol Villiers holding on to the rail. 'Reece got worried about being sued in some personal injury claim. So he installed the rails and we buy bags of grit in the winter. "Better safe than sorry", he always says.'

Cooper showed his warrant card.

'Naomi Heath? Detective Inspector Cooper from Edendale CID. This is Detective Constable Villiers. We'd like to speak to you about Mr Bower.'

'Oh, are you taking an interest after all? I got the impression no one really cared. Because Reece is who he is, I suppose.'

Cooper didn't respond to the taunt.

'Miss Heath, do you have any idea where Mr Bower is now?'

'None at all.'

A small porch led to an inner PVC door with obscured windows. A combined lounge and dining room had windows to the front and rear to take advantage of the spectacular views. From the dining area, a hatchway opened from the kitchen. Cooper glimpsed oak units, a gas range, and another window with a westerly view.

They had gas-fired central heating here, which he couldn't get at his cottage in Foolow. They probably needed it in the winter too.

'As a matter of fact, we're all very concerned about Reece,' said Naomi. 'Something must have happened. He wouldn't just have run off like this.'

'When was the last time you were in contact with Mr Bower?' asked Cooper.

'Before he left, of course. It was on Sunday, the day before yesterday. During the morning he packed an overnight bag, and he went off with it at about eleven o'clock.'

'What did he say to you when he left?'

'He said he was going away and I might not see him for some time.'

'Have you noticed any change in his behaviour recently?'

'He was a bit more moody than usual, perhaps,' she said.

'Had you been arguing before he left?'

'Reece had got angry the previous night. He'd

knocked back quite a few drinks – he likes his malt whisky a bit too much, you know. He said a lot of things, but I'm used to it. I usually just let it go, and he forgets about it next morning.'

'What was the argument about?'

She shook her head. 'It wasn't an argument, exactly. He gets upset about things. And because I'm here, it's as if I'm to blame for it all. Do you understand what I mean?'

'I think so.'

'He'd been having problems at work. A lot of it I couldn't even grasp. I think he was under pressure from his manager on one hand, and getting hassle from some of the employees on the other.'

'What sort of hassle?' asked Cooper.

'Oh, I don't know. I just think it was something that someone said to him at work.'

'What did they say to him?'

'He wouldn't tell me. He can be reticent like that at times.'

'Mr Bower is secretive?'

Naomi shook her head. 'No, just a bit uncommunicative. When things are really bothering him, he tends to keep them to himself.'

'So you think Mr Bower had enough of it and decided to get away for a while?'

'That was the impression I had. He wouldn't tell me any more. It was as if he'd made some decision and wasn't going to talk about it.'

'And you really haven't heard from him since?' asked Cooper. 'No phone calls, not even a text message?'

'No, nothing. That's what worried me. I can understand him wanting to be on his own for a while, but
he would have got in contact by now, I'm sure. I expected
him to be back on Monday, to go to work. But it's been
two nights now, without a word. That's just not right.'

'Did he take a mobile phone with him?'

'As far as I know. He always has his iPhone on him.'

'We'll need the number.'

'Fine.'

'Didn't Mr Bower give you any hint at all about
where he was going?' put in Villiers.

'No.'

'But you must have some possibilities in mind.'

'What do you mean?'

'Some idea of where he would go, if he wanted to
disappear or be on his own for a while. People normally
go to a location they know quite well. Somewhere
their family or friends live, perhaps. Their old home
town, or just a place they went on holiday once . . .'

Naomi shook her head. 'I don't know. I can't think
where he would go.'

Cooper sighed. They weren't really getting anywhere
with her.

'We'll need the addresses of all Mr Bower's family,
and any particular friends he might have gone to.'

'All right, I'll get them,' she said.

Cooper looked at Villiers as Naomi got up and left
the room. Villiers nodded at a display of photographs
on a corner table. Holiday snaps, Reece and Naomi
smiling at the camera with a blue sea and sunlit roof-
tops in the background.

'The Mediterranean,' said Cooper. 'That's no good. He wouldn't have risked crossing the border.'

'There's one on a caravan site,' said Villiers. 'Looks quite recent. Maybe they couldn't afford a foreign holiday this year.'

'Can you see—' began Cooper.

But Villiers was ahead of him. She'd already eased the photo out of the plastic pocket and turned it over.

'Bridlington,' she said, as she slipped it back.

Naomi came back into the room with an address book. 'I've marked the family members and his closest friends. There aren't many of those, just a few golfing buddies.'

'We'll also need the number of his mobile phone so we can track it. His bank account details, particularly debit and credit cards. And please make a list of the clothes he was wearing and what he took with him in his overnight bag, if you can.'

'I can do that.'

Cooper paused. 'Miss Heath,' he said, 'it's impossible for us to assess Mr Bower's state of mind. Since you were the last person to speak to him, do you think there's a possibility he might have intended to harm himself?'

'No, not at all—' She'd begun to shake her head automatically, but stopped abruptly. 'Well, I can't deny it's crossed my mind. Normally I wouldn't say Reece was the type of man to do something like that. Even if he isn't happy in his job, he has his family here. We have two children, for heaven's sake. He has all that to live for. But who can say, really? There's no way to see inside someone else's head and tell what they're thinking.'

'No, that's quite true.'

And Cooper meant that sincerely. He'd often wished there was a way of seeing inside someone's head and learning what they were thinking. He was wishing it now. He would love to know what Naomi Heath really thought about the disappearance of her partner. The only thing he was sure of was that she wasn't telling him everything.

'How long have you two been together?' asked Villiers.

'About four years.'

'And you have children?'

Naomi Heath smiled. 'Yes, we're one of those complicated families.'

'Complicated?'

'I have a son from a previous marriage. His name is Joshua. And Reece and I have a younger son together, Daniel. And of course Reece has a daughter from his marriage.'

'That would be Lacey,' said Cooper, recalling the detail from the files.

'Yes, Lacey. So, you see – it's complicated.'

'Your previous marriage—' began Villiers.

'We were divorced,' replied Naomi quickly. 'It didn't work out. We separated not long after Joshua was born. He's nine now.'

'There must be quite a difference in age between Lacey and Daniel.'

'Thirteen years. Lacey is a young woman. She doesn't

live with us any more. She's eighteen now, and she's at college. She doesn't really want to be bothered with small children.'

Cooper nodded. He could see how the relationships in this family might be quite complicated. So Lacey didn't want to be bothered with her step- and half-brothers? But how did she feel about her stepmother, the person who'd taken her own mother's place and claimed her father's affections? That could be one of the most difficult and complicated relationships of all.

'Miss Heath,' he said, 'I have to ask you: I assume you know about what happened ten years ago – the disappearance of Mr Bower's wife?'

'Yes, of course I know. In fact, I already knew about it when I met Reece. It had been in all the papers. It was big news in this area. But Reece made a point of telling me about it anyway. He didn't want there to be any secrets between us.'

No secrets? Cooper thought that was unlikely. But it was the sort of thing that people said to each other, especially in the early days of a relationship.

'Did he say what he thought had happened to his wife?'

'He said he didn't know, any more than anyone else did. He's always felt that way.'

'A witness claimed to have seen her alive,' said Cooper.

'I know. This must sound strange, Detective Inspector Cooper, but that was one of things that upset Reece the most. He'd begun to harden himself to the fact that Annette was probably dead. Then, to have the possibility raised that she was still alive, was hard for him to take. It means, of course, that she disappeared deliberately and has not been in touch for more than ten years. Reece has no idea what he did to deserve that treatment.'

'On the other hand, it was that witness statement which resulted in the case against Mr Bower being dropped.'

Naomi smiled coldly. 'It's a difficult one to understand, isn't it? None of us can imagine how we would feel in those circumstances. I'm just telling you what I gathered from Reece. He's always been conflicted about it, but I think that betrayal by his wife was harder to bear than the prospect of a conviction for a murder.'

'I see.'

'By the way, I'm really Mrs Heath,' she said. 'I kept my husband's name after the divorce. A lot of my friends thought I was mad, but I did it for Joshua's sake. He was already at school by then. It didn't seem fair to change his name or give myself a different surname from him. It would just have confused him more, and he was upset enough after the separation.'

She turned to Cooper and gestured out of the front window at the other houses in Aldern Way.

'I do get called Mrs Bower, though,' she said. 'Some of our neighbours have only moved into the area in the past few years, and they have no idea about what happened ten years ago.'

'So they don't know you aren't married? And they don't know about the court case?'

'No. Life is complicated enough, isn't it? I'd hate

having to explain it to everyone I met in the street.'

Cooper followed her gaze out of the window, the trimmed hedges and neat conifers, the well-mown lawns and integrated garages. So there were secrets, after all. That was no surprise.

Then he turned the other way. The back garden of the Reece Bower's house looked neat and bursting with colour. Beds of dahlias and carnations were in flower, a couple of apple trees were growing heavy with fruit, planters were filled with petunias and begonias.

'Reece said the police dug this garden up ten years ago,' said Naomi. 'And they didn't find a thing.'

'No signs of Annette, anyway.'

Cooper was thinking about Lacey Bower, eighteen years old now. It was difficult enough handling a relationship with a stepmother. But what if she really wasn't a stepmother at all? Not legally, anyway. It might be tempting for an embittered teenager to regard the interloper as temporary, someone who could be separated from her father at some point in the not too distant future. In Cooper's experience, teenagers were capable of anything. They hadn't learned to control some of the most powerful emotions – hatred and jealousy, the feeling of betrayal.

'Is there anyone you can think of who might want to harm Mr Bower?' asked Villiers.

'No, no one.'

It was a standard question, but the answer came too quickly. It always did. People thought they were so likeable that nobody could possibly hate them enough to harm them. It was rarely true.

124

'And what about you?' said Cooper.

She frowned. 'What about me?'

'Is there anyone who would want to harm you, Mrs Heath?'

'What sort of question is that, Inspector? It's Reece who's disappeared. No harm has come to me. I don't understand.'

'Losing your partner would seem to have caused you some harm,' said Cooper calmly. 'Don't you think so?'

She shook her head. 'I don't know what you're suggesting. It doesn't make sense.'

'All right.'

He could see she was beginning to get annoyed now. Her fingers fiddled with a spoon from the table, her knuckles whitening as if she was trying to bend it like Uri Geller.

'I hope you're doing something to find Reece,' she said, 'rather than just coming here asking me all these meaningless questions.'

'Of course we are.'

'I'm really very worried that something has happened to him. He wouldn't just have gone off like this.'

'Yes, you said that.'

But she hadn't quite said that, had she? A few minutes ago, she'd said 'We're all worried about Reece'. Now, when the same sentiment came out under pressure, it had become 'I'm worried about Reece'. One sounded like the proper thing to say. The other sounded more like the truth.

'He may get in touch,' said Villiers.

Naomi Heath turned to her, a sudden spark of something in her eyes. Hope? Excitement? A challenge?

'Do you really think so?' she said.

'Yes. I can't help thinking he'll be in touch soon, when he's got whatever it is out of his system.'

'I hope you're right,' she said.

'We'd better get back to the office now and see what progress is being made,' said Cooper, hoping she didn't recognise a lie. There would have been no progress, since there wasn't really an inquiry.

'Yes, perhaps you should.'

Cooper followed Villiers back up the drive to the road. Of course Reece Bower couldn't have married Naomi Heath if he'd wanted to. They could only marry if Annette was officially declared dead. And since the case against him was dropped because of evidence she was alive, how could that be? It was the possibility Annette was alive that was keeping him out of prison. And it was also preventing him from getting married again to the woman he now loved.

A living, breathing first wife was both a salvation and a hindrance.

12

An hour later, Ben Cooper was in Detective Superintendent Branagh's office, having fought his way
through the traffic in Chesterfield just as everyone else
seemed to be leaving town to go home. He'd been
standing gridlocked at set after set of lights, always too
close to the car in front, foot constantly on the brake.

It reminded Cooper why driving on roads in the Peak
District felt such a pleasure. Even if they were narrow
and winding and covered in mud from the wheels of
a tractor, they were much more pleasant than this. He
hoped no one ever tried to transfer him to a city.

Sitting across from Hazel Branagh, he realised how
much he was missing those big shoulders, the intimidating but reassuring presence. She looked somehow
crammed into her new office, even though it was actually bigger than her old one, and certainly airier and
more modern, with large windows looking out over
the Chesterfield. Cooper thought if he leaned a little
to the side he might catch a glimpse of the famous
twisted spire of St Mary and All Saints.

'Let's talk about the Annette Bower inquiry,' said

Branagh. 'It's much easier doing it face to face, don't you think, Ben?'

'Certainly.'

'You've read up on the case, I suppose?'

'Only the basic details. I haven't had time to go through the case files yet.'

'Do any questions spring to your mind?'

'Yes.'

'Well, ask away.'

'I did wonder what stage the inquiry had reached when it was suspended,' said Cooper.

'Yes, good question. I was planning to switch the search area.'

'Really? On what evidence?'

Branagh was silent for a moment. 'I hate to admit this. But I'm glad you're asking me, Ben. It makes me reconsider my decisions – or the lack of them.'

'I'm sure you made all the right calls,' said Cooper.

'Are you? I'm not so certain.'

Cooper waited. He could sense that Hazel Branagh wanted to tell him something, but he couldn't rush her. She wasn't someone you could hurry. If inter-rupted, she would probably just clam up.

'I suppose you would call it a hunch,' she said at last. 'I hope you won't laugh.'

'I wouldn't dream of it, ma'am.'

'No, you wouldn't, would you?' she said thought-fully. 'You have hunches yourself don't you, DI Cooper? It doesn't always appear in your reports, but your colleagues are aware of them. And they've learned to trust them too.'

He wondered who Branagh had been talking to. She always seemed to know what was going on, right down to the most junior officers. Perhaps she just picked things up from the general atmosphere in the office. That was something else she wouldn't be able to do, now she was based seventeen miles away.

'The Bowers were already living in Bakewell then,' said Branagh. 'And they still do, of course.'

'Well, Reece does – with his new partner and their children.'

'Oh yes, the new partner. They're not married, though.'

'No. Annette is officially still alive.'

'Mmm. Was the new partner involved in the original case, by any chance?'

'Not that I know of,' said Cooper. 'I haven't checked yet, though. Her name is Naomi Heath.'

'It doesn't ring a bell. There was an affair Bower was having with a colleague at work, but I don't think that was the name.'

'I'll run a check on her. Heath isn't her maiden name.'

'What is she like? How is she reacting to Mr Bower's disappearance?'

'It's hard to tell. She isn't very forthcoming. I'll speak to her again tomorrow.'

'Good.' Branagh paused. 'What was I saying?'

'The Bowers lived in Bakewell then.'

'Oh, yes. They were both keen walkers in those days. There was a particular area they liked to go to, not far away from Bakewell. I was thinking of it when the report came in that Reece Bower was missing. We'd exhausted the search of their property and the neighbouring area by then. We'd dug up the garden too.'

'Oh, yes. The garden.'

'We thought the back garden was a likely burial spot. That was where we were pinning our hopes in the beginning, because of the signs of disturbed earth. Most of it wasn't overlooked by any of the neighbouring properties. And as soon as we saw the freshly dug ground, well, it was inevitable we were going to focus our attention there. I suppose we were a bit too blinkered, and we just followed the most obvious possibilities. We should have been more open-minded. We wasted a lot of time on that garden.'

'It's looking good now,' said Cooper. 'The plants are thriving.'

'I'm not surprised. We gave it a thorough turning over and pulled out a lot of rubbish left there by the builders – bricks, lumps of plasterboard, you know the sort of thing. We dug for days and turned up nothing of significance, apart from a dead cat that had been buried by the previous owners. It was disheartening. Then we extended the search area to include some woods at the rear of the property, and along the edge of the Monsal Trail. We searched some industrial units too, I recall. Two of them were empty at the time. They were considered strong possibilities for a while. But nothing. Nothing at all.'

Cooper kept silent, listening to Branagh reliving the experience of running the Annette Bower inquiry. He understood how frustrating those circumstances could be, when every potential lead you came up with hit a dead end. As a DC, he'd been on an inquiry team assigned to interview neighbours in Aldern Way, and then employees at the industrial units. He was well aware of some of what Branagh was saying. But still, he didn't interrupt.

'There was this one other place,' she said. 'We would have gone there next – though, given the nature of the location, it would have been a massive undertaking. Hard enough to justify at the best of times.'

'What location was that, ma'am?'

'An entire valley. Lathkill Dale.'

'Why Lathkill Dale?' asked Cooper.

'The Bowers originally met on a guided walk run by the Rangers. A shared interest in nature and industrial heritage, something like that. Lathkill Dale was one of their favourite areas apparently. They went there often, when they got the chance. Does that make sense to you, Ben – going for walk in the same place time after time? Personally, I'd want to go somewhere different, no matter how close by it was.'

'Some people like it,' said Cooper. 'They form a special connection with a place and they enjoy the familiarity. They find it relaxing. I can imagine that they would want to keep going to Lathkill Dale, particularly if they'd met there. It would have a special meaning for them.'

'Mmm. That sounds a bit overly romantic to me,' said Branagh. 'Reece Bower didn't strike me as the romantic type.'

'Perhaps Annette was, though. And he just went along with it. Lots of men do that.'

'My own husband would be astonished if I developed that sort of romantic streak,' said Branagh. 'I think he would divorce me in an instant.'

Cooper rarely thought of Detective Superintendent Branagh as a wife or mother. She had always been a rather daunting authority figure to him. So the occasional reference to her family always took him by surprise. He knew, as a matter of record, that she'd been married for many years to the same man, a consultant paediatrician at Eden Valley General Hospital, and that they had two grown-up children. There had even been photographs of the family on her desk at West Street, but he'd never seen her look at them while he was in the office. When she was working, she fully concentrated on the job in hand. This sudden reference to her marriage sounded jarring. He wondered if there was more behind it.

'And then there was the child,' she was saying. 'The Bowers' daughter.'

'Lacey,' said Cooper.

'She was very young at the time her mother went missing. About eight years old?'

'That's right.'

'We couldn't interview her obviously. Not at that age. Initially she was spoken to with her father present, but she was very uncommunicative. She couldn't remember when she'd last seen her mother, or anything she'd said. I suppose it was all too overwhelming for her. Too frightening and confusing, all those questions from strangers. She seemed very close to her father

– she never let go of him, was clinging to him constantly for reassurance whenever I saw her. After the arrest, young Lacey went to stay with an aunt.'

'Annette's sister, Frances Swann.'

Branagh nodded. 'I felt very bad about tearing her away from her father, but the evidence . . .'

'Yes, it was the right decision.'

'Thank you. I've wondered, of course. I've had ten years to wonder about it, whether all I did in that moment was to make a terrible situation even worse for a small child. Her mother had gone missing, and now her father was being taken away from her. I felt I must appear to be the big, bad ogre in her eyes. I hope she's forgiven me. I'd be interested to hear how she's grown up.'

'She's on my list to speak to, obviously.'

Superintendent Branagh's face had set into a grim expression as she talked about the Bower case. Cooper could see that the memory of it made her . . . not regretful exactly, but angry.

'When the victim hasn't been found,' she said, 'one of the temptations for the killer is to claim themselves to have seen their victim alive. But Reece Bower didn't need to lie. Someone else did that job for him.'

'He was a very lucky man.'

'Either that, or he was innocent,' said Cooper. 'I suppose there's always that possibility.'

Branagh's expression didn't change. She continued to stare grimly at Cooper.

'But you don't think so,' he said.

'No, I don't.'

Branagh sighed. 'Between you and me, I see this as a chance to make amends, to explore missed opportunities,' she said. 'We may be able to put things right.'

'And it's long overdue after ten years,' said Cooper.

He'd heard the uncertainty in the superintendent's voice. She had a lot of trust in him, but she knew she couldn't order him to pursue the lines of inquiry she'd missed all those years ago. When it came down to it, the decision was his. Branagh recognised that.

'Will you do this for me, Ben?' she said.

'Yes, ma'am. I'll do what I can.'

She sounded relieved now.

'There will be questions asked, no doubt. I'll back you as much as I can. Let me know if you have any problems.'

'I'll get straight on to it.'

Cooper stood up to leave.

'DI Cooper . . .' she said as he reached the door.

'Ma'am?'

'When will you be seeing Detective Sergeant Fry?'

Cooper stared at her in surprise.

'Why would I want to see her?'

'Well . . . no particular reason.'

He knew that Detective Superintendent Branagh didn't say things like that for no particular reason.

'I'm puzzled that you should mention her, ma'am. She's been working with EMSOU's Major Crime Unit for some time now.'

'I know that, of course. But I always thought you worked together really well.' She waved a hand to dismiss his protests. 'Oh, I know you're very different, and you didn't always get on. But you were a good team. You got results.'

Cooper didn't know how to reply. It wasn't how he'd seen their relationship. But it might look different from the outside.

'I don't mean that you can't get results on your own,' said Branagh. 'Of course not. I have absolute faith in you to make the right decisions, Ben.'

'Thank you, ma'am,' said Cooper. 'I'll try to do that.'

13

Ben Cooper knew a sergeant at Chesterfield. He didn't see him very often, and they'd arranged to meet in the restroom for a coffee before he went back to Edendale. And when Cooper walked into the room, there she was. Diane Fry. Superintendent Branagh must have known perfectly well she was here. Fry had probably checked in with her on her arrival.

Fry spotted him straightaway. She was sitting at a table on her own, clutching a cup. He couldn't tell from her expression whether she was surprised to see him, or pleased, or horrified, or anything in between. There was hardly a flicker of emotion on her face as she coolly met his gaze.

Cooper got himself a drink, took a deep breath, and walked over to her table.

'Diane,' he said.

'Ben. Hello.'

'How are you doing?'

'I'm fine.'

It was typical of her not to ask how he was in return. He was never sure if it was because she wasn't interested, or she'd never learned how to be polite. It was probably both.

Some people never seemed happy with life, and you could see it in their faces. Diane Fry had that look. It was a look that suggested the whole world was a terrible place. Everyone must know how awful it was. So, if you smiled too much, you must be an idiot. Too stupid to see how bad everything was. Stupid enough to be happy.

After a moment, Fry waved at an empty chair.

'Sit down, if you want,' she said.

Cooper sat, and took a drink of his coffee.

'So what are you doing here?' he said. 'Where are you working?'

'A place called Shirebrook in Nottinghamshire.'

'No, it's in Derbyshire,' said Cooper.

'Are you sure?'

'Yes, it's just this side of the border. It's part of North Division.'

'Borders don't matter that much in EMSOU,' said Fry.

Cooper thought that didn't excuse her ignorance, but he let it go.

'Strange place, Shirebrook,' said Fry.

'I can agree with you on that. I remember it from when it was a small coal-mining town. Everybody worked at the pit. The place got pretty run down, I suppose, but it was one of those towns that had a strong sense of community.'

Fry looked at him for a second, as if trying to find something more in his words.

'It isn't like that now,' she said.

'Oh, I know. The coal mine closed in 1993. A distribution centre was built on the pit site after it was cleared.'

She looked around the room, as if assessing the officers at the other tables. As usual, she didn't look as though she approved of any of them.

'EMSOU have an operation under way in Shirebrook,' she said.

Cooper nodded. 'I think I saw an email.'

'The situation is very tense.'

'Is EMSOU responsible for community cohesion now?' he asked.

'Everybody's responsible for community cohesion,' said Fry. 'Aren't they?'

Cooper knew it was true, of course. In many ways, it was the number-one policing priority, ahead of solving crime. Good relations between communities prevented crime from happening in the first place. Certainly serious hate crimes, the type of violent offences Fry and her colleagues at EMSOU were concerned with. When tensions simmered beneath the surface, they could break out into violence at any time. The statistics showed a worrying increase in hate crime after the result of the EU Referendum, and in some areas the situation had refused to settle back to normal. In places like Shirebrook, with its large migrant population, tensions often weren't even below the surface, but openly on display.

He noticed her cup was practically empty.

'Do you have time for another coffee?' he said.

Fry shook her head. 'Sorry, we're busy here. The inquiry has become urgent.'

'You always try to be one up on me,' said Cooper. 'What's the crisis?'

'A murder case. We've got a body.'

Cooper sighed. 'Well, that's *two* up on me, then.'

'The victim is Polish. I dare say you'll get an email about that too.'

'Probably.'

Cooper watched Fry as she drained her cup. Was she the right person to be dealing with sensitive issues like a conflict between communities? He doubted it. She wasn't a community person. Surely there must be something else going on to justify the presence of DS Diane Fry and her colleagues. Had the murder happened at this time by chance?

'And what have you got on at the moment?' asked Fry.

'A missing person case linked to a previous murder inquiry. A possible manslaughter in an arson incident. A spate of armed robberies.'

But Fry wasn't really interested. He saw her eyes glaze over and she gazed around the room.

'Oh, there's Jamie,' she said, pushing back her chair.

Cooper remember DC Callaghan from his visit to Fry's new base at St Ann's police station in Nottingham, but he was surprised by Fry's eagerness to get up and greet him. She'd hardly ever let her coolness slip like that with him. Well, perhaps on one or two notable occasions. But it had taken a long time.

Jamie Callaghan nodded at Cooper without a word as he waited for Fry.

'No doubt I'll see you around, Ben,' she said. 'Good luck with the case.'

'Thanks.'

'Good afternoon, Inspector,' said Callaghan.

Well, at least he could speak. Cooper watched the two of them walk away, leaving him alone to stare at his coffee. Not for the first time, he felt he had no idea what was really going on.

When he managed to get away from Chesterfield, Ben Cooper headed west, out beyond Bakewell. He needed to escape, and there was one place he couldn't stop thinking about.

Half an hour later Cooper parked his car by the side of the road just outside the village of Monyash. A few hikers were making their way back across the fields to their vehicles or visiting the public toilets across the road.

He opened the tailgate of the Toyota, changed into his walking boots and put on his waterproof, then went through the gate, following a wide, flattened path across the grass. The walking didn't stay easy for very long, he knew.

Brown dung flies rising from a cowpat warned him there was livestock ahead. A small herd of black-and-white cattle lay cudding, their hides covered in flies, flicking their tails and twitching their yellow ear tags. He expected them to move aside from the path as he approached. But these were Lathkill Dale cattle. They were used to noisier visitors than him. They barely blinked as he passed within touching distance of their damp noses.

There were reports on file of stock fencing being cut here in several places. Cooper found it hard to imagine the reason for it, except sheer vandalism. The upper part of this dale was a national nature reserve and famous for its rare wild flowers – purple orchids and Jacob's ladder.

Soon he was approaching the remains of Ricklow Quarry, where Derbyshire Grey Marble had been worked, the stone used to make fireplaces at Chatsworth House. These slopes were said to contain fossils up to three hundred and sixty million years old.

Enormous cascades of rock covered the hillside as he picked his way through the old quarry. This was some of the roughest going he knew of in the Peak District, a slow scramble over muddy boulders made slippery by rain and mud.

Beyond the spoil heaps of Ricklow Quarry, the valley narrowed dramatically. This part of the dale had an eerie atmosphere, with moss-covered rocks amid dank, dripping trees twisted into unnatural shapes. Cooper thought of *The Lord of the Rings* – not the films, but the books he'd read as a teenager, the image he had of the hobbits' Shire. A magical place where anything could happen, good or bad.

At this point the river that gave the dale its name wasn't even visible. Limestone buttresses towered over each side of the valley. Rocks lay around, as if thrown by giants. It was a strange, mythical landscape. One dark and stormy night in the eighteenth century a vicar of Monyash had ridden his horse right over the cliff after an evening spent drinking in Bakewell. The horse survived, but he didn't. The church in Monyash had kept a glass jar on display containing a tuft of grass that was said to have been taken from the clergyman's clenched fist when his body was found.

Why were local legends like that still remembered and shared? Cooper guessed he must have been told it by his mother, or his grandmother, or some other relative. Perhaps he'd read it in a book. But were those stories still being passed on? Or would his be the last generation to look up at these crags and know about the drunken vicar and his horse and the tuft of grass?

Through a squeeze stile, a view finally opened up into the dale, with its elegantly curved limestone cliffs. He passed a fenced-off area where Jacob's ladder covered the ground in violet-blue flowers in May and June. The sheep found it tasty, so they had to be kept off in the summer. A gate would be opened later in the year to let them graze the coarse grass.

He turned a bend on the path, and there was Lathkill Head Cave. This was where the River Lathkill emerged. Well, it did some of the time. The cave had an imposing entrance, a large square opening with a rock roof like a vast lintel, and moss-covered rocks tumbled on the floor below. The vivid green of the moss was a startling contrast with the silver-grey of the weathered limestone.

Today, the cave was bone dry. There hadn't been enough rain recently. But in winter it could pour out a vast torrent of water that came from the mine workings. In the summer it was no more than a trickle and often disappeared completely in dry weather.

Lathkill. Yet another Scandinavian name. Derbyshire was thick with them. This one was said to be from Old East Norse, a legacy of the Danish invaders a thousand years ago. *Hlada-kill.* It sounded strange and exotic in the mouth now. But all it meant was 'narrow valley'.

The Lathkill was unique even in the Peak District. It was the only river that ran over limestone for the whole of its length. That gave it a distinctive characteristic. And in this case, it was an important difference.

As he stood there, Cooper noticed a nest on a narrow ledge just above his head. A neat bowl shaped from leaves and dry grass, insulated on a bed of moss. So even here in this dried-up cave, something was able to survive.

Below Lathkill Head, the valley widened as it was joined from the south by Cales Dale. Halfway along Lathkill Dale was a tufa waterfall. He thought of tufa as something specific to the Peak District, though he supposed it must occur in other parts of the world where limestone was predominant. The soft, porous rock was formed from calcium carbonate precipitated by water that had run through limestone. It looked unnatural, and in a way it was.

In the aquarium at Matlock Bath there were displays of objects left in the water that had turned almost literally to stone as they calcified. It was the sort of thing the Victorians had loved. Such oddities had appealed to them. Here in Lathkill Dale, the tufa cascade was just an indication of the nature of the landscape he was walking through. This was a place where strange things happened.

A footbridge over the Lathkill led to the Limestone Way a few hundred yards south, but it was a steep ascent up the side of the dale, with stone steps built into the hillside to help the climb. At the top, he knew there would be a wide open stretch of White Peak farmland towards Youlgrave, a landscape very different from the dale, which had begun to feel too dark, too enclosed. Too claustrophobic.

He recalled a swimming area in the River Bradford near Youlgrave. He'd been there a couple of times as a teenager with a group of friends, taking the opportunity of some rare summer sun during the school holidays. But there had been something unappealing about the fact that they were officially allowed to swim there, even if the signs spelled out that it was 'at your own risk'. The most attractive sites were the ones that were forbidden – the reservoirs and flooded quarries. They'd all needed that sense of adventure back then. Now, he was too aware of the people who'd died or got into serious trouble swimming in the wrong place. It wasn't that the world that had changed, he supposed. It was him. He'd grown up.

Cooper pulled out an OS map from his waterproof. A rock shelter was marked on the map here at the bottom of Calling Low Dale. A natural overhang in the cliff created a roof, and the shelter had been enclosed by a dry stone wall. The space was no more than six feet long and perhaps four feet wide. The vertical strata of the limestone meant water continually dripped from the roof. You wouldn't want to use it as a shelter for long.

A hill fort had stood on the long limestone ridge, enclosing an area of about ten acres inside a rampart of limestone blocks and rubble. Like many other ancient sites, it had been badly damaged by stone robbing and years of ploughing. To the north was One Ash Grange, which he'd been told was once a reformatory for misbehaving monks. Up ahead, the eastern half of the dale had been extensively mined for lead ore right up until the middle of the nineteenth century.

Cooper put away his map. Yes, he'd been to all these places before, though the details were a bit vague and confused. Before he came today, he couldn't have recalled the order he would pass them on the trail into Lathkill Dale from the Monyash road, or where they stood in relation to each other. He wouldn't even have been able to say why or even when he'd come, or how old he was at the time. He just knew he'd been here before.

Lathkill Dale was a part of his life, the way it was for many people. It had a manner of creeping into your consciousness, as if you'd always known it.

He opened another pocket and took out the photograph of Annette Bower he'd been carrying with him. He felt an odd sort of connection between them. This place had been part of Annette's life too.

But was it also the place of her death?

Diane Fry left Shirebrook and got on to the M1 at Heath. Twenty miles south, she pulled into Trowell Services.

She preferred the services on the southbound side, because it had a Burger King rather than a McDonalds. For half an hour she sat at a table in Burger King eating a veggie bean burger with apple fries on the side and drinking a tropical mango smoothie.

People ebbed and flowed around her, staying a few minutes and getting back on the road to wherever they were heading. Two customers came and sat at a table next to her, a large woman in a baggy denim trouser suit, with steel grey hair cut into a severe bob and a girl of about fifteen, in a lime green jumpsuit and a baseball cap, like a contestant in *The X Factor*. They might have been mother and daughter – but, if so, they bore no physical resemblance to one another.

Halfway through her burger, Fry's phone rang and she saw from the display that it was Angie.

'Sis.'

'Hi. What are you doing?'

'Eating. Why?'

'You sound as though you're in a railway station.'

'Something like that. What do you want?'

'Just to say, you know . . . keep it to yourself what I told you last night.'

'You know you're putting me in a difficult position,' said Diane.

'Well, that's up to you.'

Diane pulled the lettuce out of her sesame seed bun and left it on the side of her tray.

'Is this some kind of test?'

'I don't know what you mean.'

'You shouldn't have told me, you know you shouldn't.

Why didn't you just hold on to your own secrets?'

'We're sisters, aren't we? Family. We ought not to have secrets from each other, Di. We never did when we were growing up in Warley.'

'Oh, that's right. Until you left.'

She wished she could see Angie's face. She could never really tell what she was thinking, unless she could look her sister right in the eyes.

'I didn't want to leave. It was something I had to do.'

'But you didn't tell me where you were going. You let me think I'd never see you again. You became very good at keeping secrets, Angie.'

'Things have changed. I'm a different person now.'

'Not all that different,' said Diane, 'if what you told me last night is true.'

She heard the baby screaming the background. Zack. Now, that was something that had definitely changed about her sister.

'I've got to go,' said Angie. 'We can talk about this some other time, if you want. But, Sis – remember. Keep it to yourself.'

Fry dropped her phone on the table in exasperation. Last night's conversation with her sister was one she'd been hoping to forget. She'd shared her Yuk Sung Chicken and vegetarian spring rolls with Angie, conscious at first of an unusual silence. Then Angie had sat back and taken a deep breath.

'There's something I should have told you a long time ago,' she'd said. 'About a part of my life I've always kept from you.'

Diane had immediately experienced the sinking feeling in her stomach that her sister was uniquely able to provoke.

'Whatever it is, it doesn't matter.'

But Angie had shaken her head firmly. 'You have to listen, Sis. It's too late to do any harm now.'

'Are you sure about that?'

She had been convinced her sister was about to tell her some shady truths about her previous boyfriend Craig, the father of Zack. She'd always had suspicions about him, but there were times when it was best not to know.

But that wasn't what Angie had in mind.

'It goes back a long way,' she'd said, 'to when you first found me – or rather, when your friend Ben first found me.'

'What?'

That had been a painful part of their history. Diane had been trying to trace her sister for years after she ran away from their foster home in the West Midlands. It was why she'd transferred to Derbyshire Constabulary in the first place, following a trail that suggested Angie had ended up in nearby Sheffield. Yet it had been Ben Cooper, interfering with his usual naïve and clumsy style, who had tracked Angie down and arranged their meeting. It had changed her life, and not always in a good way.

'You don't need to remind me of that,' she said.

'No, you don't understand,' said Angie. 'In all this time, you've never asked me what I was doing in Sheffield. I know you wanted to skate over all that and go back to the way things were in Warley. But that just wasn't possible, Sis. Not after everything that had happened to me in the meantime. Didn't you ever wonder?'

Of course she'd wondered. Yet Angie was right – it was an aspect of her sister's life that she'd pushed determinedly to the back of her mind. She'd tried to pretend that Angie was the same person she'd lost sight of years ago, even though the truth was staring her in the face.

'It didn't seem important,' she said.

Angie had laughed then. 'Liar. You just didn't want to know, in case it compromised your principles. I kept quiet then, but it had to come out. And there are reasons I have to tell you now.'

The chicken had lost its flavour by that point in the evening. Diane had felt trapped in her own apartment, with no means of escaping whatever her sister was about to inflict on her.

'The fact is,' said Angie, 'I fell in with some very bad people in Sheffield. The worst kind you can imagine. I was an idiot, of course. I was at risk all the time. But then I did something even more dangerous – I got recruited as an informer. That was when Ben Cooper traced me. It almost caused disaster for a major operation the NCA were planning.'

'The NCA?'

'As in the National Crime Agency.'

'I know who they are. But Angie—'

Her sister had held up a hand to stop her interrupting. 'I've got to tell you now, Di. Because there's a good chance I'm going to need your help.'

149

Sitting in Burger King, Fry sighed at the memory of the previous evening. She pushed her meal aside, finished her smoothie and stood up. Immediately her table was claimed. A young man with tousled hair, sideburns and heavy framed glasses sat down across from a dumpy young woman with a plump face and dark hair.

In the women's toilets at the service area the walls were covered with adverts for insurance policies and bladder control products. A poster near the door encouraged her to text a donation to a charity in Africa.

Fry wondered what kind of adverts were on the walls of the men's toilets. Something about cars or football, she guessed.

She walked back outside, pressed her key fob, and saw her Audi's lights blink. Her car, winking at her in the darkness.

14

Ben Cooper felt himself growing calmer on the way to Bridge End Farm. The landscape always helped him to do that.

The Peak District moors had turned purple in late August, the swatches of heather coming magnificently into flower over acres of apparently empty moorland. Now, down in the valleys, the trees were starting to change colour too. They were still heavily laden with foliage, and they lumbered clumsily over the road in the strong winds. In a few weeks' time their leaves would be yellow and bronze. Autumn would strip them and scatter the dead leaves across the tarmac surface in golden tides.

The skeletal bareness of winter would be here soon, thought Cooper. Much too soon. The months when the ground was sodden, paths were churned into muddy quagmires, and the air felt chill and damp. For Cooper, every season had its moods and its appeal. But there was a period after Christmas and the New Year when even the Peak District felt miserable. He wondered if there was some event from his past that made him feel so down when late January and February arrived. Or did everyone feel that way?

The fields around Bridge End Farm looked different this year. Ben's sister-in-law Kate had persuaded his brother Matt to make a change from the traditional black silage bags. Reluctantly, he'd ordered a roll of pink silotite bale wrap and joined the trend for pink bags in support of breast cancer research. The field where the bales were stacked looked much brighter, the pink wrap gleaming in the sun next to the black bags. A couple of tourists had stopped their car up on the road to take photographs.

The swallows that nested every year in the barns at Bridge End were getting ready to leave. The house martins would stay for a while longer, but the swallows would be heading off on their journey back to Africa. It was hard to imagine something so tiny and fragile making an incredible journey like that, and returning next spring to the exact same spot. What resilience and determination it must take.

Cooper couldn't think of many people who had that sort of single-minded determination. You had to need something *very* badly, didn't you? What was it the swallows needed? To come back to their home surely. That was something everyone wanted. Had Annette Bower needed it badly enough?

At the end of dinner at Bridge End Farm that evening, Matt Cooper put down his knife and fork with a clatter on his plate.

'You're going to *what*?' he said.

'The opera,' repeated Ben.

'The chuffin' opera? What's happened to you, brother?'

Kate frowned at her husband. 'Watch your language, Matt.'

The two girls giggled. They weren't shocked any more. They were teenagers, and they thought their parents were ridiculous.

'Besides,' said Kate, 'there's nothing wrong with the opera. A lot of people enjoy it.'

'*We've* never gone to the opera,' said Matt.

'Well, perhaps I'd like to some time. Have you ever thought of that?'

Matt scowled. 'No, I haven't.'

Ben studied his brother for a moment. Matt was never the sunniest of characters, but he'd been in a particularly bad mood all evening. He'd been curt when Ben arrived at the farm, then monosyllabic over dinner, and finally short-tempered over trivialities. Something was definitely wrong.

'I'm sure it will be wonderful.' Kate began to clear plates off the table. 'I hope you enjoy yourself, Ben.'

Ben stood up. 'I'll help you with the washing-up.'

The girls disappeared to their rooms and, as he walked across the passage to the kitchen, he heard Matt switch on the TV. Kate handed him a tea towel, but didn't seem to want to meet his eye.

'I'm sorry, I didn't expect that to cause a family disagreement,' said Ben, though inside he felt as much like laughing as Amy and Josie. 'What does my brother have against opera?'

'It's nothing to do with the opera,' said Kate.

'Oh.'

They worked together silently for a while. Through the kitchen window, Ben could see the outlines of the farm buildings in the darkness, standing out against a clear, starlit sky. Beyond them he could make out the shape of the hill that he'd become so familiar with growing up at Bridge End. He couldn't even remember the name of that hill now. It was probably something 'low', he supposed. But as a family, they'd always just called it 'the hill'. It was so much a part of their lives that it didn't need a name. It was *their* hill.

Out in the yard, he heard the dog bark. Not a warning of intruders, but a welcoming bark. He guessed that Matt had gone out of the house. He'd left the TV on and disappeared to where he felt most comfortable – out there in the open, with his tractor and his dog.

Kate looked up. 'Matt is very worried,' she said eventually.

Ben realised she'd been waiting for her husband to go out, so that there was no chance of him overhearing their conversation. She knew Matt so well. Probably better than Ben did himself now.

'Matt always worries,' he said. 'He wouldn't be happy unless he had something to worry about.'

She smiled sadly. 'This is different, Ben.'

'So what is he worried about this time? Something to do with the farm, I suppose? Are the yields down this year? Has the price of feed gone through the roof? He hasn't mentioned anything.'

'No, it's nothing like that.'

'Nothing to do with the farm?'

'No.'

Now Ben was getting concerned himself. Matt hardly thought of anything, apart from the farm. Well, except his family, of course. His heart sank, and he put down the tea towel.

'Is it one of the girls?' he said. 'Is something wrong with Amy or Josie? Because you know I'd do anything—'

She shook her head. 'Not that either.'

'Well, it can't be Matt,' he said.

Kate laughed. 'Why not?'

'Well, he's as strong as an ox. He never has anything wrong with him. Not physically anyway. He just needs fuelling occasionally and he keeps going on for ever, like his old Massey Ferguson.'

Now she looked shocked. 'What do you mean "not physically"? Are you suggesting your brother is psychologically unstable?'

'No, he's just a thick-headed bumpkin, like he always was.'

Kate laid her hand on his arm and gazed out into the darkness. A light was on in the machinery shed, and a figure could just be made out moving around inside, its shadow thrown fitfully against the walls and out into the yard. Ben glimpsed the dog, Bess, wagging her tail at the unseen figure.

'It's me,' said Kate. 'I found a lump. The doctors say it's possibly a malignant tumour so I've had a biopsy done and now I'm waiting on the results.'

'I'm really sorry to hear that.'

'Oh, I'll be fine,' she said. 'That's an excellent

prognosis if you catch this sort of thing early enough. I'm not worried. Well . . .' She hesitated. 'I *am* quite nervous, but I'm sure it will work out okay. Matt isn't taking it so well.'

'That's why he's like a bear with a sore head,' said Ben. 'He has no idea how to deal with these things. He never did have. Matt had no idea how to deal with Dad's death, or Mum's illness. It's not his forte.'

'You were right about him being physically strong. But his feelings are a lot more complicated, much more difficult to understand.'

'He definitely has them, though. He just has difficulty finding a way to express them.'

'You know him better than anyone, Ben,' said Kate.

'Do I? I was just thinking the same about you. Matt and I have grown apart over the years, especially since I moved to Edendale.'

'Nevertheless,' said Kate, 'I think you're still the only one he can talk to about some things.'

'Are you sure, Kate?'

'Certain.'

She took the tea towel off him. Ben nodded, and left the kitchen. He went down the passage and out of the back door into the yard. It was dark on this side of the house, but he knew every inch of the place. He'd often wandered around these buildings in the dark as a child, and even right out into the fields among the animals. He'd loved the sense of solitude and openness to the sky. It was like stepping into a different world where all the cares of the day fell away from him. He wondered if it was the same for Matt,

156

whether he still did that now to get away from his troubles, if that was what he was doing when he went out to the machinery shed to talk to the dog.

Ben found his brother sitting on an upturned oil drum, with the dog at his feet. Matt looked up without surprise when he came in.

'I suppose Kate told you,' he said.

'Of course she did. Why didn't you tell me?'

Matt shook his head. 'It seemed too . . . personal.'

'Well, what a surprise. But I *am* your brother.'

'I'm sorry. It's just the thought of losing Kate. I can't stand it.'

'Lose her? It's not like one of your cows getting sick, Matt. They're not going to put her down with a humane killer. They can do wonders these days. If it is malignant, Kate herself says the outcome is generally pretty good for an early diagnosis like hers.'

'I know, I know.'

'Besides,' said Ben, 'she needs your support right now. Not having you stomping around in a bad temper all the time.'

Matt said nothing, but stroked the dog's head thoughtfully. Ben could see it was an action that calmed him down.

'You're right, obviously,' he said.

'I know I am.'

Ben found another oil drum and rolled it over. They sat next to each for a few minutes in silence. This was the way it had often been between them, even when they were teenagers. It was in these long silences that they felt closest to each other.

'Talk to me about something else,' said Matt in the end.

'Like what?'

'You usually have some interesting case going on. A murder inquiry, something like that.'

'You want to hear about a murder? Really?'

Ben mentally ran through his recent cases. He ruled out the death of Shane Curtis. An arson attack on a farmer's barn would only send Matt off on another angry rant.

'Do you remember the Annette Bower case?' he said. 'It was about ten years ago.'

That made Matt think. His memory was pretty good for scandalous events in the area. Farmers gossiped about things like that down at the market, or in the village pub.

'Was that the woman whose body was never found?'

'You got it.'

'Was that actually a murder? I seem to remember—'

'Her husband was charged, but it never got to court.'

'That's it. Somebody claimed to have seen her alive, so there couldn't have been a murder.'

'Well, perhaps not,' said Ben. 'On the other hand, perhaps there was.'

Matt snorted. 'That's what I like. It could be one thing, or it could be the other. No one really knows. It makes my life seem a lot more simple.'

Ben slapped him on the shoulder. 'I'm glad about that.'

His brother blinked. 'There was a lot of talk about that case. The woman's disappearance.'

'Annette Bower?'

'Yes. Bakewell, wasn't it? Everyone thought the husband was guilty.'

Ben sighed. 'Yes, but there was too much reasonable doubt after the sighting of her.'

'There was a lot of bad feeling going about. I remember it well, now. When he was let off, there were blokes who wanted to sort him out themselves, take justice into their own hands, so to speak.'

'Vigilantes?'

'If you want to call them that,' said Matt. 'Sometimes the system lets people down, you know. There was a feeling it had happened in that case. People thought that woman had been killed and no one would be punished for it. That's wrong, isn't it?'

'Yes,' said Ben. 'It *is* wrong.'

He saw a light go out in the kitchen of the house. Kate still stood there in the darkness, staring out towards the shed, no doubt wondering what was going on, what the two brothers might be talking about. She'd be amazed if she knew.

'I wouldn't be surprised,' said Matt, 'if that Bower bloke went missing himself one day.'

Ben turned and stared at his brother. His face was half hidden in the shadows of the shed, his head tilted down towards the dog, which gazed back at him with adoring eyes. Ben couldn't quite believe what he'd heard. It was so rare for his brother to come up with anything he could have called an insight.

A strong wind was blowing across the fields, bending the trees and sending the sheep scurrying to find shelter behind a stone wall. Both the trees and the sheep were used to this kind of wind up here. Even when the weather was calm, the trees stayed bent in a southerly direction, like mime artists pretending it was windy.

Instead of heading home to his cottage in Foolow, Ben Cooper had driven up the hill from Bridge End Farm and had kept driving until he found himself on the moors, right on the edge of the gritstone area known as the Dark Peak.

Although he'd been born and raised in the farming country of the White Peak, he'd always been drawn to the Dark Peak landscapes. The Dark Peak might look empty and desolate to some eyes, but it seemed to Cooper that it was just waiting for you to put something into it. It was a landscape for the imagination. His ancestors had peopled it with all kinds of mythical creatures and supernatural events; every rock had a story attached to it, every pool of water had its own legend. Everyone who'd lost their life out there was remembered, every incident had its place in the folk memory.

The changing colours of the season, the transformation of light as it passed across the hills, the shadows moving under the twisted rocky outcrops – everything spoke of a land that was alive and breathing. The Dark Peak was only empty for those who had no imagination. Cooper had sometimes been told that he had too much.

The sky was a deep black and you could see the stars clearly here. Thousands and thousands of them – some glittering brightly, some no more than a milky haze across the galaxy. That was something he would surely miss, if he ever had to live in a city. So much light pollution prevented you from seeing the stars and a few minutes standing gazing at the night sky really helped to put things into perspective. He felt so tiny in the face of that infinite universe.

Cooper shivered. In the summer, it might still have been light at this time, or at least illuminated by that peculiar half-light that came with dusk.

But the nights were drawing in. That's what his mother would have said. She'd said it every year, about this time. You could have filled the date in on your calendar in advance. The leaves were turning brown, and Christmas cards were in the shops. It was already September, and the nights were drawing in.

People thought the weather was the most important part of the seasons. But day length was the crucial factor for nature. Though there were still thirteen hours of daylight at this time of year, the hours were getting shorter by four minutes a day. Cooper had hated that knowledge as a child. It had always felt like his life was slipping away from him, slowly and certainly, an inch at a time.

He shook himself and realised that he'd been sitting here for a long time. He looked at his watch. Dawn would come at about six twenty a.m. He hoped it would bring a bit more light into his world.

15

Day 3

Next day, Stage Three of the Tour of Britain had entered the western side of the Peak District from Cheshire. Hundreds of racing cyclists were right now on the A537 Cat and Fiddle road to the west of Buxton, the longest and highest climb of the race. At the summit, the riders would turn along the A54 and head back down towards the Cheshire Plain, taking them out of Derbyshire.

Ben Cooper had known it was about to happen – it was in the bulletins months ago, but he'd forgotten. At least the race didn't come as far as Bakewell and Edendale. The traffic chaos would be unimaginable.

Arriving at West Street, he passed a uniformed officer in the corridor, just on his way out to start a shift. Instinct made Cooper turn and look back at the officer. Some joker had stuck a handwritten sign on the back of his high-vis jacket. Instead of just 'Police', it said 'Police, Fire, Ambulance, Paramedic, Care Worker, NHS, Mental Health, Social Services, Samaritan, Parent, Marriage Counsellor, Traffic Warden, Car Mechanic,

Livestock Handler'. They'd run out of space for all the other jobs.

Cooper opened his mouth to call to him, but changed his mind. The officer's sergeant or one of his colleagues would tell him before he went out in public. Jokes like that were for internal consumption.

Last week, Cooper found a printed notice taped to the wall of the men's toilets. It said:

ACTION TO BE TAKEN IN THE EVENT OF A MORALE ATTACK. The area must be evacuated immediately before any officers catch morale. A senior officer must remove the source of morale as soon as possible. Work can only be resumed when morale has been returned to its normally low level. Be vigilant – morale is a constant threat!

These notices wouldn't have appeared a few months ago. Now, no one took the trouble to take them down or find out who was producing them. The senior command staff had probably decided it was a harmless way of letting off steam.

At least morale in the CID room seemed to be normal. Or as normal as it ever was.

'Hey, I have a mate at Bolsover LPU,' said Gavin Murfin when he saw Cooper. 'He says Diane Fry and her EMSOU mates have been hanging around all week.'

'Yes, I saw her in Chesterfield last night,' said Cooper.

Luke Irvine frowned at the name. 'Diane Fry? She's a bunny boiler.'

'All women are potential bunny boilers, Luke,' said Murfin. 'They're just waiting for the right moment to strike.'

'I'll tell your wife what you've been saying about her,' warned Becky Hurst.

Murfin sniffed. 'It won't matter. She boiled my bunny years ago.'

'I happen to know you're very happily married, Gavin,' said Cooper. 'And you have been for twenty-five years.'

'It's a façade. You should know better than to believe everything you're told.'

Hurst smiled now. She knew Murfin better than that too. But she wasn't about to forgive Irvine.

'Anyway,' she said, 'what do you know about Detective Sergeant Fry, Luke? You were only the office boy when she was based here.'

'Get lost,' said Irvine.

'Don't worry, you'll get promoted to a proper police officer one day.'

Cooper didn't have time to get involved in this one. That was what he had a detective sergeant for, wasn't it?

'DS Sharma, unless there's anything urgent I'll be in Bakewell later this morning,' he said. 'You can phone me if there are any problems.'

'We'll be fine, inspector. There's just one thing . . .'

'Yes?'

'I'd like to do a media appeal, to see if we can get any information from the public on the robbery suspects.'

Cooper nodded. 'Good idea, Dev. Go ahead and set it up.'

'Thank you, sir.'

Cooper went back to his office. He forced himself to phone his brother to make sure everything was okay after the previous night. He would rather have spoken to Kate herself, but that might look as though he was going behind Matt's back. He fully expected his brother to be irritable and bad-tempered. But he was very quiet today.

'Yes, Kate is fine,' he said. 'We're all fine, thanks.'

It was so uncharacteristic that it sounded to Ben like an apology – or as close to one as his brother was ever likely to get.

'Kate's just heard she has an appointment with the consultant on Friday morning for her results,' said Matt.

'You'll let me know how it goes, won't you?'

'Of course.'

While he was listening to Matt, Cooper scanned the morning's updates.

A couple in their eighties had been visited by a man claiming to be a police officer investigating a theft. He'd flashed a photo ID card, which he said was a police warrant card. While in their house he'd stolen a wallet containing cash and various bank and debit cards. The previous day, a man matching a similar description and claiming to be a police officer had visited the home of an eighty-three-year-old man, but was refused entry and left when asked for identification.

Elsewhere, a flood of complaints from residents about

cars being parked on grass verges and street corners with For Sale signs on them turned out to be someone running a second-hand car sales business without going to the trouble and expense of buying premises to operate from.

Several small roads around Kinder Scout had been closed temporarily for the filming of a TV motoring show. The crew would be there for about a week. Nothing to do with CID, but it was best to know.

And there were internal problems too. He was alerted by a memo that engineers were currently on site, trying to resolve the problems that callers to the 101 non-emergency number had been experiencing. People had been facing delays in getting through to call handlers, or in some cases had been cut off during their calls. Cooper was very glad he didn't have to deal with that problem.

Finally he began working his way through the case files from ten years ago. He wanted to analyse the strength of the evidence against Reece Bower. Though it was an old case, Bower's guilt or innocence might well prove relevant to his disappearance.

Yet there was also that idea suggested by his brother last night, that Bower's disappearance might be due to some delayed vigilante action by local people anxious to bring justice where they thought an injustice had been done. He didn't know where to start looking for vigilantes, so the case files seemed the only place to begin.

He began by taking out the photograph of Annette Bower and laying it on his desk where he could see it. Her picture helped to remind him that this was all about a real human being who might have lost her life, not just about a collection of evidence and witness reports. It was easy, sometimes, to lose sight of a victim as a person. Cooper was determined that Annette would be real. He wanted to feel that he knew who she was.

'But who exactly were you?' he said to the photo.

Her details showed that she was thirty-two years old when she disappeared. She'd been born locally as Annette Slaney, educated at Lady Manners School in Bakewell, before gaining a degree in Health and Human Sciences at the University of Sheffield.

When she graduated, Annette had taken a management job at a hospital in Sheffield, which was perhaps where she'd met Reece Bower. They'd married nineteen years ago, and had Lacey just over twelve months later. Annette had gone back to work part-time after the pregnancy, later moving to a new job at Eden Valley General. The Bowers had also moved house about that time, from Dronfield to Bakewell, moving further into Derbyshire.

Her interests were listed as walking, running and swimming. She'd been a member of two sports clubs and had learned to play the cello. Her life seemed pretty blameless. But, at some point, everything had gone wrong.

Cooper gazed at Annette's photograph for a few more moments, looking into her eyes, imagining that she was right there in the office, on the other side of the desk, asking him to find out what had happened to her. He bowed his head in acknowledgment. No promises, but he would do his best.

The first statement he turned up was from Reece Bower himself. He'd made the 999 call to report his wife's disappearance when she failed to return home from a run on the Monsal Trail, accompanied by their yellow Labrador. The dog had come back on its own, and he'd assumed that she'd lost the dog and was still searching for it. That was why he'd waited some time before making the call. No, Annette didn't normally take her mobile phone with her. She carried an iPod and wore headphones, and she didn't want the extra weight. She also felt she didn't need it when she was going to be so close to home anyway. And she had the dog, said Bower, so she felt safe.

'But *was* she safe?' said Cooper to himself. 'Perhaps not. And we only have her husband's word for that.'

The second statement was from Annette's mother, Catherine Slaney. She talked about her daughter's turbulent relationship with her husband. In her interview, she seemed to want to put suspicion on Reece. But she agreed that Annette had left her husband once before, two years previously, after an argument over an affair that he'd been having with a colleague. Annette had stayed with her parents for four weeks before returning to her home in Bakewell.

Cooper flicked through the interview reports to find the colleague in question. Surely she'd been interviewed? Yes, here she was. Her name was Madeleine Betts. She admitted the relationship with Reece Bower, but told the interviewing officer that Reece had ended the affair so that his wife would return home. She had since moved to a different job within the hospital and no longer saw Reece Bower at all. She had never met Annette, she said.

One more witness report came from a dog walker who had been on the Monsal Trail that morning. She said she'd been accustomed to seeing Annette Bower jogging on the trail, but couldn't say whether she'd seen the missing woman around the time of her disappearance. The witness stated that she hadn't noticed anything unusual in the area, except the man in the red Nissan car. She said he was acting suspiciously and had driven off in a hurry when he saw her. She was unable to give a description of the man.

Cooper made a note. He wondered if that sighting had ever been followed up. It was nebulous, to say the least. But it was still a potential lead.

Then he read through the interviews quickly again. On the surface, there was no evidence against Reece Bower, in fact, no indication of a potential crime. Annette Bower had simply vanished. No one could say how, or why.

So what about the forensic evidence? This was where the case became more interesting, and more awkward for Reece Bower.

First up was a report from a forensic imagery expert, who had analysed CCTV footage. Footage showing a vehicle travelling through Bakewell on the morning of 29 October was said to show a car identical in model and colour to Bower's blue Vauxhall, though the number plate was indistinguishable.

Specially trained cadaver dogs on loan from South Yorkshire Police had searched the Bowers' home. The dogs were trained to sniff out traces of blood and human remains. The dogs, two springer spaniels, had identified areas of interest in the Bowers' back garden, where signs of recent digging were evident.

A report from Detective Inspector Paul Hitchens summarised the contents of ten hours of interviews conducted with Mr Bower. During the interviews he'd noticed scratches and grazes on Bower's hands. When asked about them, Bower said he had scratched his hands while gardening.

Forensic pathologist Dr Felix Webber had been asked to examine Reece Bower. Webber said the scratches and abrasions on Bower's hands had happened around the time Mrs Bower went missing and the injuries were consistent with gardening activities, but could have had a number of other causes.

A forensic scientist had been called in to conduct a search for DNA at the property in Aldern Way and in the boot of Mr Bower's car. She confirmed that she had been unable to find any trace of Annette Bower's DNA anywhere in the building or in the car. She said that as she opened the boot, she noticed a fresh smell coming from inside which could either have been an air freshener or a cleaning agent.

A further examination of Reece Bower's car found a substantial amount of mud and traces of vegetation on the chassis and embedded in the tread of the tyres, despite the fact that it had been washed at a hand car wash in Bakewell two days previously. Bower was unable to account for the mud, but suggested it had been dropped on the road by a farmer's tractor.

Cooper nodded to himself.

'That's perfectly possible.'

In the next statement, Annette Bower's sister, Frances Swann, said that Annette had confided in her about difficulties in her marriage. She had spoken about the possibility of divorce, even after the affair with Madeleine Betts was long over. Their finances were difficult and she was worried that her husband was getting into too much debt. Mrs Swann had last heard from her sister in a phone call two days before her disappearance, when she had sounded perfectly normal, with no sign of stress or any unusual state of mind.

Mrs Swann went on to say that she and her husband Adrian had arranged to visit the Bowers that afternoon, as they often did. Annette was out when they arrived, and Reece told her his wife had gone for a run with their dog and hadn't yet returned. Her husband Adrian was with her, but he'd taken their two Jack Russells for a walk while Frances began to prepare a meal for them. During the time she spent in the kitchen of the Bowers' home, she'd noticed a drop of blood on the tiled floor. She had no explanation for how it had got there. She expected her sister to return home soon, but she hadn't. Mrs Swann had persuaded Reece to walk up to the nearby section of the Monsal Trail to look for Annette. The Labrador, Taffy, had re-appeared alone while he was out. On his return, Frances had pressed her brother-in-law to phone and report Annette missing, which he eventually did.

'*Which he eventually did*'? That was interesting. Cooper had read a lot of witness statements, and the inclusion of a term like 'eventually' suggested that Mrs Swann had been very insistent on it.

There were other statements, including one from Adrian Swann confirming his wife's version of events, and one from Reece Bower's manager who admitted that Bower had seemed stressed recently, though the standard of his work hadn't suffered.

And there was a final statement, dated well after the others, from Annette Bower's father, Evan Slaney, claiming to have seen his daughter alive and well in Buxton long after her husband was supposed to have killed her.

Cooper was frowning over the details of the sighting when he was interrupted.

'How is it going?'

He looked up. Carol Villiers stood over his desk gazing at the sheaf of reports. Cooper hadn't heard her either knock on the door or come into the room.

'It doesn't look good,' he said.

'Reece Bower was never actually tried. So a review of the case might produce a different opinion from the CPS. Don't you think so?'

Cooper shook his head. 'There would have to be some new evidence. They wouldn't consider it otherwise.'

'What if the credibility of the crucial witness statement was demolished?'

'You mean her father, Mr Slaney.'

'Yes, he's the one who claims he saw Annette alive.'

'You think we might be able to prove he's lying?'

'Or mistaken.'

'He was very confident and consistent in his interview,' said Cooper. 'Who's going to accept now that he was just mistaken?'

'Lying then.'

'For what reason? He had no motivation to lie, no reason to protect Reece Bower.'

'Not that we know of.'

'Okay,' said Cooper dubiously. 'So what do you think the strongest elements of the case were against Reece Bower?'

'Well, for a start, the forensic examination found bloodstains on the floor of the Bowers' kitchen,' said Villiers. 'Only tiny spots. Most of them were invisible to the human eye. It was one particular drop of blood that drew attention.'

Cooper nodded. 'That single speck started the whole thing. The entire case rested on it in a way.'

'It was identified as Annette Bower's blood, though. Her DNA wasn't on record, but they got a sample from a hairbrush for comparison. It was definitely Annette's blood.'

'Reece Bower's story was that she'd cut herself on a knife a few days previously, while she was chopping vegetables. That was never disproved.'

'How could it be?' said Villiers. 'It was consistent with the pattern of the blood. And since Annette Bower was never found, alive or dead, she was wasn't able to either corroborate or contradict that version of events.'

'Entirely circumstantial, then,' said Cooper. 'Not real proof.'

'Everyone who knew the Bowers confirmed that

their marriage was going a rough patch. Their neighbours, Annette's sister, her parents, even some of their colleagues at work. Everyone agreed that the couple had been having arguments.'

'If all those people knew about their arguments, they were hardly a secret,' Cooper pointed out.

'I suppose not.'

'Is there a member of the family we don't have a statement from?'

'Only the daughter, Lacey,' said Villiers. 'She would have been eight years old at the time of her mother's disappearance, though.'

'It's very young, but not too young to remember something about it. Children of that age often notice more than adults realise, or expect. It's possible she could recall some detail that was important.'

'But there's no statement on record.'

'She wouldn't have been questioned at the time, or only in a superficial way.'

Cooper sensed a gap in the information. If she had been spoken to at all following the disappearance, an eight-year-old girl like Lacey would have been treated with kid gloves by the inquiry team. She would have been asked questions only in the presence of a responsible adult – in those circumstances, almost certainly her father. After Reece Bower was arrested and charged with murder, she went to her aunt's to be looked after.

'Annette Bower's sister, Frances Swann . . .' he said.

Villiers checked the list. 'She has an address at Over Haddon.'

'Do we know anything else about her?'

'She's a teacher at Lady Manners School. I don't know what subject. Her husband works for the Health and Safety Laboratory at Harpur Hill.'

'Adrian Swann?'

'Yes. Do you know him, Ben?'

'I've come across him. He's a specialist in high-velocity projectile delivery systems.'

'Mmm, whatever *they* are,' said Villiers. 'Well, the Swanns have two children of their own. One of them would be about the same age as Lacey.'

Cooper looked down at the sea of reports and statements.

'What am I missing, Carol?'

'I don't know.'

They sat and stared at each other for a while. Then Villiers picked out a witness statement from the pile.

'This man driving the red Nissan,' she said. 'He was never traced, it seems. There were public appeals, but no one came forward so he couldn't be identified.'

'If he ever actually existed.'

'You think he was invented? But it wasn't Reece Bower who reported seeing the Nissan, it was a member of the public who saw it behaving suspiciously near the Monsal Trail.'

'What does "behaving suspiciously" mean? Someone sitting in a car might look suspicious to a wary passer-by with an active imagination.' Cooper shook his head. 'It sounds like a red herring to me.'

'It worked in distracting the focus of the investigation for a while. It's almost as if Bower had planted that bit of witness evidence himself.'

'This man has an awful lot of luck,' said Cooper.

'Do you think his luck has finally run out?'

'We can't know,' said Cooper, 'until we find him.'

'Well, we've run some checks on Reece Bower,' said Villiers. 'He's not using his phone, or his credit cards. Or at least, he hasn't since Sunday, when he disappeared. However, he did draw out four hundred pounds in cash on the Friday, two days before. I suppose he could have picked up a pay-as-you-go mobile somewhere.'

'Even so, four hundred pounds wouldn't last him long, unless he's staying with someone.'

'True. So where are you going to start, Ben?'

'Mr Slaney is an obvious starting point. But I also want to talk to Naomi Heath again. I think it's interesting that she still lives in the house that Annette disappeared from. She would have to believe in Reece Bower's innocence to do that, wouldn't she?'

'Do you want me to come along?'

Cooper hesitated. 'I think DS Sharma needs you here, Carol.'

'Okay. Is there anything I can do in the meantime?'

'Have you started working your way through the address book?'

'Yes, but there are a lot of names. Is it okay if I share some out to Luke and Becky? There are so many to check.'

'Yes, of course. And you could find another address for me – Lacey Bower's. She's a student in Sheffield.'

'The teenage daughter?' said Villiers. 'I'll get on to it.'

*   *   *

Ben Cooper felt he could no longer justify taking Carol Villiers away from Dev Sharma's team. They had too much else to do. But he needed some assistance and there was a compromise solution: Gavin Murfin.

'How are you, Gavin?' he asked when Murfin came into his office.

'Top notch. What's up, boss?'

'Gavin, there was a forensic pathologist involved in the Bower case who I don't know. His name was Felix Webber.'

'Oh, old Fingers Felix. We bumped heads a few times.'

'What is he like?'

'He's a miserable bugger, the real life and soul of the funeral, if you know what I mean. I had to visit him a lot at one time. When he was there, a morgue was definitely a morgue, and not a place for chat. But he liked cops, had a bit of respect for the job, if you know what I mean.'

'Not like Dr van Doon?' said Cooper.

'Well, aye.'

'So where is he now?'

'Felix Webber went independent, set up his own consultancy practice in Derby. He wrote a couple of books, did some media interviews, and got quite a name for himself. Then he became chair of one of the committees at the Royal College of Pathology.'

'A high flier, then.'

'I think he must be doing well. He's gone right upmarket. Lives inside a Sunday supplement – white quartz worktops and a table made of fir planks.'

'So you've kept in touch?'

'Well, I've been to his house,' said Murfin cautiously.

'Through your job as a private investigator?'

'I used to get information from Webber. I could phone him and talk him into giving me a few nuggets, a bit of independent advice, but I can't get through to him now.'

'Why not?'

'He's far too important these days. He doesn't even chew his own food, let alone answer his own phone.'

Cooper laughed. 'You're with me today, by the way.'

'Just like old times,' said Murfin.

'First I want you in Chesterfield. You need to go to Reece Bower's place of work, a steel fabrications company. Naomi Heath suggested one of his colleagues had made a comment to Reece that upset him and may have made him leave. If that's so, I want to know who it was and what they said to him.'

'Got it, boss.'

'I don't think it's a huge outfit. It shouldn't take you long to narrow it down to a specific individual.'

'No problem.'

'And there's one other person I'd like you to track down and talk to,' said Cooper.

'Who's that?'

Cooper tapped the statement from Annette Bower's sister.

'This woman, Madeleine Betts. She works at Chesterfield Royal Hospital.'

'And after that?'

'You can come and join me in Bakewell. But phone me first to find out where I'll be.'

16

In Bakewell town centre Ben Cooper could find only one CCTV camera, and that pointed at the entrance to a pub on Bridge Street, pretty useless for present purposes. Even if it had existed ten years ago, there was no way of tracking the movements of the Bowers' vehicle. There weren't even any speed cameras to catch sight of his blue Vauxhall, except for some on the A6 towards Buxton.

This was Cooper's second visit to Bakewell in two days. But at least he'd managed to avoid market day, which was Monday.

There had been no answer to his calls to the number kept on file for Evan Slaney. Perhaps he was away, or just at work. Cooper didn't have a business address for Slaney, so he had no option but to head first to Reece Bower's house in Aldern Way.

When Naomi Heath appeared at the door of the house in Aldern Way, her make-up couldn't disguise the fact that she hadn't been sleeping well. Her eyes were sunken and smudged with dark shadows.

'Oh, Detective Inspector Cooper,' she said. 'On your own this time?'

'I do have a few more questions,' said Cooper.

'Come in, then. What other information can I give you?'

'I was hoping you could tell me how Mr Bower left,' said Cooper. 'It says in the initial reports that his car is still here.'

'Yes, it's in the garage.'

'Can I have a look at it?'

'I'll get you the keys. They're on the hook by the door.'

'Thank you.'

Reece Bower's present car was a silver BMW. Not a new model, but about three years old. No doubt he'd got rid of the blue Vauxhall long ago. Cooper opened the boot and moved aside a bag of golf clubs to examine a blue Berghaus waterproof and a pair of Hi-Tec walking boots. The waterproof was dry, and the boots were so clean that they couldn't have been used recently. He found nothing else – not even a spare wheel. Of course, BMWs had run-flat tyres.

Inside the car, he checked the glove compartment, all the storage areas, and even under the seats. There was nothing of interest. Nothing to see at all, except a packet of tissues and some change for parking. Reece Bower was either a very tidy man, or the car had been cleared out deliberately. It hadn't been valeted though. That was something at least. If necessary, he could get a forensic examination carried out.

The garage itself contained all the usual stuff. Cooper

knew many people with garages who used them for anything except parking their car in. They were more secure than a garden shed for storing your lawnmower and power tools, warmer and drier for stacking cardboard boxes, handier for plugging in a chest freezer. All of those things were here, but the garage was big enough to take the car as well. It probably took a bit of manoeuvring down that drive, but it did just about fit.

'This is Mr Bower's car,' said Cooper, 'so do you have a car of your own, Mrs Heath?'

'Yes, a Mini. It's on the other drive.'

'Does Mr Bower drive that sometimes?'

'Not unless he really has to. He doesn't like it. He says it's too small to be a proper car. But it suits me.'

'So if he didn't take his car, how did he leave?'

'He set off walking down the hill towards Station Road.'

'Did you hear him call for a taxi?'

'No.'

'Well, he wouldn't have got very far on foot. Could he have been meeting someone?'

'Who would that be?'

'I don't know,' said Cooper. 'I was hoping you might know.'

'I haven't any idea.'

Cooper found himself gazing out of the back window at the flourishing garden. He had to keep reminding himself that this was the same house that Annette Bower had disappeared from ten years ago. He had no sense of a sinister history to this property, the way

181

he did in some houses. But then, the search had found nothing. If Annette was anywhere, she wasn't here at the house in Aldern Way.

'You mentioned yesterday that you thought Mr Bower had been getting hassle from some the employees where he works and that something one of them said may have upset him enough to make him want to get away for a while.'

'Yes, I did say that.'

'I think you may know what people were saying to him.'

'Well, they make jokes about him,' she said. 'Usually behind his back, but some of them to his face. They don't seem to have any respect for him. Being in middle management is an unenviable position, I suppose. You have the responsibility, but without the power or the authority. Sometimes it just gets a bit too much for Reece.'

'What sort of jokes do they make?' asked Cooper.

She hesitated. 'I'd rather not say.'

Cooper studied her carefully. 'Are they to do with the time he was charged with the murder of his wife?'

Naomi lowered her eyes. 'Yes, I believe so. I can't tell you exactly what they say – Reece doesn't go into the details. All I know is that they make him angry. I think, when they see Reece getting annoyed, it just makes them worse. They like to wind him up more if they get a reaction. It's like kids in the playground, isn't it? They pick on the sensitive child.'

'So you'd say Mr Bower is sensitive?'

'On that subject, yes. Wouldn't you be? It was a very traumatic experience for him.' Then she looked at Cooper more closely and seemed to recall who he was. 'But you're a police officer. Perhaps you don't see it like that. Your people did their best to get him convicted.'

Cooper walked down the hallway to the front door, then turned to Naomi.

'Are the boys at school?' he said.

'Yes, Daniel and Joshua attend schools here in Bakewell. You're not going to drag them into this, are you? They have problems enough.'

'No, that shouldn't be necessary.' He paused. 'We'll be speaking to Lacey, though.'

Naomi frowned.

'Good luck to you, then.'

'Why?'

'I don't know what sense you'll get out of her.'

'Does she talk to you, Mrs Heath? Or to her father?'

'It depends what you mean by "talk". She's a teenager. Teenagers lie to their parents all the time. It's a miracle if they tell us the truth now and then. The only view we get of what's going on in their heads is the impression we have from the outside. The truth can be something completely different. But I'm sure you know that.'

At the top of the drive Cooper found a middle-aged woman in a red padded jacket standing near his car with a Yorkshire terrier dog on a lead. She didn't seem to be walking the dog, just standing there as if waiting for it to do something. Or waiting for something else perhaps.

'Hello,' she brightly when he approached. 'You've been to see Naomi.'

It was a statement rather than a question. So she must have been watching him for a while.

'You must be a neighbour,' he said.

'Yes, my house is there, across the road. Are you with the police?'

'Yes.'

'He's gone off, hasn't he? Reece, I mean.'

'That's right, Mrs . . . ?'

'Taylor. Evelyn.'

'Do you know Mr Bower well?'

'Not that well, I suppose. But they're a very nice couple,' she said. 'He obviously dotes on her and can't do enough for her. I wish all husbands were like that, actually. And they have that young boy.'

'Daniel, their five-year-old?'

'Yes, you see them together. Happy as any family I've ever seen.'

Cooper nodded. 'What about the other children? Naomi has a son a few years older.'

'Oh, he's fine. A bit quiet perhaps. The younger boy is very sweet.'

Perhaps this was a woman who just liked small children. But he had to ask her about one more . . .

'Oh, and there's the teenager, of course,' she said, before he could get the question out. 'The girl, she's about eighteen now, I think.'

'Yes, Lacey. Do you see much of her?'

'She was here on Sunday. I saw her going down the street when I was walking Henry. That's the dog, by

184

the way. Other than that, I can't remember the last time. She has a life of her own, I suppose. You know the way they are at that age. Even when she was living here, she only seemed to use her dad as a taxi driver to get her where she wanted to be and pick her up again at the end of the night.'

'Do you have any idea how she gets on with Mrs Heath?'

'Mrs H— Oh, that's Naomi, isn't it? We always forget they're not married. I suppose it isn't unusual these days.'

'Very common, in fact,' said Cooper. 'Does it trouble you that they're not married?'

'Oh, not at all. It's entirely up to them. But how did Lacey get on with Naomi? I'm not sure they ever did, or they're ever likely to. Come on, Henry.'

She walked off with the dog and Cooper turned to his car. He felt as though he was being watched from the houses along the road. And perhaps he was. Who knew what lay behind those hedges?

He headed the Toyota back down Aldern Way and Castle Drive, remembering which way to turn at the grit bin to get back on to Station Road.

This had been the site of Bakewell Station when Midlands Railways trains came through on their way from Matlock to Buxton. It was unusual for a station to be built half a mile out of town, and so high on the hillside. The line had begun climbing here towards its summit at Peak Forest Junction. The station building was still there with its four tall stone chimneys, though it was being used as offices for an electronics company.

The lines had been removed and the gap between platforms had been filled in to create the Monsal Trail. The goods shed, signal box and cattle dock were long gone. The iron and glass canopies over the platforms were a distant memory. Now interpretation boards had been installed to show what the station used to look like.

So Reece Bower wouldn't have been leaving by train anyway. The last one had stopped here in the 1960s. The former station forecourt was now a car park for walkers and cyclists using the trail. Bower could easily have been meeting someone here, a friend who'd waited for him to leave the house and picked him up by car.

A small industrial estate had been built on the site of the goods yard. Waste management, cardboard baling, plumbing supplies, an MOT centre. He recalled that one of these units had burned down in a fire a few years ago. He wasn't sure which one it was, as the units all looked intact now.

Then Cooper remembered that Annette Bower was supposed to have disappeared while she was just a few yards away on the Monsal Trail running with her dog. Officers working on the initial inquiry had conducted a search of all these industrial units, in case Annette had wandered in and been injured, or something worse had happened to her.

Cooper parked on the station forecourt and walked through a passage on to the Monsal Trail itself. The trees were dense on the eastern side of the trail, and the verges of the old track bed were thick with nettles and brambles, overlain with an impenetrable tangle of cleavers.

Officers also searched this area intensively in the search for Annette Bower. For a while, there had been expectations that her body would be found in the undergrowth. He could imagine the curses of the search team as they struggled through the nettles, sweating under their baseball caps, probing the ground with their poles for an obstruction. It must have taken them days. And it had all been in vain.

Cooper looked up and down the trail. In one direction, a bridge carried Station Road over the trail, while in the other the trail vanished into trees beyond the industrial estate. He wondered how far the search parameters had been extended. As SIO, Hazel Branagh would have been very thorough, he was sure of that. But the Monsal Trail stretched for a total of eight and a half miles, from the Coombs Road Viaduct south of Bakewell all the way into Wyedale.

The hill the station had been built on was called Castle Hill, but there were no signs of a castle now, not even any discernible earthworks. Only a golf course.

A golf course? Of course, Bakewell Golf Club. Naomi Heath had mentioned Reece Bower's golfing buddies. Was this the club Reece Bower was a member of? It seemed likely, since it was so close to his home. Perhaps the names of some of those buddies would be in the address book Naomi had given him.

Gavin Murfin was leaving the steel fabrications company where Reece Bower worked. It was located on a business park just off the A61 north of Chesterfield, and he couldn't find a way directly back on to the bypass, so he pulled into the side of the road to check his satnav.

It was rare to get a bit of peace and quiet without any rushing about, so Murfin took his time over it, even closing his eyes for a few minutes to take a short nap. There was too much dashing backwards and forwards these days, not like when he was a young DC and could spend the afternoon in the pub. At least Ben Cooper trusted him out on his own now and then.

When he opened his eyes again, Murfin wiped a trace of spittle from his mouth, sighed, and put the Skoda back into gear.

Madeleine Betts worked at the Royal Hospital, which meant he had to drive back through Chesterfield, round a couple of roundabouts, and out towards a place called Calow. The route took him past the familiar sight of floodlights and a football ground – the Proact Stadium, home of Chesterfield FC. There had been times in the recent past when Murfin thought his own club, Derby County, might end up playing the Spireites in League One and he'd have to spend more time in Chesterfield than he really wanted to.

Off the bypass, he found plenty of signs for the hospital. But it was a big, sprawling place and he had to ask for directions at the front desk.

When he arrived at his destination, Madeleine Betts was waiting for him in an office where they could talk privately. She looked at Murfin suspiciously, but he was used to that. She made a fuss about inspecting his ID as a civilian support officer and didn't seem impressed.

'They let me ask questions and write things down,' he said. 'But I can't nick anyone now, more's the pity.'

'Do sit down,' she said, with a frown.

'You know, I don't like hospitals much,' said Murfin as he eased himself into a chair.

'Too many sick people, I suppose?'

'No, I think it's all the rushing about. I can't stand accidents, or emergencies.'

She smiled thinly at his attempts to break the ice. And there was definitely ice, a couple of inches of frost at least. Madeleine Betts looked like one of those women who'd been disappointed in life so often that she'd forgotten how to smile. Murfin had met quite a few of them.

He coughed and pulled out his notebook, brushing ineffectually at a small stain on the cover.

'It's about Reece Bower,' he said, lifting a corner of his eye to catch the flicker of a reaction sparked by the name.

'I thought it might be,' she said.

'When his wife disappeared, you told the investigating officers that the two of you had ended your relationship some time previously.'

'Yes. Annette had left him, you see. Reece ended our relationship, so that she would come back to him. I'd moved to work in a different department by then, and I no longer saw Reece at all.'

Murfin nodded. Her wording was almost exactly the same as the statement she'd given ten years ago. He'd checked it before he set off. He was wondering whether Betts had written it down somewhere, maybe in a diary. No one's memory was quite that good. Had she prepared her replies in advance? It was a pity he couldn't threaten to take her back to the station. He'd already told her he wasn't able to do that.

'And is that still true, love?'

'I'm not your love,' she replied sharply.

Murfin smiled. He heard that a lot these days.

'There's time yet,' he said.

Betts scowled and pursed her lips. Murfin squinted at her curiously. She wasn't his type at all. Too humourless. But he supposed there could a certain attraction about the cool blonde look, the toned muscles and stylish clothes. There had been an attraction for Reece Bower at least.

'So have you been seeing Reece?' he repeated.

'No, I haven't seen him since then.'

'Any contact at all?'

'I just said—'

'No, you said that you hadn't seen him. You might have spoken to him on the phone, sent a few text messages back and forth, that sort of thing.'

'No.'

'So . . . Mr Bower's phone wouldn't show any contact with you recently at all,' said Murfin. 'Is that right?'

'Yes.'

He turned a page of his notebook and made a note on a new sheet, forming the words slowly and carefully, then staring doubtfully at them for a moment before adding a large question mark. Madeline Betts watched every movement he made with an expression of horrified fascination.

'Have you found him?' she said finally.

'Who, Reece? No, love.'

Of course, she wanted to ask whether his phone had been found, but she daren't do that. It would look too obvious.

Murfin beamed again. He liked people to be in doubt. And this woman had underestimated him from the start.

17

Ben Cooper was waiting to make an awkward right turn in front of the bookshop in Bakewell. The road up the hill past the church reached Burton Moor, the only route to Over Haddon without heading further on towards Monyash.

From the top, he was looking down over Lady Manners School towards the house near Haddon Road.

In the valley, Haddon Hall nestled among the trees where the River Wye meandered through water meadows to join the Derwent. Haddon had been abandoned by the Vernon family as their residence in the early eighteenth century in favour of Belvoir Castle. The result was an unspoilt medieval mansion, which had remained unmodernised throughout the eighteenth, nineteenth and twentieth centuries. It was a bit of a miracle that it had escaped the fate of so many grand country houses.

The Vernons had sometimes exercised their power through crude and violent methods. In the ancient 'trial by touch', a suspected murderer was made to touch the body of the victim. If the suspect was guilty, the victim would begin to bleed again. It was said that one local peasant panicked so much at the prospect that he tried to run away – only to be pursued by a posse and lynched in a field near Ashford-in-the-Water. The Peak District had been like the Wild West in those days.

Over Haddon was a small village perched on a ledge above Lathkill Dale, with a population of less than three hundred. At the bottom of a narrow road running down from the village, a clapper bridge crossed the Lathkill.

Cars parked along the side of these narrow village roads made driving a hazard. When two cars met from opposite directions, it was sometimes a test of politeness as to who would gave way. After three o'clock on a weekday, it was best to avoid the villages altogether. School-out time meant lines of extra cars as parents waited to collect their children.

The Swanns' home was an eighteenth century stone cottage, with a conservatory added and a path leading into a cottage garden. Tubs and planters clustered round the front door and on a paved terrace.

Cooper had been obliged to phone and make an appointment with Frances Swann. Often he could call on people at work, but she was a teacher and schools were sensitive about the police coming on to the premises unless it was necessary. She had taken the opportunity of a free period to come home.

'Thank you for seeing me, Mrs Swann. I understand you teach at Lady Manners School.'

'That's correct. I'm in the Modern Languages department.'

Cooper didn't ask what languages she taught. He

had no doubt she was fluent in several languages that he had never managed to learn. He also knew that being in the Lady Manners catchment area was one of the reasons that property in this area tended to be so attractive to buyers, and therefore expensive.

Frances Swann had sharply defined cheekbones, which might have made her face look attractive when she was younger. But age had narrowed her eyes and made her lips purse in disapproval. Cooper imagined she could be quite fierce, a forbidding presence in the classroom, a stern instructor if he got his French conjugations wrong.

Cooper was glad Gavin Murfin wasn't here with him. Frances Swann would probably have disapproved.

She led him through into a dining room. They passed a kitchen with a Belfast sink and an Esse range set into a deeply recessed fireplace. The dining room had a wood-burning stove, though it looked more expensive than the one in his own cottage at Foolow.

Mrs Swann's manner was brisk, and Cooper got the impression she would like to get him out of the house as soon as possible.

'I'm afraid we haven't heard anything from Reece, if that's what you're going to ask me,' she said.

'Well, that was one question,' he said.

'I have no idea why he should have left Naomi. We're not privy to what goes on over there now, not the way we were when my sister was still here.'

'You were a frequent visitor to the Bowers' house in Aldern Way at that time, I gather?'

She looked at him sharply. 'Oh, I imagine you've

been reading all the old paperwork. The details of the case against Reece.'

'It isn't all that old,' said Cooper. 'Ten years.'

'Yes, I'm aware of that. I still think about it, of course. Almost every day I think about Annette. This latest business has brought it all back. No doubt people will be talking about it all over again, and asking questions.'

'People like me, I'm afraid.'

'Well, it's your job, I suppose. At least you have an excuse. A lot of people don't have that pretext. Their interest is just prurient.'

'I'm aware that you were the first person to raise the alarm about your sister's disappearance, although it was Mr Bower who actually made the phone call.'

'That's true.'

'And your concern started when Annette failed to return from a run.'

'It wasn't like her,' said Frances. 'She knew we were coming. She would normally have been back at the house getting ready. When I say "normally", I mean always. Except that one occasion.'

'So you were sure from the start that there was something wrong.'

'Yes, I was. Certain. Much more than certain than Reece seemed to be. That was why . . .'

Her voice tailed off. She had probably been over this part of the story many times, when she was questioned a decade ago. But clearly she hadn't forgotten it. The details must still be sharp in her mind.

'That was why you had suspicions about Reece,' suggested Cooper.

'I felt a little guilty about it at first. Having those suspicions seemed unworthy. He was my brother-in-law, after all. But I couldn't keep the suspicions to myself – not once I noticed the blood.'

'Ah, yes. A splash of blood in the kitchen.'

Mrs Swann gave a small shudder at the recollection.

'It was hardly a splash,' she said. 'A speck, that's all. But I knew it was blood.'

'And what was your conclusion?'

She sighed. 'It's difficult to admit, even now. But the sight of that one speck of blood formed an absolute certainty in my mind that Reece had harmed Annette in some way. I know it doesn't sound logical seen objectively. It probably doesn't make any sense to you, when you're looking from the outside and at this distance from the events. But it was very different for me. My conclusion was a culmination of several factors.'

'What factors, Mrs Swann?'

'A number of comments Annette had made to me about the ongoing state of her marriage, the fact that they'd been arguing recently and that Reece had been drinking more than usual. And his apparent lack of concern that afternoon about her disappearance. He kept saying she would be back soon, coming up with all kinds of unlikely explanations. I didn't believe a single one of them.'

'And then there was the blood,' said Cooper.

'And then the blood,' she agreed. 'And it *was* Annette's blood.'

'Yes, it was. The DNA tests proved it.'

'So I was right,' she said.

'But your sister's body was never found,' said Cooper as gently as he could.

She was silent for several moments. He saw that her composure was beginning to break down and he didn't want to do that to her. But sometimes there was no choice. Mrs Swann clenched her hands together.

'No, and that's the worst aspect of all,' she said. 'You can't imagine what that's like. No one can.'

'I'm sorry.'

She turned away. There was nothing Frances could say to that. And nothing else he could say to make it better when 'sorry' just wasn't enough.

'I have to ask this, Mrs Swann,' he said.

'I know you do. Go on.'

'At the time, did you have any ideas about where your sister's body might be found?'

She took a deep breath. 'Yes, when they began to search the garden, I was confident something would be found. I'd noticed that fresh digging myself. I remember one of the investigating officers seeing it . . . what was his name now?'

'Detective Inspector Hitchens?'

'That was it. And from that moment, when I saw the expression on his face, I expected a discovery. I had to leave the house then, of course, and return here. I sat waiting for the phone to ring, or a knock to come on the door. Can you imagine? I could have been waiting for a very long time, couldn't I? Ten years or more. I might still be waiting now for a discovery that never came.'

'They dug almost the whole garden up, but didn't find Annette.'

'That's right. I thought the police would do more, you know. A lot more.'

'What do you mean, Mrs Swann?'

'I wanted them to start a search in Lathkill Dale,' said Frances. 'Reece and Annette went there often, and it seemed the sort of place Annette would head for if she wanted to be on her own for a while, to think things through. If Reece hadn't killed her after all, it seemed likely to me that she'd gone there and met with an accident of some kind.'

'In that case, she would have been located years ago,' said Cooper.

'I know, but it would have made me feel easier in my own mind.'

'And what do you think of your father's conviction that he had a sighting of Annette in Buxton?'

'Oh, that.' She sighed. 'It's hard to know what to think, or who to believe. Of course, I've always wanted to believe that Annette is alive and just doesn't want to come home – although I don't understand why she wouldn't have got in touch in all these years. On the other hand . . .'

'You still suspect that Reece killed her.'

'In my heart of hearts, yes. It's ruined my relationship with my father, you know. He's become very cut off. He talks to Adrian more than he does to me. I think Adrian trusts him. They're men together with a shared interest. So I doubt they talk about things like this.'

'Mrs Swann, I take it you don't have any of the same suspicions about the disappearance of Mr Bower?'

She laughed rather nervously. 'Oh, no. Reece has gone somewhere. I have no idea where, and I don't particularly want to know. There won't be any good involved, I'm sure of that.'

'I see. How close is your relationship with Naomi Heath?'

'We don't have a relationship,' said Frances, suddenly cool.

'And your husband?'

'Adrian would tell you the same.'

Through an open door, Cooper glimpsed what looked like a study or workshop in an adjoining annexe. On a table stood an amazing object that caught his eye immediately. It was a carved tawny owl, almost life-sized.

'That's beautiful,' said Cooper.

'Yes, Adrian is putting it in for the show this weekend,' said Frances.

'What show?'

'The Festival of Bird Art in Bakewell. The National Bird Carving Championships are held there every year.'

'So your husband is a bird carver.'

'A very good one,' she said.

'So I see.'

'Would you like a closer look at it?'

'Very much so. Can I touch it?'

'I don't think he would mind. He likes people to appreciate his work. Adrian is a member of the British Decoy and Wildfowl Carvers Association. He's entering the Advanced Class of their competition this year for the first time. The owl is his entry for the Bird of Prey category.'

Gently, Cooper touched the perfectly carved feathers on the wings of the owl.

'It's wonderful.'

'Decorative style is the most challenging. A carver is trying to recreate a lifelike depiction of the bird. A finished piece can be almost indistinguishable from the real thing. It's very different from decoy carving, or the interpretive style.'

Cooper wondered if she was repeating word for word what her husband had told her, if she was genuinely interested in his passion for bird carving.

'Adrian says "Inside every piece of wood there's a bird waiting to be released",' she added.

That seemed to confirm it. Cooper looked around the workshop and saw a small wooden cabinet.

'Are these his tools in the canvas roll?' he asked.

'Yes.'

Two rows of carbon steel chisels and gouges lay neatly in their pockets, along with a fine-toothed rasp, a sharpening stone and a small mallet. Alongside was a set of seven-inch knives with long handles, some straight and some with curved blades.

'Those are Mora,' said Frances. 'A Swedish make. They're high quality woodworking tools.'

'They look pretty lethal to me.'

She laughed. 'That's not the way Adrian would see it. These knives are for creating, not destroying. Just look at the tawny owl. It's a wonderful thing, isn't it?

He brought it to life using only his hands, and these tools.'

Cooper dutifully admired the owl again.

'Do you see much of your niece these days?' he said.

'Lacey?'

'Yes, Lacey.'

Frances sighed. 'I'm afraid it's a difficult relationship.'

'But she stayed with you for a while, didn't she?'

'Well, we did our best for her after her mother went missing and her father was arrested. I suppose that's always the way with teenagers. They don't appreciate the efforts of people who are looking out for them. Perhaps, when she grows up properly, Lacey will see things differently. I do hope so.'

'Do you have a current address for Lacey?'

'Not an up-to-date one. She moves around a bit. Lacey has gone her own way, you see. She lives in a flat in Sheffield now.'

'What is she doing in Sheffield?' asked Cooper.

'She's at college, studying.'

'I see.'

'We used to have a mobile phone number for her. Lacey doesn't have a landline. In fact, she rarely makes phone calls. She usually communicates by text. But I think she must have changed her mobile, and we've heard nothing from her for a while. You could probably get her address from the college.'

'Thank you anyway, Mrs Swann.'

'Are you going to talk to her?'

'I'm going to try.'

Frances Swann showed him to the door. He had the feeling there was something else she wanted to say, but she didn't manage to get it out until he was right on the threshold.

'Do you know,' she said. 'Every time I hear about a body being discovered, I find myself praying that it will be someone else who is dead, not my sister. That's a terrible thing, isn't it, Detective Inspector Cooper? A terrible thing.'

As he left the house, Cooper's phone buzzed, and he saw a call from Gavin Murfin waiting. He rang Murfin back as soon as he got in his car.

'I'm on my way into Bakewell now,' said Murfin.

'Good. Can you meet me at the address for Evan Slaney off Church Street?'

'No problem.'

'How did you get on with Madeleine Betts?'

'She's a bit of a frosty one,' said Murfin. 'She says she's had no contact with Reece Bower and doesn't have any idea where he is.'

'Did you believe her?'

Murfin hesitated. 'Well, I don't think she knows where he is. But my nose tells me she's keeping something back.'

'Okay.'

'I had no luck at the steel fabrications company by the way, boss.'

'Nothing?'

'No one admits to saying anything out of the ordinary to Reece Bower before he went missing. I talked to everyone who had contact with him in the last few days before his disappearance. I think they were genuine. They admitted pulling his leg a bit when he first went to work there, like. But he didn't react to it, they said.'

Cooper didn't know whether he was disappointed, or if he'd subconsciously expected it. The story had sounded like an excuse, a means of passing off an obviously stressed state and deflecting questions.

'That sort of stuff does get tired very quickly,' he said. 'People lose interest when it isn't a novelty any more.'

'Right. Actually, they all say Bower was pretty good at his job. They're missing him, Ben. They wanted to know when he might be coming back to work.'

'I can't answer that,' said Cooper. 'It might be never.'

18

Jamie Callaghan was staring at the passing traffic on the motorway as Diane Fry drove towards Shirebrook from the Major Crime Unit's base at St Ann's in Nottingham.

'They shouldn't have to put up with that,' said Callaghan. 'No one should.'

Fry had been reviewing the previous day's interviews with him, the accounts of Tammy Beresford and the Polish couple Michal and Anna Wolak.

'No, perhaps not,' she said, not sure which of them he was referring to.

Callaghan glanced at her. 'Is that all you can say? I expected you to feel more strongly about it.'

'Did you? Why?'

Callaghan shrugged. 'I don't know. I just thought it would seem more like you. All those immigrants coming in, changing your whole town beyond recognition. And the trouble they cause . . . it's not acceptable.'

'Don't you think,' said Fry, 'there are always two sides to a story?'

'Well, more than two. When an incident occurs, every single witness has a different account of what happened.'

'Exactly. So why are you taking Tammy Beresford's version of events as gospel?'

'Well—'

They had reached the exit at Junction 29, and tucked into the side of an HGV as she cruised through the roundabout on to the A617 towards Mansfield.

'You sympathised with her, didn't you?' she said.

'She's a victim,' protested Callaghan.

'Yes, but who's to say whether the other side might be victims too, unless we talk to them?'

Callaghan raised an eyebrow. 'DS Fry, you sound like—'

'What? Who?'

He sank back in his seat. 'Never mind. It was just something I've heard. Nothing important.'

'It's probably best to keep it to yourself then,' said Fry.

Callaghan laughed. 'That does sound more like you.'

Fry thought of all the times she'd observed the behaviour of victims and felt a twinge of contempt at their weakness. Often she'd wanted to tell them that it wasn't so bad as all that, that they should have a bit of backbone and pull themselves together.

She'd seen plenty of genuine victims, individuals whose lives had been destroyed by some horrible crime. But so many people were just self-obsessed narcissists who deliberately overdramatised their situation because they longed to be the centre of attention. They were the same people who dialled 999 because they'd broken a fingernail or to complain their kebab was cold.

'I'm more interested in firm evidence,' she said.

'The attack on Krystian Zalewski has got to be a hate crime,' said Callaghan.

'Does it? Why?'

'Because he's Polish.'

'That doesn't make sense, Jamie.'

'It's what people will be saying, though.'

Well, that was true. It was what DCI Mackenzie had been well aware of right from the beginning, from the moment the identity of the victim was confirmed. Mackenzie had been praying that Zalewski's murder would be anything but a hate crime. Callaghan almost seemed to want it to be one, to confirm all his preconceptions.

'Evidence,' she said again.

'Well, we've got the presence of the far right extremists in the area. That's a fact. And we know Geoffrey Pollitt has right-wing sympathies, to say the least. So there's a clear connection.'

'Did you get the information Mr Mackenzie asked for?' asked Fry.

Callaghan tapped a folder.

'It's all here.'

An EMSOU intelligence officer had compiled a report on right-wing activities in the south-east fringes of Derbyshire.

'There's an active BNP unit in the vicinity, you know,' said Callaghan.

'BNP? Seriously?'

'They're very small in numbers, but they're still out there campaigning. The BNP leadership is trying to present an image of themselves as a legitimate political party, so most of the time they stay on the correct side of the law. But there are always a few loose cannons who go on a freelance mission.'

'And they may have headed to Shirebrook?'

'It's an obvious target for them, given the cultural mix. In the past, many of their meetings have been held at a pub in Shirebrook.'

'How many people attended these meetings?'

Callaghan checked the reports.

'Oh, forty or fifty. Not much more.'

'Most pubs around here get twice as many as that for a quiz night,' said Fry.

They were turning off towards Shirebrook, passing a hand car wash under the canopy of an old petrol station, just like the one Krystian Zalewski had worked at. You could get a wash, wax and dry from £5. Fry noticed the car wash was open seven days a week. How many staff did they need for that? Or did these men work every single day?

Frowning, Callaghan was still looking at her.

'Obviously we can't tolerate organisations like the BNP,' she said. 'But we have to be careful, Jamie. If you say anything publicly, you're liable to be subject to a complaint under the Police Conduct Regulations or the Code of Ethics.'

Callaghan sighed. 'Always by the book. Okay, just between you and me then, the BNP were infiltrated by members of the Metropolitan Police's undercover intelligence unit. They weren't just there to observe, either. They worked actively to disrupt target organisations.'

'With black propaganda?'

'I imagine so.'

Fry shrugged. 'Well, that means we can't necessarily believe what we hear. It may be misinformation.'

'Sometimes it feels as though our hands are tied by rules and procedures,' said Callaghan.

'That always seems to be the way. But there's a reason for it.'

Callaghan paid no attention.

'Look, there's an incident logged here, not far from Shirebrook. A group of activists were brought in because they'd been handing out leaflets – there had been complaints from the public about them – which was considered to be inciting race hatred. The local cops sat them down and were nice to them, made them a cup of tea and all that. The trouble is, the legality of the wording on their leaflets was open to interpretation, so it had to be passed upstairs.'

'Of course.'

'Well, they couldn't be detained while that process went on – we all know it can take for ever to get a legal decision. So they were asked to leave their remaining stock of leaflets at the station. They refused. In the end they went back to their pitch in the town centre and handed out a different leaflet. There was nothing anyone could do about it. And that's typical, Diane.'

'I know. But there are ways of dealing with organisations like that.'

'Oh, yes, there's a bit of management jargon shoved in here,' said Callaghan. 'Do you want to hear it?'

'If you must?'

'It says here: "We rely on communities to identify suspect individuals, and we work through multi-agency support systems to contain any potential threat." In other words, we're hoping someone else will do the job.'

As they entered Shirebrook, Fry noticed flags flying from the lampposts on a business park. The red Cross of St George on a white background – England flags.

She had switched off and was no longer listening to Callaghan as she drove. She had never told him about her experiences growing up in the Black Country. In fact, Fry had never told anyone about it.

Being a foster child had been bad enough, moving from one place to another with Angie because foster parents found her too difficult to deal with. After Angie ran away and disappeared from their home in Warley, Diane had become close to a foster brother a couple of years younger than her. Vincent, a quiet boy born to an Irish mother and a Jamaican father, had been adopted by their foster parents, Jim and Alice Bowskill, and had stayed with them when Diane went off to do her degree and start a career in West Midlands Police.

Life was tough for a mixed-race boy back then. At school, she'd done her best to defend him from the racist bullies. But the racism and bullying had pushed Vince in the direction many boys went. He'd made the wrong friends, been attracted to a way of life the Bowskills deplored. His life had fallen apart, despite their best efforts.

Maybe there was no easy way for a boy like Vincent Bowskill to fit into society when everyone had to be put into a category. It had broken her heart when she lasted visit Vince in his dingy flat in a tower block in Perry Barr, with signs of drug use lying around his sitting room, including a crude crack pipe, converted from a Ventolin asthma inhaler.

And Fry had not forgotten the role played by the right-wing extremists. Then it had largely been the National Front, with its opposition to inter-racial marriages and their slogan known as The Fourteen Words: *'We must secure the existence of our people and a future for white children.'*

Since those days, there had been a multitude of spin-off organisations. There were new issues for them to campaign. Anti-Muslim, anti-immigration, anti-EU. Their continued existence created a deep anger in Diane Fry that she was fighting very hard to keep contained.

'And what about the pre-planned operation?' asked Callaghan as they drew into Shirebrook market square. 'The raid is scheduled for tonight, isn't it?'

'We don't say a word until after the raid,' said Fry. 'Not a mention of slave trafficking, or we could jeopardise the whole operation. The Czech gang are still under surveillance and we can't risk alerting them.'

'No, we wouldn't want the Drenko family to escape.'

'Not after all this time and effort.'

Fry parked the Audi and switched off the engine.

Slave trafficking. It had been a big and complex enough inquiry for the Major Crime Unit already, without the murder of Krystian Zalewski complicating the issue.

She wondered what else could go wrong in Shirebrook that would make her job even more difficult.

19

Up the hill above All Saints Church in Bakewell was the Old House Museum. Wattle and daub walls, a vast open fireplace, and a Tudor toilet. And near the museum, on a narrow back street, was the address of Mr Evan Slaney.

Ben Cooper sat and waited in the Toyota until he saw Gavin Murfin's green Skoda pull into the road. Murfin had trouble finding somewhere to park and had to walk down from about a hundred yards up the hill.

'Why are these towns always built on hills?' complained Murfin when he reached Cooper.

'It's the Peak District,' said Cooper. 'Where else would you build them?'

'I'm surprised people don't grow up with one leg longer than the other. They must always be on a slope.'

'Come on, Gavin. We're going to talk to Mr Slaney. He's Annette Bower's father, okay?'

'Got it.'

Evan Slaney's cottage was surprisingly small, with tiny windows on to the street that were overshadowed by the surrounding buildings. It was also crammed with furniture and antiques. Cooper first thought of it as bric-a-brac, but he could tell from the sheen and the careful placement that they were probably quite valuable.

Bookshelves lined the walls of the sitting room and there seemed to be a lot of antique lamps. Victorian, Regency, art deco. They were being used to light the room instead of the normal ceiling lighting. They cast a dimmer light, and their positions threw shadows everywhere.

Cooper was cautious about stumbling over some item on the floor, or a corner of a tasselled rug. In this sort of light you could imagine ghosts and shapes that weren't really there at all. Perhaps that was why Mr Slaney liked it. Sometimes the harsh light of reality could be much too painful.

'It's been a long time now,' said Slaney when he let Cooper and Murfin in. 'A very long time.'

'Since your daughter's disappearance, sir? It's been ten years.'

'As I say. A long time.'

Evan Slaney was a tall man in his sixties with a permanently disdainful expression. His hair looked a slightly unnatural shade of brown, which probably came from a bottle. Cooper found it hard to imagine him handling these antiques with any gentleness.

'We're not reopening your daughter's case as such,' said Cooper.

Slaney gave him a thin smile. 'Not "as such". I see. Then it's to do with my son-in-law. Or my ex son-in-law. I don't know which it is – do you?'

'I'm not sure what you mean, sir.'

'Well, it depends whether my daughter is alive or not, doesn't it?'

'And what do *you* think now, sir?' asked Cooper.

'Now? If you've read the reports, you know what I think.'

'From the reports, I only know what you thought ten years ago. I'm asking you what you believe now.'

Slaney clenched his jaw. As if to calm himself, he stroked the shade of a Chinese porcelain lamp made in the shape of a dragon.

'I still believe I saw Annette,' he said. 'I've never lost that belief, Inspector.'

'I'd like to go over your sighting of her again, if you don't mind.'

'Again? After all these years? Why?'

'It may be relevant.'

'Relevant? What a mealy-mouthed expression.'

Cooper didn't react. Slaney paced a free patch of rug and stopped suddenly. He glared at Murfin, then back to Cooper.

'I'm sure you know this already,' he said. 'But one day I was doing some shopping at Waitrose in Buxton. When I came out of the store there were a lot of people around. As I reached my car, for some reason my attention was drawn to a woman on the other side of the car park. I recognised her immediately. It was like a thunderbolt.'

'How exactly did you recognise her?'

'Don't you recognise a person you know well from the way they stand or move, from a little gesture, or how they hold their head? Besides, she was wearing a coat she'd had for some time. I was so certain that I shouted her name across the car park. People stared at me – I must have seemed like an idiot. But of course she didn't hear me. And she'd loaded her shopping and driven off by the time I could get to her.'

'The car . . .?' said Cooper.

'It was a white Ford Focus. That was the same make and model she drove when she was with Reece. They always had two cars, and she preferred it to the Vauxhall. It may sound ridiculous to you, but that small detail was the one that convinced me completely. I knew it was Annette. I thought she must have changed her name, started a new life, and was living somewhere locally.'

'But you've never heard from her, sir?'

'No.'

'Not in ten years. Don't you think—'

'No, Inspector, I don't think what you're going to say. Call it faith, if you will. But I believe Annette is alive and living somewhere. Oh, not in Buxton any more. I think she's gone far away from all of us.'

That last phrase could be interpreted in different ways. It sounded to Cooper like a euphemism for someone who'd died. That's what people did these days. They talked about a person having 'passed', about a pet having 'gone over the rainbow bridge', as if they'd just gone to a better place. It seemed as though they used anything to avoid the word 'dead' and having to acknowledge their loved one no longer existed.

And he could understand that. He'd found himself doing it sometimes, not long after his fiancée Liz had been killed. That act of faith could be comforting. But, at the end of the day, she was still dead.

Slaney was watching Gavin Murfin moving around the room, wincing occasionally as he came too close to an antique lamp. He looked like a man who'd just let an unruly child into his collection and was regretting it.

'Did Reece Bower did seem different after that, sir?' asked Cooper.

'After Annette's disappearance?' said Slaney. 'Of course. We were all different. Not only had we been through a difficult experience, but we'd suffered a great loss. It was inevitable that we would be changed by it. You can't just get over something like that. *I* never have. I've found it difficult to feel really happy. I'll never be content with life again.'

'But Mr Bower? How did he change?'

Slaney pursed his lips in thought. 'He became more morose, perhaps. He always rather serious, but whenever I saw him after that he seemed to be brooding about something. Not that I saw him often, you understand. We weren't very close, Reece and I. But I did think, in view of what happened, he might have showed some, well . . . appreciation.'

'Appreciation? Oh, you mean gratitude for the fact that you saved him from standing trial? Because you helped him avoid conviction for murder?'

Slaney flushed angrily. 'That was never the way I saw it.'

Cooper was interested to see the way Slaney reacted to a provocation. If he could make Annette's father lose his temper, he might get something more from him. But he had no justification for doing that. Mr Slaney was a witness, after all. Cooper just couldn't be certain in his own mind which side of the case he was on. A witness for the defence, or for the prosecution?

'Morose and brooding,' said Cooper. 'That's how you described Mr Bower.'

'I suppose it was to be expected, after the ordeal he went through.'

'Certainly sir.'

That was possible, of course. But killing someone changed you too, no matter how much you thought they deserved it, no matter whether you believed you'd got away with it. Killing made you a different person. It changed you for ever.

Could Reece Bower have become such a different person that he was consumed with remorse for what he'd done years earlier? It was an impossible question to answer. Perhaps only Bower himself could know.

'And do you have any suggestion of what's happened to Reece, Mr Slaney?' asked Cooper. 'What does your faith tell you about his whereabouts?'

Slaney shrugged. 'I haven't any idea. Do you believe his disappearance is connected with the previous case?'

'We think he might have been scared off by the possibility of some new information coming to light.'

'Oh. You mean he'd been tipped the black spot, then.'

'The black spot?' said Murfin. 'Some local Derbyshire custom I'm not aware of?'

'No, it's from Robert Louis Stevenson,' said Slaney. '*Treasure Island*.'

'Of course.'

Cooper saw Evan Slaney smirk at his visitor's ignorance. Murfin responded by bumping into the dragon-
shaped porcelain lamp. Slaney let out a pained cry,
but Murfin caught it and steadied the shade before
the base tipped over.

'Oops,' he said. 'No harm done.'

Cooper waited a beat of a second. Slaney was off
his guard now.

'Are you aware of your daughter and her husband
having a particular connection to Lathkill Dale, Mr
Slaney?' he asked.

'What?' Slaney seemed startled.

'Lathkill Dale,' repeated Cooper.

'Yes, they walked there often. It's right on the doorstep, you know. They also liked to visit a cafe in
Monyash, I think.'

'The Old Smithy, is it?'

'Something like that.'

Cooper stood by the window, and had to bend to
peer through it into the street. These old cottages were
made for smaller people, he supposed.

'What do you do for a living, sir?' he asked.

'I'm an accountant by profession,' said Slaney. 'I
worked for a partnership in Chesterfield for many years,
specialising in financial accountancy. But I'm a
consultant now. It means I can take on as much work
as suits me. Or as little.'

Murfin had reached the bookshelves and was running
a finger along the spines. Cooper noticed that one shelf
was full of Sherlock Holmes stories. *The Hound of the
Baskervilles*, *A Study in Scarlet*, and several volumes of

short stories. There were even some modern interpretations of the great detective. *The House of Silk, The Servants of Hell.* The collection was impressive.

'You're a big Holmes fan, I see.'

'He's an eternal character,' said Slaney. 'So rational. So astute. If he was alive now, Conan Doyle would be very proud of the way he's endured.'

'Didn't Conan Doyle get fed up with his character and try to kill him off in that fight at the Reichenbach Falls? It was his readers who wouldn't accept Holmes was dead.'

'Yes, they believed in him too strongly to accept his death.'

'Exactly.'

Slaney studied him. 'I can see what you're driving at,' he said. 'I'm not an idiot.'

'And?'

'And? Well, I'm still sure it was Annette I saw.'

Cooper nodded. 'Thank you, sir. That's what I wanted to know.'

'You should be following other lines of inquiry, Detective Inspector,' said Slaney. 'It's Reece's disappearance you ought to be investigating.'

'Oh, we are,' said Cooper. 'We are.'

Slaney didn't looked convinced. He led his visitors to the door.

Outside, it still felt dark and full of shadows, as if the whole world was lit by dim antique lamps that threw shapes against the walls that weren't really there at all. Cooper found himself wishing for some sun, if only a little of it.

'Actually, we don't have Sherlock Holmes any more, do we?' said Slaney as Cooper and Murfin stepped over his threshold. 'All we've got left are the bumbling Lestrades.'

As he left Bakewell, Cooper tried to analyse why he felt so sure that Evan Slaney was lying.

There were certain signs to look for, of course. In interviews he'd heard them so many times. Repetition, as if a lie had to be spoken several times before it was believed. Lack of vehemence, lack of detail, inconsistency. None of those had been discernible in Mr Slaney.

But there had definitely been a lack of eye contact. Generally, if someone was lying they would not look you in the eye. In normal conversation people made eye contact for at least half of the time, so anything less prompted suspicion. Cooper had become so used to it now that he usually left an interview knowing instinctively whether it had verged on the negative side.

And that was definitely his impression on leaving Mr Slaney. It was more than just the difficulty of seeing his eyes in the gloom of his sitting room. Slaney had been looking elsewhere most of the time. He'd been gazing at the lamps, at the floor, at the window – anything but meeting Cooper's eye.

There could be all kinds of reasons why people told lies. Sometimes they just wanted to present themselves in a better light and that was all. Some felt a need to be seen as braver, cleverer, or more successful than they really were. And the further they strayed from the truth, the more they had to lie. So dishonesty became a part of their day-to-day routine, a central theme in the narrative of their lives. Cooper had met people who hardly seemed to be aware they were lying. For them, deception took less effort than telling the truth.

There didn't seem any point mentioning it to Gavin Murfin. Instead, Cooper called West Street and discussed his feelings with Carol Villiers. He knew Carol would understand what he meant.

First she had some information for him. Lacey Bower's address in Sheffield.

'No luck with Reece's address book, though,' she said. 'We've spoken to a few of his golfing friends, but we're drawing a blank so far.'

'Thanks anyway.'

'And I certainly can't find anyone with a phone number in the Bridlington area.'

'Well, that was a very long shot,' laughed Cooper, remembering the holiday photographs in Reece Bower's house.

'Mrs Heath seemed quite happy for us to pursue the idea. She didn't discourage us from thinking of friends he might go to.'

'It's still a possibility, to be honest,' said Cooper. 'But wherever Reece Bower is, I don't think it will be Bridlington.'

'So what do you think the chances are that Annette Bower is actually still alive?' asked Villiers. 'Could Mr Slaney be right?'

'If Annette just decided to disappear, she wouldn't stay around here, would she?'

221

'The supposed sighting of her was in Buxton though.'

'But nothing since,' said Cooper.

'No, that's true.' Villiers paused. 'You said "supposed sighting". I take it you have doubts about its authenticity.'

'There's always room for doubt, Carol.'

'You don't find Evan Slaney a reliable and truthful witness?'

'I don't know about truthful,' said Cooper. 'He may think he's telling the truth, but that doesn't necessarily make him reliable.'

He turned the Toyota on to the Sheffield road at Baslow and headed north towards Owler Bar.

'It's odd, isn't it?' he said.

'What is?' asked Villiers.

'That Annette Bower's body has never been found after all these years. It's the wrong way round, in my experience.'

'I'm not sure what you're saying, Ben.'

'I've always thought the worst thing to have was an unidentified body. You know what I mean – so many bodies remain unidentified for years, sometimes for ever. The world is full of people who will never be missed by anyone.'

'Sadly, yes.'

'But Annette *is* missed,' said Cooper. 'Missed, but never found.'

20

Lacey Bower's flat was in a high-rise block of student accommodation on the edge of Sheffield city centre.

Cooper checked the details of the address Carol Villiers had given him.

'The flat is on the seventh floor.'

'Great, that's my lucky number,' said Murfin.

'And it looks as though the lift isn't working.'

'Oh, shit.'

Cooper had to stop a couple of times on the way up the stairs to let Murfin catch up and rest for a minute.

'Nearly there, Gavin,' he said on the fourth floor.

'I can count, you know,' said Murfin, eyeing the number on the landing with a sour expression.

'You don't have to go through the fitness tests any more, now you're a civilian, do you?'

'Damn right. Even when I did, I used to cheat anyway.'

'Cheat?'

'I used to lie about me age. I told them I was seventy-six.'

Cooper laughed. 'Come on, only a few more flights.'

There was loud music coming from behind the door of Lacey Bower's flat. Something Cooper didn't recognise and wouldn't understand if he could hear it properly. But he didn't expect to recognise much that eighteen-year-olds listened to. His nieces were well into their teens and they mentioned names that were a mystery to him. There was nothing better designed to make him feel old.

'Who is it?' called a voice through the door.

'Police,' said Cooper. 'We just want to talk to you.'

The door opened a crack, with a chain firmly in place, and a pale face appeared half covered by a fringe of straight black hair.

'ID?'

Cooper showed his warrant card, which she studied carefully.

'Can we come in for a few minutes?' he said.

'I suppose so.'

She took the chain off and let Cooper push the door open. She walked across the room and turned off the music without being asked. She had an iPod docked into a set of speakers and a laptop open on a table.

'I was just doing a bit of work,' she said.

'You're at college.'

'That's right. I'm studying Travel and Tourism. Maybe one day I'll be able to get right away from this place.'

'Travel and Tourism? Is that a degree?'

'A BTEC Diploma.'

'Right. Is it going well?'

'Okay. If I work hard and don't get distracted.'

Lacey looked at him curiously.

'You're not quite what I expected from a policeman.'

'We come in all kinds of shapes and sizes,' said Cooper. 'Just like real people.'

Lacey glanced from him to Murfin, who had only just made it through the door and closed it behind himself. Cooper could see a different thought forming in Lacey's mind.

'My colleague isn't actually a police officer,' said Cooper. 'He's civilian support.'

'That explains it,' she said. 'One of those old fogeys working on a cold case squad.'

Murfin grinned. 'Don't worry about me, love. I've got a skin as thick as the concrete in this tower block.'

'I wasn't worried about you. You look like you're about to have a heart attack, but as long as you don't do it here I couldn't care less.'

'I'll try to survive for your sake, love.'

Lacey perched on the arm of a sofa pushed against the window. The extent of the view was fantastic, looking out over the western side of Sheffield to the outskirts of the city and the first hills of the Peak District in a haze on the horizon. Two good things about Sheffield: it was built on hills, and the national park was right on the doorstep.

'Lacey,' said Cooper, 'are you aware that your father is missing?'

'Yes, I know. I've known since Monday.'

'How did you find out?'

'Naomi Heath. She sent me a message through the college.'

'She doesn't have your phone number?'

'Dad does,' said Lacey. 'But I've told him that if he lets Naomi phone me I'll ditch my phone and change my number.'

'Do you have any idea where your father might be?'

'Oh, I don't know. All kinds of places. You could try that woman he was having an affair with at work.'

'Madeline Betts?' said Cooper. 'We've checked with her. She hasn't seen him.'

'Some other woman, then. How would I know? I don't keep track of what he's up to.'

'You don't approve of your father.'

Cooper felt he was stating the obvious. Lacey was eighteen and it was perfectly normal at that age.

She pulled an exaggerated expression of disgust. 'What's to approve of?'

'So have you been to Bakewell recently?' asked Cooper.

'Yes, actually. A couple of days ago. I'd booked a place at a psychic investigation.'

'A what?'

'A psychic investigation,' repeated Lacey more slowly.

'A ghost hunt?'

'If you want to call it that. There's a group that organises investigations at special locations. This one was at Bakewell Town Hall. It's an interesting place, you know.'

'No, I didn't know that. You mean interesting ghosts?'

'Spirit manifestations.'

'Did you go home while you were in Bakewell?'

'Home?' she said. She swept an arm around the flat. 'This is my home.'

'I mean the house in Aldern Way, as I'm sure you know. Where your father lives, the house you lived in yourself until you came here.'

'No, I haven't been back for a while.'

'Any particular reason for that?'

'Have you been there?' said Lacey.

'Yes, I was there just this morning.'

'And did you meet Naomi?'

'Of course.'

'Then why do you need to ask?' she said. 'There's your reason, right there.'

So she neither approved of her father nor of his new partner. Or perhaps it was *because* of his new partner. And Lacey knew about her father's affair with Madeline Betts too. That was interesting. It was supposed to have ended years ago, when Lacey was a small child.

Lacey was watching him still.

'Do you have any theories about where's he's gone?' she said, narrowing her eyes.

That was smart of her. Cooper made a mental note not to underestimate her just because she was eighteen and listened to music he didn't understand.

'We are currently exploring the possibility that Mr Bower's disappearance is connected with your mother's ten years ago,' he said, waiting with interest for her reaction.

'Oh, I get you,' she said.

Now she looked more subdued. So she cared about

her mother more than her father. Cooper glanced at Murfin to see if he'd recovered.

'You were very young when your mother went missing,' said Murfin on cue. 'It was very confusing for you. When it happened, you didn't know who you could trust, not even the police.'

Lacey looked at him more closely, frowning.

'Have I met you before?' she said.

'I was on the inquiry team at the time.'

'You came to the house, didn't you? With that inspector.'

'Yes, I did.'

Lacey smirked. 'Ten years. You've put on weight.'

'I'm ten years older,' said Murfin, 'that's why. But you're ten years older too. You're not that same eight-year-old girl who didn't know what was happening. You're an adult now.'

Cooper nodded in approval. Lacey was looking uncertain. She didn't know how to react to Gavin Murfin, or perhaps to the memories that he was evoking. A familiar face or the sound of a voice could take you back so easily to a time you'd almost forgotten.

'You spent some time with your aunt and uncle in Over Haddon, didn't you?' said Cooper. 'After your father was arrested, you went to stay with them. That must have been strange. They're very different people. Your Aunt Frances is a teacher, and a bit of a disciplinarian, I bet. Your Uncle Adrian is a very talented woodcarver. I've seen the tawny owl he's carved for the show . . .'

'The owl is beautiful,' said Lacey, gazing into the sky over the city.

'Yes, it is. Beautiful.'

She was quiet for a moment. Cooper moved a step closer. Just one small step.

'I'm sure you must have thought about it a lot since then,' he said. 'About your mother, I mean. You must have spent some time wondering what happened to her.'

'What do you think I am?' she snapped. 'Obviously I have. I spent years going over and over it in my mind, trying to work out what it all meant, thinking up scenes in my head where Mum would turn up at the door one day, smiling and looking just the same as she always did. It never happened.'

'No, I'm sorry.'

'Well, I don't do that now. She's gone. One way or the other, she's gone for good and that's it. I know she's never coming back.'

Her voice cracked, and she turned away, pushing a lock of hair from her face as she gazed out of the window. Was she picturing her mother somewhere out there in those hazy hills?

'My boss was in charge of the case then,' said Cooper. 'Detective Superintendent Branagh. She was what we call the senior investigating officer.'

'I don't know her,' said Lacey over her shoulder.

'You might not have met her. Though I gather you saw Detective Inspector Hitchens and some other officers, including my colleague here, who was a detective constable on the case.'

'What's your point?'

'You weren't asked any questions at the time, Lacey,

because you were so young. So we were wondering whether you had any memories from the time your mother disappeared.'

Lacey looked over her shoulder at him. If there had been a tear in her eye when they spoke about her mother, she'd surreptitiously wiped it away.

'Memories?'

'Anything, even if it doesn't seem significant.'

She hesitated, as if deciding whether she could trust him.

'I do remember a cave,' she said.

'A cave? What cave, Lacey?'

The repetition of the word 'cave' seemed to be having an effect. Lacey's shoulders drooped and she hugged her arms to her body. She looked suddenly smaller, as if she'd somehow shrunk to that eight-year-old in her own mind.

'It might have been nothing,' she said.

'Can you tell us about it? Is it still clear in your mind?'

'Not really. I haven't thought about it for a while.'

'What exactly do you remember?'

'Well, just this cave,' said Lacey. 'Water was pouring out of it.'

'Yes . . .?'

'That's it, I'm afraid. I just remember standing with my dad, looking at the water.'

'And that's all?'

'Yes. I'm sorry.'

'Well, we might have a location in mind,' said Cooper. 'Would you be willing to go there with us to have a look, to see if it jogs your memory? It would be very helpful if you could identify the cave.'

'I suppose that will be all right.' She glanced at her laptop. 'I do have work to do just now.'

'It won't be today. I'll let you know when we need you.'

'Okay then. But it's only a vague memory, you know. I'm not sure it will help.'

'Why do you associate that particular recollection with your mother?' asked Cooper.

Lacey shrugged. 'I can't say. It must have been about that time. The two things are imprinted on my mind together. My mum going missing, and the cave. I don't know what it means. I never have done.'

'Have you never asked your father about it?'

'No. No, I couldn't do that.'

'Why not?'

'We never talked,' she said. 'At least, we never talked about what might have happened to Mum. It was all unspoken. I suppose we dealt with it in our ways. Me, running through fantasies in my mind, fantasies where Mum came back home to us. And Dad, well . . . Dad getting on with life in his own way. Meeting Naomi Heath, moving her in to the house, taking on her child, having another one with her. You know, all that stuff. Mum became something that happened in the past as far as he was concerned. But she wasn't for me. That's why we couldn't talk about it. You can't communicate with someone who's on an entirely different plane of existence.'

Cooper listened with interest. Wasn't that what Lacey

had been trying to do with her psychic investigations? Communicate with people on a different plane? She wanted to make contact with the dead. Yet she couldn't talk to her own father about what troubled her most.

That had also been Lacey's longest speech so far, and her most vehement.

'Do you think you actually know what happened to your mother, Lacey?' he asked.

'No,' she said.

But she didn't look certain. Not at all.

'And have you ever told anyone else about your memory of the cave?'

'It was a secret,' she said. 'I didn't know if it was true, or something I'd imagined. So I haven't mentioned it to anyone.'

'Not anyone?'

'Well, hardly . . .'

She paused. Murfin made a small movement, but Cooper shook his head and he relaxed.

'Who did you tell, Lacey?' said Cooper gently.

'Just one person. There is only one person I've ever been able to talk to about anything to do with my mother.'

'Your Aunt Frances?'

'No, not her. I can't stand *her*.'

'Who, then?'

She scowled down at her hands, apparently deciding how much she should tell him. Cooper knew not to press her at this moment. People had to be allowed to make their own decisions when it was so important to them.

232

'Like I said, there's only one person,' said Lacey. 'My grandfather. And *he* let us all down.'

When they left Lacey Bower, Murfin paused in the corridor outside the flat. The music had already started up again behind the door. It was louder than ever. Cooper thought they should probably get out of here before the neighbours came round to complain.

'I don't supposed they've got the lifts mended while we've been in there,' said Murfin.

'No chance.'

'Okay. Let's do it.'

Murfin was panting and sweating by the time they reached the ground floor and got out into the fresh air.

'So is seven still your lucky number?' asked Cooper.

'I'm seriously rethinking it.'

'Can you rethink a superstition?'

'In this case, definitely.'

Murfin was looking anxiously around the street as he waited for Cooper to unlock the Toyota.

'No pie shops, Gavin,' said Cooper.

'What? There must be millions of them in Sheffield.'

'Just get in the car.'

Cooper began to work his way through the streets of Sheffield, heading for those Derbyshire hills he'd seen from the seventh floor of the tower block. He wondered what it would be like to live up there permanently, to be able to glimpse the Peak District in the distance but not to be in it. He wasn't sure he could bear it for very long – even if the lifts were working.

'Gavin, first thing in the morning, I'd like you to

check out some industrial units in Bakewell, near Reece Bower's home,' he said. 'See if anyone who was working at the units when Annette Bower disappeared is still there.'

'What am I looking for?'

'The owner of a red Nissan. I'll leave the details on your desk.'

'It was ten years ago, Ben.'

'I know,' said Cooper. 'It's a long shot. But it's a lead that doesn't seem to have been followed up properly at the time.'

Murfin sniffed and fiddled uncomfortably with his seat belt.

'Is there a problem, Gavin?' asked Cooper.

'No, boss.'

They drove in silence for a few minutes. Murfin had left his car in Bakewell, so they had to make a fifteen-mile detour.

'What about this ghost-hunting thing?' said Murfin after a while. 'That's a load of rubbish, if ever I heard it.'

'Some people believe in it, Gavin.'

'That's true. My missus for one.'

'Does she go to psychic investigations?'

'Not likely. She does her own haunting. But sometimes it seems as though everyone else goes.'

Cooper wasn't surprised. Derbyshire was full of ghost sightings, and it had been for centuries. Some people called it 'the dead centre of England'. That might be because of its geographical position in the middle of the country. Or it might not.

'You don't think young Lacey is hoping to see her mother's ghost? To make contact, like?'

'I hadn't thought of that,' admitted Cooper.

'She'd be better going to a medium in that case. They can produce anyone you like from beyond the grave. Or so they say. People fall for it all the time.'

'I don't think Lacey Bower is so gullible,' said Cooper.

Cooper thought about Evan Slaney's cottage with all his ancient lamps and dark corners. He imagined Mr Slaney sitting there during the evening with his Conan Doyle stories, perhaps projecting himself into the gas-lit world of Holmes and Watson. Was Mr Slaney still convinced he'd seen his daughter alive? Cooper wasn't sure. But he was less confident of being able to get Mr Slaney to admit any doubt, after all this time. When you'd stuck to a conviction for ten years, it must be very hard to admit that you were wrong. Perhaps impossible.

And what of Annette Bower herself? She had disappeared into the shadows ten years ago. And somewhere between those shadows was his answer.

Before they could get back to Bakewell, Ben Cooper took a call from Dev Sharma at West Street.

'Inspector, we have a significant find reported. I believe it's relevant to your missing person case. Mr Reece Bower.'

'Has he been found?' asked Cooper.

'No, not exactly,' said Sharma. 'But I'm afraid it looks like bad news.'

21

The ruins were just visible through the trees. To reach them, Ben Cooper had to cross a wooden footbridge, with the River Lathkill no more than a trickle below it.

The house had been standing derelict for more than a century, slowly collapsing and decaying into the hillside. It had been a two-storey limestone structure once, with mullioned windows and a wide set of steps up to the front door. A few walls still remained, a doorway and a fireplace. But its roofless shell was only a broken memory of a home.

Carol Villiers was already on scene, despatched by Dev Sharma to cover until Cooper arrived.

'I'm told it's called Bateman's House,' she said. 'Apparently, it was built as a home for the company agent.'

'The lead mining company,' said Cooper. 'Mandale Mine.'

'That's right.'

'It was probably quite grand in its day.'

'I wouldn't want to live here now.'

The whole valley here exuded an atmosphere of

mining history. The six and a half miles of Lathkill Dale might look untouched to the casual visitor, but for many centuries it had been mined for lead. The shafts, drainage channels and spoil heaps had all been absorbed into the natural landscape.

Cooper looked at the steps, imagining the lead miners gathering at the end of each week, exhausted and filthy, to collect their pay from the agent.

'This is the interesting bit,' said Villiers.

Behind the house was the entrance to a shallow mineshaft. He could reach the bottom down an iron stairway bolted to the wall. It was a steep descent, and the only safe way to go down was backwards, clinging tightly on to the handrails. It wasn't very deep, but at the bottom he felt immediately anxious as he turned to look up at the sky and get a glimpse of the trees.

This had been part of a working mine. Now it was a tourist attraction. A hand-cranked electric generator had been installed, and visitors could wind the handle to produce enough light to peer over a wall and view a second, deeper shaft.

The second shaft wasn't easily accessible. The single light bulb powered by the generator lit the sheer, rocky walls and a glitter of water, a stream running deep below. But the bulb was too weak to show anything much on the bottom.

Now two crime scene examiners in scene suits were working in the shaft. They'd set up their own lights, and one of them had climbed an aluminium ladder down to the bottom. Cooper was almost blinded by the flash of his camera bouncing off the walls.

'Two visitors who came to look at Bateman's House had brought their own torch,' said Villiers. 'They shone it into the shaft to see the water. And they saw this instead.'

'A wallet,' said Cooper.

'It's Reece Bower's. His credit cards are still in it, and some cash, even a few business cards. So there's no doubt about it.'

'Lots of latent prints,' said Cooper, examining it through the sides of the evidence bag.

'And DNA,' said Villiers.

'Where?'

She pointed at a dark stain in the creases of the brown leather of the wallet.

'Blood,' she said.

'So it is.'

'But the SOCOs say there's no sign of a struggle here in the shaft. It's more difficult to tell on the surface, because the ground is pretty trampled by visitors.'

Cooper climbed back up the ladder and looked around him at the deep valley and the slopes dense with trees and tangled undergrowth. He would have to organise a search. And it wasn't going to be small scale.

'Carol, call the duty controller at Derby Caves Rescue Organisation,' he said. 'We'll need them.'

'Okay.'

The DCRO base was located in the Fire and Rescue Centre at Buxton. Their rescue vehicle was kept there, ready and loaded with the equipment necessary for most eventualities. Almost all of their search and rescue operations took place in the limestone areas of the

Peak District, either in the caves and mines around Castleton or in this area between Eyam, Monyash and Matlock.

Cave Rescue covered a vast area, though. They could be called on by police forces throughout the Midlands, as well as in South Yorkshire and Greater Manchester. They were all volunteers, of course. But Cooper knew they would come.

'Lathkill Dale isn't an insignificant area,' he said. 'There are at least six miles of it. We'll have to work our way along the dale methodically, or it will be chaos.'

'We need some more bodies to do that,' said Villiers.

'I'll call Hazel Branagh. I'm sure she'll authorise it.'

Cooper would have liked to call in the air support unit, but the helicopter had been grounded by a laser attack. He should say *another* laser attack. There had been eleven attacks on NPAS aircraft in the area around its Ripley base in just one year. Pilots found it difficult to cope with a dazzling light in the cockpit. And many of the lasers being used as weapons were too high-powered even to be legal.

There was another daunting prospect. A search of this extent could produce a huge amount of material, which might or might not be potential evidence. It would all have to be examined to establish whether it was connected to Reece Bower.

At the serious end of crime, in a large murder inquiry, money was rarely a major issue. But in lower priority cases, forensic resources were too expensive to be justified. Even with the new forensic centre opened at Hucknall in Nottinghamshire to pool resources between neighbouring forces, Cooper had to think twice about whether he could justify the cost.

'Why would Reece Bower come here to Lathkill Dale?' said Villiers.

'If he was here at all. When he was alive, I mean.'

'You think it's possible somebody dumped his body close by?' Villiers shook her head. 'But why here, of all places?' she said.

'If you were trying to think of a hiding place, it might spring to mind.'

'What – a place that's visited by hundreds of hikers every week?'

'But there's so much of it,' said Cooper. 'Walkers only visit a small part of the dale. Most of them stay on the trail. They might visit Bateman's House, if they know it's here. And they might head up the track and look at the ruined engine house. Who goes further than that? Not many.'

'I suppose that's true.'

'And the people who do come up here,' he added. 'They're generally the kind who could be relied on to report what they found, rather than just pocketing the money and disposing of the rest.'

'Do you think so?'

'I'm certain of it.'

As they walked back to the trail, Cooper noticed a broken section of bridge, a length of timber cracked halfway between two posts, splinters of wood fresh in the break.

'It was probably rotten,' said Villiers when she saw him examining it.

'No, it isn't. The wood is perfectly sound.'

'Something smashed it, then.'

A road wound steeply down from Over Haddon past a tea rooms to an old mill and a ford over the river. Cooper went back to his car parked at the bottom of the road.

'I'll have to go and tell Naomi Heath,' he said. 'And I'll see if she can tell whether there's anything missing from the wallet.'

'Rather you than than me,' said Villiers.

'It has to be done.'

Jackdaws chattered in the trees above the mill. The first yellow leaves had begun to fall, drifting downhill towards the river.

'And what about the daughter?' said Villiers.

'Lacey? Her too. I want her down here in Lathkill Dale. Let's see what else she can remember.'

At West Street, Cooper had another call waiting for him from Detective Superintendent Branagh.

First she wanted him to bring her up to date with the Reece Bower inquiry and what progress he was making. She gave her go-ahead for the search of Lathkill Dale, but Cooper could tell she was concerned about the extent of it, and how long the search was going to take. That translated to how much it was going to cost. But budgets were a superintendent's job to justify, thank goodness.

After he'd filled her in on the details, Cooper could tell that there was something else on Branagh's mind.

'Ma'am?'

'Ben, I need you to meet with EMSOU,' she said. 'Their intelligence unit have come up with some information they want to share with us.'

'In relation to one of our cases?'

'No, theirs.'

'Ma'am, I'm at a critical stage in the Reece Bower inquiry,' said Cooper. 'It's no longer just a missing person. We've had some significant finds in Lathkill Dale which suggest we might have to upgrade it to a murder inquiry.'

'Yes, I know,' said Branagh. 'I do read the reports. And I appreciate that I was the one who sent you there in the first place. I hate to take you away from it and put more work on to you. But, to be honest . . . well, there isn't anyone else. No one that I would trust this much.'

From anyone else that might be a meaningless platitude, just so much fake praise. But Cooper had never heard Detective Superintendent Branagh use platitudes. She had never felt the need. So he had to believe her.

'Who should I speak to, ma'am?'

Branagh hesitated, and in that second of silence Cooper knew whose name she was going to give him.

'Detective Sergeant Fry is in the area,' she said.

'Yes,' said Cooper, 'I know.'

Diane Fry answered Cooper's call promptly.

'Did you say you know where Shirebrook is?' she began, without any pretence of small talk.

'Obviously.'

'Can you get there tonight?'

'Tonight? To Shirebrook?'

'Yes. Meet me in the market square. You know my car. I've still got the black Audi.'

'It's about thirty miles from Edendale,' said Cooper. 'Right over the other side of Chesterfield. It would take me about three quarters of an hour.'

'I'll see you later then,' she said, and ended the call.

Cooper opened his mouth to ask why she wanted him in Shirebrook, but she'd already gone. How should he respond to her demand? He could just not go, in which case somebody else might be given the job and he would never find out what she wanted to tell him. And the times she'd offered to share information or ask for his help were rare enough that he didn't want to pass up the opportunity.

And what else was he doing tonight? The answer was 'nothing', of course.

22

A light rain had begun to fall. Ben Cooper could feel it on his face, though it was leaving hardly any impression on the concrete.

Cooper had parked his RAV4 in one of the car parks behind the shops and walked through into the marketplace. It looked pretty bleak.

On the way into Shirebrook he'd passed a dilapidated pub. A sign on the wall had said POKOJE DO WYNAJECIA OD £65 W TYM RACHUNKI – Rooms for Rent £65 a week including bills. POLEC LOKATORA A OTRZYMASZ £25 – Refer a friend and receive £25 cashback. Near a pond by the side of the road the notices said ZAKAZ WEDKOWANIA, ZAKAZ WSTEPU – No fishing, no public access.

At one time, these signs would have looked very odd. They would certainly have had local people scratching their heads. But everyone in this area had learned a few words of Polish by now. The *polski sklep* had become as traditional a feature of the British high street as WH Smith or Boots. Even English people had been tempted to buy Polish bread, pierogi, kielbasa, sauerkraut, or pickled cucumbers.

Cooper saw Fry's black Audi and climbed into the passenger seat.

'It's hardly the Peak District, is it?' said Fry.

'But still Derbyshire.'

'So you said.'

'It's quiet too.'

'There's a Public Space Protection Order,' said Fry.

'I know. It's a shame.'

'Why?'

'The trouble with PSPOs is that they give local authorities the power to criminalise behaviour that isn't normally criminal. And they aren't just directed at an individual, like an ASBO is. Their geographical definition makes anyone liable to prosecution in a particular area. It kills a place like this. Shirebrook used to be full of pubs. Now most of them seem to be closed.'

Cooper watched buses come into the stops and a few people getting on. The number twenty-three to Mansfield, the number eighty-two to Chesterfield. A man passed along the pavement riding a mobility scooter with two England flags attached to the back of the seat.

'My dad was stationed here when he was a young bobby,' said Cooper, 'many years ago, before the Miners' Strike in the mid-1980s. Shirebrook was a very different place then. The strike tore it apart. You remember what the Miners' Strike was like.'

'I don't think we had the Miners' Strike in Birmingham,' said Fry.

Cooper snorted. 'You just weren't interested, I suppose. You were more concerned with other things.'

'Probably.'

'But in places like Shirebrook, it meant everything. For a lot of these old ex-miners, the strike is still fresh in their memories. Still a raw wound. They blame everything that's happened to them since on the Thatcher government and the closure of the pits.'

'That's ridiculous,' said Fry. 'It was more than thirty years ago.'

'Thirty years is nothing. Not to some of these people.'

'I can't believe that.'

Cooper had often had to remind himself that Diane Fry came from a different background. She wasn't just from the West Midlands and a city girl. She'd also been a graduate entrant to the police service, with a degree in Crime and Policing from Birmingham City University.

Yet these days Fry was starting to look over-qualified. Even Cooper's modest A levels had become unnecessary, since Derbyshire Constabulary had recently reduced the qualifications for entry. In fact, there were no longer any educational requirements at all, not even the old minimum of a level three NVQ. Now it was enough to demonstrate training or experience that the Chief Constable might consider the equivalent. It was all about expanding the pool of potential recruits and encouraging people from under-represented groups to apply. The change had been made in time for the next recruitment window, which opened for applications later in the month.

'I've read up on your murder case,' said Cooper. 'Krystian Zalewski, found dead from stab wounds in his flat. He was apparently attacked in an alleyway off Shirebrook marketplace.'

'That's right.'

'And you have no witnesses to the attack?'

'Not so far. Zalewski lived on his own, and he didn't seek treatment for his injuries, so he died in his flat.'

'If nobody saw it, and Mr Zalewski lived alone, who reported finding the body?' asked Cooper.

'No one,' said Fry.

'How could it be no one?'

'The landlord downstairs came in to open his shop early next morning and found a stain on his ceiling. A red stain, and it was spreading. Not surprisingly, it took a while before it dawned on him he had blood dripping through the floor of the flat above. But then he went up to check. He has a duplicate key of course, but the door was bolted on the inside. So the landlord made a call. That's Mr Pollitt.'

Cooper thought he detected a peculiar emphasis on the name 'Pollitt' as if it caused a bad taste in her mouth and she was spitting it out.

'And response officers came and broke the door open,' he said.

'That's it.'

'But I gather that EMSOU were here before that.'

'Possibly.'

'Possibly? Is that all you can say?'

'I'm restricted in what I can tell you,' said Fry. 'But when Krystian Zalewski was killed, we thought it was connected to an existing operation.'

'An existing operation?'

'Yes.'

'So what did bring EMSOU to Shirebrook,' asked Cooper, 'if it wasn't the murder?'

'Come with me. I'll show you.'

'Where are we going?'

'Not far.'

Just to the south of the town centre was the Model Village, the estate built for miners and their families. Rows of terraced house with narrow strips of front garden. Back alleys lined by brick privies and scattered with wheelie bins. Lines of washing filled many of the front gardens, where grass had been allowed to grow rank. One or two had squeezed a trampoline in for the children, leaving no room for anything else.

Cooper recalled his father talking about the Miners' Strike of 1984–85. Shirebrook had been the scene of fighting between pickets and police escorting working miners. Women and children had shouted 'Scab' at men going to work, the wives of working miners had their windows smashed, and their children were bullied at school. A striker had been injured in an attack. At a mass meeting, NUM members had decided they would refuse to work with men who crossed picket lines, but by the February of 1985, Shirebrook miners had become so desperate that most of them went back to work.

They drove past a parade of shops, turned a corner, and reached the furthest part of the estate. Fry pulled up a few short yards from the end of the road.

'We're about to raid an address here,' she said.

'Why?'

'Incident reports showed that police officers have been called to this address almost twenty times since it became an HMO,' said Fry. 'That's a house in multiple occupation.'

'I know what it means.'

'For months now we've had surveillance on a Czech gang believed to be involved in slave trafficking. We've been working closely with the National Crime Agency, of course.'

'Slave trafficking?' said Cooper.

'It's a modern form of slavery. Victims are housed in appalling conditions, living in garages or in cupboards. Some have to forage for food in bins. They can't wash, they don't get clean clothes – they may be charged a pound a time by their gangmasters just to use the toilet. Most of the men are sent out to work in factories, or used as domestic servants. They're threatened with violence or beaten to keep them frightened and submissive. Ben, the trafficking network is like a spider's web that goes right across the continent of Europe.'

'It's almost unbelievable that it happens here in the UK.'

'Not unbelievable once you've seen it at first-hand.'

'Are we about to do that?'

'Perhaps.'

Fry drew out a folder with a series of photos.

'Katerina Drenkova is the godmother of the gang,' she said. 'She organised the trafficking and controlled the finances. Her husband and son were the enforcers, Ladislav and Pavel Drenko. They assaulted and threatened their victims with baseball bats.'

She shuffled the sheaf of photos to show two more men.

'These two victims tried to escape,' she said. 'Two Czech men, Josef Hajek and Mikolas Zeman. Hajek turned up at A & E with a head injury after one of the Drenkos hit him with a baseball bat. He was interviewed by local police at the hospital. Hajek had been constantly threatened by the Drenkos that if he tried to leave, or did something at work to lose his job, he would get a beating.'

'Where did he work?' asked Cooper.

'At a car wash. The manager described Hajek as a good worker, but said he always seemed to be hungry. He always turned up for work in the same clothes, and had er . . . poor hygiene habits.'

'I see.'

'Mikolas Zeman was trafficked into the UK by someone else and sold to Katerina Drenkova.'

'Sold?'

'That's the way slavery works, Ben.'

'I know, I know.'

'When Zeman was trafficked, he was told he'd have a better life here in the UK. He'd be able to get work and he'd have a roof over his head. It looked like a good option for him, a new start. A more comfortable way of life than in his village in the Czech Republic. It didn't turn out that way, of course. He and five other men shared one room at the house owned by the Drenkos, with three sleeping on the floor and two in a single bed, like sardines. Others had to sleep on the floor in a garage. They urinated into bottles and had to eat outside. One of the men was treated as a household servant, doing the cooking and cleaning. Others were sent out to work in factories.'

'And car washes.'

'Yes. Anyway, the NCA launched a seven-month surveillance operation, and a series of raids were subsequently carried out on addresses across the Midlands. We estimate that several dozen men were trafficked over about six years. The gang will be charged with conspiracy to traffic for the purpose of exploitation, requiring a person to perform forced or compulsory labour, and acting as a gangmaster.'

'I don't think those offences even existed when I was in training.'

'The Modern Slavery Act 2015,' said Fry. 'I'm sure you'll have had the updates.'

'Of course I will.'

'The NCA's financial investigations found bank accounts worth hundreds of thousands of pounds. So slavery can be quite profitable for the owners.'

Fry looked at her watch. Moments later, several cars and a van load of uniformed officers raced into the street. They piled out and entered the garden of a house about six doors down.

'There are officers in the back alley too,' said Fry.

One officer wielded the battering ram and broke down the door in three or four blows. His colleagues ran in and began leading people out and loading them into the van.

Cooper was surprised how many people came out of the house. He lost count of them after six. They were all males of working age too. Not your normal household of two parents and two and a half children. He looked to Fry for a cue.

'Okay, we can go in now.'

A concrete path ran through a few yards of grass that could barely be called a lawn. A wheelie bin stood by the white PVC front door, which had splintered under the impact of the battering ram. Fry and Cooper stepped through the gap into a hallway. The carpet was trampled with mud, and a line of men's work boots stood against the wall.

The interior of the house was overheated. It smelled rank and stale, thick with the stink of cigarette smoke and the sour dregs of beer. Downstairs the walls were a uniform dull grey, with net curtains and roller blinds at all the windows. The kitchen was barely seven feet wide. If he stretched, he could almost have touched both walls at once. Not that he would have wanted to. They looked as though they had absorbed years of grease and food splashes. The smell of cooking practically oozed from the paintwork.

'I've been in plenty of houses like this,' said Cooper. 'What's the big deal?'

'Upstairs,' said Fry.

The stairs creaked ominously and the carpet was frayed into tattered ribbons, as if by the constant passage of many pairs of hobnailed boots.

The same smells met Cooper on the landing. Upstairs, heavy floral patterns predominated. Massive red flowers on the wallpaper, even bigger blue flowers on the rugs. In the two first floor bedrooms upstairs, he could hardly see an inch of carpet. Three mattresses lay on the floor of each room, the piles of disarrayed blankets suggesting that they were regularly used. Clothes were hung on rails and behind the door, cardboard boxes were full of shoes and underwear, a yellow high-vis jacket hung over the side.

'Some of these properties have owner-occupiers and have been made really nice internally,' said Fry. 'Well, where else could you buy a three-bedroom house for seventy thousand pounds?'

'Not in Edendale, that's for sure.'

Cooper thought of the Swanns' home in Over Haddon. That was a three-bedroom property too. But the difference in price between the two houses was probably somewhere in the range of three hundred and fifty thousand pounds. What was it they said about property? Location, location, location . . .

'But a lot of these houses are rented,' said Fry. 'Landlords charge about four hundred and fifty pounds a month. If you can get nine or ten people in them, that's very cheap.'

'So where's the third bedroom?'

She pointed upwards. 'Attic.'

The trap door opened to reveal an extending ladder. In the attic, Cooper couldn't reach the walls, but he had to duck to avoid hitting his head on the ceiling.

'It's the same in here,' said Cooper. 'Mattresses and blankets.'

'This is more than just a house in multiple occupation. These men were being exploited.'

Cooper came back down the ladder and stood on the landing.

'Why have you shown me all this?' he said.

'Detective Superintendent Branagh asked us to bring you in and make sure you were up to speed with the operation.'

'But why?'

'Because,' said Fry, 'the next house we raid may be in your area.'

'And what do you suggest I do in the meantime?'

'We want LPUs like yours to gather information,' she said. 'It's only by obtaining intelligence on the ground that we can get a complete picture. You and your team are best placed to do that.'

'I suppose we are,' admitted Cooper.

Outside, the occupants of the house had been driven away in the police van. As Fry and Cooper left in her Audi, they drove through a new housing development that had been built right next to the Model Village.

Cooper noticed that the roads were called Sunflower Close, Orchid Way, and The Spinney. Now, that *could* be in Edendale.

23

Back in the marketplace, only the takeaways were open. A car was parked outside the Shirebrook Xpress on the corner of Market Street, someone picking up a pizza or a couple of burgers. Cooper could smell the waft of frying chips from Deep Pan Kid, where the only movement was from two women in orange tabards behind the counter. A solitary black-and-white cat strolled across the empty market square.

Fry took him round the back of the row of shops and showed him the taped-off stairway.

'This is where your murder victim lived?'

'Yes. We thought Krystian Zalewski might be a slave-trafficking victim,' she said. 'One who had tried to escape from his captors and had been punished.'

'A punishment that went too far?' said Cooper.

'Exactly. But when a knife is involved, it can easily end up worse than you expect.'

'But you're not sure now that it's the right explanation.'

'No. He'd been living in this one-bedroom flat for four months on his own. There are plenty of HMOs in the area, but this isn't one of them. The landlord, who owns the shop downstairs, says he never saw anyone else coming to the flat.'

'But the access is from this stairway in the backyard,' said Cooper.

'True. And the landlord locks the shop at five o'clock and goes home, so he wouldn't know who came here in the evening, or during the night for that matter.' Fry shook her head. 'In some ways, it's a classic set-up. Krystian Zalewski had very little contact with anyone else. He was living in a place where people could come and go without being observed for sixteen hours of the day.'

'And he worked at a car wash,' said Cooper.

She nodded. 'A car wash. On the surface, that seemed to clinch it. But his employers say they had no problems with him, never noticed anything to give them cause for concern. Zalewski was a hard worker, always turned up on time. But he showed none of the indications of being trafficked. He was clean, had a change of clothes, didn't seem ill-treated or malnourished. In fact, he brought sandwiches to work every day and sometimes offered to share them with his co-workers.'

'Sounds pretty normal.'

'Yes, it does. We've had officers visit the Polish shops, and the staff at Zabka recognise him. They say he came in regularly and bought groceries. Basic stuff, but enough to keep a single man fed.' Fry raised her hands in a gesture of futility. 'No, Krystian Zalewski wasn't being trafficked. He was just a migrant worker, trying to make a go of it. But because he was such a loner, we couldn't be sure.'

'I wonder how he was regarded by the local people,' said Cooper.

'That we don't know. The landlord is the only person we've found who can claim that he knew Zalewski. And he only collected his rent once a week.'

'No other conversation at all?'

'Oh, he spoke to his tenant a couple of times to explain to him what was supposed to go in the wheelie bins. He hadn't quite grasped the idea of recyclable and non-recyclable.'

'Have any of us?' said Cooper.

Fry ignored the remark.

'The owner of the shop was a complication,' she said Fry. 'His name is Geoffrey Pollitt and we already had him under observation.'

'You'd been tracking him? Why?'

'It was over quite a different matter. He has far right connections.'

'A known extremist?'

'He's a middle man. Two years ago he bought a lock-up shop on the marketplace at Shirebrook. The tenant's lease hadn't been renewed when its term expired, so the shop was standing empty, with its shutters permanently down. When we went to have a discreet look, we realised there was a large storeroom at the back of the shop, with delivery access from one of the side streets.'

'It must have rung alarm bells when there seemed to be links between slave trafficking and the far right.'

'You're not kidding. We would have moved in on Pollitt eventually, but we were in the process of gathering information.'

'Which can take for ever,' said Cooper.

'We have to be cautious.'

'And the death of Krystian Zalewski put a spanner in the works.'

'It meant we had to respond, of course. It gave us a justification for turning over the flat and visiting Mr Pollitt.'

'And?'

'And nothing. Before he worked at the car wash, Zalewski was employed at the distribution centre just outside Shirebrook. There are thousands of Poles and other East Europeans working there, most of them on zero hours contracts through agencies. Zalewski got into trouble, broke too many rules about timekeeping, and the agency let him go. There's nothing in it as far as the slave trafficking inquiry is concerned.'

'You sound disappointed.'

'Not disappointed, but frustrated,' said Fry. 'It means we still have no idea who killed him, or why. We're back to square one.'

'That *is* frustrating,' said Cooper.

Fry looked at him. 'What are you smiling at?'

'Oh, I was just thinking . . . I have a murder case with a suspect and a motive, but no body. And you have a body, but no suspect and no motive.'

'And that's funny?'

'It made *me* smile,' said Cooper.

*　　*　　*

When Fry had left, Cooper stayed in Shirebrook for a while. Slave trafficking? He knew that slavery wasn't a new phenomenon in Britain. Far from it. Most people thought of the eighteenth-century slave trade, the trafficking of black Africans to North America and the Caribbean. Yet the British had known slavery many centuries before that.

There had been a history teacher at Eden Valley High School who loved to cover the early centuries of the British Isles, as if they were somehow simpler and easier to understand than the Reformation, or the Repeal of the Corn Laws. He'd explained how, more than two thousand years ago, the Romans had brought their slave-based economy to their new province of Britannia. Right here in Derbyshire, the lead mines had been worked by Celtic slaves, the famously warlike Britons cowed into subservience and sent to hack out minerals by hand.

Vikings had begun the slave trade in Bristol, shipping British captives to slave markets in Ireland. And at the time of William the Conqueror's Domesday Book, ten per cent of the population of England were recorded as slaves. Slavery had always existed – and according to Diane Fry it was still flourishing right here in his own county.

He didn't envy Fry the cases she had to deal with now. The crimes he handled were somehow more normal and made more sense, even the sudden deaths. Organised crime on the level that she'd been talking about was rare in his part of Derbyshire, thank goodness. Not that it didn't exist at all. Perhaps he just hadn't found it yet. The thought wasn't comforting.

Cooper decided to take a stroll round Shirebrook. At the top of Patchwork Row he found a clutch of important buildings – the library, the Salvation Army hall, the working men's club. On The Row itself were the Piekarnia Olawa bakery and a bistro for Polish home-made dinners.

Many of the pubs seemed to have closed. For some reason, the Miners' Welfare was still open, despite the fact that the pit had closed decades ago. Next to the Miners' Welfare stood a funeral directors'. You could take that as symbolic, he supposed. The mining industry in Derbyshire was long since dead and buried.

He turned and looked across the road. The police station seemed disused too, but it wasn't. Officers were still based there, the Safer Neighbourhood Team who did such a great job out on the streets policing their local community. That must have been where Sergeant Joe Cooper was based back in the day, when he was a beat bobby. It looked the right sort of solid old building, probably rather tatty and gloomy inside. In those days at least. But perhaps it still was.

In Shirebrook they had Polish-speaking volunteers now to help out on occasions such as the annual Remembrance Sunday parade in November. Derbyshire's Police and Crime Commissioner himself had been seen in Shirebrook marketplace one day, hearing the views of local people as part of his 'Listening to You' campaign. Joe Cooper would have been completely unfamiliar with both of those phenomena. Neither Polish speaking volunteers nor PCCs were part of his policing experience. If he was still alive, Sergeant Cooper would be flabbergasted at the way the job had changed in some parts of the county.

The new Police and Crime Commissioner had pledged to visit all three hundred and eighty-three towns and villages in Derbyshire during his term of office, promoting his appearances on Twitter with the hashtag #D383. Cooper hadn't heard of any plans for the Commissioner to visit Edendale yet.

He breathed in the smell of hotdogs from a burger van parked in a corner of the car park at the Ex-Servicemen's Club on Carter Lane.

Cooper supposed pro-EU feeling in Shirebrook must be as rare as a lump of locally produced coal. Some said this neglected corner of the East Midlands acted like a canary in the mine – a warning of what could happen if the mass movement of people into the UK wasn't controlled.

Of course, it was only a minority who caused the trouble. There had always been a problem minority, even in the old days when it was a proper community, before the start of the Miners' Strike. But this minority stood out more. They behaved differently, they spoke differently.

A Polish man had stabbed another East European in the chest and was later jailed, causing further animosity from people who felt Shirebrook wasn't safe any more. The rise in antisocial behaviour, street drinking and violent disorder became intolerable for some, prompting a series of street protests from locals who wanted to take their town back.

Cooper recalled one wet Saturday, when the market-place here had been full of residents standing in water-proofs and under umbrellas to protest about a spate of violence and antisocial behaviour in the town. Speakers had called for more action by the town council and police over a situation they described as 'a potential time bomb'.

Gangs of men drinking in the town centre were said to be frightening women and pensioners. Following the rally in the marketplace, residents had marched to the distribution centre outside the town, where they held another demonstration.

A lot of the talk was about the loss of jobs after the closure of the pit, leaving a generation without alternatives for employment other than to join the armed forces and risk their lives in Afghanistan and Iraq. The BNP sold itself as a party for the working class, as opposed to the politicians of the establishment elite. *British Jobs for British workers* was a familiar slogan.

For three years the BNP had run their annual Red, White and Blue Festival near Codnor, an event which had cost Derbyshire Constabulary more than half a million pounds a year to police. It was a relief to everyone when it was cancelled one year and moved away from the county. It was money that could now be better spent, if it was still in the budget.

Meanwhile, Shirebrook's population had risen by several thousands. The rest of the East European work-force was scattered around the area in towns like Mansfield and Worksop. Some landlords had taken advantage of the influx to cram beds into old miners' cottages and rent them out to groups of workers. Groups of men like those he'd just seen could be very intimidating for neighbours.

Was Shirebrook unique in its transformation? It had changed from a struggling ex-mining town wallowing in a sad nostalgia for its industrial heritage, and it had become this fractured, anxious place that looked so quiet outwardly, but was seething with tensions underneath.

A juddering noise surprised him and Cooper looked up. A helicopter passed overhead and landed near the distribution centre.

For a moment, he wondered what job you could do there that would make you wealthy enough to afford your own helicopter. It would have to be a lot more than the minimum wage, even with overtime.

'Polec Lokatora a Otrzymasz.' Perhaps he could refer a friend.

But there was no one here in Shirebrook marketplace to ask. Just the sound of a gentle rain, falling on to a hard surface.

24

Day 4

Next morning, Ben Cooper found a video clip waiting for him, an extract from last night's local TV news. When he clicked to play it, DS Dev Sharma's face appeared in close-up on his screen.

Sharma was standing outside the Singhs' shop on Buxton Road, making an appeal for information from the public to help identify the robbery suspects. He gave a clear description of them as far as it was known, and a photograph was shown of a motorcycle crash helmet similar to the distinctive red one worn by a suspect.

He did an excellent job too. He was calm, articulate, and exuded confidence. Cooper had authorised the appeal, but he had no idea that Sharma would come across so well in front of the cameras. No doubt senior command officers would be watching this already.

When he left his office, Cooper discovered that Dev Sharma had also brought a youth into custody at West Street. A skinny teenager who sat in an interview room in the custody suite with a solicitor and a woman Cooper recognised as a Social Services caseworker.

'Who is that in the interview room, Dev?' he asked in the CID room. 'He only looks about sixteen.'

'Not even that,' said Sharma. 'He's a couple of months away from that age.'

'But who is he?'

Sharma looked at Cooper with a solemn expression. 'Troy Curtis. He's Shane Curtis's brother.'

'And?'

'He was the other arsonist.'

'Damn.'

'His mother is very upset.'

'I can imagine.'

Cooper looked at Sharma to see how he was dealing with it. 'This sort of case can be the hardest. Are you okay with it?'

'I'm fine.'

'It's perhaps worse when you have your own children.'

Sharma nodded. 'I haven't told you yet. Asha is expecting our first child. He's due next April.'

'Congratulations,' said Cooper. 'That's wonderful.'

'Thank you.'

'You said "he"?'

'Yes, I always knew it would be a boy first.'

Cooper laughed. 'A lot of fathers say that.'

'We'll have more than one, of course. But the first one changes everything, doesn't it?'

'I suppose so.'

If his marriage to Liz had gone ahead, Cooper might have been the one announcing his first child by now. In fact, it could have been months ago. He could be a father by now. And it would have changed everything. Yet it wasn't to be. And everything had changed in an entirely different way.

Cooper swallowed. He hoped it didn't look rude, but it might be time to end the conversation.

'Well done with the media appeal by the way,' he said, watching Sharma's rare smile break through.

Then Cooper turned away.

'Gavin,' he said, 'we need to get Lacey Bower down here from Sheffield. Preferably today. I want to take her into Lathkill Dale and see what she can remember.'

'I'll get on to it.'

'Is that the daughter?' said Hurst, overhearing.

'Yes.'

'Well, if I understand it, her mother disappeared ten years ago and her father was charged with murder. Now her father has gone missing too, and it looks as though he's the victim of a violent crime?'

'Yes, you've got it, Becky. Why?'

'We should be treating her with extra care, shouldn't we? She's only eighteen. She's vulnerable.'

'Everyone's "vulnerable" these days,' said Murfin. 'I once heard some do-gooder say that criminals who get prison sentences are "vulnerable to committing more offences". What rubbish.'

'Your opinions were always so old-fashioned,' said Hurst.

Murfin sniffed. 'What you call old-fashioned, I call common sense.'

'We'll treat her with care,' promised Cooper.

'Perhaps I should go with Gavin.'

'Only if you have the time, Becky. I know you have a lot on. We all do.'

Cooper turned back to Dev Sharma.

'Pass my congratulations on to Asha,' he said. 'I'll leave you to your suspect for now and I'll be in my office for a while, but then I'm going out.'

Sharma raised one eyebrow as he turned to watch Cooper go.

Cooper could hardly bear to read through all the day's memos. For a moment he thought of deleting them from his inbox unread. But there was always a chance that one of them was important and actually related to his own job and once he started reading, it was easy to relax and become absorbed in the minutiae of everyday life in Derbyshire Constabulary.

An amount of money retrieved through the Proceeds of Crime Act had been used to cover the cost of new radio equipment for the ShopWatch scheme in Edendale. The equipment allowed retailers to communicate with each other and police to share information about thefts or suspicious behaviour.

Shoplifting was a problem that not only affected retailers but had an impact on shoppers and people visiting the town. The POCA cash had come in after an application to the courts for criminals' assets to be seized and sold. Some of the money generated also went to pay compensation to the victims.

In a recent joint operation with other agencies, more than seventy vehicles had been stopped across Derbyshire as part of a crackdown on rogue traders who preyed on vulnerable people, trying to con them into paying for unnecessary or overpriced work on their homes. The day of action had been co-ordinated by the intelligence unit as part of a week-long campaign.

CID hadn't been involved in the operation, but there were countywide alerts to respond to reports of suspicious activities, especially in the villages, where dodgy traders targeted the elderly and housebound. That might actually have an impact on his team.

Cooper had hardly made any progress through his inbox when the door of his office opened. Carol Villiers again.

'What's going on, Ben?' she said.

'What do you mean?'

'Don't forget I've known you for a very long time. We grew up together and we were in the same class at school. You were never able to keep a secret back then. It was always written all over your face.'

Cooper laughed. 'I thought I was better at it now.'

'Yes, you are. You've had a lot of experience,' she said. 'And it probably convinces most people. But I know you better than that, Ben. So what's going on with this inquiry? Why are we giving so much attention to Reece Bower? At the end of the day it's just a missing person case.'

'You're right, Carol.'

'Of course I am. So?'

'We're pursuing lines of inquiry which were overlooked ten years ago.'

'Overlooked?'

'Well, that's not the right word. Interrupted.'

'You mean interrupted by the witness who claims to have seen Annette alive?'

'Yes.'

'So we're picking up where Detective Superintendent Branagh left off.'

'You know she was SIO at the time?'

'It's in all the files,' said Villiers.

'She was DCI Branagh then. I was just a divisional DC. I only saw Hazel Branagh from a distance. But everyone knew how frustrated she was when the CPS pulled the plug. She felt so strongly she couldn't hide that.'

'I imagine the whole team felt the same,' said Villiers. 'It was a major inquiry by the sound of it. A lot of effort went in to putting the case together against Reece Bower.'

'And to finding Annette's body. They were thwarted on both counts. All that time and effort went to waste. No one likes that.'

'So Superintendent Branagh is bringing in a fresh pair of eyes,' observed Villiers. 'I understand that. But why were you so keen to pick up an old case?'

Cooper thought about his answer for a moment. He couldn't have explained the reason for it at the time. During his conversation with Hazel Branagh, it had just felt the right thing to do. Otherwise, he would have been disappointing her.

'Because I know that frustration,' he said finally. 'You're right, Carol, it affects everyone, even when you aren't directly involved. The Annette Bower case is one of the first major inquiries I can remember in

Edendale. There's a great sense of satisfaction when you're part of a team which brings an inquiry to a successful conclusion. But you share the despair and disappointment when it all comes to nothing. I feel exactly the same way that Superintendent Branagh does. I'm glad she asked me to do this. I wouldn't have wanted her to pass it to someone else. I owe an obligation to Hazel Branagh. She's been very good to me over the years.'

'So you're paying back a personal debt?'

'Something like that.'

'It's okay, Ben. I can relate to that.'

'We can manage anyway,' said Cooper. 'The barn fire is manslaughter at most, possibly an accidental death. Shane Curtis may even have been involved in starting the fire himself. The robberies – it's just a matter of time until they make a mistake or we get some correlation in the witness statements.'

'There's the murder of a Polish man in Shirebrook,' said Villiers.

'Not our case. It's in Bolsover LPU, and EMSOU are on the case anyway.'

'So they are.'

'Carol, did you finish going through the address book Naomi Heath gave us?'

'Sorry, Ben. DS Sharma didn't think it was a priority, considering our workload.'

'It's okay.'

Cooper watched Villiers leave. He worried that if Carol didn't get a promotion soon she would be passed over in favour of Becky Hurst, who was bright and ambitious, just the kind of officer who attracted attention from the command structure.

Hurst would deserve it, of course, though she might need just a bit more experience. But he hated the idea of Carol Villiers becoming a sort of female Gavin Murfin, middle-aged and embittered.

Murfin appeared as if on cue, arriving back from his morning visit to Bakewell.

'Any luck?' asked Cooper.

'One of the old guys at a car repair business says there was a lad who used to come there ten years ago to visit his girlfriend. He had a red Nissan. I think that's all it was, boss.'

'The original inquiry team must have followed that up surely?'

'I suppose so,' said Murfin.

'What do you mean "you suppose so"?'

Murfin shifted uneasily. 'To be honest, I remembered this as soon as I saw the units. We went to check them out back then. I was with Bill Osborne.'

'Your old DS?'

'Bill was a bit of a character, like I said.'

'A character? Gavin, are you telling me Detective Sergeant Osborne was bent in some way?'

'No, no . . . it's a bit more complicated than that. It *was* ten years ago. And Bill was old school.'

Cooper frowned. He had a feeling he wasn't going to like this at all. Murfin looked as guilty as hell.

'Gavin, you'd better sit down and tell me all about it.'

Murfin collapsed wearily in a chair. 'Well, when the two of us went to the industrial units we soon tracked down the lad with the red Nissan. It turned out he was the son of a mate of Bill's who'd gone a bit off the rails, like. He wasn't a bad lad really. At least, that's what Bill said.'

'And DS Osborne didn't want this person interviewed for some reason?'

'He was just visiting his girlfriend,' said Murfin. 'She worked at one of the other units, in the office.'

'Come on, let's have it, Gavin.'

Murfin sighed. 'He'd been involved in a bit of a domestic dispute. He'd been in court and he was put on probation. One of the conditions was a restriction on his movements. He wasn't supposed to go within five miles of Bakewell. But he badly wanted to see her. If he'd been reported, he would have gone to prison for breach of his probation order. He had nothing to do with Annette Bower's disappearance, Ben.'

'So you and Bill Osborne covered it up?'

'Bill told the incident room we couldn't trace the owner of the red Nissan. It wasn't important.'

'And you went along with it?'

'It was ten years ago,' repeated Murfin.

'So you said.' Cooper tapped a pen on his desk. 'Where is DS Osborne now? He retired, didn't he?'

'Yes, he was only a few months away from his thirty at the time. So I reckon he didn't really care all that much about, you know—'

'Disciplinary hearings?'

'Right.'

'But the interests of the inquiry didn't matter either, I take it?'

'He went abroad,' said Murfin, as if it was a defence. 'He lives in Portugal now.'

'I'm going to have to put this in my report,' said Cooper. 'I'm sorry, Gavin.'

'Bill Osborne was very good to me,' said Murfin as he stood up to leave the office. 'You understand, Ben.'

Cooper sighed. That was one of the difficulties of his position. He understood all too well.

He put on his jacket, and put his head round the door of the CID room.

'Are you okay with the arson inquiry, Dev?'

Sharma turned to him. 'It seems fairly straightforward, Inspector. Reckless endangerment of life. A charge of involuntary manslaughter at the most. Our two suspects are juveniles, so they'll go to youth court for remand.'

Cooper nodded. 'Keep me up to date with how you're getting on. What about the armed robbery?'

'DC Hurst is following some lines of inquiry and we're gathering the intelligence together. I'm hopeful of an arrest soon.'

'Great job.'

Cooper was conscious of the quizzical look DS Sharma gave him as he left. No doubt Sharma wanted to ask him the same questions that Carol Villiers had. But in Sharma's case, they didn't know each other well enough.

Derbyshire Cave Rescue Organisation were already on the scene this morning. Cooper recognised their yellow Iveco rescue vehicle with the red-and-white checkerboard pattern and blue lights parked at the rendezvous

273

point he'd established in Lathkill Dale. The back doors of the rescue vehicle were open, revealing an equipment storage area.

Cooper knew he was lucky to get their assistance for an extended period. A call-out could take them away to a serious incident at any moment, anywhere.

The DCRO controller had a grey beard that stuck out in tufts around the straps of his red helmet. He'd been on operations in Lathkill Dale before.

'Actually, that shaft behind Bateman's House originally housed a water-powered pumping engine that was installed at sough level to drain the flooded mines,' he said. 'They put it thirty-six feet down, then built the house over it to hide the pump.'

'To hide it? Why?' asked Cooper.

'To guard against industrial espionage, so they say. The pump's design was unique at the time. It was supposed to be secret.'

'Really?'

'So they say. Top secret. Mind you, it didn't work. Not in the long run.'

Cooper had always thought of the Peak District as beautiful on the surface, but with a sense of darkness lurking underneath. That feeling was often associated with the history of places. Even the most picturesque village could have a sinister and disturbing past. The signs of it were everywhere, if you cared to look.

But here in Lathkill Dale, in this pretty valley with its wooded slopes and crystal-clear river, there was genuine darkness underneath, the real blackness of the tunnels those old lead miners had worked in.

They said that lead mining had begun in Derbyshire as early as the Bronze Age. Mandale Mine was a survival of mining activity that had lasted into the late nineteenth century. Among the undergrowth here were the remains of shafts, engine houses, ponds, and an aqueduct. And some features whose names had been forgotten, and sometimes their purpose. Coes, soughs, goits, leats, stopes and gin circles.

It was the geology of Lathkill Dale that eventually put an end to lead mining. The mine companies had dreamed of riches from the deeper veins of lead. They had one massive problem, though – underground flooding. The water that poured into the dale and sank through the limestone found its way into the mine workings in vast quantities. Engines and waterwheels were installed to power underground pumps. But nature won in the end. The vast amount of water continually flooding through the mine workings eventually forced the closure of Mandale Mine.

Attempts to drain the mine by the waterwheel and a viaduct had been a disaster. So too had the notorious Over Haddon gold rush of 1894. People could be such optimists.

One consequence of the mining was that the water table had been lowered. In dry weather the River Lathkill ran dry. Even in the average summer there was little more than a trickle. The water surged back to the surface at Bubble Springs. But it also emerged here, from these soughs, the drainage tunnels dug by the miners to channel floodwater out of the mineshafts.

*   *   *

Cooper had managed to gather a makeshift team together to make inquiries around Lathkill Dale.

'We need to find out if anyone saw Reece Bower in this area on Sunday, or anyone related to the case,' he said. 'I'm particularly interested in sightings of Evan Slaney.'

'Slaney?' said Luke Irvine.

'Annette Bower's father. You've all got copies of his photograph. But anything else you can come up with may be valuable.'

'What if someone stole the wallet from him and decided to dispose of it here in Lathkill Dale?' said Irvine. 'That would make our efforts pointless.'

'I don't think that can be what happened, Luke. Consider the blood on the wallet, and the cash and cards still in it.'

'Well, it's a line of inquiry.'

'No, it's a line of speculation,' said Cooper. 'Not the same thing.'

'But—'

'Luke, can we get on? There's a lot of ground to cover.'

'Yes, boss.'

Cooper looked at Villiers.

'The schools are back, aren't they?' he said.

'Yes, autumn term started this week.'

'Thank goodness.'

Just over a year ago, a thirteen-year-old girl had fallen from a crag in a nearby dale while catching Pokémon on her mobile phone. She'd cracked her skull on a rock in the river bed and never woke from the resulting coma. In the past, there had been drownings in reservoirs or flooded quarries, children lost in caves or trapped in abandoned mine workings. But this year, they'd managed to get through the school holidays without a single fatality.

'At least we won't have any kids wandering about getting in the way,' he said.

Cooper looked at the map and considered the bottom end of the dale. A long series of eleven weirs led down towards Conksbury Bridge, the deepest of them known as The Blue Waters because to its colour. At Conksbury was the site of a deserted medieval village. Sometimes visitors would park at the bridge and walk up river towards Haddon. He mentally marked that end as a lower priority. It would have to wait until last.

Several members of Cave Rescue had come down the trail in their yellow-and-red oversuits with torches and helmet lamps.

'There's a cave here.'

'Let me look.'

The ground rose slightly, then dipped steeply into the cave mouth. The rocks above the cave lay tilted diagonally in cracked and broken strata, as if the earth had sunk on the downstream side. It was a distinctive opening, a dead black drop into the unknown.

And Cooper knew this cave.

He'd visited here as a child, been taken for a Sunday afternoon walk along the river by his grandparents one day during the summer holidays. The old man had his own way of warning children away from dangerous situations. Halfway along the dale, they'd stopped at this exact spot, and Granddad Cooper had pointed at the cave mouth. 'A monster lives in there,' he said. 'If small children get too close to the cave, they get sucked inside by the monster. He eats them all up, and he spits their bones into the river.'

In his recollections, Cooper could see himself staring wide-eyed into the dark cave mouth, picturing the monster. He had no details, but his imagination could fill in the gaps. It was something big enough to eat a child, a thing that lived in the dark. Not human, but no kind of animal he knew of either. He pictured teeth, claws, and a pair of red eyes which might even now be staring at him out of the darkness, waiting for him to get too close. He'd taken a step back nervously. And he remembered Matt laughing, sniggering at the thought of young Ben being sucked in by the cave monster. Or scoffing at the knowledge that his younger brother actually believed the old stories.

Cooper shook his head, trying to clear the memory. He looked around, found he'd taken an unconscious step back from the cave, as if he still believed in that child-eating monster.

'And he spits their bones into the river,' he said quietly.

'What did you say, Ben?'

He turned and saw Carol Villiers had come within earshot. Embarrassed, he pointed at the cave.

'We need to get this checked out.'

'How far in does it go?' asked Villiers.

'I don't know. I've never been inside.'

The controller rubbed his beard. 'We'll take a look,' he said.

Across the trail, a muddy path strewn with dead leaves led up to the remains of the mine itself. Cooper noticed signs along the edge of the trail marking the locations of abandoned shafts. The signs said 'Danger, please keep out'. They were polite, anyway.

Further up the dale, Lathkill Head Cave was still dry this morning. A few feet inside, the roof lowered suddenly, leaving only space for a tight, muddy crawl over huge boulders. That crawl might be possible for a fit person when the river was dry, but in wet conditions you would probably need breathing apparatus to avoid drowning in the icy cold water pouring over your head.

'Someone find out what the weather was like in October ten years ago,' said Cooper.

'I'll get right on to it,' said Irvine, pulling out his phone.

'I remember,' said Murfin. 'It had been chucking it down off and on for a couple of weeks. It was like monsoon season. It was one of the reasons the SIO held off starting a search in Lathkill Dale. She was hoping for the rain to stop.'

'Superintendent Branagh didn't mention that.'

'It would have been a nightmare trying to slide about in the mud on those slopes,' said Murfin. 'Our blokes would have been trampling any forensic evidence out of existence in that quagmire. And besides, there was water pouring out of those channels.'

'The soughs.'

Murfin nodded. 'Trust me, it was *wet*.'

'Thanks, Gavin.'

Right now, you would never imagine that a river emerged here. Yet on that day in October ten years ago, a huge volume of water would have been gushing out over these rocks. There would have been no way of getting to the mouth of the cave without getting your feet wet, and battling across the rush of the water.

Carol Villiers came up and saw Cooper staring at the cave entrance.

'No, Lacey Bower said it was a cave with a lot of water flowing out of it. She was quite clear about that.'

Cooper bit his lip. 'This is it. This is the cave the water flows out of. It's just not flowing now, not at this time of year. Water seeps down into the limestone, and there hasn't been much rain, so at the moment it's dry. In the winter, in wet weather, the rock can't absorb all the water that runs into the dale. So it emerges here, from this cave. That's why it's called Lathkill Head. It's where the River Lathkill starts.'

'I've checked the weather anyway,' said Irvine. 'The day that Annette Bower actually disappeared was relatively fine. Rain early in the morning, but it cleared up. The next day was wet, and so was the rest of the week. Gavin was right. The climate was against the inquiry team.'

'And in favour of Reece Bower,' said Cooper.

25

For a few minutes Diane Fry stood and watched young Eastern European men and women file in and out of the Zabka supermarket in Shirebrook.

After a while she walked inside and looked at the shelves of sauerkraut and sour cabbage. All the adverts by the door were in Polish. A notice said '*Zakaz – Spozywania Alkoholu w Obrebie Sklepu* – Consumption of alcohol prohibited in the shop.' Shelf after shelf of tins and packages had unfamiliar names. From what she could hear, there seemed to be few British shoppers around, and none of them entering the *polski sklep*.

She felt conspicuous. Though she hadn't opened her mouth, she had the feeling that everyone knew she wasn't Polish. She didn't feel comfortable staying any longer. She wasn't planning on buying anything anyway.

Jamie Callaghan was waiting for her when she came out of the shop.

'I just wanted to remind you,' he said, 'according to the files, Geoff Pollitt also owns four other properties in and around Shirebrook. They're all HMOs.'

'It sounds as though they're due for a visit.'

Callaghan looked puzzled. 'If Pollitt is a right-wing extremist, why is he renting out property to migrant workers?'

'I guess money overcomes prejudice,' said Fry.

'He's an unpleasant piece of work, isn't he?'

'You can say that again.'

'What a pity we can't connect him to the Krystian Zalewski murder.'

'There's time yet.'

Fry watched a couple of hatchbacks slowly touring the marketplace, then driving out again past the tattoo studio on Market Street.

'What kind of vehicle does Geoff Pollitt own?' she asked.

Callaghan checked his notebook. 'He has a white Saab registered to him. He also drives a plain blue Renault Trafic panel van. He uses that for his business, but there's no signage on it.'

Fry pursed her lips as she looked at the deserted marketplace. There weren't any children at this time of day, and even the cat was missing. She noticed a young man wearing jeans and a hoodie knocking on the door of Pollitt's shop, glancing over his shoulder as he did so. After a moment, the door was opened and he slipped inside. What could he be buying in that shop?

Of course, Geoff Pollitt was probably just inviting people in to look at the bloodstain on his ceiling. She wondered how much he was charging for the privilege.

The thought made her feel sick. There was prurience, and there was exploitation. And Geoff Pollitt had crossed the line. But then, according to the intelligence on him, Mr Pollitt had crossed the line several times.

Fry left Jamie Callaghan still canvassing shoppers at the *polski sklep* with the assistance of a Polish-speaking community worker. That should keep him busy for some time.

Geoff Pollitt answered the door of his shop when she knocked. She'd wondered if there was some secret knock, but whatever she'd done seemed to have worked. Pollitt's face peered at her with no recognition at first, then disappointment, then irritation.

'I'm busy,' he said.

'The shop seems to be closed, Mr Pollitt,' said Fry. 'What are you doing, stocktaking?'

'Maybe.'

'It's all right. You can lock the door again once you've let me in.'

He grumbled to himself as he took the security chain off the door and opened it a few inches further.

'It's not very convenient.'

'That's a shame. But I'm sure your community spirit will overcome any inconvenience.'

'Community spirit,' sneered Pollitt. 'That's a joke.'

'I'm not laughing.'

'I've kept a diary, you know,' said Pollitt. 'A record of all the incidents. All the East Europeans who've been up in court. Years of it, all logged.'

Ah, so Geoff Pollitt was the record keeper DCI

Mackenzie had referred to. All the court cases and newspaper reports cut out and kept in a scrapbook. That shouldn't have been a surprise to her, but it was. She hadn't pictured him reading newspapers.

'Did you know that eight million people living in this country were born abroad? Getting on for a million of them are Poles. Polish is the second most spoken language in England. You've seen all the signs written in Polish. You'd think you were in Warsaw.'

'Have you ever been to Warsaw?'

'Don't talk daft. Before we had the protection order, gangs were constantly hanging around in the market-place. They intimidated women and old people. There were groups of men sitting on walls and benches and under the trees drinking all day. It frightened a lot of folk off from coming down into town. It's bad for business. Shopkeepers were having to clear up cans and bottles every morning, and it was all Polish booze. Drinking in public is part of their culture, the Poles and Lithuanians. They even have sessions in the canteen at the distribution centre now to teach them about English laws, about our culture and the way to drink alcohol.'

'Is that a good idea?' said Fry. 'I'm not sure our culture and levels of alcohol consumption are much of an example for anyone.'

But Pollitt was in full flow. It was if she'd turned on a tap of bile and now she couldn't stop it.

'Why should folk here put up with it?' he said, ignoring her comment.

'With what?'

'Antisocial behaviour. Isn't that what you lot call it? The fact of the matter is, they're making noise, they're smoking weed, they're threatening people with knives,' he said.

'Can you give me an example?'

'Example?'

'A specific incident when someone was threatened with a knife by a Polish worker. It was reported to the police, surely? But we don't have anything on record.'

'Folk here don't always talk to the police,' said Pollitt. 'They haven't always helped. Like by trying to hide the identity of foreign criminals.'

Fry knew the notorious incident he was referring to. The previous year, Derbyshire Constabulary had gone to court in an attempt to withhold the identity of a young Polish man convicted of a sexual offence in his own country, because they feared reprisals against him in Shirebrook. His offence had only come to light after he was fined for breaching the ban on drinking in public.

On that occasion, the police argued that the rapid rise in the migrant population had created a deep-seated mistrust of foreign nationals among many of the local population, and that tensions were running high following incidents involving drunken Polish men, culminating in the stabbing of a British man and a knife attack on one drunken Pole by another. The judge had taken a different view, ruling that the young Pole was in no immediate danger. The man had left Shirebrook nevertheless. Maybe he felt the risk to his safety was greater than the judge suspected.

'So you want to get rid of all the East Europeans?'

'Aye. But that's just the beginning,' scowled Pollitt.

'What do you mean?'

'I don't need to spell it out. Everybody knows what's going on. We're just not allowed to say. We're not supposed to speak the truth these days. So we say nothing and take action instead. That were always the way of it, right through history. Nobody takes any notice of ordinary people until we get out in the streets, smashing their windows and giving them a good kicking.'

'So who's next for a kicking after East Europeans? Black people? Muslims? Anyone who happens to be mixed race?'

'Mixed race?' spat Pollitt. 'What does that mean? Nothing. It's one of your mealy-mouthed words. Fact is, you're either white or you're not. Anything else is just pollution.'

Fry felt herself growing hot. She gritted her teeth and her fists clenched in her pockets. This had been a big mistake. She would have to leave the shop soon or she might regret the consequences.

'I want you to know we're watching you, Mr Pollitt,' she said. 'Just in case you had any plans for putting your ideas into action.'

'Oh, like I'm going to let you lot know if I do.'

With a smile he watched her leave, as if he'd won the encounter. Glad to be out of the shop, Fry went to sit in her car and looked for something to distract herself. She opened the intelligence file she'd been given on Shirebrook. What sort of place was this really?

A summary of statistics showed a population density here almost three times that in Derbyshire as a whole, and a high percentage of lone pensioner households. It was the most deprived area of the county, with worrying levels of child poverty and a large proportion of adults without qualifications. Mortality rates were considerably higher than average too, with early deaths from cancer being prevalent.

Fry nodded to herself. So life expectancy was low in Shirebrook? Krystian Zalewski probably hadn't known that. But he'd soon found out.

Also in the file was a map of the area affected by the PSPO, with the whole of the town outlined. A thick red line ran all the way around Shirebrook, taking in the town centre, the Model Village, and even the business park where the distribution centre was located.

On paper, the shape of the PSPO resembled an enormous sack, narrowing to a neck at Upper Langwith, as if all the problems could be contained within it. She sighed. Some hopes.

Twenty-six miles away Lacey Bower was standing on the trail in the depths of Lathkill Dale. She hunched her shoulders right up to her ears and shook her head at Ben Cooper.

'I told you, I just have this vague memory,' she said. 'Really vague, but it's there in my mind.'

'Lacey, you were at school that day,' said Cooper.

She looked completely out of place in Lathkill Dale with her pale features and her lock of black hair over her face. She'd thrown on a huge baggy sweater which hung off her shoulders. It was odd that she should look so incongruous, when this dale had been one of her mother's favourite places.

'I know, I know. It's weird, isn't it?' she said. 'I was sure I could remember it, but when I asked Aunt Frances about it she told me it wasn't possible. She said it couldn't be from that day, just like you. Yet I remember being there with my father. I see it quite clearly. How can that happen?'

'It must be a false memory,' suggested Carol Villiers. 'It happens sometimes after a traumatic event.'

Lacey just shook her head even more vehemently.

'No. Do you know what I think it is? I think Dad went back there later, to the same place. And that time he took me with him.'

Cooper was watching her closely.

'You've got to show us the exact spot, Lacey,' he said.

'I don't think I can, though.'

'Think carefully. Cast your mind back to that day. No matter how young you were, there must be some more detailed impressions.'

'There was just this cave.'

'And water pouring out of it.'

'That's right. I was standing with my dad, looking at the water. I've told you all this.'

Cooper felt frustrated. It was like trying to drag a coma patient back to consciousness with familiar objects and sounds, attempting to jolt their memories with a favourite tune. He needed to find a way of inserting a catalyst into the brain through the functioning senses.

'Try harder, Lacey, please.'

Lacey stood on the trail and turned in a full circle, staring at her surroundings as if she was seeing the valley for the first time. Or perhaps she was re-living a distant memory that she'd thought was a dream, or a nightmare. Cooper hoped the recollections were becoming clearer, but he didn't have any great hopes.

'Nothing,' she said. 'Absolutely nothing.'

It was time for a bigger prompt. Cooper gestured for her to follow him.

'Come with me a little way up the trail.'

'If I've got to.'

'It might help.'

'Yeah. And it might not.'

He led her a few hundred yards up the dale. She followed slowly, with Carol Villiers coming up in the rear. They reached the spot where Lathkill Head came into view.

'Was it *this* cave, Lacey?' he said.

She peered at the gaping entrance and the slabs of rock.

'There's no water,' she said.

'Sometimes there is,' said Cooper. 'It's been dry, recently, but at the time your mother went missing, there would have been a lot of water flowing out of this cave. A whole river of it. Try to picture it.'

Lacey screwed up her face, stared hard at the cave, looked all around her, touched the stone wall by the entrance. At least she was trying. Cooper kept his fingers crossed.

'No, this isn't it,' she said finally. 'Definitely not. I've never seen this cave before in my life.'

Cooper knew he had no justification for keeping Lacey Bower any longer. She was adamant that she couldn't remember anything more that would be useful. He went back to the rendezvous point where the DCRO were still actively engaged in a search.

A few yards from the track was the tail of a deep sough, one of the channels built for draining water out of the mine. The top of the sough must be some-where up the hill near the ruins of the mine buildings. The route of it seemed to pass under the trail to emerge here and discharge into the goit, a long walled channel that fed into the river. Some levels of Mandale Mine had been lower than the valley bottom, though. There, water had to be pumped up to reach the sough.

Pheasants cackled in the woods and chased each other through the undergrowth. A buzzard cried plain-tively overhead. As he reached the edge of the goit, a vole scuttled out of sight into a hole in the rock.

The goit alone was about three hundred and fifty yards long with walled sides. How long was the sough tunnel itself, though?

Cooper dropped down into the goit between the stone walls and entered the portal of the tunnel. As he stepped inside, something touched the top of his head. He raised a hand to brush away a cobweb, but found something more solid. He shone his torch upwards and found a small forest, tendrils of vegetation hanging from the roof, the roots of nettles and ivy that grew on the surface. They'd crawled their way between the stones looking for nutrients, only to find themselves hanging in futile darkness.

In places the stonework gleamed with moisture. Just as the tunnel turned and lost the light from the entrance, it became rougher underfoot and he found himself stumbling over stones. Ahead, the sough appeared to be blocked. As he walked carefully back to the entrance, he estimated he'd walked about eighty yards to the blockage.

Cooper pulled a strand of vegetation from his hair and found the DCRO controller standing on the trail, watching him.

'It's dry at the moment, but that sough flows with water in the winter,' he said. 'It drains water out of the mine workings.'

'Can we get to the other end of it?' asked Cooper. 'There must be another section past the collapse.'

'Yes, we can reach it from the adit. That's a horizontal entrance into the mineshaft. Deeper in from the adit there's a winze, a passage connecting two levels of the mine.'

'Where is that?'

'This way.'

He was led up on to the northern slope above the trail. To the north-west of the sough outlet was a wheelpit, built to house a large waterwheel. Mine tubs had passed above it on a leat, arched over with ashlar stonework. The remains of a rectangular engine house emerged from the gloom, a three-storey fragment of stone with an arched window opening, like the ruins of a church, standing nearly twenty feet tall among the trees.

Halfway up the daleside was a circular chimney. Further on was an abandoned coe, a miner's hut, and the ruins of a powder house. The aqueduct was long gone. It had been supported by six stone piers, which still existed on either side of the trail. Near the water-wheel were a few remains of the smithy and an ore house.

The DCRO controller told Cooper there were several other known mine entrances in addition to the sough. They included two capped shafts and two adits, inclined entrances linking to the shafts below.

From here, two long rakes had been driven through the side of the dale and deep into the hillside as far as the Monyash road. Most of the length of these tunnels must have collapsed by now, he guessed. But who could tell? There was no way of knowing how far the rakes were accessible without sending in a properly equipped team.

They crested a rise under a cliff of limestone, and there was an iron grille in the rock face, closing off a shaft. It was fastened by a bolt into an iron bar. It looked as though it lifted on a hinge like a large cat flap.

'This is the main adit,' he said. 'We haven't checked this one yet. But, as you can see, it's closed with an iron grille, so no one can just wander in.'

'We'll have to enter it anyway.'

'Understood.'

Cooper knew it would be foolhardy to go in there

alone, even with the right equipment. Yet people often did. The DCRO could testify to that. They rescued solitary cavers from time to time. Even the most experienced could get into trouble on their own.

He looked into the adit, with its low roof and stone walls chiselled and hacked away by miners. It sloped steadily downwards into complete darkness to a point where it reached the shaft. He could hear the hushed voices of the cave rescue team whispering off the stone, a trickle of water running somewhere in the blackness.

He borrowed a helmet, turned on the light, and stepped up to the entrance, ready to enter the mineshaft.

26

In Shirebrook, Diane Fry and Jamie Callaghan had been sent to visit a member of the public who'd phoned the 101 number in answer to the press appeals, claiming to have information about the Krystian Zalewski murder.

The young woman was working in a hairdresser's, though the fascia outside the shop said it was a beauty studio. Several pairs of eyes turned to watch Fry and Callaghan as they entered, women twisting in their chairs to get a better look. The air was thick with chemical smells. Shampoo and hair spray, perming lotion and nail varnish remover. Hot blow-dried hair and a hint of ammonia.

The staff were almost indistinguishable from each other. They all had short, dyed blonde hair and were dressed in black.

Fry held up her warrant card.

'Nikki Frost?'

'Yes?' said one of the women.

'I'm Detective Sergeant Fry. This is Detective Constable

Callaghan. You phoned and said you had some information about an incident.'

She said she was expecting them and left her colleagues to attend to the customers for a few minutes. They squeezed into a back room with a kitchen area and shelves stacked with styling products.

Nikki looked nervous, so Fry made her sit down while she herself perched on a stack of cardboard boxes. Callaghan leaned against the wall in the doorway. They were crammed together in a densely perfumed space that had hardly any oxygen.

'It's about the man who was killed earlier this week,' said Fry. 'His name was Krystian Zalewski.'

'Someone brought in one of those leaflets you've been giving out. Then I saw all the police tape that had been put up at the end of the alley, and I sort of put two and two together.'

'Are you saying you were there in the alley when Mr Zalewski was attacked?'

'I suppose so. I must have been.'

Fry sighed. 'You'd better start from the beginning, Miss Frost.'

Nikki's hands were trembling slightly. Her black-painted fingernails jerked like a nest of beetles disturbed from under a stone.

'I was on my way home that night,' she said. 'I'd been at a spinning class. I can burn about seven hundred calories in a forty-five minute session.'

'Spinning?'

That puzzled Fry. She had an image of an old woman

in a shawl bent over a wooden spinning wheel turning out yarn, and it didn't seem to fit.

'Indoor cycling,' explained Callaghan. 'You do time trials and sprints and flats to motivational music.'

'Really?'

'I go to a gym in Mansfield,' said Nikki. 'I usually get there by train, because it's only a five-minute walk from the station at the other end.'

'Shirebrook has a railway station?' asked Fry. 'I haven't seen it.'

'Yes, it's on the Robin Hood Line. Trains pass through here on the way from Nottingham to Worksop. But there's no service to Shirebrook on a Sunday so my friend gave me a lift to the gym and we went to Pizza Hut for something to eat afterwards. Later, she dropped me off in the car park on King Edward Street, near the butcher's. From there, I walked into the marketplace.'

'Did you see anyone on the way?'

'Not really. I have a friend who works at Deep Pan Kid, and I waved through the window as I passed. I'm not sure she saw me, though. Then I cut through the alley to get home. I live just off Thickley Close, you see.'

'And what happened, Nikki?'

'Well, it was very quiet. It does get really dead in Shirebrook at that time, since they enforced the order, you know, with all those posters—'

'The Public Space Protection Order.'

'That's it. Well, there was no one around, and most of the shops were shut. I suppose I ought to have been more careful . . .'

She shot a sideways glance at Jamie Callaghan, a look full of doubt and a hint of fear. It was enough to cause Callaghan to shift uncomfortably and change his position against the wall.

'No, it wasn't your fault,' said Fry. 'You should be able to walk home safely on your own, Nikki.'

'I know, you're right. Everyone says that. But still—'

'Just take your time, and tell us what happened next.'

'I turned into the alley. It was quite dark there, but I could see the street lights at the other end. Then I heard the sound of an engine.'

'An engine?'

'Not a car. There were a few of those around the marketplace, but this was different. It was a motorbike, and it was close. It must have been at the end of the alley. I had this feeling that something was wrong, that I could be at risk, that I ought to turn round and run. But I kept on walking, just putting one foot in front of the other like an idiot. That was my mistake. One man jumped out from a corner and grabbed my bag. Another one came into the alley. They were both wearing motorbike helmets and leathers.'

'Did you call out, Nikki?'

'Not at first. I don't know why. Maybe it was shock or something. You don't know how to react in that situation. You hear about it happening to other people, but when it happens to you, it's different. I was thinking that they were just messing about, that it might be my brother and one of his mates having a joke on me. I couldn't believe it was really true that I was being mugged.'

'I know it's difficult, Nikki, but did you notice anything else about these two men?'

She shook her head. 'I couldn't see their faces. Like I said, they wore helmets with those dark visors. One of the helmets was red, I remember. I think the other might have been black. But it was dark, you know . . .'

'Yes, of course. Did they speak to you?'

'No, just tried to pull my bag away from my arm. I hung on to it like grim death. That was probably stupid, wasn't it? There wasn't much of any value in it. They say you should just let go, so that they don't hurt you.'

'So you struggled with them. How long?'

'It seemed a long time, but it must only have been seconds.'

'Did they threaten you? Did you see a weapon at all?'

'It didn't occur to me at the time. But since then I've been thinking about it. One of them did have something in his hand. He was holding it at his side like this.'

Nikki bent her right arm away from her body with fist clenched.

'Was it a knife?' asked Fry.

'I couldn't say. Not on oath. But considering what happened afterwards . . .'

'Okay, Nikki. So what did happen afterwards?'

'Another man came into the alley. I don't know whether I'd called out or screamed by then, or if he'd seen the men trying to grab my bag, but he ran to help me. That's what he did. He came to stop me being robbed.'

'And this was Krystian Zalewski?'

'I think it must have been. I didn't know him, of course. He was Polish, wasn't he?'

'Yes, he was Polish.'

Callaghan moved restlessly and seemed to be about to speak. Fry gave him a look and he relaxed again. It would have been better if he wasn't here at all, but she was stuck with him.

'Why didn't you come forward to tell us about him before, Nikki?' she asked. 'Didn't you see his photograph in the local paper?'

Nikki flushed, a mottled red spreading up her neck that looked oddly out of her place with her image. The cool blonde dressed in black, blushing like a child.

'Yes,' she said. 'But I didn't recognise him. It all happened so quickly that night, you know. Really fast.'

'So what exactly did you see of Mr Zalewski?'

'Not much,' said Nikki. 'He ran up behind me shouting something I didn't understand. When the two men turned towards him I managed to pull free, and I legged it. I mean, really legged it. I was terrified, and I wasn't stopping to look back. So I had no idea what happened afterwards. I saw the photograph, but I suppose I just didn't make the connection at first.'

'I see.'

Nikki looked up at Fry with a slightly puzzled expression.

'To be honest, I didn't read the whole story,' she said. 'I saw his name, and I thought . . . well, I thought it was just another row between the Poles. They get drunk and start fighting each other. You know what it's like. It happens all the time. I reckoned it was a row that had gone too far and one of them had got unlucky.'

Fry recalled the statistics. Two prosecutions for affray in the past three years, the dramatic reduction in incidents of drinking in public and drunk and disorderly offences. Even Geoff Pollitt's impeccable record-keeping showed nothing like the picture of Shirebrook this woman was suggesting.

'We have no reason to think the men who tried to rob you were East European,' said Fry.

'But it's what you expect, isn't it? After everything else that's happened around here in the last few years.'

'Perhaps.'

'Have you caught them?' asked Nikki, a small tear glinting in her eye for the first time during the interview.

'No, not yet.'

'I'd hate to think they've got away with it,' she said. 'That would be awful.'

Fry remembered the map of the Public Space Protection Order, with that thick red line running all the way around Shirebrook.

'They weren't contained within the sack,' she said.

Nikki looked baffled. 'What?'

'Never mind.'

'I suppose you'll ask me why I didn't report the attempted robbery at the time, too,' said Nikki.

'Yes, I was going to ask that. It's a serious incident. You should have contacted us straightaway. Why didn't you dial 999?'

Nikki shrugged and looked embarrassed.

'I didn't want all the fuss,' she said. 'I suppose that's the truth. It didn't seem worth going through all the bother of dealing with the police and giving statements and all that. I thought it was something that passed without any serious consequences. And I didn't lose anything. I kept hold of my bag.'

'But you did lose something, didn't you, Nikki? You lost something during the struggle in that alley.'

Nikki Frost stared at Fry as if she was a magician.

'Yes, I did. I didn't realise it until I got home, and I wasn't entirely sure where I lost it. For all I knew, it might have been at the gym, or in the toilets at Pizza Hut, or in my friend's car. But you're right, I did lose something. I lost an earring.'

'Thank you, Nikki. I'm glad you came forward in the end.'

'There was one other thing,' said Nikki. 'I saw an appeal on the TV last night.'

Fry frowned. 'Yes?'

'An Asian detective, it was. I didn't catch his name.'

'Something to do with Krystian Zalewski? I'm not aware of it.'

She shook her head. 'No, it was something else. A robbery at a corner shop in Edendale.'

'I don't understand. Why do you mention it?'

'There was a bit of CCTV. It showed two men robbing the shop. And there was a red crash helmet one of them was wearing. It looked familiar. I think it was like one I saw that night in the alley.'

The DCRO controller shone his torch through the iron grille of the adit. A totally incongruous object lay on the uneven stone floor of Mandale Mine, reflecting the light from his torch.

'Wait a minute,' said Ben Cooper. 'What's that?'

'A mobile phone,' said the controller in astonishment. 'It looks as though someone has thrown it through the grille. Why would anyone do a thing like that?'

'Why indeed?' said Cooper.

The controller unbolted the grille, and it lifted like a giant cat flap to be secured by a couple of hooks on the walls. Two Cave Rescue members entered the adit to reach the shaft. Their torches and helmet lamps illuminated the whole area.

'Don't touch it,' said Cooper.

He pulled out an evidence bag form the pocket of his jacket and pulled on a pair of gloves. Stooping, he gathered up the phone and slipped it carefully into the bag. It was an iPhone 7. He pressed the home button, but nothing happened. Then he remembered that the button was a pressure sensitive fingerprint scanner. It wouldn't work while he was wearing gloves, or even inside the bag. He tried the power button on the side, but still got nothing. The battery was most likely dead.

It would have to go back to the lab for examination. In the meantime, he had little doubt who it belonged to.

'Are we okay to go in now?' asked the controller.

'Let's do it.'

You were supposed to check out the area when you arrived at a scene, make sure you knew where all the entrances and safe exits were. That kind of knowledge could save your life in a dangerous situation. But how could he do that here? No one knew how many entrances there where to these mine workings, which passages might lead to the surface and which were blocked at some point before they got there.

Entering the shaft, Cooper felt the instant change of temperature as the chill struck through the rock. He sensed the alteration in sound too, as the peace of the woods was lost and the noise of his own movements became amplified, the sound of his breathing too loud in the enclosed space. He watched his breath cloud in front of his face, and a drop of moisture glittered in his torchlight as it fell from the roof.

The mineshaft itself was quite large. Downstream from the adit entrance Cooper could see the arched and fragile top end of Mandale Sough, which finished in the collapse he'd reached from the other side.

A DCRO team set off to wade through the passage. They were soon lost from sight. Some levels of Mandale Mine were a long way from the entrance.

'You can just about creep through a gap here,' said the controller. 'There's a capped vertical shaft to the left, and the sough continues for some way to the right. Further on, the passages become lower, and a lot wetter.'

Cooper saw remnants of blackened timbers against the walls of rock.

'What are those?'

'Down there is a section where we carried out a rescue a few years ago. We brought the timbers in to hold up the roof while we led some trapped cavers to safety.'

'Hold the roof up?'

'Well, you never know. Parts of the mine are unstable. It's inevitable, given the amount of water flowing through it. You've seen the collapse in the sough. It could happen in any part of the mine just as easily.'

'So this search is risky.'

'As long as we take proper precautions, we'll be fine. But some areas are inaccessible, you understand that, don't you? We'll have to wait until the teams come back.'

Cooper hated waiting. But after what seemed a long time, helmet lamp beams appeared and the DCRO teams began to return and report to the controller.

He shook his head at Cooper.

'There's nothing down here.'

'So it seems.'

'One of the teams did find something, but it turned out to be an animal. You'd be surprised how often that happens.'

'I suppose so.'

Cooper knew that many of their call-outs were for animals. A dog, a calf, or half a dozen sheep that had fallen into old mineshafts. A dead badger rotting in a passage. A caver once spotted what he thought could have been human remains down a mine working. A small DCRO team investigated and found the suspicious object was actually a very old and decrepit cuddly toy.

The controller wiped across his forehead below the rim of his helmet.

'A few years ago,' he said, 'the RSPCA and the Fire Service called us out after a calf fell into a recently collapsed mineshaft. The shaft was about fifty feet deep, and the top ten feet or so were through loose soil and rock. Very dangerous to descend. We decided to remove the loose material around the shaft top and stabilise it to see if we could make a safe descent to bring the animal to the surface in a sling. It took hours of digging by hand and with a JCB to make the top section of the shaft safe and install a platform. We were sending up bags of loose material to the surface to clear it out. But we did eventually reach the calf.'

'Did you get it out?' asked Cooper absently.

He shrugged. 'A decision had to be made. Its position, its injuries, and the state of the shaft meant the safest and kindest thing to do was kill it humanely and leave it where it was. The team doctor tranquillised the calf and killed it with a captive bolt gun.'

'So it's still there?'

'Obviously. If you were exploring in there and came across its skeleton, you might get a shock.'

'The fact is, people don't always recognise a dead body,' said Cooper. 'Not if it's the remains of someone who's been dead for a long time.'

'That's true. It's more likely they'll get it wrong the other way round. Believe me, if there had been human remains in Mandale Mine for the past decade, someone would have come across them by now. Mine explorers do come in from time to time.'

Cooper nodded. That made sense. Was he on a wild goose chase?

But he looked again at the phone. For most people, this was as personal an item as their wallet. It was as if someone had chosen deliberately, planting clues that pointed directly at a specific owner – in this case, Reece Bower. But where was he supposed to find the owner of the wallet and the phone? It must be somewhere they hadn't they searched yet. Nearby, he was sure, there must lie a body.

27

The front desk had called up to let Cooper know there was a member of the public downstairs asking to see him. His first reaction was to tell them he needed to make an appointment – he was busy, after all. But when he heard that his visitor had information about the Bower case he gave in to his instincts and had the man brought up.

When the door opened, Cooper found himself looking at a man in his seventies, slim and sprightly looking, with bushy white hair which stood out from his head in untidy wings as if he'd just been walking against a strong wind.

'Eric Oldfield,' he said, holding out his hand. 'You're the detective inspector, are you?'

'Yes, sir. DI Cooper.'

'You look a bit young to me. But then, all bobbies look young at my age. Some of them I've just passed only looked about fifteen. I'm never sure whether they're actual police officers or just on work experience.'

Cooper smiled as he waved the man to a chair.

'I gather you may have some information for us.'

'Well, there's something that's been troubling me for years,' said Oldfield. 'I don't know if it means anything.'

'What is it?'

'It goes back to when that woman from Bakewell disappeared.'

'Do you mean Annette Bower?'

'That's the one.'

'It was ten years ago.'

'Yes, ten years,' he repeated, as if Cooper had said something profound and moving. 'I should explain that I'm a widower, twice over. A little over ten years ago I met the woman who became my second wife. Margaret was the real love of my life, I realised. We met at a local history group and we were soon head over heels in love with each other. It all moved very quickly. It didn't last, I'm afraid.'

Cooper let Mr Oldfield have a quiet moment. He looked as though he needed it. It seemed unnecessary to ask what had happened to Margaret. He'd introduced himself as a widower twice over. That spoke for itself.

'The Annette Bower case . . .' prompted Cooper gently.

'Oh, yes. It was in the news an awful lot at the time, wasn't it?'

'Yes, it was.'

'I didn't really follow it,' said Oldfield. 'We were so busy with our own lives that we didn't take much notice of what was going in the outside world, especially if it was something unpleasant. We didn't want anything to intrude into our happiness. We were so focused on building a home and being with our new families. We were very much in love, you see. That's the way it is, in the beginning.'

He sounded very apologetic. Cooper wanted to tell him it wasn't something he should feel the need to apologise for. It sounded the kind of life that everyone dreamed about. It was certainly what he'd dreamed of himself, building a home and starting a family. For him, it had never happened.

Cooper fought down a pang of envy. This man didn't seem so happy now, did he? And he was talking about the past. Perhaps that dream had fallen apart too.

'This Annette Bower. At first they said her husband had killed her, didn't they?' said Oldfield.

'Yes, he was charged with her murder,' said Cooper.

'But then they reported she was alive after all, and it went very quiet. It seemed he hadn't killed her, she'd just gone off somewhere. Her husband was found innocent.'

'Well, not quite,' said Cooper. 'But go on.'

'So I forgot about what I'd seen. It didn't seem to matter after that.'

'What *did* you see?' asked Cooper.

'I recognised a photograph of the man, the husband.'

'Reece Bower is his name.'

'I believe I saw Mr Bower that day, on the day his wife disappeared. In fact, I think I saw him twice.'

Now Cooper was interested. 'Really?'

Oldfield nodded. 'It was an odd thing, actually. When you're out there, you sometimes pass the same people going out and coming back. You say "hello" the first time, as you do when you meet a fellow walker. Then when you pass them again, you don't know whether to say "hello" a second time or just to smile or nod. Some people laugh as if it's a huge joke, or an amazing coincidence that they've run into the same person twice. But there's only one route, isn't there? You're bound to pass the same people.'

Cooper held up a hand. 'Slow down, please. Can you start from the beginning?'

'Sorry. I get carried away.' Oldfield took a breath. 'I'm a bit of an amateur photographer. I was out taking photographs of the old mine workings. Margaret was with me, of course. I took quite a few photos of her too. I got them out to look at them yesterday. It brought back all these memories.'

'The old mine workings . . .?' prompted Cooper gently.

'Yes. And while I was taking photos, a couple came past us. She said "hello", but he just nodded. That's the way it is sometimes. He looked a bit bad-tempered, so we let it pass. Had a bit of a giggle about actually, once they were out sight. And then the really funny thing . . .'

Cooper waited. He was sure there was a point to the story, if he was patient enough. And he felt Eric Oldfield was finally getting to it.

'The funny thing, Mr Oldfield?'

'It must have been about half an hour later, or perhaps a bit more. I was taking some shots of the viaduct buttresses. We'd walked off the trail a few yards, down towards the river, so I could get all the buttresses in one shot, looking towards the mine. And when I looked up from the viewfinder, there he was. The same man. The one who'd scowled at us when the woman said "hello". Only this time, he was on his own.'

Now Cooper felt a surge of excitement. This was what he'd been waiting for. He touched the photograph of Annette in his pocket, picturing her smile, and the friendly expression. She could certainly have been the woman who said 'hello' to everyone she passed on a walk. Did she also fail to make the return trip?

'Are you absolutely certain it was the same man?' said Cooper.

'Yes, certain. I even recognised the blue waterproof. He still looked bad-tempered too. He was walking very quickly, as if he wanted to get away. I had the impression he would have broken into a run if he could, but he didn't want to draw attention to himself or look ridiculous. Do you know what I mean?'

'I think I do,' said Cooper.

'And it was him. The man who they said had killed his wife, but hadn't. The man who has gone missing now. I know it was ten years ago, but I remember it clearly, every detail. It was such a happy day. I treasure the memories.'

'Why have you only come forward with this now?'

'Well, it was all in the papers again, wasn't it?' said Oldfield. 'And I read them now, more than I used to. There isn't much else for me to do, you see. Not these days.'

His expression had changed. He looked almost tragic. Some of the memories weren't quite so happy, clearly.

'I think I know,' said Cooper. 'But just tell me – where exactly was this? Where did you and your wife see this man? Where were these mine workings?'

'Oh, didn't I say? It was in Lathkill Dale, of course.'

Jamie Callaghan was making calls as he and Diane Fry left the hairdresser's in Shirebrook and drove down towards the Model Village.

'Apparently, the media appeal was in connection with a series of small-scale armed robberies they've had in North Division over the past few weeks,' he said. 'Nikki Frost was right – the most recent one was at a corner shop in Edendale. Two men dressed in leathers and crash helmets, who made their escape on a motorcycle.'

'This Asian detective she mentioned – is his name Sharma?'

'Yes, DS Devdan Sharma. Do you know him?'

'I've met him,' said Fry.

'It must be a coincidence,' said Callaghan. 'The red crash helmet, I mean.'

'Possibly.'

Fry didn't like coincidences, but she knew they happened. If this one involved Edendale divisional CID, it could be awkward. With luck, evidence would come to light that would rule out a connection.

Officers were still examining the house in the Model Village that had been raided the previous night. The presence of the police was no longer the spectacle for the residents that it had been a few hours ago, and when Fry found DCI Mackenzie inside he looked much more calm and relaxed.

'Anything useful turned up here, sir?' asked Fry.

'You might say that,' he said. 'We found some documents in the pocket of one of the men's jackets. One of them is some kind of agreement he signed for the rental of the house they were living in. It has the name of the owner-landlord. But there's also the name of an agent mentioned. It might be a name you'll recognise.'

'Let me see.'

Fry studied the paper. It was written in Polish, but the names and signatures were perfectly clear.

'Well, look at that,' she said. 'Our Mr Geoff Pollitt, no less.'

Dev Sharma looked pleased with himself today. When Cooper entered the CID room at West Street, Sharma was carefully carrying a large cardboard evidence box as if it contained the crown jewels.

'What have you got, DS Sharma?' asked Cooper.

Sharma smiled, a rare smile of genuine pride and pleasure in the job.

'A motorcycle crash helmet, sir,' he said.

Cooper hardly needed to look. 'Red, with white stripes and black stars?'

'Yes, how did you know?'

'Just a guess.'

'It's a match for the one worn by a suspect in the TV footage of the robbery at the Singhs' shop,' said Sharma.

'I thought it might be. Good work.'

'Thank you, Inspector. We've also brought two suspects in for questioning.'

'Even better,' said Cooper. And he felt genuinely happy for Dev and the team that they'd done it without him.

'They carried out one robbery too many. It was bound to happen. They all push their luck too far.'

'Where did this happen, Dev?'

'Down in the Matlock LPU. They robbed a small sub-post office and village store. Same MO – two men in crash helmets who got away on a motorcycle.'

Sharma explained the circumstances. This time the team had got a lucky break. They didn't come very often, so they all felt suitably grateful. And it was all down to the introduction of new technology.

The police station had continued to change in many ways. A new feature downstairs was the docking station for the body cameras. There were more than seven hundred cameras issued to officers across Derbyshire now, partly paid for by a Home Office Police Innovation Fund.

In this case a response officer in the Matlock area had been equipped with a body-worn camera, a Reveal RS2-X2 with a front-facing screen, attached to his equipment vest with a Klickfast mount.

More importantly, the officer had decided to switch it on when he got out of his car. The camera had caught several good images of the suspects on its high-definition video footage before they climbed on to their motorbike and escaped down the A6.

'A clear shot of the number plate,' said Sharma. 'The make of the bike, everything.'

'And the helmet,' said Cooper.

'Exhibit number one. We went straight round to the registered address in Clay Cross, found the bike outside with the engine still warm – and two suspects inside sharing out their stash. The crash helmet was in the hall, the weapons were in one of the bedrooms, and the house was full of items from their robberies, though it will take us some time to sort through it. We've also picked up potential leads to at least two other suspects.'

'Names?' asked Cooper.

'Two brothers. Wayne Crowley, aged twenty-six, and Earl Crowley, twenty-three. It will all be in my report.'

'Thanks, Dev. I hope the interviews go well.'

Cooper couldn't resist a twinge of envy. Two suspects whose luck had run out. In fact, fortune had swung the other way, and Dev Sharma had benefited. It would look good on his record when the time came.

An hour or so later, Cooper saw Dev Sharma pass his office with Luke Irvine and Becky Hurst. They looked tired and no longer quite so jubilant. Cooper put his head out into the passage.

'How are the interviews going with the robbery suspects?' he said.

'As you might imagine, sir,' said Sharma. 'A lot of "no comments". And when we do get them talking, it seems to be all about their political views.'

'Political views?'

'They're rather right wing.'

Cooper could understand now why Sharma had brought both Irvine and Hurst in for the interviews.

'Basically, they're racists,' said Hurst. 'They got on a rant about immigrants and the EU.'

'It's an issue about immigration, not racism,' put in Irvine.

Hurst laughed. 'If you say so, Luke.'

Irvine's face flushed. 'It makes me really angry when people have this knee-jerk reaction and want to condemn everything as racist. It's an attempt to shut down any discussion of immigration. It's an attack on free speech.'

Hurst appealed to the rest of the group.

'Did you see how angry Luke got? As soon as the word "racism" is mentioned they always insist what they say isn't racist, don't they?'

'He might have had some justification,' said Sharma.

'Come off it, Dev.'

'Well, freedom of speech—'

'Bollocks to your freedom of speech,' said Irvine.

Hurst's eyes widened, and Cooper could see she was about to answer in the same vein.

'That's enough,' said Cooper. 'All of you. Have you asked them if they're members of a right-wing organisation?'

'We'll ask them in the next session,' said Sharma, 'if we get a chance. To be honest, I'm experiencing a bit of a problem. The two brothers we have in the custody suite are from Manchester and their accents are very thick. I'm having difficulty understanding them.'

'Really, Dev?'

Sharma nodded.

'I'm embarrassed to say I may need a translator,' he said.

'What about the search of their address?'

'It's going to take long time to go through their haul of stolen goods,' said Sharma. 'They have all kinds of stuff at the address in Clay Cross, besides a pile of cash. They don't seem to have got rid of anything.'

'Perhaps they were waiting for the attention to die down,' suggested Cooper.

'Either that or they've been so busy carrying out robberies they haven't had time to sell anything. But there's one interesting item I'd like to show you.'

'Okay.'

Sharma came back to Cooper's office a few minutes later carrying an evidence bag.

'There were a lot of mobile phones taken from robbery victims,' he said. 'We happened to pick this one out. A Samsung Galaxy. It's an interesting one, I think.'

'Why?'

'There are a lot of text messages and emails on it. And they're all in Polish.'

'Polish?'

'One of the lads from scenes of crime is half Polish. He recognised the language, though he couldn't translate it completely. The incoming messages are all for someone called Krystian. And here . . . look at the email address.'

Cooper peered at the screen. 'Zalewski.'

Sharma nodded. 'That rang a bell, so we checked with the phone company. The number belongs to Mr Krystian Zalewski. His current address is in Shirebrook, Derbyshire. Well, when I say current—'

'He's the murder victim,' said Cooper.

'Right. The one EMSOU are scratching their heads over. I hear they've been pulling in members of the BNP.'

'They're working on the possibility of a hate crime.'

Sharma laid the phone on Cooper's desk. 'Well, it looks as though he might have been the victim of a street robbery. But one that went badly wrong.'

'Our suspects? They've never injured anyone in previous robberies. Threats, yes. People frightened and shaken up afterwards. But there have been no injuries. Why was this incident so different? Why did someone end up being stabbed to death?'

'He must have tried to fight them off, I suppose,' said Sharma.

'In a previous incident, when a victim resisted, they simply ran off. These lads weren't up for a fight. They relied on surprise and speed, intimidating a victim into cooperating, then getting away fast.'

'I don't know the answer,' said Sharma. 'We might be able to get to it during the interviews. We'll be adding a charge of murder, it seems. That might shake them up enough to get one or both to talk.'

'Of course.' Cooper leaned back in his chair. 'I suppose they must have picked up his phone after the attack. It was stupid of them to keep it.'

'Well, they're not the brightest of criminals, sir,' said Sharma.

For a moment, Cooper stared at the phone in its evidence bag on his desk. He could hardly believe that one of his team's inquiries had helped solved Diane Fry's murder case.

Cooper didn't have long to wait for the expected reaction to his latest message.

'Are you expecting a visitor, sir?' said the front desk. 'Detective Sergeant Fry is here from EMSOU Major Crime Unit.'

'Yes, I'm expecting her.'

'I'll send her up. She says she knows the way.'

Cooper hesitated. 'No, she's a visitor. Escort her up.'

'Will do.'

Cooper waited, wondering what he should do in the meantime. Straighten his desk, or leave it as it was to show that he was busy? He got up and moved one of the chairs back from the desk a bit.

A few minutes later, Diane Fry was sitting opposite him with a look of incredulity sharpening her features.

'You seriously think you've solved our case?' she said. 'That's a bit much even for you. Your little team can't compare with the expertise and resources we have at EMSOU.'

'I didn't think it was a competition,' said Cooper mildly. 'We're on the same side, aren't we? I'm offering our assistance.'

'The crime happened in Shirebrook,' said Fry. 'It's a long way from your Local Policing Unit here in the Eden Valley.'

Cooper didn't like the way she said 'Local Policing

Unit'. Somehow, she added a hint of a sneer to the phrase.

'There are no borders in Derbyshire,' said Cooper. 'People can drive from Edendale to Shirebrook without passing through Customs, you know. It takes less than an hour, even through Chesterfield.'

Fry frowned. 'What does Chesterfield have to do with it?'

'Never mind.'

'So what exactly have you got for me?'

He dropped the evidence bag on the desk with a smile of triumph.

'A mobile phone,' he said. 'Very useful, mobile phones. I've got one in my own case. It can tell you an awful lot, as long as you find it in good condition and get access to it.'

She leaned forward. 'Whose phone is this?'

Cooper knew she must have figured it out as soon as she saw the contents of the bag. There was no point in dragging it out any further.

'It's Krystian Zalewski's,' he said.

In Lathkill Dale, the DCRO had come back with a report of high carbon dioxide levels in the upper entrance of Lathkill Head Cave. A group descended the cave with a CO_2 meter to measure the atmosphere. On the surface, the reading was barely 0.01 per cent. The highest levels were found in a choke between two chambers called where readings went up as far as 2.31 per cent, where there was little air flow near the stream.

'In the choke, the extra exertion of climbing over

320

the rocks would increase the effects of CO_2, and the lower levels of oxygen. A short trip is fine in those conditions. But if you stay in too long—'

'I understand.'

The remnants of his own team had wandered back into Lathkill Dale and arrived at the rendezvous point. Only Carol Villiers and Gavin Murfin were left now, and he could see from their faces that there was no good news.

'We interviewed the people at the Lathkill Hotel in Over Haddon,' said Villiers. 'We also went to the Mandale campsite, and the Reckoning House camping barn. Nothing.'

'Have you checked the car park at Over Haddon?'

'Yes. Nobody has seen any suspicious vehicles. There were only a few cars there and we accounted for them all.'

'It was amazing,' said Murfin.

'What was?'

'I went in the toilets there. Do you know there are pot plants in the gents? And they'd been watered recently too.'

'Okay, you can call it a day. We can manage here.'

'See you tomorrow then, boss.'

The afternoon was getting late. Cooper knew he was no use here for now. He had to leave the search to the experts and hope they came up with something. It was time for him to get back to the office and do his own job. But he wanted to get one last look inside this mine.

'Inspector—'

'I won't go far in,' he said.

Cooper's urge was to go deeper in, and deeper, to keep going through the tunnels and shafts of the mine until he found what he was looking for. But if he got trapped or lost, it would only create more problems for the search team and put others at risk. He had to take some responsibility.

'Inspector, we need you to come back out, please. It might not be safe without proper equipment.'

'All right, I'm coming,' he said.

He couldn't resist taking one last look at the tunnel, a final sweep of his torch. The depth of the darkness was unnerving. It was easy to imagine anything in here. Yet anything, he felt, would be far better than nothing at all.

28

The twelve-mile drive up the A6 from Bakewell to Buxton was always spectacular, whatever the time of year. As autumn approached, it came into its best with the changing colours of the trees. On the final stretch, the River Wye ran right alongside the road as it twisted and turned through the limestone quarries and railway bridges near Pig Tor and Cowdale.

A massive restoration project had been going on in Buxton to renovate the Georgian Crescent. It had been built by the fifth Duke of Devonshire as part of his scheme to establish Buxton as a fashionable spa town, but had stood empty for years. An eighty-bed five-star hotel and thermal spa was due to open next year, a project estimated to have cost forty-six million pounds. Judging from the signs on the safety fencing, this was where Martina Curtis's National Lottery money was being spent. All those scratch-card purchases were helping to restore The Crescent in Buxton.

The bell of St John's Church was ringing the hour as they arrived. Parked in the square outside the opera house was a miniature red double-decker bus that took tourists round the town.

They mounted the steps of the opera house among a tide of people and entered the tiled lobby. The various parts of the auditorium were reached by a maze of narrow passages and even narrower stairs. Signs pointed to the stalls, dress circle, upper circle, gallery, and a series of boxes on either side of the stage.

They had seats in the centre of the dress circle on Row A, looking down into the stalls. He found he had to lean forward to see what was happening at the front edge of the stage.

'Do you want to rent a pair of opera glasses?'

'Why not? It's only a pound.'

For a moment he wondered how much Chloe Young had paid for the tickets. The programme was expensive enough.

Cooper couldn't remember much about his last visit here. But the interior of the building was vaguely familiar.

Stained glass on the promenades, ladies bar on Upper Circle floor with a portrait of Arthur Willoughby, a Victorian gentleman. Brass lights, a brass rail on the parapet at the bottom of the aisle. Iron radiators painted gold. A theatre manager's box to the right of the stage, and a box containing the lighting controls.

It was a long drop from the dress circle to the stalls.

'It was designed by Frank Matcham,' said Chloe. 'He was the architect of many famous Edwardian theatres. I think of it as being like a miniature London Coliseum. Grand, but on the scale of a dolls' house.'

'I'll have to take your word for it. I've never been to the London Coliseum.'

They settled themselves in the plush green seats. Cooper looked up at the ornate, domed ceiling. He'd never visited the Sistine Chapel in Rome, but he imagined it was painted something like this. Flocks of cherubs and angels floating on clouds and an immense amount of gilt had been used in the decoration of the interior. Gold edging glinted everywhere. Buxton Opera House was a little jewel box of a building.

Panels on either side of the stage commemorated William Shakespeare and Arthur Sullivan. Criterion Strawberry ice-cream tubs were for sale at £2.50, orange lollies £2. He found a tiny gents down a set of steps by the Stalls Bar.

Cooper found himself fascinated by the boxes. On this side, Box C stood over the stalls, while Box D directly overlooked the stage, with Box F above it. They were tiny, containing no more than two or three seats.

The orchestra filed into the pit and he knew they were close to the start. He spent a couple of minutes reading the synopsis of the story in the programme. But soon the lights went down and the curtains opened, revealing a candlelit church. The cast seemed to be dressed in ornate costumes with ruffles, frock coats and swords, but he couldn't quite place the period and location.

'When is this performance set?' whispered Cooper.

'The year eighteen hundred in Rome. Didn't you read it in the programme?'

As a screen spooled out the words in English, Cooper did his best to follow the plot. It seemed to be about a painter called Cavaradossi who helped a fugitive to escape justice and attracted the attention of a sadistic police chief, Scarpia. He was quite a villain too. Heartless and malevolent, pursuing his prey ruthlessly. He was always introduced by dark, demonic music that contrasted with the arias of Cavaradossi and his lover, Tosca.

After torturing him, Scarpia ordered the execution of Cavaradossi, but promised Tosca that the firing squad would fire blanks if she gave herself to him. Thinking she'd achieved their freedom, Tosca stabbed the evil Scarpia. But the police chief had lied, and Cavaradossi was killed. Tosca ended up throwing herself off the ramparts of the castle.

Tosca was described in the programme as 'a roller-coaster story of love, lust, murder and political intrigue'. As Becky Hurst had said, pretty much the usual.

'How long does it go on?' he asked Chloe.

'This is only the first act.'

'I know.'

'About two and a quarter hours, with intermissions.'

Cooper was impressed by Scarpia's gloomy study with a hidden torture chamber where Cavaradossi's screams came from, and he liked the sound effects – from the distant cannon fire during the *Te Deum* in Act One to the tolling of church bells and the sudden rattling shots of the firing squad.

He could see that Scarpia had a manipulative mind. The police chief had calculated that he could succeed in his objective by turning the strength of Tosca's passion to his own advantage. There was a moment towards the end of Act One, when the chorus came in on Scarpia's *Te Deum* that made Cooper sit up. There was one familiar aria later in the piece. Tosca's *Vissi d'arte*.

Above, and to the left, Cooper could see people in the boxes overlooking the stage. The upper box looked a bit high for comfort – though it would be ideal if you felt like throwing fruit or rotten eggs on to the stage after a performance.

He frowned, then looked again at the upper box. There were three people in it, one male and two females. He could only see them from the shoulders upwards. But as one woman leaned forward on the rail to look down at the stalls, Cooper felt a stab of recognition.

During the second act he was leaning forward to look over the low parapet when Young pulled him back.

'Careful,' said Young. 'You're not thinking of jumping, are you?'

'Just thought I saw someone I recognised,' said Cooper. 'I need to see if it's really them.'

She put a hand on his arm.

'Ben, wait for the intermission at least.'

Reluctantly, he eased back into his seat for the rest of the opera, occasionally casting a glance at the box to make sure the group of people were still there.

Cooper was struck by the scene in which Tosca quietly took a knife from the supper table and concealed it. As Scarpia triumphantly embraced her, she stabbed him, crying 'Questo è il bacio di Tosca!' – 'This is Tosca's kiss!'. The supertitles scrolled out her words in English:

Is your blood choking you?
And killed by a woman!
Did you torment me enough?
Can you still hear me? Speak!
Look at me! I am Tosca! Oh, Scarpia!

When he was dead, she forgave him, lighting candles and placing a crucifix on his body.

By the time Tosca made her fatal leap from the wall of the castle crying *O Scarpia, Avanti a Dio!* – 'O Scarpia, we meet before God!', Ben Cooper was watching Box F carefully.

Even before the thunderous applause had died down, he jumped up from his seat.

'I'll catch you in the bar,' he said.

'Ben, wait—'

But he couldn't wait. He needed to know for certain. Everything hinged on this moment, in the same way that Reece Bower's life had been changed by that positive sighting of Evan Slaney's.

He found himself on a narrow stairway between Box D and Box F. A door led into the Upper Circle, where a man was sitting at the end of a row, close to a speaker and a set of spotlights.

He heard the door of Box F slam. Cooper ran up the stairs. But when he opened the door, there was no one there. Too many doors, too many stairs.

Quietly, he cursed to himself. He'd spent so much

time looking at the photographs of Annette Bower that he'd impressed a very clear image of the missing woman in his mind. And he was sure he'd just seen her.

Diane Fry watched an old couple make their way down the street in Shirebrook. Jamie Callaghan was handing out more flyers with the appeal for information. Some passers-by swerved sharply away from him as if he was selling insurance. Others took a flyer, glanced at it, then dropped it in a bin a few yards up the road.

Fry shook her head. The idea that some of these people were still fighting the Miners' Strike from 1984 didn't make any sense to her. She had a suspicion Ben Cooper was right, though. He knew this place and she didn't. She would probably never know it, no matter how much time she spent here. She would always been an observer, an outsider, just like she'd been in Edendale. Someone who didn't belong.

She recalled her last meeting with Ben Cooper in Edendale. That case of the suicide tourists. And for a while she thought it had been the last meeting between them too. It had been the way Cooper said 'Goodbye, Diane' in that casual yet final way. She left Edendale feeling a period of her life had come to an end, and surprised by a sudden turmoil of mixed emotions she couldn't explain.

How could two words do that to her? They were simple enough. Just an ordinary 'goodbye'. He was distracted by something else as she was leaving and he hadn't looked at her as he spoke. That was all it was. That was all.

It was ridiculous that she should start trying to read deeper meaning into everything people said or did. Not now. She'd avoided it all her life, had watched people doing it and had shaken her head in pity. Such futility in attempting to second-guess what someone else was thinking, so much pain you could cause yourself by dwelling on the possible meaning of a word, an expression, a casual gesture. It was a tragic waste of time and emotional energy, not something Diane Fry would do. She was immune to all that. She left it to the Ben Coopers of the world.

She turned and unlocked the car.

'Come on, then, Jamie,' she said.

'Where are we going?' asked Callaghan in surprise.

'The pub?'

He smiled. 'If you say so, Sergeant.'

Ben Cooper was still distracted as he came out of Buxton Opera House with Chloe Young. Walking through the tiled lobby and down a flight of steps, he looked everywhere, staring at the crowds of opera goers.

'That execution . . .' Young was saying. 'Well, I suppose he was just a painter.'

Cooper stopped suddenly. 'There she is.'

'What?'

'It's her, I'm sure of it.'

'Ben—'

He let go of Young's arm and ran down the steps,

dodging between the crowds. He caught up with a group of three people, two women and a man, who were heading towards the taxi rank.

Breathless, Cooper came up behind them and touched one of the women on the shoulder. She spun round with a small cry of surprise.

'Who are you?' she said.

The man pushed himself in between her and Cooper.

'What's going on here, friend?'

Automatically, Cooper pulled out his warrant card and held it in front of the man. But he was looking only at the woman. Now that he stood right in front of her, he realised that she looked nothing like Annette Bower. Well, a bit perhaps. She was the same height, same build, and had the same colour of hair. The style of it was different, but that was to be expected. What he noticed most that she was too young. He'd been looking at photographs of Annette Bower from at least ten years ago.

'So you're police? What have we done?'

'Nothing, sir,' said Cooper.

He spoke to the woman. 'I'm sorry to startle you. Can I ask your name?'

'Hannah,' she said. She was starting to relax now and smiled at him quizzically. 'Hannah Moulton. These are my parents.'

'I think I made a mistake,' said Cooper. 'I've confused you with someone else.'

'That's all right.'

'Are we free to go, then?' asked her father.

'Of course. I'm sorry,' he said again. 'There's no reason to panic.'

Cooper jumped as an alarm began to sound. He looked around for a car flashing its lights, but it wasn't coming from the street. The woman he'd approached looked flustered and began to dig in her bag. It took her a minute or two to pull out a rape alarm and turn it off. She sensed him watching and met his eye with a small shrug and a rueful smile. Sometimes there was no reason to panic. It could just be a false alarm.

'Sorry,' she said.

'No problem.'

Cooper stood and watched the group get into a taxi. People passed him on either side, with the occasional wary or amused glance.

He turned and found Chloe Young standing behind him, shaking her head in bemusement. She looked as though she didn't know whether to laugh or not.

Across the road from the Opera House, geraniums gleamed in hanging baskets lining an arcade. A young man was half-heartedly asking passers-by for change. He was wearing a slouch beanie hat that made him look like an overgrown garden gnome.

They'd decided to try the theatre menu at the Old Hall Hotel. Chloe had been tempted by the salmon terrine and the pan-fried sea bass with crushed new potatoes, samphire and lemon butter sauce. Cooper chose tian of crab and apple salad, followed by fillet of pork with black pudding mashed potato, creamed cabbage, and whole grain mustard sauce.

According to the plaque on the wall outside, Mary Queen of Scots had stayed here between 1576 and

1578. Well, not exactly in this building, since the present hotel was built in 1670. It was likely that a lot of other events had happened here in the last three hundred and fifty years. Cooper was pretty sure he'd been to a wedding reception at the Old Hall some years ago. So it had played a part in his own life, in a way.

He looked across the table at Chloe Young. She was eyeing him speculatively over a forkful of sea bass.

'I suppose I seemed to have behaved a bit oddly in the opera house,' he said.

'I'm not sure. Isn't that the way you normally behave?'

'Only when I've got a bit too involved in an inquiry.'

'And how often is that?'

He laughed. 'Quite often, to be honest.'

'I thought that might be the case.'

'I'm sorry.'

'No, don't apologise. I like it. It means you're dedicated. Passionate about your job. That's a good thing, in my book.'

'And you're the same?'

'Yes, I think I am,' said Young. 'Though I try not to embarrass myself in public too often.'

Cooper laughed. 'You didn't get the murder victim from Shirebrook, did you?'

'Not in my mortuary. It's in a different area. But I heard about it. Sad case.'

'Mmm.'

He was conscious of Young watching him closely as he ate. Her eyes were keen. She didn't miss very much, he was sure.

'Is something else bothering you, Ben?' she said.

'Oh, just that it's Friday tomorrow.'

'The start of the weekend? People usually look happier about that.'

'No, sorry. I mean – it's my sister-in-law, my brother's wife Kate. She has an appointment at the hospital.'

'Nothing serious, I hope?'

'It could be.'

'I see. Well, she'll be in good hands.'

'I hope so.'

'You care about her, don't you?'

Cooper was taken aback.

'I care about them all – Matt, Kate, their two girls Amy and Josie. They're my family.'

'There's no need to feel embarrassed about that. I like it.'

There was more meaning in her gaze than he dared to acknowledge. Cooper felt a sudden rush of emotion, a feeling that he would like to spend the rest of his life with this woman. But it was too soon. He had to take it more slowly.

He toyed with his mashed potato, seeking a way to change the subject. He let a few moments pass, hoping it would feel more natural.

'So how are you liking being back working in Derbyshire?' he asked.

'I love it,' she said. 'It's like coming home.'

He felt himself relax. 'I'm glad you feel that way.'

'I'm starting to think that I'd like to live further out this way rather than in the suburbs of Sheffield. Totley is nice, and it's close to the Peak District of course. But it isn't quite the same.'

'No. I can't imagine ever living in a city now.'

Young studied him as he ate his pork.

'You know I have a brother?' she said.

'Yes, you've mentioned him. Martin?'

'That's right. He works near here, at the Nestlé bottling plant.'

'Oh, the one at Waterswallows, where Buxton Mineral Water is bottled?'

She nodded. 'They claim that the whole process from rainfall to bottle takes five thousand years. The water fell on Derbyshire at the end of the last Ice Age, slowly filtered down through about a mile of limestone, then was naturally pumped up again.'

'Is that true?'

'Martin thinks it is.'

'Five thousand years,' said Cooper. 'I thought the last Ice Age was longer ago than that.'

'Me too. Though actually the scientists say we're still in an Ice Age now.'

'It feels like it sometimes.'

'Well, that's the way I think of Derbyshire,' said Young. 'A long, slow process of absorption, until you think what you're looking for has long since vanished. Then up it comes again, out of the landscape.'

'Ah, like my missing body. It might just pop up again, after ten years.'

She smiled. 'You never know.'

'It would be nice. But I'm not depending on help from the Peak District landscape. It doesn't always yield up what it's absorbed.'

They ordered dessert. Warm chocolate and vanilla

ice cream, glazed lemon tart, coffee and chocolate truffles.

'Nestlé relocated the Buxton Spring Water bottling plant a few years ago,' he said. 'It was right here in the centre of Buxton before that, on Station Road. It had been there for a hundred years or so.'

'Yes, that's right. The new factory is on the edge of the national park, so Martin says they clad it in recycled stone and gave it a wavy roof to fit in with the setting.'

'But the water comes from right here, at St Ann's Well,' said Cooper. 'Didn't they have to build a pipeline from the old site to supply the new plant?'

'Yes, more than two miles of it.'

Cooper paused over his coffee, imagining water flowing two miles underground below Buxton. Then he pictured the water being pumped out of the flooded mine workings in Lathkill Dale. Miles of underground tunnels and soughs. Would they yield up what they had taken? Would they even give him a clue exactly where to look?

He realised that Young was still gazing at him. In fact, she couldn't seem to take her eyes off him.

'I think you need to relax more,' she said with a lift of an eyebrow.

'How do you suggest I do that?'

'I'm sure we could think of a few ways.'

Cooper felt a warm glow that had nothing to do with the heat from his coffee.

'That's better,' she said. 'Your eyes look lovely when you smile.'

29

Day 5

Evan Slaney sat uncomfortably in Interview Room One at West Street. In the harsh lights, without the shadows of his lamps, Slaney looked pale and vulnerable.

Sitting across the table from him, Ben Cooper produced two photographs from the evidence log.

'Do you recognise this, sir?' he said, sliding the first one across.

Slaney barely glanced at it. 'Well, I can say with confidence it's a mobile phone.'

'Yes, it's an Apple iPhone 7.'

'Who does it belong to?'

'It belonged to Reece Bower,' said Cooper. 'As does this wallet.'

Now Slaney leaned across the table, touching the edges of the photograph with his large right hand.

'Those marks. Is that . . . blood?'

'Yes, sir,' said Cooper. 'That's blood. In fact, it's Mr Bower's blood.'

He withdrew his hand quickly with a frown of distaste.

'That's horrible.'

'You might be interested to know that we've checked all the calls and messages on Mr Bower's phone. Do you know who his last message was sent to?'

'I have no idea.'

'To you, Mr Slaney.'

Slaney sat back in his chair. 'To me? His last message was to me?'

'It seems so. He texted you asking you to visit his house on Sunday morning.'

'Yes, I remember,' said Slaney. 'I was rather taken aback. We hadn't spoken for a long time.'

'He doesn't say in the text what he wanted to see you about.'

'And I have no idea what it was either.'

'Did you go?'

'Yes. Well, I nearly didn't. I thought long and hard about it, but in the end I decided it might be something important. As I say, it was so unusual for him to contact me.'

'Did it occur to you it might be about Annette?'

'To be honest, yes. Only because it was pretty much the last thing we talked about. I couldn't think of anything else that he would have to say to me.'

'What time did you arrive at Aldern Way, sir?'

'About ten a.m. It was Naomi who let me in. Reece was out in the garden at the back, mowing the lawn and burning some rubbish.'

'How did he seem?'

'I thought he was very stressed about something, really vague and absent-minded. He looked surprised to see me, even seemed to have forgotten that he'd invited me.'

'So what did he want to tell you?'

'Nothing, so far as I could tell. It was all very mysterious. I came away none the wiser. In fact, I wondered if there was something he was anxious to talk about, but he didn't want to mention it while Naomi was there.'

'You think Naomi shouldn't have been there? He wanted to see you on your own?'

'And it went wrong for some reason, yes. It was very odd. And of course that was the last time I saw him.'

'He went missing later that same day,' said Cooper.

'That's shocking. Awful.'

'I need you to tell me the truth, Mr Slaney.'

Slaney laid his hands on the table, as if to draw attention to them. Cooper couldn't help looking, and noticed something odd straightaway. He could see that Slaney's right hand was distinctly larger than his left. The knuckles were thicker, the fingers longer, the palm spread more widely on the surface of the table.

He supposed some occupations might cause the development of one hand so much more than the other. He doubted accountancy was one of them, though. No matter how many years you spent tapping an electronic calculator, it wouldn't give you a hand like that. It looked as though it could crush a rock.

'Well, you're right,' said Slaney. 'I haven't been completely honest with you.'

'I'm sorry if I don't look completely surprised.'

'You guessed?'

'I can usually tell when a person is hiding something, though I may not always be able to tell what it is.'

'Does that come from experience, Inspector?'

'Yes, but often with the wrong sort of people.'

'This may not be exactly what you want to hear, though.'

'Try me.'

'He made a fool of me, you know. He convinced me I'd seen Annette.'

'Who did? Reece Bower.'

'He's a very clever man. *Was* a clever man, perhaps I should say. He fooled Annette for a long time too. She thought his affair with Madeleine Betts was over.' He laughed bitterly. 'She thought that was his *only* affair. Oh, yes. He was a charmer. Very persuasive. But they say that about psychopaths, don't they? They can be charming. That's what makes them such successful manipulators.'

'How did he convince you that you'd seen Annette, sir?'

'He was on at me about it constantly,' said Slaney. 'Showing me photographs of her, telling me over and over that we had to keep our eyes open, that one of us would see her walking down the street one day. We'd get a glimpse of her going into a shop or disappearing round a corner. And we'd know it was her from that momentary flash of recognition. Looking back now, he practically brainwashed me into expecting to see her at any moment. To be perfectly honest –

and I didn't say this to the officers who interviewed me at the time – but I thought I saw Annette twice before that last occasion.'

'In Buxton?'

'Yes. They were just as Reece said – momentary glimpses of a woman walking down the street. One time I thought I saw her turning a corner as I was driving through the traffic lights on Terrace Road. By the time I managed to stop the car, she'd vanished into Spring Gardens. I looked in the shops, walked through the shopping arcade, staring at strange women until I was in danger of getting myself arrested. I gave up in the end. And when I got back to my car, I'd got a ticket on my windscreen for illegal parking.'

'But you were convinced you'd seen her,' said Cooper.

'I wasn't sure that first time. I tried to be logical and kept telling myself I'd imagined a resemblance in a complete stranger. I tried to laugh it off. And then it happened again, and even a third time.'

'Was it the same woman?'

Slaney shrugged. 'How can I know now? I spotted her once sitting in the window of a restaurant at The Quadrant with another woman, and then finally there was the incident outside Waitrose. By the third time, I was fully convinced it was Annette I'd seen.'

'Because of the make of car she was driving and the coat she was wearing.'

'That's right.'

'But you only reported the one sighting. That final one . . .'

Slaney smiled sadly. 'I didn't want those police officers to think I was mad.'

Cooper recalled his own feelings after he thought he recognised Annette Bower at the Opera House the previous night. Like Evan Slaney, he'd spent too long looking at photographs of Annette. And he hadn't mentioned it to anyone, not even to Chloe Young. Now she probably *did* think he was mad.

'As you can imagine, I was very angry,' said Slaney. 'Angry not only that he was probably responsible for my daughter's death, but that he allowed me to believe she was still alive all these years. As far as I'm concerned, he killed Annette twice.'

'So Reece Bower used you.'

Slaney nodded. 'Looking back now,' he said, 'I have a feeling the photographs that Reece showed me were all deliberately a bit vague or out of focus. There were no posed shots. They just caught my daughter from odd angles from which she was only just recognisable. The human memory is an odd thing, isn't it? Given the right sort of prompting and manipulation, we can convince ourselves we remember anything.'

'You must have felt very betrayed.'

'Certainly.'

Cooper leaned forward and watched him closely.

'And was that why you killed him, Mr Slaney?'

Evan Slaney's face fell into an expression of incredulity. It looked so cartoonishly ludicrous that, despite himself, Cooper almost laughed at the sight of it.

'Me?' said Slaney. 'No, you've got that completely wrong, Detective Inspector. I hated Reece for that. But

I didn't kill him. I could never conceive of doing such a thing.'

Cooper sat back in surprise. For some reason, he felt he believed what Slaney was saying. But he couldn't be wrong, could he? There was just some evidence missing.

There was a knock on the door and Cooper was called out of the interview. Dev Sharma stood in the corridor.

'What is it, Dev? It must be important.'

'We haven't completed the search of Mr Slaney's house yet, but I thought you'd like to know about this straightaway, sir.'

Cooper saw he was carrying a small plastic evidence bag.

'What's in the bag?'

'A knife,' said Sharma.

Cooper looked more closely. 'But not just any knife,' he said. 'If I'm not mistaken, it's a woodcarver's knife.'

'The blade is about three and half inches long, with a birch wood handle. The make is Mora.'

'Where was it found?'

'In the hollow base of an antique lamp. A Chinese porcelain dragon.'

Cooper put his foot down as he drove through Baslow towards Bakewell. He arrived at the house in Over Haddon just as Frances Swann pulled up in her white Citroën.

'This is very inconvenient, Inspector,' she said. 'I've had to leave a class. I hope it's as important as you suggested in your call.'

'It could be.'

'So what is it you want?'

'To see your husband's wood-carving tools.'

Her face creased in bafflement. 'The tools?'

'Yes.'

'But you've already seen them. I don't know what else I can tell you about them.'

'Perhaps I should call your husband to come out,' said Cooper. 'Would you prefer that?'

'No, don't do that. Come inside.'

This time Cooper knew where Adrian Swann's workshop was. The carved owl seemed to watch him as he entered and went to the cabinet where the tools were kept. Frances followed him as he unfurled the canvas roll.

'Is there anything missing?' asked Cooper. 'Can you tell?'

Frances peered at the tool set. She seemed reluctant to get too close to it, as if she wasn't allowed to touch it. He could imagine that Adrian Swann might be very possessive about his tools. They gleamed as if they were polished and oiled regularly and a mislaid tool could be a disaster.

'Yes, you're right.' Frances pointed. 'There should be another knife. One with a straight blade. The curved-bladed knife is there, but not the straight blade.'

'How big is the missing knife? Seven inches?'

'About that, including the handle. The blade itself isn't very long. Adrian uses the knives for the fine detail on the birds, you know. I don't understand why it isn't there, though. He's very particular about his tools. He'll be very upset if it's missing.'

Cooper drew out the knife with the curved blade and turned over the handle.

'Mora,' he said.

'I told you,' said Frances. 'A Swedish make.'

'Who has access to these tools?'

'No one but Adrian or me. The only other person he would let in to handle his tools is my father.'

'Mr Slaney?'

'Adrian learned woodworking from him, years ago before we even married. Adrian has gone on to be much better. Dad was never really an artist. He preferred something primitive. He was never happier than when he was chopping wood. When he and Mum lived in the house at Rowsley, he kept their wood burners stocked with logs.'

'What happened to your mother?' asked Cooper.

'She died. She was killed in a car crash eight years ago, about two years after Annette went missing. It broke my father up, as you can imagine.'

'So she wasn't around to support his sighting of Annette in Buxton?'

'No. That was my father's personal conviction.'

Cooper put down the tool.

'I'm sorry, Mrs Swann,' he said. 'I'm afraid we'll need your husband to come in some time anyway.'

When he returned to Edendale, Cooper had Evan Slaney brought back into the interview room. He showed Slaney a photograph of the knife in its evidence bag.

'What about this, sir? Do you recognise it?'

'Well, yes. I know what that is.'

'Do you own a knife like this yourself?' asked Cooper.

'No. But my son-in-law uses them. I mean Adrian Swann. It's a wood-carving knife.'

'Do you know how it got into your house?'

'In my house? No. Adrian has been there a few times, of course, but he would never have brought his tools. He keeps them in his workshop at Over Haddon. He's very particular about who handles them.'

He met Cooper's eye. In fact, his eye contact throughout the interview had been noticeable. Cooper was rapidly coming to the conclusion that this man was telling the truth now, in a way that he hadn't done before.

'Mr Slaney, did you have a surprise visitor recently?' he asked.

Slaney stared at him. 'Why, yes I did. Have you spoken to her? Did she tell you she'd been here?'

'Who are you talking about, Mr Slaney?'

'My granddaughter, of course.'

'Lacey?'

'Yes, Lacey Bower. She's grown into a fine young woman. I'm pleased that she hasn't forgotten her grandfather, but I was surprised. I hadn't heard anything from her for a long time, not even a birthday or Christmas card. She has her own life to live, of course. I understand that. So it was quite a surprise when she turned up on my doorstep.'

'Did she give any particular reason for her visit?'

'Does she need one? But, no. We only exchanged small talk, very inconsequential chat. I asked her how her college course was going, but I didn't really understand the details. I know Lacey is struggling financially as a student, but aren't we all?'

'Did you think she'd come to ask you for money?' asked Cooper.

'Well, she has done in the past. When Lacey first went to live in Sheffield, she asked me if I could help her with the deposit on a flat. I had to refuse, I'm afraid. Times are hard for everyone.'

'But she didn't ask on this latest visit?'

'No, not at all. Lacey seemed a bit restless, to be honest. She didn't want to stay very long. She probably had better things to do than spend time with her old granddad in his gloomy cottage.'

'Did she stay long enough for you to make her a cup of tea?'

'Coffee,' said Slaney. 'She asked for coffee. I also happened to have some of her favourite cake in. She likes Genoa.'

'I see.'

Cooper recalled a discrepancy he'd noted in Lacey Bower's statements. He hadn't thought it was important at the time. On Wednesday, Lacey told him that she'd only ever mentioned her memory of visiting the cave to her grandfather. In fact, she'd specifically claimed never to have told her Aunt Frances when Cooper had asked her about it.

But yesterday, in Lathkill Dale, Lacey had let slip a different version of events. *I was sure I could remember it, but when I asked Aunt Frances about it, she told me it wasn't possible*. That was what she'd said. And they couldn't both be true, could they? So which should he believe?

Evan Slaney was staring at him across the table.

'I don't understand how this could be relevant, Inspector.'

'But I think I do,' said Cooper.

He stood up from the table.

'Are you going to charge me?' asked Slaney.

'No, sir. I have a few more inquiries to make, then I expect we'll be able to release you.'

'Well, thank God.'

Cooper left the interview room and walked slowly back to his office. He needed to think carefully about what had just entered his mind. Could it be true? Someone had been leading him up the garden path. And it didn't quite lead to the garden he expected.

He sat for a long time with a coffee going cold on his desk and letting his calls go to voicemail. Cooper was recalling his conversation with the neighbour in Aldern Way. The woman with the Yorkshire terrier called Henry. He'd forgotten her name now. But when he asked her about Lacey, hadn't she said something important. *She was here on Sunday, of course*. But Naomi Heath claimed not to have seen Lacey for weeks, and the girl had said the same. Almost exactly the same, in fact.

And there was Frances Swann, who'd lost contact with Lacey and didn't even know her address or phone number. Yet Lacey had let slip that she'd seen the carved owl sitting in Adrian Swann's workshop, ready for the show this weekend. How had she seen that, unless she'd been to the Swanns' house in Over Haddon recently?

Finally, Cooper thought about the knife, the nine-inch wood carving drawknife that was missing from Adrian's desk. Frances Swann had told him the only other person who would have access to the tools was Evan Slaney. Why had she volunteered that information? Had she calculated that Slaney would be so angry about the knowledge that he'd been manipulated by Reece Bower that he would blindly draw suspicion on himself?

But how could Frances possibly have known that it would lead to the discovery of the knife at Slaney's home?

How indeed. There was the crucial question. It ought to have been impossible for her to know that. She had claimed to be unaware of what had happened to the knife, just as she'd claimed ignorance of Lacey's where-abouts.

And along the way Cooper had become more and more convinced that Evan Slaney was guilty of killing Reece Bower. Now it dawned him that he'd been wrong. And not only wrong – he'd been manipulated towards his conclusion. Naomi, Frances and Lacey, they had all played their part in leading him towards that desti-nation. Up the garden path to what seemed an obvious outcome.

Cooper could have kicked himself. He'd been stupid.

Worse, he'd been gullible. During these last few days, he'd been the instrument of a conspiracy between three clever women. Naomi, Frances and Lacey. Together they'd taken their revenge on one man, and set up another to be the suspect.

And yes, they'd used a third as their pawn. Detective Inspector Ben Cooper. He hadn't believed everything they told him. But he'd believed far too much.

30

By late afternoon, a scene-of-crime team had finished digging out the flower bed in the Bowers' garden on Aldern Way. Reece Bower's corpse had been wrapped in layers of black plastic bin liner, tied with clothes line. The outline of a human body was clear, even through the plastic. Whoever had done the tying had made the line far too tight, as if afraid that Reece might escape from his makeshift shroud.

Cooper knew the smell would be overpowering when they opened those bags. He turned away and saw Dr Chloe Young waiting by the house to get access to the body. Sometimes, she had the worst job.

Naomi Heath perched uneasily in an armchair in the sitting room of the house she'd shared with Reece Bower, with a uniformed female officer standing over her. She was moving her hands restlessly on the arms of her chair, her head turned away from the window so that she couldn't see what was going on in the garden. It was too late for her to be in denial, though.

Cooper stood directly in front of her.

'You knew where he was, didn't you?' he said.

After a moment, she nodded. It was a curt nod, so quick and precise that he could have mistaken it for an involuntary twitch, a nervous response to his question. But he could tell the truth from her expression.

'Of course you did,' he said. 'You killed him.'

She didn't answer. Cooper nodded at the officer, who put the handcuffs on to Naomi's wrists and led her to a car waiting on the drive. No doubt the neighbours in Aldern Way were already at their windows to see her being taken away.

Carol Villiers came in from the garden, where Dr Young had finally got access to the body.

'Naomi Heath,' said Villiers with a note of surprise.

'She either killed Reece Bower herself,' said Cooper. 'Or at least, she was involved in his death and the disposal of the body.'

'Surely she must have had help. She couldn't have dragged his body out there on her own and buried him. That would take at least two people. And somebody tied those knots really tight.'

'Somebody angry, perhaps?'

'Yes.'

'But not Evan Slaney,' said Cooper. 'Not him.'

'Who would have thought a woman like Naomi was capable of it?'

'If you put people under enough stress, they're capable of pretty much anything,' said Cooper.

'I suppose so.'

'She was very clever, actually. She let me form my own conclusions.'

'By suggesting it was something to do with new

evidence about the disappearance of Annette Bower?'

'Yes,' said Cooper. 'And of course there was, in a way. The new evidence was Lacey.'

He waited for Chloe Young to finish with the body. She smiled at him faintly.

'Another one?' she said.

'Sorry.'

'This one is fairly fresh. A few days, I'd say, but the speed of decomposition has been affected by the plastic wrapping, which was fairly airtight.'

'Cause of death?' said Cooper hopefully.

'That's easier. He was stabbed.'

'Any sign of a weapon?'

'No, it was removed after the attack and before he was buried. Some kind of bladed weapon certainly, but not the usual kind. From the wounds, I'd suggest a knife with a short but very sharp blade. It wouldn't take any great strength, because a weapon like that could have been wielded by anyone. But you would have to get in very close to the victim to use it, Ben.'

Young looked at the well-kept garden and the French windows leading on to the patio.

'Not your normal sort of crime scene, is it?' she said. 'You wouldn't expect to get a murder in a place like this.'

'Actually,' said Cooper, 'in my experience, this is exactly the sort of place you're likely to get a murder.'

Later, when Naomi Heath had been processed through the custody suite at West Street, Cooper and Villiers went in to record the first interview.

Cooper watched Naomi's shoulders relax as she spoke about the events of the previous Sunday. She looked positively relieved. It dawned on him this may have been what she'd been wanting to tell him all the time. She'd just been waiting for right moment to get it off her chest.

But as she spoke, he changed his mind. Naomi wasn't relieved. She was proud.

And Cooper had to admit she'd pulled it off well. She'd always talked about her partner in the present tense, as if she never doubted he was still alive. It was a difficult thing to do, when you knew perfectly well someone was dead and not just missing. They might already be past tense in your head and your heart, but they still had to be present in your words. It took an unusual level of control to maintain that pretence.

But who had helped Naomi? Someone angry – that was what he'd said when Bower's body was found.

And there was another pressing question. Who'd left Reece Bower's phone and wallet in Lathkill Dale? It would have been a risky undertaking. During the day there were always walkers up and down the trail. A car would have been seen, an individual might have been spotted acting in an odd manner. It was hard to imagine who would have the nerve to risk that.

Wait a minute. There was one person who lived within walking distance of Lathkill Dale. It would have been no trouble for her to walk down the road one night and distribute the missing items in the dark, when no one was around.

*   *   *

Frances Swann was brought into Interview Room Two. The custody suite was starting to fill up, though Cooper didn't think he'd quite finished yet.

There was no pretence about Mrs Swann. On the contrary, it seemed that she intended to be quite open about her part.

'It was such a sense of betrayal,' she said. 'He was still having the affair, you know.'

'The same affair? With the work colleague, Madeleine Betts?'

'Yes. He'd either restarted it, or perhaps it never ended, I'm not sure. Annette didn't know that. Nor did poor old Naomi. He took *her* for a fool, all right.'

'How did you find out about Annette? I mean, about what really happened to her?'

'Lacey told me.'

'Lacey was only eight years old at the time.'

'It's old enough,' she said. 'Children at that age might not understand everything that's going on, but they still have the memories. Sometimes it's only years later that they manage to put the pieces together.'

He went back in to Naomi Heath, who was still waiting in the next room, a cup of water on the table in front of her. That was all she'd asked for.

'And Mr Slaney?' Cooper said.

'Evan Slaney was just as much at fault with his delusions. It was he who prevented Reece from being brought to justice. If it hadn't been for Slaney, it would all have been over and done with ten years ago. And we wouldn't have had to go through this nightmare.'

'He feels betrayed,' said Cooper.

'Oh, we were *all* betrayed, Inspector.'

'And you managed to keep up the pretence that Reece had just disappeared,' said Cooper in amazement.

She smiled. It was a tight, humourless smile.

'I learned that from an expert,' she said.

'But it was Lacey who brought the knife that day,' said Cooper. 'She got it from her uncle's workshop.'

'Possibly.'

'Oh, I know that's true.'

'Then why are you asking me?'

'What I want to know,' said Cooper, 'is who actually stabbed him?'

'I couldn't say.'

'Couldn't say? You were there, Mrs Heath, so you must know. Who stabbed Reece Bower?'

She didn't answer directly.

'It was an accident really. When it happened, we panicked. I don't suppose we were thinking straight, any of us. You do stupid things in the heat of the moment, don't you? And with three of us together, it seemed to make things worse. None of us was able to think it through logically. Someone said we should hide the body.'

'So you buried him?'

'We couldn't have taken him far. A body is heavy, as we found out. Oh, I suppose the three of us could have lifted him into the boot of a car with a bit of struggle, but the cars were out at the front on the drive, right by the road. All our neighbours would have seen what we were up to.'

'Yes, I'm sure they would.'

'So there was only one option. The back garden isn't overlooked. Frances remembered the police searching it when Annette disappeared. *They* thought it was the most logical place to dispose of a body. And so it was. And that's what we did.'

'All three of you?'

She nodded. 'We spent a lot of time digging. I can't believe how shallow the grave was when we finished because it seemed to have taken us so long. And then not all the soil would go back in again. It seems obvious, but we hadn't accounted for that. It took us another hour to disperse it throughout the garden so it wouldn't be noticed.'

Naomi stared into the distance, somewhere beyond the confines of the tiny interview room.

'It's funny, you know,' she said. 'Once you set out on a job like that, there's no going back. We couldn't put him in the hole, then change our minds and dig him up again, could we? The evidence was too damning. We'd already moved him, put him in the bin bags, dragged him out into the garden. There would have been no way of explaining all that when the police came knocking. When *you* came knocking, Detective Inspector Cooper. Besides, we thought, without a body . . .'

'There would no murder charge?' said Cooper.

'Well, Reece got away with it.'

'It wasn't because there was no body. He would have been tried, and probably convicted, if it hadn't been for the sighting of Annette alive and well in Buxton.'

'Oh, Annette's father,' said Naomi. 'What a gullible old idiot.'

'Tell me one thing,' said Cooper.

'What? Isn't it all clear for you?'

'There will be a lot of questions yet, I'm afraid,' said Cooper.

'Oh, of course. You have to build a case. Make sure the Crown Prosecution Service have a reasonable likelihood of a successful prosecution.'

Cooper read in her sardonic smile a reference to the failure of the charges against Reece Bower ten years ago. They were probably the exact phrases that someone had used then, perhaps the SIO herself, Hazel Branagh, as she explained why the prosecution would not go ahead after all. Naomi Heath wasn't around at the time, but the words would have been remembered very clearly by Frances Swann, he imagined. They were the words that had killed any chance of justice for Annette Bower.

'What I want to know,' said Cooper, 'is why you didn't just dispose of Reece's wallet and phone – or even bury them with him in that shallow grave? Why did you decide to plant them at locations in Lathkill Dale? Whose idea was that?'

'It was Frances's idea,' she said. 'She wanted to force you into searching the dale. Frances always believed you would find Annette if you looked hard enough, if you searched thoroughly, in the proper way that didn't happen all those years ago.'

Naomi looked straight at Cooper. He saw satisfaction in her eyes.

'And you know what?' she said with triumphant smile. 'It worked.'

Back in his office, Cooper was reflecting on the interviews and waiting for Lacey Bower to be brought in from Sheffield. He was convinced the three women had been in on the death of her father together but though the circumstantial evidence was strong, he wasn't any closer to knowing who had struck the fatal blow. That was a crucial question.

He suddenly jerked upright and looked at his watch. It was time to put in the call he was dreading.

He dialled his brother's number at Bridge End Farm, and it seemed a long time before the phone was picked up.

'Hello.'

'It's Ben. What did they say, Matt?'

And Matt said just one word:

'Malignant.'

31

Six days ago

Frances Swann stared at Reece Bower as if he were a complete stranger. His face looked drawn and haggard, but there was a strange light in his eyes, as if he was getting a thrill from the story he was telling her.

'I can't believe my ears,' she said. 'Is this some kind of joke?'

'No joke,' he said. 'It's all true, Frances.'

'So Lacey was right. You've lived a lie all these years. You've made us *all* live a lie.'

Frances turn to look at Naomi. She was sitting back in an armchair as if it was a perfectly normal day, an afternoon with the family. Yet when Frances looked closer, she could see Naomi's body was rigid. Her knuckles were pale, the tendons stood out on her neck, and a red flush was rising to her cheeks.

Reece made a dismissive gesture, as if it was all a fuss over nothing.

'Don't make a big drama out of it,' he said. 'So Lacey has let the cat out of the bag. But we've all got to carry on as normal.'

'Why? For you?'

'Yes, Frances.'

'And what about Annette?'

Naomi spoke for the first time. Her voice was distant.

'Reece, tell us exactly what happened.'

'Okay, okay. Well, it was a quiet day. It was a Thursday, late in October. The schools were back and the holiday season was over. I remember it had been raining in the morning, but Annette fancied she could tell from the sky that it would clear up. She liked to think she could read the clouds. So we got in the car and set off to Lathkill Dale for a walk. Because it was so quiet we managed to get right down to one of the parking places just above the mill. That was lucky. Otherwise, it's murder coming back up that steep hill to the car park.'

He paused, licked his lips, as if reflecting on what he'd just said.

'And she was right,' he continued. 'It had cleared up by the time we got out of the car. Annette was always right.'

'Was no one else around in Lathkill Dale?'

Bower shook his head. 'The rain had kept everyone else away.'

'Go on.'

'Well, we walked some way up the dale, then Annette wanted to divert off the path to look at the old mine workings. But there must have been an unmarked shaft . . . She fell, just disappeared from view. I don't know how far, but it was a long way down. I could hear her screams as her body bounced off the stone. And then there was a thud, far away. She was quiet

361

after that. Very quiet. So quiet that I didn't have any doubts . . . Yes, I called out to her, but there was nothing. I knew then.'

'Knew what?'

'That she was dead, of course. Dead, and completely out of sight where no one would find her. I couldn't believe my luck.'

'Your *luck*?' shouted Frances.

The blood was roaring in her ears now. Reece's face seemed to swim in and out of her vision, as if she was drunk. But she was stone cold sober. It was fury bubbling up inside her that made her feel intoxicated with rage.

Reece held up his hands placatingly.

'It was the best way out. You've got to understand that. Our marriage was over. We were doing nothing but arguing, and she was getting violent. Annette had been on and on at me all the way to Lathkill Dale in the car, and all the way up the trail too. Do you know, we passed a walker coming the other way, and she smiled at him and said "hello". Then, as soon as he was out of earshot, she started in on me again. It was intolerable. I couldn't have stood any more, Frances. She was out of control. If it hadn't been for this accident . . . well, it would have ended badly.'

'Accident?' hissed Frances. 'You call that an *accident*?'

'That's what it was. I didn't know the shaft was there. It should have been sealed up. It wasn't my fault.'

'She could have been *saved*,' said Frances. 'All you had to do was make a call.'

Reece shook his head. 'There was no signal.'

'What a pathetic excuse. You deliberately left her there to die.'

Now he'd begun to plead. 'Frances, I might have made a wrong decision in the heat of the moment. It was an accident, really it was. But it seemed so . . . so neat, somehow. It was a solution to all our problems. Imagine if she'd been badly injured? She fell a long way. She might have been paralysed, brain damaged, left a cabbage in a wheelchair. It was much better that she was dead than that. So I had to leave her there.'

Frances stared at him, wondering if he actually believed what he was saying. He was so self-centred that he probably did. It was all about his own convenience. Even the death of his wife had been a stroke of good luck to avoid a messy divorce, or worse.

'And afterwards?'

'I knew you were coming that afternoon, Frances. So I made up the story about her going for a run. I took Taffy out myself and left him on the trail. I knew he would find his way back home. But then things began to go wrong . . .'

Frances sensed Lacey come up quietly to stand next to her. Lacey's breathing was very shallow. She had that faint wheeze in her air passages that she suffered when she was stressed.

'Oh, the murder charge must have been *very* inconvenient,' said Frances.

'I was terrified,' said Reece, trying to make himself look small, like a helpless boy.

Frances sneered. That sort of thing didn't work with her.

'But then Evan had that sighting of Annette in Buxton,' he said.

'I always thought you seized on Dad's story a bit too eagerly.'

'Wouldn't you? It was my only chance. I didn't think it would have reached that stage. Not a murder charge, without a body.'

And then Reece smiled.

That was the final straw.

Naomi leaped up from her chair and ran at him, screaming. She raked her fingernails across his cheek and he lashed out with his fist, knocking her backwards. Frances ran forward to grab him, and Lacey was right there with her, pummelling at her father. In a second, Naomi jumped up again, blood spraying from a cut lip. Frances heard screaming that seemed to go on and on, but she could see nothing in the red haze that seemed to fill the room.

It felt like a long time before the haze cleared. Naomi had collapsed and was hanging her head towards the carpet. Lacey was kneeling over her father, who lay prone and still in a shaft of sunlight from the French windows.

When Lacey stood up, Frances saw a red stain spreading rapidly on his white shirt. And something else. A wooden handle protruding from his side, just below the ribs.

'Is he . . .?'

And Lacey said: 'Yes, Auntie. He's dead.'

32

It was market day in Shirebrook. But the market traders were already packing up to go home, loading their unsold goods into a small fleet of Transit vans, while council workers began to dismantle the stalls.

DCI Alistair Mackenzie had bought himself a burger from a fast-food van. The smell of fried onions was turning Diane Fry's stomach.

'So that's it,' said Mackenzie through a mouth full of burger. 'Job done.'

'Krystian Zalewski was trying to prevent a street robbery,' said Fry. 'He came to the assistance of a woman who was struggling with two men. That was how he got stabbed.'

'And the woman ran off when the attackers turned their attention to Zalewski.'

'Nikki Frost, yes. She ran away as fast as she could and went home. I don't suppose we can blame her for that. She had no idea what happened after she left. And she didn't know Zalewski either. Even when she saw his photograph in the local paper, she didn't recognise him. She only made the connection when

365

someone pointed out the spot where he'd been attacked. It was then she realised he was her rescuer, and he was dead. I feel very sorry for her.'

Fry felt as though her last words were lost in the cacophony of diesel engines and steel tubes being thrown on to the back of a trailer. Mackenzie looked at her with an expression of dissatisfaction.

'And how come Divisional CID got the suspects in custody before we did?' he said.

Fry took a deep breath. She'd been asking herself the same question.

'They just had a lucky break,' she said. 'It happens, sir.'

'A body-worn camera?'

'That's right.'

'Technology.'

'And luck,' repeated Fry. 'It was just a coincidence.'

'A coincidence? More of an inconvenience.'

'I appreciate that, sir.'

'Did you have any suspicion that it would turn out this way, Diane?'

'No. It was a complete surprise to me,' said Fry. 'I'm sorry.'

'No need to apologise. They were circumstances out of your control. Out of anyone's control.'

'We're on it now. A murder charge takes precedence.'

Mackenzie wiped his hands on a paper napkin and dropped it into a litter bin. A man on a mobility scooter buzzed past them, just missing Mackenzie's toes. There seemed to be a lot of mobility scooters in Shirebrook. A lot of old people's bungalows. A lot of England flags.

'DS Fry . . .' said Mackenzie.

'Sir?'

'Please try to make sure the next thing that happens is neither a coincidence, an inconvenience – or a surprise.'

'Of course.'

'So are we finished in Shirebrook? We've got the suspects locked up, we've got the statements we need. It's just a matter of doing the paperwork and putting our case together for the CPS.'

'There's just one more job I want to do here,' said Fry.

Mackenzie raised an eyebrow, but didn't question her. 'Do you need DC Callaghan?'

'Not really.'

'Well, keep him anyway, Diane. I'll leave you to it. See you both back at St Ann's.'

Fry watched him head back to his car. The stalls were almost gone now, the Transit vans had left. The marketplace would be empty and deserted again soon, just the way it had been when she first arrived in Shirebrook. Had anything changed in these last few days? It wasn't very likely.

When Ben Cooper and Carol Villiers arrived back at the rendezvous point in Lathkill Dale, the DCRO controller came forward to meet him. The man took off his helmet and ran a hand through his hair. There were streaks of mud on his face like camouflage paint, and more stains in his beard.

'We've looked in all the accessible places,' he said. 'There's nothing there.'

'Well, that just means we'll have to look in all the inaccessible places,' said Cooper impatiently.

'Where do you mean?'

Cooper hesitated. 'I'm not sure. But that's where we'll have to look.'

'Well, if you can show us, we'll look. Otherwise—'

He looked around the dale, with its steep slopes covered in trees and dense undergrowth, rising to limestone cliffs.

'Where is the main mine building from here?' asked Cooper.

The man pointed. 'Up the slope and towards the right. There's no path from here though. You'll have to hack your way through.'

'I'll manage.'

'*We*,' said Villiers. 'I'll come with you, Ben.'

A few minutes later, Cooper was working his way up the hillside with difficulty. Villiers had moved ahead of him and was ten yards further up the slope, pushing aside the branches of an overgrown elder tree and tramping down a patch of nettles. She was stamping on the weeds as if she really hated them, which perhaps she did. Some people were prone to get a bad reaction to nettle stings.

He looked down at his feet as he felt his toe catch on a root and had to stretch out his arms to keep his balance. He laughed at his awkwardness and wondered if Carol had seen him almost fall.

But when he looked up again, Carol Villiers had gone.

*　　*　　*

With a cold feeling gripping her heart, Diane Fry pushed open the scuffed door and walked into Geoff Pollitt's shop in Shirebrook marketplace.

'Wait out there, Jamie,' she called. 'I just want to have a word with Mr Pollitt alone.'

Callaghan hesitated. 'Are you sure that's a good idea, Diane?'

'I won't be long.'

Pollitt straightened up from behind the counter when she entered. He didn't look directly at Fry, but gazed past her to see who she'd brought with her. When he saw she was alone, he smirked.

'Can I help you with something, Sergeant?' he said.

'Why, what exactly are you selling?'

'Nothing that would interest you. Maybe you should try next door at the pet shop? They sell peanuts for monkeys.'

'We raided a house down at the Model Village on Wednesday,' said Fry.

'I heard. Not one of mine.'

'No, but we do know about yours, Mr Pollitt.'

He went a little pale.

'You can't do. You're just trying it on.'

Fry ignored him. He was right, of course. She was trying it on. But sometimes you had to bluff a bit. She hoped she was making him uneasy. When people were unsettled, they made mistakes, perhaps blurted out the wrong thing. It was something to hope for.

'It's all over, isn't it?' said Pollitt. 'They say you got two blokes for doing in the Pole upstairs.'

'Yes, we did.' Fry looked up at the ceiling. Yes, the

bloodstain was still here. It looked darker now. That could be bacteria growing on the blood. It wouldn't meet approval from a health and safety inspection. But then, what in this shop would?

'We're not leaving Shirebrook just yet,' she said.

'Why not?' said Pollitt. 'Are you starting to feel at home?'

Fry gave a bag of cat litter an experimental kick. It gave way under the toe of her shoe and a slit let out a trickle of granules. The crunch felt very satisfying. But it wasn't the only thing she wanted to kick.

'We've been watching your shop,' she said. 'You get a lot of visitors, don't you? People who don't seem to buy very much.' She looked around the bare shelves. 'Not anything that you have on display anyway.'

'So?'

'So what are they doing here? Are you having meetings?'

'Okay, yes. I get together with like-minded people sometimes. There's no law against that, is there?'

'Like-minded in what way?'

'Do you need to ask? You know for yourself what the problems are. Everyone can see it. Quite a lot of us think we're living in depraved and degenerate times. The EU has been a disaster for us in England. Brexit is our future. The Referendum vote gave us hope.'

'Did it really?'

Pollitt's lip curled.

'You sneering liberals,' he said. 'You don't understand, do you? You don't want to hear what ordinary people think, how immigration is destroying our communities and ruining our lives. You just put your hands over your ears and shout "racist". Well, it doesn't work any more. Things are going our way. You'll see.'

She studied Pollitt, feeling the anger growing inside her. He was a man of his time, a typical product of this moment in history. But that didn't make him any less despicable in Fry's eyes. It didn't make him any less worthy of being stamped out of existence, like the cockroaches that no doubt were infesting his stock room.

Fry took a step closer. Pollitt seemed to recognise the look in her eyes and he flinched as if she'd hit him. But she hadn't. Not yet.

A few minutes later Fry opened the door of the shop and stepped out into the daylight of Shirebrook market-place.

Jamie Callaghan had been waiting impatiently for her on the pavement. He looked as though he'd been expecting the worst. He stared in horror at Fry's hand as she rubbed her knuckles with a tissue.

'Is everything okay?' he said.

'Fine.'

'Are you sure, Diane?'

Fry shrugged. Callaghan went to the door and stuck his head into the shop.

'Oh, God. What happened to him?' he said.

'I think he was visited by a group of local men who took reprisals.'

'Polish men? East Europeans?'

'I don't know. They may just have been Shirebrook

residents who took exception to outsiders attacking members of their community.'

'He can tell us himself, can't he?'

Fry turned to look at Geoff Pollitt. He glowered back at her over the hand clutching his nose.

'He doesn't seem to be talking,' she said. 'Which has got to be a good thing.'

In Lathkill Dale, Ben Cooper was lying on the ground and peering into an impenetrable darkness.

'Carol! Carol!' he called.

He called again and again. There was no answer. Only a trickle of soil and stone sliding into the hole from the dangerously unstable edge.

'I didn't even hear her fall,' he said desperately.

'It's the entrance to an old mineshaft. They must be all over this valley.'

'How far down does it go?'

'There's no way of telling.'

'We need lights.'

'The DCRO team are coming. They'll deal with it, don't worry.'

But Cooper was hardly listening. As his eyes adjusted to the lack of light, he'd spotted a ledge of rock jutting out of a hole a couple of feet down. He twisted his body round and eased himself over the edge.

'No, wait. It's not safe.'

'She's probably injured,' he said.

'Well, we don't want two of you getting hurt.'

Cooper hesitated only a second. One part of him knew that he was being given good advice, that it was foolhardy to risk his own safety, that he should wait for the rescue team with lights and proper equipment. But he was here, right now, and Carol was lying down there, hurt.

His boots touched the ledge and his fingers scrabbled on the side of the hole. He could feel grooves and scratches and smooth surfaces, as if the rock had been attacked by hundreds of hammers and chisels. He got a grasp on a crevice and steadied himself then pulled out his torch and shone its beam down into the shaft.

'I can't see anything. There's a massive tree root in the way. She must have fallen right through it.'

'It might have broken her fall at least.'

'Let's hope so.'

'But we can't get to her. Too much debris has fallen in.'

'Is there another way to get in?'

'We can try to find one,' the DCRO controller said doubtfully.

'We've *got* to find one.'

More help arrived, and they began to scour the hillside for yards around the old mineshaft, dragging aside fallen trees and hacking through tangled brambles. Long minutes passed and it was almost half an hour before a rescuer held up a hand.

'Here!'

'Yes, we've got something.'

'It looks like the remains of a mine entrance, but it may just be a ventilation shaft, or a drainage channel.'

'If it goes into the same shaft, it's what we need.'

Cooper began pulling away the undergrowth, tearing

his hands on the brambles. Quickly other people came to his side and began to help.

'Inspector Cooper, there's something here.'

'What have you got? Is it Carol?'

'I'm . . . not sure.'

There was something about the man's tone of voice that made Cooper's heart sink, and his skin felt cold.

'Let me look,' he said.

'Be careful, sir.'

'I'm fine. Stand aside.'

Cooper pulled out his torch and shone it into the hole they'd made. The light worked its way along the edge of the hole until it hit something white and very still. An officer lowered himself down into the hole.

'It's a body,' said the officer. 'But it's not DC Villiers.'

Cooper stared at him.

'Is it the body of a male?'

'Hard to tell, sir. The head and torso are buried under a collapse. The rest of the body is skeletonised.'

'It will have to wait, then. Mark the spot. We'll come back to it.'

Cooper joined him in the hole. A passage ran off in both directions, hacked through the hillside by miners, one of the last workings of Mandale Mine.

He took a moment to get his sense of direction.

'This way.'

They had to stoop in the passage. The rock walls were worn smooth in places, in others left broken and jagged. A length of rusty chain hung from an iron bolt in the wall. Rotting lumps of timber lay crumbling underfoot. Cooper tripped over a jutting stone and the officer grabbed his arm to steady him.

After a few minutes they came to a point where the passage took a sharp turn. Rocks had tumbled from the roof here and it was a tight squeeze to get through, but he managed. Ahead was total blackness. He ducked to get the headlamp pointed forward. And his heart sank. The passage ended ten yards further on in a solid wall of stone.

But wait a minute. There was light coming through from above. Just a single shaft of it, almost hidden by his helmet lamp. Cooper began to move forward again. He was breathing heavily, and not only from the exertion. The air was bad down here.

He cast his light about the passage as he moved, conscious that he might pass over the opening to another shaft at any second. And then to his left he spotted an opening in the floor, a sloping access into another shaft. What did they call it? A winze.

The space around him was full of dust now. It swirled in his torchlight and settled on his skin. He could feel himself breathing it in. It formed a sour, rough coating inside his mouth, drying up his saliva. He was beginning to feel a bit light-headed. Any longer and he would have to retreat.

But there she was. Thank God she was wearing an orange waterproof. It reflected the light at the furthest limit of his torch beam and she was lying halfway down the slope into the next shaft. She was covered in dust and branches and small stones.

'I can see her,' he called back.

'Is she conscious?'

'I can't tell. She isn't moving.'

Even as he spoke, he saw Villiers stir. She moved her arms, then her legs, and began to sit up. He heard her groan.

'Carol, stay where you are. I'm coming down.'

She looked up, shading her eyes against the glare of his torch.

'Are you hurt?'

'A bit scratched and bruised. I came right through the tree root.'

'What did you land on?'

She looked at her hands, and wiped a smear of something dark on her jacket.

'Wet mud.'

'You were lucky. It could have been a lot worse. Wait a second, I think I can get down the rest of the way.'

'Careful, Ben.'

Cooper took another step and found himself slithering the last few feet to the bottom of the shaft. Villiers put out a hand and stopped his descent.

'You shouldn't have come down.'

'So they told me. Are you sure you're okay?'

'I'll be fine.' She winced. 'Well, perhaps a twisted ankle. And some of those bruises are going to be bad tomorrow.'

'We'll soon have you out when Cave Rescue get here.'

Cooper shone his torch around. A lot of soil and vegetation had fallen into the shaft and was scattered around their feet. The mud smelled like an accumulation of decades and decades of debris that had ended up in the hole and had lain rotting in thick layers at the bottom. That was what Villiers had fallen on to. Now she smelled the same way as the mud, ripe with decomposition. And so did he, probably.

He felt the need to support himself against the wall and realised the place they were standing in wasn't on a level. It sloped slightly downwards into the hillside. In front of him, a great slab of rock formed a kind of roof. Beneath it, a roughly hewn passage vanished into the darkness.

This wasn't a carefully constructed tunnel like the Mandale sough with its delicate and beautifully balanced stone arch. Miners had simply hacked their way through the rock here to get to where they hoped the veins of lead would be. They had left only a space wide enough for an average-sized person to walk through bent double.

A trickle of water ran into the passage from the muddy entrance. More water dripped from the roof, glittering for a second in his torchlight.

'It's very dark down here,' said Villiers.

'No one wants to die in the dark.'

'Especially not alone.'

'Actually,' said Cooper grimly, 'you weren't exactly alone, Carol.'

'What do you mean?'

'I think we've found Annette Bower. Or what's left of her after ten years.'

33

Day 6

'Well done, Ben,' said Detective Superintendent Branagh. 'A successful outcome. So the system's working.'

Cooper grimaced. He couldn't say it wasn't working, or it would be a sign of his own weakness. As usual, decisions were taken way above his head and he'd been presented with a fait accompli. He just had to make it work.

'And did Detective Sergeant Fry help?' she said.

'No, we helped her,' said Cooper. 'That's the way it works sometimes.'

'The case looks sound against the Crowley brothers. EMSOU are happy. The Major Crime Unit are preparing all the paperwork, so that's a load off our shoulders.'

'I hope Detective Sergeant Sharma gets due credit.'

'Of course. I've already made sure of it.'

'Good.'

'I'm very glad we resolved the Annette Bower case after all these years,' said Branagh. 'I have to admit, it's been a thorn in my side for a long time.'

'In a way,' said Cooper, 'it was taken out of our

hands. The Annette Bower case was resolved by others.'

'The sister-in-law and the new partner. They took their own form of justice.'

'And the daughter,' said Cooper. 'We mustn't forget Lacey.'

'The CPS are still deliberating about the charges,' said Branagh. 'Joint enterprise murders are difficult to prosecute these days. If we can't establish who actually committed the act, we're going to have difficulty getting a murder conviction in court.'

'Conspiracy to murder?' said Cooper. 'Perverting the course of justice?'

'Those certainly.'

'It's funny,' said Cooper.

'What is?'

'That we have a body this time. But we still might not be able to get a murder charge to stick.'

'Well,' said Branagh, 'I'm sorry, but that's the way it works sometimes, isn't it, Ben?'

Cooper smiled sadly. He would have preferred a neater outcome than this. And he was sure that Superintendent Branagh would too.

'The post-mortem on Annette Bower's remains shows no evidence that she was murdered,' he said. 'There's very little soft tissue left, of course, after ten years. But the pathologist says her skeletal injuries are consistent with a fall of about thirty-five feet on to a hard surface, followed by a rock collapse. She had a fractured arm, several broken ribs, probably a punctured lung. If her initial injuries didn't kill her, then

Mrs Bower would have suffocated under the collapsed debris.'

'Horrible.'

'Yes,' said Cooper. 'And her husband left her there to die. We've no way of knowing whether he deliberately pushed her into the shaft, or if it was an accident.'

'Well, we can't ask him, so it's academic now, really, from our point of view.'

'I would have preferred a tidier solution.'

'It's rarely tidy, Ben. You know that.'

Cooper had really been thinking of Annette Bower herself. Would she have preferred a tidy ending, a murder charge that would have succeeded in court and brought Reece a life sentence? Or would she have been happy with the outcome, the rogue vigilante justice that he'd met with, no matter how messy the results?

He couldn't know. No matter how long he stared at Annette Bower's photograph, he'd never actually known her in life. He'd only met her in death, a muddy skeleton in the darkness of a disused shaft in Mandale Mine.

'At least the arson case was simple enough,' said Cooper. 'Shane Curtis's killers will be heading for a youth offenders' institution.'

'Will that do them any good?' asked Branagh.

'Possibly not.'

Cooper recalled seeing the boys brought into the custody suite. Shane Curtis's younger brother, Troy, looking shocked and frightened at the prospect of court.

Nothing that happened to him now would help Troy. But Dev Sharma had once summed it up perfectly. *'People are capable of making such a mess of their lives.'*

When he finished the call with Branagh, Cooper sat back in his chair, hoping that he might finally get a chance to relax. It had been quite a week. The interviews and re-interviews had taken all day, and the initial reports had been written up. It was late afternoon, now, and he'd sent the members of his team home. They'd already racked up enough overtime for this month.

But this was the way it would be from now on. The caseload at Edendale LPU would never get any lighter. The system would creak at the seams for ever, or at least for the rest of his career. He'd been running from one thing to another like a man fighting fires.

Cooper felt something in his pocket and realised he still had the photograph of Annette Bower. He drew it out, found one corner slightly creased and tried to straighten it. Was it his imagination, or was she smiling more widely than when he first picked the photo out of the file? After these past few days, he felt as though he'd actually met her.

Then there was a knock on his office door and Dev Sharma appeared.

'Have you got a moment, sir?'

Those dreaded words again. Cooper nodded.

'Come in, Dev. I thought you'd left with everyone else.'

'Not quite. I won't be long. It's just—'

'Sit down. What is it?'

'Well, I wanted to let you know straightaway,' said Sharma. 'I'm being transferred.'

'Oh? Where are you going?'

'To EMSOU.'

'The Major Crime Unit?'

'Yes. I'll be based in Nottingham. It's an easy enough drive from Derby. Only half an hour on the A52.'

'A lot easier than getting to Edendale,' said Cooper.

Sharma smiled. 'Yes. Even when it isn't tourist season.'

'The Major Crime Unit is what you've always wanted, isn't it? You told me that you'd applied for a transfer before.'

'Yes, I didn't think I would get in. It's a stroke of good luck for me.'

Cooper studied Sharma for a moment. 'Actually, I didn't know there was a vacancy for a DS at the Major Crime Unit,' he said.

'I believe there's been a promotion,' said Sharma.

'Who?'

'I probably shouldn't say any more. I'm sure there'll be an official notice. I just wanted to tell you first, because I've really appreciated working as part of your team.'

'Thank you,' said Cooper. 'Though it hasn't been all that long, has it?'

'Unfortunately, no.'

But Cooper was thinking *'Long enough, to get what you needed from us'*. He tried to put the thought out of his mind.

'We'll have a farewell dinner for you. Remind me – where did we go when you first came to Edendale?'

'The Mussel and Crab in Hollowgate.'

'That's right. It was pretty good, I thought.'

'Excellent.'

'We'll set a date, then.'

'They haven't told me exactly when I'll transfer,' said Sharma, 'but it could be soon.'

'Does Detective Superintendent Branagh know?'

'Yes. She's already approved it.'

Sharma stood up. For a moment, Cooper thought he was going to smile, but he rarely did.

'Have you finished here today, sir?'

'Not quite.'

'Do you want me to help?'

'No, go home,' said Cooper. 'It's been a long week.'

Sharma went back to the CID room, leaving Cooper alone again, contemplating yet more changes. This job certainly kept him on his toes. Like the officer with the notice taped on his back, he'd become a firefighter, a paramedic and a social worker. Not to mention the man who wrote reports and answered emails.

Cooper pushed back his chair and put on his jacket. There was one more thing he had to do before he finished the paperwork on the Bower case.

In his Toyota on the way out of Edendale, Cooper saw a call come in from Chloe Young. He pulled over on Buxton Road in front of the Silk Mill heritage centre.

'Hi, Chloe. How are you?'

'Busy,' she said. 'I thought you promised me you didn't have any bodies for me? Suddenly it's like rush hour.'

'Are you too busy to see me?'

'Well . . .'

Cooper heard the hesitation all too clearly. Had he ruined everything last time? Did Chloe Young think he was too obsessed with his job? She wouldn't be the first to think that. It was an occupational hazard for police officers.

But Young was only dealing with some business at her end. She was probably as pestered with reports and emails as he was himself.

'How about tonight?' she said.

'Great,' said Cooper. 'Where?'

'Well,' said Young again, 'probably not the opera.'

'Agreed.'

Cooper put the car back into gear and pulled out on to the road with a smile on his face. Out of Edendale, he turned eastwards. It was Saturday, so he took his time, heading down the A623 from Calver to Baslow and driving through the parkland of Chatsworth House, dodging the sheep on the road until he could cross the open expanses of Beeley Moor and work his way through villages towards the M1. He always preferred the back roads if he wasn't in a hurry and he had things to think about.

After his drive over the moors, Shirebrook hardly seemed like Derbyshire. Perhaps Diane Fry was right and it was really in Nottinghamshire, but the boundary had slipped. The miners here had dug for coal rather than the lead that came out of Lathkill Dale. But both industries were dead and gone.

Fry's Audi was parked at the back of the shops where Krystian Zalewski had lived. There were three marked police vehicles there too, and a Scientific Support van.

Under the harsh glare of security lights he saw Fry coming out of a back door of a shop, wearing a pair of blue latex gloves. She gave him a brief nod.

'We've been searching the premises of the shop-keeper,' she said without even a 'hello'. 'Geoffrey Pollitt.'

'How did it go?'

'He's in custody. We arrested him last night.'

'For what?'

Fry began to peel off the gloves.

'After I spoke to him yesterday, Mr Pollitt headed straight round to one of his rental properties in Shirebrook, which was in multiple occupation by a group of six Lithuanian agricultural workers. He planned to move them out before we could raid the address. But a team of officers was already waiting for him. While he was engaged there, we gained entry to the storeroom at the back of his shop. I said he was a middle man, didn't I?'

'For some kind of far-right extremist organisation.'

'Well, it seems that was just a hobby,' said Fry. 'His income came from a share in the proceeds of organised trafficking. He arranged accommodation and provided various other services in this area for the Czech gang I told you about. It was quite a lucrative business.'

'So will that be a conspiracy to traffic charge? You mentioned the Modern Slavery Act.'

Fry shook her head. 'That's for offences that take place outside the UK. No, Pollitt will be charged under the Serious Crime Act with participating in the activities of an organised crime group. There may be money laundering offences under the Proceeds of Crime Act too. The CPS will decide on that. If he's convicted, Pollitt could get a maximum of five years in prison.'

Cooper looked at her, wondering that she didn't look happier. But Fry was never satisfied. From her manner, you would think someone had stolen all the glory.

When the glove came off her right hand, Cooper noticed some fresh grazes on her knuckles. They looked raw and had been bleeding quite recently.

'How did you do that to your hand?' he said.

She looked down and shook her hand, as if she hadn't even been aware of it until now.

'Oh, I think I must have banged it on something during the search. There's a lot of rubbish stacked in that storeroom.'

'But you had gloves on,' said Cooper.

'Of course I had gloves on. What did you expect?'

Cooper watched her curiously. He prided himself on that sense of knowing when someone was lying, or trying to hide the truth from him. He couldn't remember getting that feeling with Diane Fry before. She was more likely to blurt out the truth, even if it wasn't very palatable.

'So did you bring the information I asked for?' she said. 'Or did you just come to do your shopping in

Shirebrook market? They do a good burger at the fast-food stall, DCI Mackenzie tells me. But if you're having fried onions, stay well away from me.'

'I brought the information,' said Cooper.

He passed her the folder.

'Thank you.'

She opened her car door and threw it on to the passenger seat without looking at it.

'Everything's working out okay, then?' said Cooper, raising an eyebrow.

'I'm sure everything is working out fine for *you*,' said Fry.

'Diane, are you all right?'

'Oh, I've just been having a bad week,' she said.

Cooper laughed. If it had been him, if he was going through a really bad week, he would have gone for a drive over the Snake Pass, or taken a long walk on the moors, whatever the weather. There was nothing like a good blow to clear the mind and make you feel better. There wasn't any point in suggesting it to Diane Fry, though.

Fry looked out at the streets of Shirebrook – a few parked cars and a deserted market square, dark but for the lights of the *polski sklep*.

'I'm still trying to understand the real nature of this place,' she said.

'It's a bit late now,' said Cooper.

'Is it?'

'You'll be going straight on to something else, won't you? You'll have another case to deal with, somewhere else in the East Midlands. So you'll soon forget about Shirebrook. There'll be a new challenge.'

'True.'

'Besides,' said Cooper, 'you've never understood the real nature of any part of Derbyshire.'

Fry was silent for a moment. 'Or of anything in it,' she said.

Cooper stared straight ahead. By 'anything' did she mean 'anyone'? It would be a startling admission coming from Diane Fry. But she hadn't said that, had she? No, not quite.

'You do understand the way back to Nottingham, though?' he said.

'Of course I do.'

'Have a safe trip, then.'

Fry got into her car and slammed the door. Cooper watched the black Audi drive away. He didn't need Dev Sharma to tell him who had been given the promotion at EMSOU. The credit for a successful conclusion to the Krystian Zalewski murder hadn't all gone to Sharma.

Well, that was the way it worked sometimes.

34

But how did you end up here, in the dark? The details are vague in your mind now, and hardly seem important. When you're about to die, the reasons for your death become strangely irrelevant. They're questions for someone else to answer, problems for those you're leaving behind to sort out for themselves. Once you're gone, it's all going to happen without you.

But will those people be in the dark, as much as you are now? The thought makes you groan and twitch with anxiety. At least there should be justice, a retribution of some kind. You pray silently for a reckoning. Without it, your death will be such a waste.

You open an eye, but you can still see nothing. The creaking has become a rumbling, like a mountain moving under its own impetus. You feel water seeping into your clothes, cold and clammy. It's flowing round you, coming higher and higher. It parts around your body like the waves of the ocean breaking against an island.

Now you think you might drown first, before the final crushing fall. Your breathing gets faster until you're gasping for air, your pain released in an animal grunt. You're lying on the hard rock, panting like a beast. And this is how your life will end.

A question stays in your mind, surfacing now and then in the blackness, a bursting rocket in the dark. Why has no one come? Why did he leave you here? You know the answer, of course. But the question keeps coming, the words playing over and over in your head. The answer is important to you.

A sudden, deafening roar and a cascade of dust. A rock crashes on to your leg. You feel the bone shatter. You're too exhausted to cry out now, too close to the edge to respond to the pain. Your mouth is full of grit that chokes your breath and trickles into your lungs. You have only moments left.

Will anyone else know the answer to your questions now? Or will you be lost and forgotten, written off for ever, a person who might never have existed? Perhaps no one will ever care. No one will come to find you, here in your tomb in the darkness.

Yet that's your final, dying hope. That someone will come to look for you one day. Even after you're dead in the dark.